PARALLEL WORLDS

THE HEROES WITHIN

Edited by

L. J. HACHMEISTER & R.R. VIRDI

First Edition

Cover design by Nicole Peschel

Edited by L. J. Hachmeister and R.R. Virdi

Source 7 Productions, LLC

Lakewood, CO

CONTENTS

INTRODUCTION

BY L. J. HACHMEISTER

Authors write for a variety of reasons. Some, for hobby, others for their profession. What motivates us can be monetary in nature, to build worlds, or a burning passion to express ourselves and connect with others. And, of course, everything in between. I think for all of us, though, the story, no matter why we initially write it, and no matter how distant we think we are from the characters, is part of us. Many times, it parallels our own world.

This anthology sparked from a conversation between me and fellow author R.R. Virdi. We both found it fascinating how heroes and villains are essentially born from the same place, and what truly enlivens a story is sourced from our own experiences. We also discussed how some of the best stories are the ones where we know something about the author, and what motivated them and the plight of their characters. This connection brings us all closer together, allows us to see the world through another person's eyes.

These nineteen stories are all very different, ranging from epic stories with inspirational heroes to darker tales of the beleaguered rapscallion that must overcome the impossible obstacles to right their world. In the end, though, they represent us, and the heroes – and worlds – inside us.

1

DEAD END RHODES

SARAH A. HOYT

Of all the criminals in the known universe, borgers are the worst.

They are the worst both in law and in my own mental hierarchy of crimes. I loathe murderers, kidnappers, slavers and all those who treat other humans as objects for their convenience.

But borgers *make* people into objects. They steal the brain, discard the body, and entrap all that remains of a living human in a glassteel body, cut off from its normal senses. They murder the person and keep what remains entrapped in a body so unlike that of humans that the poor creature goes insane. As far as we can tell, and of course, the operation is so highly illegal that our statistics are probably flawed, borgers end up wasting seventy five percent of those they take and on whom they manage the operation, because the resulting cyborg is too crazy to function, even for limited purposes.

Borging is so heinous, and so severely punished, that if you are even caught near a cyborg you haven't denounced to the authorities so they can give the poor soul the peace it deserves, you'll be executed as a borger. Even if you had nothing to do with the making of it.

Why do the borgers do it? Profit. Money. There are certain

asteroids and moons in which the atmosphere will eat through skin, the radiation kill any human, the temperature boil anyone not encased in layers of glassteel. Cyborgs are powered by batteries created by an alien race. They don't eat. They don't sleep. They don't excrete. Many of them can't even think in any sense. But they can do the repetitive and boring actions needed to mine rare metals. And they do.

I'd cross the galaxy – and have – to kill a borger.

So you'll wonder why I live with a cyborg, and why he's technically my boss in my mobile investigations business.

Sometimes so do I.

The poor soul who is the head of our investigation business calls himself Nick Rhodes, which is not his name. He assumed Nick Rhodes' identity, after being borged. I think the self-identification came from watching too many sensis in the series. He believes that he is a veteran of some ancient war on Earth called World War One or The Great War or The War to End all Wars, and that he lives in a city called New York, in a country long forgotten, in a world that was the cradle of humanity and like all cradles ultimately abandoned. He believes he's a private investigator. That last is real.

As I said, most people go insane when borged. But at least he can think. Boy, can he think.

To keep him happy, the inside of our spaceship – a serviceable two floor Flitja of ancient model – is set up as the house of Nick Rhodes in the sensi serial of the name.

I slept in the front bedroom upstairs, and he in the back. Yes, I know he didn't sleep, but I'm not sure he knew. Our office was in the front of the spaceship, just off the airlock he insisted on calling "the foyer". In back was the kitchen, which baffled him, until he'd convinced himself all kitchens in New York in the 20th century came with automated cookers and huge refrigeration units as well as dried food storage with foods from all the human worlds. He'd written these into the memories of Nick Rhodes' from the sensis and would now regularly cook for me, since he could not eat.

Awareness of his condition remained, but in his mind it was Nick Rhodes who had been set upon, in a back alley, and turned into a cyborg. Fighting the condition would only distress him.

I came into the office, early morning, before him, and took my place at the desk that, in *Nick*'s memory belonged to his secretary Stella D'Ori. My computer carefully disguised as a typewriter, I sat about reading the morning mail, answering it, confirming appointments, charting our course when we left this world, when the current case was – hopefully – solved.

Nothing in my background had prepared me for this. I'd been a socialite in interplanetary society, known for my dancing. Sensis of myself dancing with some gallant or other had graced the press of all the human worlds, particularly in my native Human Commonwealth worlds. I'd lived without a care for money or survival, until I got married. But my father had disapproved of my marriage and disowned me, and this was now how I must earn a living. I managed, more or less.

Nick came into the office while I finished the last of the correspondence. He wore a suit that would befit the 1930s in New York city, this one in a soft brown, with a pale yellow tie upon the immaculate white shirt. The surfaces of his cybernetic body left exposed as between his hat and collar gleamed, soft golden glassteel. He removed his hat and hung it on the coat tree, and though his face was, of course, motionless, I imagined he smiled at me as he rumbled "Good Morning, Stella," in a voice that sounded less electronic every day.

I said, "Good morning, boss," as he sat at his desk and turned on the privacy shielding.

He had no need to sit, of course, just as he had no need of wearing clothes to disguise his sexless body. But he did anyway. The shield, that made the area in which he sat into a nebulous, swirling, impenetrable confusion, not unlike wind-blown clouds, was a necessity. And like everything else, Nick had rewritten it into his memory, deciding that Nick Rhodes – the fictional hero –

had used this shielding to disguise the horrendous facial scarring from The Great War and avoid scaring his customers.

The ringing of someone at the outer entrance to the airlock – not functioning as such while on the ground in a planet with Earth atmosphere – announced the arrival of the client who had brought us here: the man who had paid enough for the services of our detective agency for us to come to Peura Planet and land in its paltry spaceport and endeavor to solve the client's problem.

Because Nick's brain had become renowned throughout the Galaxy, people assumed his pseudonym was a nod towards the old serial adventures by some recluse celebrity or genius. There were speculative articles on who he really was, but despite my presence, right there, and my once-well-known looks, no one had landed on his real identity. Perhaps because I'd changed so much these last five years, living with a cyborg.

Just as well.

The client was middle aged, prosperous – he would have to be – wearing a relatively fashionable one-piece in blue-grey with dark red accents. For this region of the galaxy practically avant-guard. My father had worn a similar one twenty years ago, but we'd been in a far more populous and wealthy area.

He was well built, with steel-grey hair and eyes, which seemed to coordinate with his suit.

He rushed into our office, ahead of me, and stopped, staring at the privacy shield. Then turned to me. "What is this?" he said. "I thought I'd paid for an audience with Nick Rhodes. How am I to know—"

"If you know who we are," I said. "You know Mr. Rhodes always meets clients from behind a privacy shield. Please, won't you sit down, Mr…." I faked hesitancy but of course, I remembered the name. Without his wired advance we wouldn't have come this far. As well, though, to make him think he was one of many and unimportant.

"Mr. Peura."

He gave me a half-annoyed look, as though he didn't like to be reminded that he was not special, and realizing he wouldn't be the first to meet Nick Rhodes face to face, without the shield.

I saw him consider protesting, and give it up, then throw himself down on the chair in front of Nick's desk as though he held a grudge against it. He glared at the privacy shield.

Behind it, Nick's chair – specially made to accommodate Nick's weight – creaked, and out of long habit, I could visualize him shifting, leaning back, waiting for the client to speak.

It took a moment. Peura was not unusual in feeling uncomfortable talking to the blankness of the privacy shield. I turned my chair slightly so that I could see him, and so that he could see me and smiled slightly, encouragingly.

If he thought my costume of bright, short dress, the ribbon holding back my platinum hair, were strange he said nothing. I presumed he thought I was keeping the atmosphere to match Nick Rhodes sensies. He wasn't wrong. He was just wrong about the reason.

"It's my son," he finally said. "He's gone missing." As though having said it he'd performed a major and difficult task, he took out a hanky in one of those nano-cleaning fabrics out of his pocket and mopped up his forehead. "I don't know what to do."

The chair creaked. The shield shifted and rotated slightly, indicating that Nick had sat up straight, and Nick said, "I presume you've contacted the authorities."

Peura swallowed hard. I could hear the sound and see his Adam's apple move. "There aren't… many authorities out here. Most of the investigators work for me. You see, I own the mining rights to this world, that's why it's named after me. All three cities in this world are built around mines. Hence their names: Mine One, Mine Two, Mine Three. The security are my security guards, who are supposed to keep peace for me. I don't know if you understand that they aren't police as such. More company security."

I understood him perfectly well. He was the local boss thug and all the thugs in the world responded to him. He didn't say that, of course, but it was understood.

"Of course when I realized my son had disappeared," he said. "I had all my security men look for him. Of course..." He hesitated and mopped at his forehead again. "They're not exactly what I'd call brainy, you know. They're more... more."

"More hired muscle?" Nick rumbled, his voice, from behind the privacy shield sounding more gravely than usual, in a way that disguised the mechanical timbre.

I expected Peura to take offense, but he made a strange laugh-cough sound at the back of his throat, as though he were afraid of laughing, or perhaps unused to it. "You could say that," he said. "You could say that. What they are is convicts, from... well, from more civilized worlds, who have trouble keeping them behind bars, and so they rent them out to these far-flung worlds to act as security. Well, that is no big difference. Most of the miners are too. They're brought here for punishing labor that would give the government bad press in their worlds."

I felt the encouraging smile fade from my face. And I heard Nick shift in his chair. I'd heard of the system, but I didn't have to approve of it. I didn't know if Nick had. I never understood, in any case how he reconciled the fictional ancient New York city in his mind with the real world of multiple human planets with their differing law codes and different ways of getting around those laws. I don't know what Nick thought of this penal arrangement. I knew in the fictional New York, in the long-vanished country of the United States, prisoners had done some work, and it was judged not to be slavery, and was in fact paid, if at a lower rate than any other.

I didn't know if Nick perceived the difference between that and what was going on here. As for how I felt about it, well, I did tell you I hate slavers, right? This was not much different from outright slavery.

Sure, in the more "civilized" worlds these men might be given some limited sentence, but once that became "let's rent convicts to people who desperately need labor in lawless outer worlds" the sentences had a way of being extended, of becoming fluid, of having years added to them arbitrarily for misbehavior or infraction, with no court supervision. If the rumors were right – and I'd recoiled from verifying them as one flinches from a sore tooth, because when it is something the United Human Planets, the Human Hegemony and the Human Commonwealthagree on, it's nothing I can change – temporary punishment became life-long slavery, and what was supposed to be a quiet way of punishing really bad criminals became the normal punishment for everything from misdemeanors to felonies.

Worlds have different ideas of what is criminal. Some are so barbaric as to forbid means of personal defense to individuals. You can get a hefty sentence for possessing a zapgun in a dozen of them. Others forbid certain foods and drugs. Others yet reserve punishment for murder or kidnapping or crimes commited against others. But all of these worlds rented their "convicts" to people like Peura in distant worlds, where no one would supervise their treatment.

I narrowed my eyes at Peura. He didn't notice. He was staring ahead at the privacy shield intently. He sighed. "You see, my son wasn't... we weren't on the best of terms. He wanted to go off world and study... he wanted to be a starship pilot. I told him no, because he was my only son and would one day inherit all this. But he wasn't happy about it, so he'd often go into town, this town or another to drink. He often came home very late. But one night, a month ago, he didn't come home. And no one has been able to find any trace of him."

"I presume you have traced his movements until he disappeared though?" Nick rumbled.

"Oh, sure. He was out with a group of… well, he'd say a group of friends, I think, from the spaceport. Not locals. People who landed here, you know, we import… That is not only do my family and I require some luxuries from other worlds, but we import a lot of our food for the men in the mines. Narcis, my son, he was… He didn't like associating with the miners, not that I can precisely blame him, you know. I mean, they are servants and people with a bad past. In fact, we discouraged our children associating with them from the beginning.

"So he has friends among the people who do regular supply runs. One such party was in town, young men from one of the companies that supplies food and liquor. We have... well, with men such as the ones we get here, you have to provide some diversion, so we have bars in the cities, and he and his friends were at one of the bars, drinking into the night. Until they all left.

"No one seems to have seen them on the street as such, but the young men he was with said that he had left them at the door and headed down towards the other bar in the town, while they went back to the spaceport. They did clock in at the right time. But Narcis was not seen again."

That was the crux of the case. The rest was summarized. He hadn't been able to keep the young men here, of course. Their employer, a world called Cinzan, had called them back and to their distribution route. Cinzan was mostly an outpost that purveyed luxury goods, anything from mink stoles to liquor to sex bots. You wanted it, and it was sinfully decadent? You could get it from Cinzan.

And whether they were on Cinzan or in their spaceship, or in one of the many isolated planets to which Cinzan shipped, we could call them at Peura's expense. Peura had secured from Cinzan the promise the three men who had been in the ship would be available for our interrogation, if we so wished.

Other than those men, and the miners who had once been convicts, the Peura world contained women – also convicts, and imported as either wives or comfort women, in close numbers to the men, so as to avoid trouble – and the Peura family.

That consisted of Mrs. Analie Peura, a second or third or perhaps fourth wife, who he admitted "Is about the age of my daughter Reelen."

That age turned out to be twenty-seven to Peura's sixty or so.

Both women lived in the world "But take frequent shopping

and destressing trips to other worlds," he said. "You know how women are."

Nick made a rumbling, uncommitted sound, then said, "Did your son also travel often?"

"When he was younger," Peura said. "Of course I sent him to study abroad, see a bit of thc universe. But lately, since he'd become obsessed with becoming a space pilot – of all the crazy ideas – I told him he could not go anywhere, and I gave such orders to the spaceport as well."

"Would there be any chance the Cinzan men smuggled him abroad the ship?" Nik asked.

"No. There was no extra passenger when they arrived to Cinzan. In fact—" He paused, as though evaluating what he was about to say, as though something about it bothered him. "In fact, when they arrived, they were minus one crew member, who got sick, and whom they had to space en route."

"I see," Nick said, in a tone of deep understanding.

Something about it must have stung Peura who lashed out, "I'm glad you do, because I don't. If you think somehow being minus one crew member tells us that my son went to—"

"I didn't say that," Nick interrupted. "Only that any deviation from normal routine is interesting in cases like this, that's all."

Peura mumbled "Cases like this," under his breath. "Have you seen many cases of someone disappearing into thin air at a bar door, in a world as thinly populated and controlled as this one?"

"More than I'd like to tell you about."

"Well, then you should have an answer for me very shortly, and my son back home in double time, right?"

"I will do my best. If you could send your wife and daughter to me." I could tell from the creaking that Nik had turned to me, behind the privacy shield. "Stella?"

He always turned to me for hours and scheduling, as though we had an open social calendar, and people coming and going and only I could keep track of such complex affairs. Or maybe it was that I needed to eat and sleep, and therefore my mortal needs hemmed in our availability.

"In an hour and two hours respectively would work," I said, crisply.

"Then so be it. In one hour and two hours respectively."

"I don't know if I can get them to obey commands," Peura said. "And I don't know what they can tell you. Do you think if they knew where Narcis was they wouldn't have told me by now?"

"It's possible they don't know they know," Nick said, which is the kind of infuriating pronouncement he was likely to make. "Do what you can to make them come."

The words had the tone of a dismissal, and were, and I can't blame Peura for being put out. He was paying us a lot of money to come out here and find his son, and, to his mind, all we were doing is bothering him and his family.

I accompanied him to the airlock and out to the stairs down from our spaceship. As the outer door retracted, and he left, walking huffily away from us, towards the gates of the spaceship, I caught a glimpse of a red sunset over arid-looking terrain, all reddish soil and low-growing trees. The air smelled hot and spicy, like an open furnace.

I closed the door and went back to our temperature-controlled office. Nick had taken down the privacy shield and was sitting back in his chair, with his feet on the desk, his hands crossed on his chest over the creamy yellow tie.

"You know he has a point, don't you?" I said. "He expects us to do more than question his relatives."

Nick made a sound. I wasn't sure what it was supposed to mean. It sounded somewhat like clearing your throat, if your throat were full of gears, I guess. He made it when he didn't wish to discuss something, which usually meant when I was right.

I went to my desk and barely had the time to sit down when he said, "Stella, did you research this world when we got the request from Peura?"

"There was no time," I said. "Remember, we were under way

and quite close to here, and we'd have had to stop and find a parking orbit with a friendly planet to do so. Also, the charges would be high because they'd be channeled through that planet. If we'd turned the job down, they wouldn't be reimbursed, either. And as you know, the galactic databases are—"

"Yes." He said. He didn't say that Peura had also paid us a very good price for our coming out here, with an extra bonus for coming straight out. And I didn't belabor the difficulty of accessing the galactic data bases while we were underway. I had never fully explored how Nick interacted with modernity, other than asking me to read him things from my "research" which usually meant a quick search of electronic information sources.

"See what you can find out," he said.

I saw. It wasn't much. Peura was wealthy and owned not just this planet but this solar system, which consisted of this large world and a lot of tiny worlds – asteroids really – orbiting closer to the system's sol-type star.

His wealth was inherited, but his father had come from nothing and it was he who had initially bought the system and devoted his efforts to mining rare metals. I skimmed the names of the metals – it's like they're discovering new ones every week – but the important thing is that they were used in everything from building glassteel to making some of the essential parts for the coms that allowed communication across space.

The current Mrs. Peura was the fourth. The first three lived in different – and distant worlds – the last one in Dover, capital of the Human Commonwealth, as a socialite of some renown.

His daughter Reelen had attended some kind of academy in New Oxford, the world where most well-to-do sent their children to school, and managed to get through fifteen years of schooling with completely average grades without betraying either an interest or an abhorrence for any of the subjects.

His son, Narcis, had also attended school at New Oxford, but surprised me by having excellent grades in mathematics and physics. No wonder he wanted to be a pilot. He had an excellent chance of qualifying.

There was a holo with records, and I activated it.

A slim young man manifested in front of my desk. Blond, unruly hair, a charming smile, and the kind of clothes that meant he cared more for fashion than his father did.

"Narcis Peura?" Nick asked, from behind his desk.

"Yes," I said, and reported.

Nick didn't answer. He never did. Sometimes as he sat there, with his feet on his desk, the lights behind his eyes cycled on and off, on and off, on a rhythm. Not quite off; brighter; then low, then bright.

I'd just done relating what I'd heard when the doorbell rang.

I went out and admitted a young woman who smiled at me, eyeing me up and down. "Why, aren't you pretty. Just like an historical sensi. Does he make you dress like that?"

I shook my head, then shrugged. Nick didn't make me dress like that, but I'd often wondered at the contradictory reactions that would form in his mind if I'd appeared in normal getup. He seemed to handle it well enough from our guests, but the few times I'd tried to step out of character, he'd been confused and hurt. It was not a good thing to make him suffer more than necessary. Even if he was a cyborg.

"I'm Stella D'Ori," I said. "And you are?"

"The sane one of the two you asked to see," she said, and smiled again. I was no longer sure it was a nice smile. "Reelen Peura. Pleased to meet you, though of course, despite your pseudonym being very apropos, I probably should ask for your real name?" She raised an eyebrow expectantly. I ignored it, stepping around her to close the door, then leading her into the office.

She, like her brother , obviously kept up with the off-world fashions. She wore a one-piece that looked – rather artfully – like a little blouse and a tutu kind of skirt in masses of tulle. Not tulle, of course, nor was the blouse silk, but both some kind of bio-fabric that looked more like the real thing than the real thing could look.

I thought I'd look rather good in that, gliding across a dance floor, but it had been too long, and now it was never going to happen again.

She made for the chair behind my desk. Heaven only knows why. Some people do. Maybe they think my desk is ornamental. I cleared my throat and gestured her towards the chair in front of Nick's desk. She pouted harder, but obeyed, arranging her skirts before sitting down, and crossing her legs in a way that made the semi-transparent pant portion of her costume outline her legs with just the hint of veiling imperfections, to make them look like sculpted masterpieces.

I smiled a little and didn't say anything. Nick was past noticing that kind of trick, but she couldn't know that, and one had to admire a woman for doing her stuff, right?

In fact, she was arching that eyebrow towards Nick and saying in a slightly throaty voice, "Man of mystery, uh? Or too ugly to show your face?"

"We'll go with too ugly," he said, which would be the real Nick Rhodes' response of course, since he was supposed to have been disfigured in war. But said that way, in his gravelly voice, it sounded like flirting.

She had a throaty laugh too. She pulled a cigarette from somewhere. I'd never gone for them, but they were popular again with my generation. We were assured that there were no carcinogen effects of smoking the new, improved cigarettes. Perhaps. They had gone around as a fad several times since ancient times, and then become unfashionable, or banned, or were considered too dangerous. One never knew where the medically approved or disapproved roulette was going to land. All we could do was roll with it.

But I didn't smoke, or drink to excess, or dope, preferring to know that whatever was thinking my thoughts and making my decisions was myself. My husband, who had been the same, used to say that we were the last two sane people in the universe. A thought of Joe came and went. It hardly hurt at all anymore. I twirled the ring I still wore on the fourth finger of my left hand. Inside it, it said *To Lilly From Joe.* And it was stupid to wear it, I know. Both Lilly and Joe were as good as dead.

"Well, darling," Reelen said, a smile in her voice as she shook the cigarette to light it. "I suppose you want to know about darling boy's disappearance."

"Yes," Nick said. "If by that you mean your brother. We were in fact hired to investigate his disappearance."

"I think he did a bunk," she said. "And paid the men from Cinzan a rather large sum not to tell daddy about it. He loathes living here, not that it is a big prize, mind you, and despises the idea of becoming master to a lot of convict miners one day. He's always dreamed of being a pilot, you know, out among the stars."

She looked wry and amused, but shrugged and smiled. "He'd probably make a rather good one, too." She took a puff on her cigarette.

Nick was quiet a long time. Reelen took a few puffs from her cigarette, exhaling, letting the smoke out in the kind of lazy curl one has to practice.

I could see her gathering herself to leave, when Nick said, "And you? You never entertained dreams of escaping?"

For a moment, for just a moment, I felt as though the façade of the well-composed girl was just that: a mask between her and the world, and it had come down just a little.

Then it went up again. "It is not the same is it? Daddy doesn't care what I do. And because I was never stupid enough to vent my crazy dreams at him, he never restricted me to the planet. I'm allowed to go and shop in other worlds. My allowance permits me to buy all kinds of fripperies." She pinched at the not-tulle skirt with her free hand. "And daddy could not be happier if I married and went away to another world. He'd probably endow me generously at that. I'm the spare. It is the heir who is to be bound to this world forever, and to supervising our precious mines here and in the asteroids. Daddy says it's no work for a woman." She took a deep pull on the cigarette and exhaled lazily. "At that, he is probably right."

Nick nodded. He got little more from her after that. She laughed at the idea that she felt resentful because she wasn't allowed to pursue a career. "What? A career darling? But I am like the lilies of the field who do not toil, and yet, Solomon, in all his glory was not as finely arrayed. Don't be ridiculous. I am perfectly willing to believe toil is what happens to other people so I get to live as I please. At least, unlike *poor* Anelie I didn't have to marry into it."

If it hadn't been for that brief glimpse of a real person behind the mask, I'd have felt like throttling her before the interview was done. She told us all her favorite planets to go shopping in; the stores she patronized there; the sensis she'd taken in recently. I didn't know why Nick wanted to know such things, but I supposed there was a reason. I often couldn't understand why he asked questions, but it always made some sort of sense in the end.

Of her brother she said only that "I hope he did make it to somewhere he wants to be, and got to try for a pilot. The way he's been going on, going out and boozing it up with anyone who visits, or going down into Mine One City and getting drunk and fighting with the miners over one of their women... It's not healthy. It will end in tears. So I hope he's happy wherever he is. Daddy should stop worrying. Narcis will come home eventually, or make enough money to hire a manager. Or maybe close the damn mines and be done." That last was said with spiteful force, and once again the mask slipped a little, and I thought she was very angry at the mines, and perhaps at her father. Whether this had anything to do with her brother's disappearance, I didn't dare guess.

When she had left I told Nick that. The lights in his eyes dimmed and relit. "Obviously," he said. "What else to you think is interesting?"

"She's not as vacuous as she appears?" I said.

"Obviously also," he said. There was a pause. "We might have to pursue this in the Cinzan end."

I agreed, and frankly, though I couldn't say why, I hoped we did. I wanted out of this world. It felt like something was badly wrong on Peura Planet, and it was – for reasons I could never fully identify – making me think of Joe which was always bad, also.

But the doorbell rang and I let Analie Peura in.

While she might have been the same age as her stepdaughter, Mrs. Peura was quite a different article. She was also blond, but her hair had the kind of sleek, carefully cut look that told me she probably didn't rely to trips outside the world to get it cut. Something like this required weekly, if not daily, attention. Also, while her step children were blond, she was the kind of silvery blond that required mods. Probably a permanent mod. Nothing so crude as dyes for Anelie Peura.

She wore a severely cut black one piece that seemed simple, but as she moved, betrayed that it had probably cost more than some small asteroids. It made her look like a perfect woman, with an extra dose of "what the boys want."

I realized I was getting irritated with her and told myself to calm down. After all, it wasn't as though Nick would notice, or care, except particularly, in the sense that he knew – or had memories of – what men liked, and adding it to his estimate of her character.

I made the introductions and she sat in the chair in front of the desk, folded her sculpted hands in her lap, and looked ahead, not making any comment on the privacy shield. Either her husband had told her what to expect of she understood that someone in Nick's position – or the position he supposedly had – had to have shielding.

"It must be very difficult for you," Nick said, sounding somehow as though he were empathizing with her. "To be out here, with two step-children almost your age."

She smiled. It wasn't a nice smile. "Oh, so Reelen has been little miss pleasant, as usual?" she asked. "You mustn't mind. She's very young for her age, if you know what I mean, and was thoroughly put out at my husband requiring she come here and submit to interrogation. You'd think she'd be thrilled at meeting a real-life celebrity, but apparently not. And then, you know, she was disappointed in love."

I tried to think back through the public profile of Reelen Peura, and the magazines that had featured her. I didn't remember any man being particularly featured, much less any broken relationship.

Nick obviously didn't remember my reporting any such thing either, because he said, "I don't remember any relationship being mentioned, in the public—"

"Oh, no," Analie said. "It wasn't public, of course. Would you believe, my darling stepdaughter who spends half her waking hours making jokes about how I had to marry for money – as though I would have done something like that without some real regard for my dear Peura – fell in love with one of the miners?" She laughed, deep in her throat, a laugh that conveyed a sense of derision. "Yes. A convict miner, sent out here to serve his sentence. Mind you, he was not a pauper. Well to do, and educated, a pilot, sent here on a minor charge of smuggling. Chocolate, if I remember, to one of the worlds where it's forbidden. He told her he'd not done it on purpose, that it was just a moment of forgetfulness. As if. Well. He told her once he went back – he was only here for two years – he would send for her to come to his world and they would be married. But he never did.

"And if she thinks I don't know one of her long-drawn out trips all over was looking for him… Well, all I have to say is that when you have the money that Reelen does and you're reduced to pursuing the man who jilted you, you've lost all your pride and possibly need your head examined, too."

Yeah, I definitely didn't like Analie. Which was just as well, since she didn't tell us anything at all relevant. She talked about her life before she'd married Peura and how she very nearly, and almost became a famous international sensi star. But then she'd fallen in love – she said – with dearest Peura, and become his fourth wife, instead.

Judging by her performance, I'd say the sensi world had lost nothing. If she couldn't help sinking her claws into her step-daughter the first chance she got, I doubted she had what it took.

After she left, I told just that to Nick, who pulsed his eye-lights at me. "Her claws?"

"With gossip," I said.

"Well," he said. "Yes. But it is very interesting, don't you think so."

I didn't see what he thought was interesting in two women forced to live in closer proximity than they found comfortable hating each other, but then Nick was not someone I could really understand. Not having emotions, all his life had become very cerebral. Perhaps he thought that the way women behaved to each other was, in and of itself, interesting. There was no saying. Perhaps he didn't remember what women were like, in real life? Or perhaps he saw us more clearly now.

"I think we're going to call Cinzan to begin with. And then I might need you to break into some records that aren't publicly held," he said. "And find a few things. Would that be possible?"

It was possible. I'm no more a computer hacker than I am a gene designer. Of the two I probably could figure out the later easier, since I'd taken some biology courses in school. But in my five years doing this I'd acquired some contacts who could do my hacking for me and would. Some out of gratitude for Nick's help in the past, some out of the memory of who he used to be. Or who I used to be.

I concentrated on the dialing codes to get an answer at Cinzan and after trading ID -- and explaining my business with two layers of functionaries -- was connected, by relay to the *Do Drop In*, the spaceship that had last touched down in Peura, before returning to Cinzan, and which was now en route to some place called Daisy Wheel.

"Well, hello," the man who answered said with a grin. "Why you are a sight for sore eyes."

His name was Richard Doyle. He and his team mate, Ignacio Fontes were the surviving crew members of the *Do Drop In*. For this trip they'd been joined by a third, Fernan Jones, who stayed in the background while his teammates answered Nick's questions.

Nick had the privacy shield on, of course, which prompted Ignacio to say "Thank you for not just having the sight off on your end. Your secretary sure is good to see after a few months on an all-male route."

They looked to be in the middle of our office, two of them sitting down, in chairs that looked like they were riveted to a bulkhead. The third moved in the background, going in and out of focus, depending on where he was.

Nick took them over the events of the night: they'd met with Narcis Peura, who was a nice guy, and they'd gone out and had some drinks.

"Old Peura is smarter than he looks," Doyle said, with a grin. "He runs that world better than most. Instead of handing out rations, he hands out coupons and he has stores that work on the coupons, where they can buy what they want. That allows them to take wives, and believe they're living independently. The lifers at least, those who will never be released. It's better for them that way, I suppose, and Peura hasn't had any of the rebellions that other worlds have had."

"And people who are short-termers can also buy on credit," Fontes put in. "So that when they leave, some of the poor sods are indebted to their eyeballs. And have to send him money, after they're released."

The rest was as had been described to us. They'd drunk with Narcis, and then said goodbye to him at the door, never to see him again.

"Then on the way back poor Mike got sick. And we weren't sure what he had, or if it was contagious, and at any rate, we didn't have the room in the freezer, so we spaced him."

"Mike?" Nick said.

"Michael Argon," he said. "Our former teammate. Good old Mike. But it's the life of a spaceman, right? At any time, we could go too."

And that was about all I got from them, which was nothing I couldn't have got from records.

I told Nick that after they left and he said, "Sure, and it might end up with you going to Cinzan and looking at their records, to make sure they really didn't smuggle Narcis there. Thing is, Stella, if they smuggled him anywhere, it was with him intending to go to pilot school, so if you can get into Peura's accounts and see if there has been some unusual flow of money out, or some credit extended to someone who sounds like Narcis? I don't think he would have left without taking the money to study. But if he did, it's perhaps a good idea to also look into whether he's been accepted at pilot school under an indenture arrangement?"

Having given his orders, he got up and left his desk, presumably to go to the kitchen to cook for me.

Meanwhile I dialed someone I used to know. James Brighton and I never dated, which in retrospect probably counts as sinfully wasted opportunity. Jim was a slim, dark man, who attended the same schools I did but didn't come from the same class. In fact, while I was there on daddy's money, he was there on a scholarship because of brains and native curiosity.

He'd studied electronics and social communication and… who knows?

What I knew is that on leaving school he'd become one of the news mediators. One of the real ones. The people who take any current event and dig and dig, until they find gold or muck and sometimes both.

Most people who get a name in that field, sooner or later decide the digging is too much work and start just making up stuff, until they're found out and their career crashes and burns.

Not Jim. The average career in the field was three years, but he'd kept at it for eight. And of course, being where he was and what he was, he kept an excellent team of hackers at his disposal.

Nick had saved him from a stick situation. Well, not Nick, precisely, but the man Nick used to be. In memory of that man, and out of kindness for me and our old friendship, Jim did me what favors he could. Oh, he wanted payment, in the form of whatever we found at the end of the road, the real version of the events, which he could then add to a mind that must be like one of those multidimensional computers they're supposed to be building: in layers and with infinite capacity. But he never pushed and was never grouchy about being asked. I could only imagine that sometimes the cost was onerous enough. I wondered sometimes if he knew what the real situation was, and that was why he kept doing us these favors. But even if that were true, I wouldn't dare ask. There is knowledge so dangerous you don't want even a well-intentioned friend to know. It would just endanger him to no purpose.

He materialized in the middle of the office, sitting at his desk in Haven, a town in New Oxford. He'd never left, saying a center of knowledge and investigation was just right for his sort of business.

He'd not visibly aged in the nine years since we'd been at school. There were some silver threads in his dark hair, and perhaps a few fine lines around the eyes, but he still looked slim and youthful as he had in college days.

His clothes were also much as in college days: a loose pair of pants, and a rumpled pullover top. He was sitting at a desk crowded with various coms and other tech I didn't know the name of, and appeared to be typing on a different keyboard with each hand. There was a tall pot on his desk, and a cup by it. I knew both would contain coffee.

For a man known around the Human Worlds by reputation in one of the best paying and toughest jobs, you'd think he'd at least pay a secretary and someone to straighten for him.

Heck, he probably did. An army of them I should imagine. But I doubted any of them dared try to straighten his work space or moderate his work habits.

He looked up, right after accepting my call, and smiled, "Hello…" a brief hesitation. "Stella. Before you ask, yes, we're private. What do you need?"

I told him where we were and whom our case concerned and asked him for everything he could find on the family, including any unusual money draws from Peura's accounts that might be traced to Narcis. I also asked to find out if anyone of Narcis description had enrolled at piloting school, including under a false identity.

In these days of retinal scans, it's pretty hard to maintain a false identity, but it's not impossible. The trick is to corrupt the records, not to change the retina.

On a whim, I tacked on a question, "Is it possible for you to find a pilot convicted of smuggling chocolate who was sent here and released in the last, oh, year or so?" I didn't think either Analie's or Reelen's memory went further than that. Not as a fresh wound or grievance, at least. "I'd appreciate data on him."

Jim grinned. "I'm sure I can get you that. You'll let me know what really happened as soon as you can, right?"

"Of course," I told him.

Just as I hung up, Nick buzzed from the kitchen to tell me dinner was ready. He sat across the little table from me, watching me eat. He'd done chicken in a cream sauce, with asparagus and these little red fruits that people say come from Earth and that have an almost but not quite sweet flavor. It was excellent as always.

My husband Joe liked to cook, but his efforts were more hit and miss, even with the benefit of the cooker. After all, our cooker was not top of the line, and it was necessary, often, to alter the programming on the fly. I'd guess Nick, being mostly machine, himself, had a special sensitivity for when things needed to be tweaked.

He sat across the small table from me, his eyes glowing duller and brighter, which usually meant he was thinking.

I know I said cyborgs neither eat nor excrete, but that's not precisely the whole truth. There was a maintenance routine that Nick performed, I'd guess at night, while I slept. There is synthetic cerebrospinal fluid and also a kind of synthetic blood that is used only in extremely rare instances for human patients, and more commonly for cyborgs. To buy that in the quantities needed to replace what is lost to routine cleaning is not… easy, though we'd managed so far.

The process he undergoes every night puts the fluids through a machine that removes the impurities, and reinjects it into the body, with nutrients and whatever replacement is needed to keep his brain going.

I was glad he did that out of my sight, as I imagined it would be rather disturbing to watch. But maybe not. Maybe he just lay down, and hooked himself up, and processed random thoughts while the machine worked.

But he always watched me eat, and though he never asked me how I liked it, he must catalogue my expressions well enough to make my favorites again more often than not, while never repeating the things I'd enjoyed less.

After eating, I processed the dirty dishes. When we returned to the office, he asked me if I could bring up an image of Michael Argon. I wished he'd reminded me to ask Jim about him, but of course, I also didn't think it would be that hard to find a picture.

It wasn't. Minutes later I brought up a hologram of the late Mike Argon. Like Narcis, he was tall and slim, with an unruly shock of blondish hair. The resemblance ended there. It was obvious that Mike Argon had grown up in a rough neighborhood. He had a scarred face, which meant he both fought a lot and lacked the money to regen. He also had a tattoo on his left arm, from wrist to shoulder, which showed a spaceship in full flight. It was so detailed, you could read the name of the spaceship as the *Never Late*.

Shortly after, Jim called back.

There was no sign of any extraordinary money outflow from Peura accounts, and he would bet money – he said, and Jim never bet money – that Narcis had not been in the *Do Drop In* when it took off from the spaceport at which we currently sat.

I said, "Maybe another ship, then? I mean, they have an entire spaceport. They must have more traffic than one ship at a time."

"I don't think so," Jim said cheerfully. "Not from anything I can trace. I think that spaceport exists to bring in ore from the asteroids and send whatever supplies are needed there."

"That is odd," I said. "As none have taken off or landed since we've been here."

The other thing that Jim had found was the pilot who had been convicted of smuggling chocolate. His name was Mars Rosen, and he'd finished his sentence six months ago.

"But here's the funny thing," Jim said. "He has never returned to his favorite haunts. The family got a letter from him, but that was all. He said he was going to take a crew job on the *By Your Leave* out of Cinzan, but they never heard of him. Your Reelen has looked extensively for him, but he hasn't been found.

Later when I reported to Nick, I mentioned that it was weird we'd seen no shuttles.

"Maybe," he said, "or perhaps Peura doesn't want us knowing about his business."

And then he asked me to look up Doyle and Fontes and tell him if they were only children.

As it happened, they weren't, and I whistled under my breath as I found out both of them had had brothers who were convicted of drug infractions on two different planets and had been put into the rental system. It was harder to find out to whom their services had been rented, but when I reported to Nick, I said, "Do you think that's it? They had some vendetta against Argon? Maybe he was dealing drugs."

Nick shrugged, which is an embarrassing habit for a creature who isn't human. "Unlikely. After all, Cinzan deals in drugs. You just have to be careful where you take them, and I'm sure they are."

Then he gave me instructions. This case had been unusual in that I'd not left the ship much. Normally I am Nick's legs. My husband would have made a joke about what fine legs they are too, but Nick, of course, never does. What I mean is that normally I go out and see and hear and find the things he can't know. I suspected in this case he'd been protecting me from what was obviously a rough neighborhood. He shouldn't have been. While I'd started out not very good with weapons, I could hold my own with anyone now.

Still I dressed to disguise the fact that I was obviously female, slim and young by putting on a padded suit and boots and a helmet.

"Peura wanted me to send you with an escort," Nick said. "Meaning someone who'd follow you everywhere. But I told him no. Which means he'll probably have you followed. You know what to do."

I knew what to do. The area outside was paved with concrete. There were warehouses in the far southern quadrant. I wondered what they contained. Food for the miners in the asteroids? They must be starving without their regular shipment. What could Peura be hiding?

It's not easy to lose a tail in a miner town with one street. It's also not easy to tail someone. I spotted him long before I got to the outskirts of the town. Mostly because it's really hard to tail someone on flat ground. His attempts to meld with the trees didn't work. He was a tall, well-built man. Which meant I was going to have to do something he'd regret.

I did it before I got to the bar that was the last known location of Narcis. I turned down a blind alley and waited long enough he couldn't help following me. And then I'd jumped him and injected him with a heavy soporific that would give him a headache in the morning.

It wasn't something I liked to do, but it would only give him a mild hangover. And I couldn't have him tail me as I headed back to the spaceport from the bar.

I kept in mind what Nick had told me to look for and found it in the vast wilderness, with the low trees. It was a large reservoir, low to the ground, hidden among the trees. I wouldn't have noticed it had I not been looking. It was probably used to collect infrequent rain for watering. I thought if it were for drinking water, it would be guarded, and the cover on it would be tighter.

Climbing to where I could pry the cover off wasn't easy, but shining a light in there revealed exactly what Nick had said. Let's say Argon was none the better for the wear. But his tattoo was visible, and *Never Late* was still readable.

I beat it to the spaceport, but once there, having gen-identified myself past the automatic gates, the curiosity about those warehouses came again.

I heard no sound from them and saw no movement or light, so I headed that way, at a fast clip, keeping to the shadows.

There are instruments that detect and disable security systems, and the systems on those warehouses weren't… well, they weren't what you'd have in a more heavily populated world.

The first one I got in was filled with barrels. It took a little prybar work to figure out they contained synthetic cerebrospinal fluid and synthetic blood, of the exact kind we used. My first thought is that one of those barrels would avoid the dangerous business of securing it for a year. My second thought wasn't a thought, but something that made my hair stand on end at the back of my neck.

The second warehouse contained parts. I knew those parts. The third warehouse was an operating theater. There were tables, and what looked like an automated crematorium.

To say I beat all speed records back to the ship was to say little. I got in and secured the door, and told Nick all I'd found.

"Borgers," I said. "There's borgers operating in those warehouses."

"Of course," Nick said. "I figured as much. Not every prisoner, but some of them, perhaps the ones he knows won't be missed, or have family that can be fobbed off with letters and some remittances will be borged and sent to the asteroids to mine."

"He being Peura?"

"None other."

"But you can't think he borged his own son."

"Oh, no, not him. That would be Doyle and Fontes. My guess is that both their brothers were borged and they figured it out somehow. I don't think the borging operation runs around the clock. In fact, I'm fairly sure he gets people to come in from outside and do that. Perhaps the two pilots heard rumors. Perhaps Narcis found out and talked. At any rate, what they did was kill their third team mate, and somehow fake his data, so that Narcis read as him going back into the spaceport."

"Corrupting stored data isn't that hard."

"No, it's just one outdated scanner, I understand. They probably disposed of Argon, and went back, got Narcis and convinced him they could take him with them, so he'd go willingly."

"And they borged him?"

"They probably tried. It's not an unskilled job. I think they just killed him. I don't think they made a borg, because if they had they'd have sent him back into the streets, to denounce his father with his presence, and perhaps his words. I doubt a shipment has gone to the asteroids since he disappeared. If it has, then maybe the borging was successful, and maybe he's there. But I bet you they will find traces of his DNA in that operating theater."

We called the authorities, of course, at the same time we took off. There was no point staying there, when they came to town looking for borgs.

Nick was wrong. Narcis had indeed been borged and was in the asteroids and coherent enough to testify before they put him out of his misery. His testimony was the death sentence of Fontes and Doyle. Peura also met a death sentence for borging even if he'd not done it personally.

Reelen, suddenly the sole heir of the system, sent us a fat check. Not for finding her brother, but for finally finding out why Mars Rosen hadn't come back for her. Yes, he too had been borged.

As for us, we stayed away from all worlds for a while, floating in the night of space, bound by our routine.

When we didn't have clients, Nick read in the office, while I did my filing, called Jim to report what had happened, and caught up on news and trivia.

Two earth-days out of Peura system, I woke with my bedroom door opening. Nick stood in the doorway, his eyes lights dimming and brightening.

"Yes," I said. "Nick? What do you need?" I thought perhaps he'd run out of fluid or something had gone wrong with the machine.

The voice that answered me was curiously hesitant, "Lilly," it said. Nick rushed into the room, fell to his knees beside my bed. He has no expressions, of course, but I got the feeling he was searching my face. "Lilly!" he said. And then, after a long pause, "I remember. I remember. I'm sorry."

"There's nothing to be sorry for," I said, while he lay his hard, smooth head on my shoulder. "You didn't choose to be borged. Someone else did it to you, Joe. There was nothing you could do. And you're still helping people."

"But, oh, Lilly," he said. "You don't deserve this."

"No. But that's not how life works. It's not what you deserve. It's what you can do. Sometimes the only thing you can do." I ran my palm gently on the hard steelglass surface that hid my late husband's still living brain. "I just do what I can."

He'd forget again. He'd done it before. But for these brief moments I had Joe. I didn't know if that made it all better or worse.

Because he couldn't, I cried for both of us, holding the unyielding mechanic body that held all that remained of my love.

BIO

Sarah A. Hoyt, under various names, is the author of over 30 books —she gets tangled up when she tries to count them and always misses a couple—in science fiction, fantasy, mystery, romance, and historical fiction.

. . .

Her first published novel, *Ill Met by Moonlight*, was a finalist for the Mythopoeic Award. *Darkship Thieves*, the first novel of her popular Darkship Thieves series is a Prometheus Award Winner.

She's published over 100 short stories in magazines such as *Analog*, *Asimov's*, and *Weird Tales* (and others, some no longer in existence), as well as an array of science fiction, fantasy, and mystery anthologies.

Sarah was born and raised in Portugal and now lives in Colorado, near her two grown sons, with her husband and a varying clowder of cats. English is her third language, but she can swear fluently in seven. When not laying down words on the latest manuscript, she can be found refinishing furniture, walking, or studying history.

2

LOOK ME IN THE STARS

CHRISTOPHER HUSBERG

A voice said, Look me in the stars
And tell me truly, men of earth,
If all the soul-and-body scars
Are not too much to pay for birth. - Robert Frost

My name is Elizabeth Towner. (If you're reading this--call me Lizzie!)
I'm probably the last person on earth.
This is my blog.

* * *

Thursday, December 21st, 2023

In(de)finite Hiatus

Remember when I said that checking this blog, and writing in it and everything, was worth it? Because of the whole hope idea? Remember that whole thing about choosing to fight?

I think that's done with, now. I think I'm over it. I won't be updating the blog any time soon. You can only hold a one-sided conversation for so long, right?

Look for me, in the stars or otherwise.

Posted by lonelysurvivor7 at 08:17:00 PM 0 Comments

Labels: none

* * *

Wednesday, December 20th, 2023

A Parallel

I picked up a book I haven't read in some time, today. Found this:

... and I even remain alone to write the sad tale of the destruction of my people. But behold, they are gone... And whether they will slay me, I know not.

That's from something I used to read all of the time. Something I, and a lot of other people, used to think was scripture. But everyone else is dead, so I guess they don't think at all anymore, and as for me, well...

I guess I don't know.

People would tell me this book was written for "our day," that the prophets who wrote in it saw each of us and knew what we would be doing and what we would look like and everything. I wonder if this guy speaking, Moroni, saw me when he wrote this. I wonder if he knew how alone I would feel.

Even if he didn't, though, I... I think I might know how *he* felt. And that's something.

Posted by lonelysurvivor7 at 10:40:00 AM 0 Comments

Labels: the book of Mormon, annihilation, loneliness, Moroni

* * *

Friday, December 15th, 2023

Life's a Bitch and Then You Die

This is true, except for that last part. At least for some of us. At least for one of us. Life's a bitch. No denying that, because sometimes your little brother gets leukemia. Sometimes he suffers and you watch him get really thin and lose his hair and turn white as chalk and he sobs and sobs from the pain and then he's gone. Or sometimes your dad touches you, makes you used and worthless and even though you want to kill him you still love him weirdly because he's your daddy and he calls you his little princess and you just want to make him happy. Sometimes your mom dies before you can say you're sorry. Sometimes you hurt the people you love.

I wonder if it's just as bad if you don't hurt them when you should.

Am I the only one who doesn't get to die after all of this? Am I the only one who still has to live, alone, no one left to abuse me? No one left to abuse? Maybe this is the real definition of loneliness: I have no one left to hurt.

Life *is* a bitch. Coin's still in the air about the dying part, though.

Posted by lonelysurvivor7 at 04:38:00 AM 0 Comments

Labels: none

* * *

Wednesday, December 13th, 2023

People I've Killed

In no particular order:

- Samantha Marie Pickett
- Jimmy Lenkersdorf (Lankersdorf? Lenkersdorfer??)
- Man at the gas station
- Sean and Shana Willis
- Krysta Towner

Posted by lonelysurvivor7 at 2:22:00 PM 0 Comments

Labels: people I've killed

* * *

Wednesday, December 6th, 2023

A Question, Revisited

Been a while, I know. I just haven't been in the mood to talk, lately. I haven't been in the mood to think, either, but that seems about all I can do.

Had the first snow of the year a few days ago, and it actually stuck. A few inches are still on the ground right now, even though the sky is clear. Looks like this will be a cold winter. I'll need to stock up for that. I haven't had any encounters recently—not close-up, not at a distance. They're always thin out in the winter. I'm not sure many of them survive the cold.

I think, maybe, perhaps, it's *possible,* that they're dying out. I see fewer and fewer of them each summer. Isn't that a good thing, you ask? I guess so. But can I ever be sure? Can I ever live free of them? Even if most of them die—er, *again*—some could still lurk in the shadows. Some could still sneak up on me. And it only takes one. Then I'll be gone, too.

But let's say, let's just *say* they all die. Let's say one day I am truly free of them. I'm not sure what I would do then, either. Not sure how things would change. I think I'd be more alone than I ever was. I mean, what am I supposed to do when *they* leave me, too? What will I do with my hours of checking, patrolling, recon? Read more books? There are only so many books left in my world.

I used to ask a lot of questions. Way too many questions, actually. I would whisper them at night, in bed, shivering. I would scream them during the day, desperate for a response, angry and alone. I would think them to myself, would hear them echo inside, bouncing against my skull.

I guess, mostly, I asked them when I prayed. When no one else is around, you kind of get used to talking to God. I used to pray a lot, like a million times a day, when this whole thing started. At some point, I stopped. You can only hold a one-sided conversation for so long.

But I did pray a few days ago. It was the first time since... it was the first time in a long time. And this time, I didn't ask any questions. Not that I didn't want to. Just didn't even think about it at first. I started talking, blabbering on about what's been happening, what I've been doing, what I've been thinking. Wish I could say it was a conversation, but it was just me, monologuing. When I realized I hadn't been asking any questions, I tried to think of something to ask, but I was fresh out.

How's that for irony?

Being honest, a part of me still yearns for a response. Maybe there *is* a God. He or She, I don't care. Part of me wants to think I have Heavenly Parents, you know? Wouldn't that be nice? Part of me wants to remember that I'm their daughter, that I mean something to them. I used to *know* those things. I used to believe them, with fire and feeling and without any doubt. But I've forgotten too much, I think. Because now I just think of where I am, of what's happened—not just to me, but to *all* of us—and I just wonder how, you know? I've never had kids, so I guess I don't know, but I just wonder *how*.

Maybe this blog is a prayer. Based on how many replies I get, there's not much of a difference. (Ha ha.)

Posted by lonelysurvivor7 at 01:55:00 PM 0 Comments

Labels: it only takes one, A Question, the meaning of life, prayer

* * *

Wednesday, November 8th, 2023

Early Thanksgiving (or: A Happy Thought)

I've been looking back through my posts—checking for comments, of course, I can't help it—and I've noticed a trend. A depressing trend. A depressing trend of depression—all of my posts seem so sad! So, here's a thing remotely happy:

Thank God for George A. Romero. If it weren't for all the nerdy but knowledgeable experts that he educated and inspired, humanity wouldn't have stood a chance when the dead rose. Of course, standing a chance doesn't equate to coming out on top, as you can tell. But, I imagine, we did better than we would have. I'm still around, aren't I?

Anyway, George, here's your shout-out. Take it for what it's worth.

Posted by lonelysurvivor7 at 08:59:00 AM 0 Comments

Labels: george a. romero, the apocalypse, happy thought

* * *

Wednesday, November 1st, 2023

My Brother

I was thinking of a video, earlier today, of me and my brother. (I was hoping I'd still be able to find it on YouTube, but whatever powers ran that ship seem to have abandoned it some time ago. Like all the other social media websites, it's long gone. Strange that this one is still around, when I think about it.) Anyway, it's this video my father took of us raking leaves in the fall; it's pretty funny. And... we were both so little, my brother and me.

Hmm.

I'm throwing a tantrum in the video. I mean a *real* tantrum. I'm screaming and crying and jumping up and down. Can't remember why, anymore. I keep saying something about a pocket dolly, or a Polly Pocket, something like that, but I don't remember now what I was talking about and it doesn't matter because that's not the point. My brother, he's only three in the video, thinks what I'm doing is hilarious. He keeps dancing around, throwing leaves at me from the pile we've made, and the whole time he's laughing hysterically, like little kids do when they just get to laughing and can't stop. So, there we are, I'm balling my eyes out, lying in a pile of leaves, and giggles are bubbling out of my brother from deep in his chest, like the laughing itself tickles on the way out. But apparently I don't take my brother's laughing very well, because what happens next is a clip my family would watch later, over and over, rewinding again and again and watching it in slow motion, all laughing around the computer together. It even became this mini internet sensation. Auto-tuned and everything, no joke. (That's right—I was an internet celebrity long before this stupid blog.) Anyway, what happens next, or what you see on the video, is my hand shooting out, right into my brother's crotch. But I don't just hit him there. Oh no, seven-year-old me apparently thinks blunt trauma is too good for him, so I grab him between his legs and *squeeze,* and I don't let go. My brother shuts up instantly, for a moment, but then his eyes kind of get wide and he lets out this high-pitched moan, like the prolonged hoot of an owl. Then he just topples over into the leaves with me.

My brother is lucky, in a way. Not about me grabbing his junk, although that did get a few million views. He's lucky for other reasons. He's lucky because he died long before any of this shit happened. He's lucky because he died when my family was still unbroken. The moment he passed, we were all with him. Even my father. My brother was nine years old, but I guess he was the lynchpin that kept our family together. He kept Mom sane. Somehow, he stopped my father from hurting people, from hurting me. And my brother made me smile, even when he was sick from chemo.

Mom held me when he died, and my father held him. I remember my father's tears, strange things I'd never seen before, things I'd never thought possible. He whispered between sobs as he held my brother close to his chest. Please God, please God, please God, please god please godpleasegodpleasegodpleasegodplease. That was the last prayer I remember hearing from my father.

My brother, despite all of the pain and sickness, smiled at me and whispered something I couldn't hear. Then he was gone. That was it. No angels, no voices, no bright lights. He was there, and then he wasn't. Mom tried to reach out to my father, to bring him into our embrace, but he shied away, clutching my brother's body.

My father seems a wounded, wild animal now in my memory, flinching away from human touch. A predator, guarding his prey.

Anyway. My brother got the best years of us. I'm glad he did. I'm glad he didn't see what we became.

Monsters all, in the end.

Posted by lonelysurvivor7 at 08:57:00 AM 0 Comments

Labels: my brother, family, sinning, death

Wednesday, October 25th, 2023

Wilderness Writing

Some of what I wrote while out and about:

I'm sitting here, gazing out at the empty road. How long has it been since a car drove along that road? It used to see traffic often —it's secluded, sure, but every few minutes or so you would see a car pass by, and you could often hear an engine even if you couldn't see anything. Now, there's nothing.

I'm afraid. Every time I come out here, into the wild, I'm afraid something will happen. Not with them—that fear is so constant I hardly notice it anymore—but I'm afraid of other things, more mundane things. Things that wouldn't have been much of a problem a few years ago. What if I broke my leg? Well, I'd die out here. What if I got heat stroke, or dehydrated? No one would be around to save me. No one to call, no emergency services, no one to helicopter me out, no one to report my death, no one to find my body.

In light of all that, I've really been trying to understand why it is I come out here at all. And it's the same reason I do anything, now. The same reason I get up every morning, I guess.

I think—I hope—I'll find someone.

Out here, in the wilderness of all places. But if there are people anywhere, why not here? If there are people out there, why wouldn't they be doing what I'm doing right now? Wouldn't God send us somewhere like this, to finally meet one another? Wouldn't God want us to stop being alone together?

* * *

The land here is beautiful. All gently sloping upwards and westwards, ridges and waves of rock moving like an ocean paused, or moving so slowly that my senses can't register it. Rounded red rocks, like strange shaley animals. One looks out below me. My guardian.

* * *

Is there anything like me left in the world? Was there ever?

Not my...best writing? Not that anyone would care; it's the best writing in the world, as far as I'm concerned, and I kind of own the vote. (I guess, by those standards, it's the worst writing in the world, too. Damn.) But anyway. There's something I did while I was away. Take it for what it's worth.

Posted by lonelysurvivor7 at 10:12:00 AM 0 Comments

Labels: the wilderness, writing, Capitol Reef

* * *

Monday, October 23rd, 2023

Back Online

I'm finally back. Although I'm not sure why; there really isn't much to come back to.

Here's what happened: I went on a sojourn into the wild (something I do every few months; it calms me, I think, puts things into perspective), and when I came back the generator was dead. No amount of pedaling on the exercise bike or fiddling with wires and buttons and switches would make it work again. A few weeks of searching later, I came across another one, and when I finally got it up and running, I found out the router had crashed, or something.

Of course. So, it took me a few more weeks to find a router that would work again. And here I am, back online. Alone, yes, but back online. And in case you're wondering, nothing's changed: I'll still be in Temple Square every Wednesday from noon to 3 PM. I would say I'd update you more on what's been happening, but, well, that's about it. Maybe I'll publish some of the writing I did out in the wild in the next post or so. We'll see. But anyway, I'm back.

If you're out there, please let me know.

Posted by lonelysurvivor7 at 07:22:00 PM 0 Comments

Labels: the wilderness, exercise bike generator

* * *

Wednesday, August 8th, 2023

Wake-up Call (or: Today I Choose to Fight)

Shit. Shit shit. I saw one today, right on the edge of the compound. Practically walked into its groaning maw as I walked the perimeter. Thing would've had me if I was a foot taller. I always envied the tall blondes in high school, the volleyball players and the slender cheerleaders, but who's laughing now? Okay, you're right, no one's laughing. But who's still alive?

(Maybe you shouldn't taunt the dead, Lizzie, you say. Or the undead, for that matter, you add. And to that, I respond: you're right. Poor form. I'll work on that.)

But there's a deeper lesson to be had, here: I'm getting lazy. I need to be more alert on patrols; I need to be more prepared. I can't let them get that close. This is the first one I've seen up close since May—so, maybe, they're getting more sparse, if the diminishing numbers I've seen are anything to go by—but that doesn't mean I can let my guard down.

Here's a weird thing, if you'll forgive a tangent: sometimes I think of this whole damn situation in terms of cancer. Maybe this will sound weird, but it helps me to get a fresh perspective on the urgency of things. Please, allow me to elaborate.

Sometimes, I think of myself as having a form of terminal cancer, and there are two basic options open to me. One: I can do everything I know I need to do, I can do the chemotherapy, the radiation therapy, I can eat right and visit the doctor regularly and do all the x-rays and body scans and whatever. I can even go above and beyond that, with crystals and essential oils and auras or whatever. And you know what, if I do these things, then I have a chance —a *chance*—of surviving. The second option: I can lie down and let the disease take me. What's scary, and frustrating, and exhausting, and really really sucks, is that the first option is a decision I need to make every day, every minute of my life; the second option is a decision I only need to make once. If I get too comfortable, or if I consign myself to my inevitable fate, or if I just start getting lazy and missing "treatments" and "doctor appointments" and so forth (are we on the same page with the metaphor, here?), then I'm dead. I'm dead in the water. (And now I'm *mixing* metaphors, which probably doesn't help with the clarity thing.) But I do have the choice. That part of my fate—that small part, that whether-I-live-or-die part—is kind of in my hands. What I do with it is up to me.

But whatever I choose, They, with a capital "T" (I'm coming back from the metaphor, now—you with me?), They-Who-Are-Dead-But-No-Longer, are still out there waiting for me. And it only takes one. One bite, one scratch, one moan, and if I'm not prepared, I'm dead. And where there's one, there are always more.

Today, all I can say is thank God for Mr. Fluffy. (Mr. Fluffy is my shotgun.)

I'll be where I usually am. But you can bet your ass I'll be more careful. Today is another day I choose to fight.

Posted by lonelysurvivor7 at 07:41:00 AM 0 Comments

Labels: I'm an idiot, it only takes one

* * *

Saturday, August 5th, 2023

What Might Have Happened

I can't sleep.

And it's been five years, to the day, I think, since I last saw my mother alive.

I've tried to reconstruct the last time I saw her. I've tried to remember what she looked like, what we were doing. I was leaving to start a graduate program in American Lit after spending most of the summer at home, with my mother, in Montana. I was young—I finished my undergrad pretty early—and I was going to road-trip it, by myself, across the country, and my Mom was worried.

By that point I was an only child, and my father was out of the picture.

We had a discussion—an argument, really—about me leaving. I'd been dating a boy, Benjamin (I always hated that he liked being called "Benjamin" —like, how pretentious are you that you insist people use all three of those syllables?), and she wanted me to stay and "pursue that relationship" or something. Benjamin had told me repeatedly that he loved me, and that he supported me in whatever I chose to do. I believed him on the first count, but I was dubious on the second. It wasn't hard to miss the flash of anger, or frustration, or whatever in his eyes when I talked about my graduate program. And just *mentioning* a PhD would send him careening into silence. Sometimes it took me hours to get him out of those moods. We were never very serious. No, that's not right. *I* was never very serious. Things between us would never have lasted—you can only hold a one-sided conversation for so long, you know? —even if all hell *hadn't* broken loose, and everyone *hadn't* ended up dying.

We talked about other things, my Mom and I, on that day. If I wasn't going to keep dating Benjamin, she wondered, then who *would* I be dating? (It never crossed her mind that I didn't plan on dating *anyone.*) There would hardly be any church-going Christians at the college at which I'd been accepted, let alone "active" Mormons. And back then I knew, even if my Mom didn't, that I would never be able to sustain a long-term relationship with someone who didn't share my religion. (My beliefs have changed significantly since then, both on religion and relationships. But religion, unlike faith, doesn't matter unless there are people to share it with, right? Same thing with relationships.)

Anyway, even if I think differently now, I didn't tell her a truth that might have helped her in the moment. I let her doubt, I allowed her worries to fester. I did that on purpose and it was an awful thing.

We argued. It was a stressful time for us. I wish I'd been kinder to her, of course I do. Especially in those last moments. But there's this thing about last moments, that they sometimes sneak up on you. With my brother, at least we knew our last moments were our last. With my Mom... I think I kissed her on the cheek as I left, but honestly, I'm not sure. I remember senseless things, I remember how my backpack snagged on the screen door as I left, but I don't remember whether I kissed my own mother the last time I saw her alive. So much happened in the days, weeks, and years that followed that I just can't remember anymore.

I told her I loved her. I said that, at least. I know I said that, I'm sure of it. I had to have said that.

I did call her that night, but not from a hotel in Iowa as I'd planned. It was from a rest stop on the side of the road, after seeing the road blocks ahead of me, and when she answered her voice was frantic and there simply wasn't time for forgiveness.

Posted by lonelysurvivor7 at 02:34:00 AM 0 Comments

Labels: none

* * *

Wednesday, August 2nd, 2023

My Day-to-Day

6:00Wake up.

6:00 - 6:20Check the perimeter.

6:20 - 6:45Check equipment, repair or restock if needed.

6:45 - 7:00Light breakfast.

7:00 - 8:00Yoga (or my interpretation of it, anyway).

8:00 - 9:30Read.

9:30 - 10:30Exercise bike, read.

10:30 - 11:00Brunch.

11:00 - 12:00Check weapons, repair if needed. Archery practice.

12:00 - 16:00Hunting/Foraging (T, Th, Sa), Exploring/Recon (M, F), Watching (W), Whatever I Want (usually: Reading [Remind me to write a post about how fictional characters are the only people left alive for me sometime, because I have a lot to say on that.]) (Su)

16:00 - 17:00Check perimeter. Snack. Gardening, and more archery practice if there's time.

17:00 - 18:00Dinner.

18:00 - 18:30Check the perimeter.

18:30 - 19:30Whatever needs doing. Read.

19:30 - 20:00Supper.

20:00 - 20:30Check the Perimeter.

20:30 - 21:00Prepare for sleep.

21:00Sleep.

Of course, that doesn't include days I go out in the wild, or days on which I'll actually shower or bathe. Reading is replaced with blogging (and swapped with the exercise bike time slot) on Wednesdays. And sleep doesn't always come easily at nine. If I'm honest, it never comes easily at all. But for the most part, that's the gist of things. So... now you know, I guess.

Today's Wednesday, obviously, so you know where I'll be.

Posted by lonelysurvivor7 at 10:29:00 AM 0 Comments

Labels: schedule, day-to-day

Wednesday, July 26th, 2023

Something Funny, But Not Really (or: I Should Have Watched More Movies)

When the apocalypse finally came along, it felt almost scripted. Hollywood had done such a thorough job of showing us what to do that we did it exactly the way they'd always said we would. Cities of looters and riots? Saw that. Entire towns that had holed up in a church to pray, only to be slaughtered on the ground they thought sacred? Check. The aged husband and wife who committed suicide together? Saw that, too. (Really. I'd rather not talk about that right now, but really.) Everyone had roles to play.

But there were some roles that Hollywood forgot to script. What was I supposed to do, for example, when so many of the people I loved the most were already long gone before the apocalypse even started? What am I supposed to do when I feel just as alone now as I ever did then? I mean, what is a Mormon woman, a woman who believed in a God and an afterlife and so much more, what is she supposed to do when she's the last person on earth? There aren't any scriptures for that. There aren't any church handbooks or sermons. Am I supposed to keep believing? Have more faith? Is that what I'm supposed to do? Because, seriously, I don't know. I really don't. I hardly knew what to do *before* the apocalypse happened, but now...

Anyway. I guess maybe I should have taken some improv classes?

Posted by lonelysurvivor7 at 10:09:00 AM 0 Comments

Labels: the apocalypse, Mormons, the meaning of life, faith

* * *

Wednesday, July 19th, 2023

On Dying in Another's Arms

This may seem hokey, and I'm honestly not sure why it should given the fact that I have nothing to be embarrassed about anymore (embarrassment is conditional, right? on other people being around?), but there's a scene from the seventh *Harry Potter* movie that I've always loved. [And yes, now that you ask, SPOILERS DO FOLLOW. Although I'll say what I always said, back when there were people to say it to: if you haven't read the freaking Harry Potter books by now, or at least seen the movies, that's your own fault. Don't expect people to go to great lengths to keep you a virgin from the storyline you've obviously avoided for who knows how long. Also, if you haven't read the books, you're a dummy. Also also, IF SOMEONE IS READING THIS WHO IS ALIVE BUT HASN'T READ THE BOOKS JUST FIND ME FFS I DON'T CARE WHAT YOU THINK ABOUT HARRY POTTER.

Anyway. So, the seventh movie. And by seventh movie, I mean the actual seventh movie, not the eighth one that is still about the seventh book or whatever. The scene I'm talking about is at the end of the film, when Dobby the house elf, who was about as faithful a friend as Harry could ask for, is killed. I won't go too much into the circumstances of how he was killed, because I'm actually much more drawn to how he *dies*, if that makes sense. Dobby dies in Harry's arms. And even though the scene is sad, Dobby seems pretty damn happy that that's where he gives up the ghost—in the arms of someone he loves.

Now, hold that thought. I'll come back to it.

I took an essay workshop class—essay as in creative nonfiction —when I was finishing up my undergraduate degree, and a friend of mine in the class wrote an essay about fainting. I didn't know this about her then, but apparently she fainted, like, *all of the time*—a few times per month, at least. She maybe had a medical condition of some kind, or she just happened to faint a lot, I can't remember exactly. But the point is, she wrote this essay about fainting, and reading it fascinated me because I had never (and still haven't) fainted, not once in my entire life. I've never been exposed to this world of volatile consciousness. I don't remember much of the specifics of what she wrote, except for one thing. She talked about how she had woken up in hundreds of places after fainting, both unfamiliar and familiar, and sometimes waking up was scary, frightening, disorienting. But something that always helped, and of the most comforting experiences, had been those moments when she woke up *in another's arms*. It didn't matter whether she knew the person or not. For those first few seconds, looking up into someone's face who cared enough about her to hold her, feeling their arms around her, she couldn't feel safer.

Waking up, falling asleep. Living, dying. I think doing each of these in the arms of someone who cares about you can make all the difference. My friend woke up in the embrace of friends and family many times; Harry held Dobby as he died.

My brother died in my father's arms. I wished then, and I wish even more so now, that he could have died in mine.

There's a feeling there, a connection, I think. In those few seconds between unconsciousness and consciousness, and especially between life and death, there's *got* to be a connection. I think of all the people in the history of the world who must have died alone, without anyone around them, no one to hold them, and I get this horrible sick feeling in my gut. And I hope that everyone who *has* died in someone else's arms knows how lucky they are—how good they had it.

Posted by lonelysurvivor7 at 10:54:00 AM 0 Comments

Labels: death, dying, love, loneliness, Harry Potter

* * *

Saturday, July 15th, 2023

It's really hard...

...to wait a whole week in between checking this thing. I try to wait, partly to conserve energy, partly to exercise some form of self-control. This week was a fail at that, apparently, given that it's only Saturday. It's silly, but every time I run the exercise bike, a bubble of hope forms in my chest. (I use an exercise bicycle generator, by the way. That's how I get power. And yes, I think it's pretty damn cool, thanks for asking. Every time, I'm worried something will go wrong—that the generator won't power up, or that the computer won't turn on, or that the router won't connect. But so far, it's worked. Halle-freaking-lujah.) The process of turning everything on and logging in seems to take far longer than it should, like I'm forced to watch everything in slow motion or something, and the bubble of hope doesn't do much during that time except press uncomfortably against my ribs. Then I'm finally connected, and of course there's nothing waiting for me except my own words on the screen.

I'm sure I'll start wondering whether this is worth it, eventually. But for now, it is. God, it *absolutely* is. It's been long enough since I felt hope, anyway, and I guess at this point I'll take it any way I can get it.

Goes without saying, but I'll say it anyway: I'll be at the same place, at the same time, as usual. And please: if you're out there, if you're reading this, respond.

Posted by lonelysurvivor7 at 07:01:00 AM 0 Comments

Labels: exercise bike generator, hope

* * *

Wednesday, July 12th, 2023

A Question

Am I really the only one left?

Is it selfish of me to ask that? I mean, if there's really no one left, does selfishness even exist anymore? (That's morbidly interesting. For me, selfishness and altruism are the same thing. Mind: blown.)

But, really, there has to be someone else out there, someone like me, somewhere. Statistically. Right? I mean, what are the odds that *everyone* in the world is dead except for me? (I opted out of a Stats class in college but... about 7 billion to one, I guess? "Never tell me the odds." Name that movie!)

I think about them all of the time, those people that might be—that *have* to be—out there. Should I be seeking them? I'm not sure what else I could do other than what I'm already doing. But then, it's been a while since I've done something for anyone but myself. Not that there are many alternatives (and there's the selfishness =

altruism thing again... doesn't *that* tie my brain up in painful knots of philosophy).

A Bishop I had once used to tell me that

life is all about relationships, Lizzie... it's about the connections we make with other people.

Okay, maybe he didn't say it directly to me. But I think I remember him saying it in church once or twice. And, now that I think about it, what he said reminds me of something else:

For what is significance? It is significance for people. *No people, no significance. That is all I have to tell you.*

Good old Annie Dillard. Emphasis mine, by the way. (I found a copy of *Teaching a Stone to Talk* a few months back. It's sitting on a shelf nearby right now, actually... so no, I didn't quote it from memory. And lay off—I was almost a grad student once, so I can quote random books whenever the hell I want.) You can probably see where I'm going with this.

But you know what? Maybe I'm better off without people. Maybe that's why all this happened, all of this, so that I could be alone. That might be what's best for me in the end, anyway.

That, I could almost believe. But now I'm getting into things that I'm not too keen on talking about, even with you. One day, maybe, but not today.

Until then, I'll be here. Temple Square, Salt Lake City, Utah. Noon to 3 PM.

P.S. I've updated the links at the top of the page. Click on them to read more about me (and how I'm still alive—with two people to thank for it in particular), how to find me, and what the hell happened to everyone else in the world.

Posted by lonelysurvivor7 at 08:35:00 AM 0 Comments

Labels: A Question, Annie Dillard, the meaning of life, The Empire Strikes Back, Bill and Grady

* * *

Wednesday, July 5th, 2023

It's Been One Week

...since you looked at me!

Barenaked Ladies? Anyone?

Anyway. It's been a week. There aren't any comments. Guess I'll see if someone is at the meeting place this afternoon, but I think I got all my hopes up about logging on and seeing a set of comments waiting for me. Not sure if I have any more hope left for this afternoon.

But this is weird, right? I mean, the internet is working... which means there have to be servers somewhere, and they must be powered and online. Which means that there must be people out there making sure they still work. Right? I mean, I'm no internet expert, but I'm pretty sure I wouldn't be able to log on and blog about "my so-called apocalyptic life" (oh, I *am* clever) if someone wasn't out there making sure things ran correctly.

I don't know. Maybe I'm finally going crazy. Maybe I'm imagining this whole thing. Some imagination! I can hallucinate anything, and I choose a blog? (Antiquated, I know, but believe me, I tried Facebook and Twitter and Reddit and Tumblr and Quantime and all the big social media outlets, but they aren't even *around* anymore. All of their main pages are down. So, here I am, *blogging,* or whatever.)

The least my imagination could do is let me hallucinate a Chris Hemsworth fantasy. I wouldn't mind being whisked away to Asgard right about now.

Anyway. I'll be at the same place, at the same time as usual. Temple Square between noon and three.

Oh, and happy Fourth of July yesterday. Freedom and things. Yay.

Posted by lonelysurvivor7 on 11:01:00 AM 0 Comments

Labels: the apocalypse, middle school, Chris Hemsworth, Barenaked Ladies, July 4th

* * *

Wednesday, June 28th, 2023

I'll Be Here

If you are reading this, or if you come across this at any time in the future, I'll be in the northern Utah area. ***I'LL BE AT TEMPLE SQUARE IN SALT LAKE CITY, UTAH EVERY WEDNESDAY BETWEEN THE HOURS OF NOON and 3:00 PM, MOUNTAIN WEST TIME, UNLESS I SAY OTHERWISE ON THIS BLOG*** (I'll keep my general location updated under the [Where Am I? (Find Me)] tab). I won't tell you exactly where I am, for obvious reasons. But come to Temple Square in Salt Lake City, and I'll find you. (The temple is the building that looks like a castle, by the way. There's a golden guy with a trumpet at the top. I'll be there today, watching and waiting.)

I'm hoping someone will read this and find me. Please comment if you read this.

Posted by lonelysurvivor7 at 10:52:00 AM 0 Comments

Labels: Utah, temple square, survivor

* * *

Tuesday, June 27th, 2023

Is anyone out there?

My name is Elizabeth Towner. Call me Lizzie, if you can call me anything. I'm in the northern Utah area. I'll be at Temple Square in Salt Lake City today (27 June) between the hours of noon and 3:00 PM, Mountain West Time.

If there is anyone out there, please, let me know.

Also: this is not an automated message. I'm still here. Please, if you are reading this, contact me.

Posted by lonelysurvivor7 at 09:48:00 AM 0 Comments

Labels: none

* * *

Monday, June 26th, 2023

Is anyone out there?

My name is Elizabeth Towner. I'm in the northern Utah area. I'll be at Temple Square in Salt Lake City today (26 June) between the hours of noon and 3:00 PM, Mountain West Time.

If there is anyone out there, please, let me know.

Posted by lonelysurvivor7 at 09:21:00 AM 0 Comments

Labels: none

* * *

Sunday, June 25th, 2023

Is anyone out there?

My name is Elizabeth Towner. I'm in the northern Utah area. I'll be at Temple Square in Salt Lake City today (25 June) between the hours of noon and 3:00 PM, Mountain West Time.

If there is anyone out there, please, let me know.

Posted by lonelysurvivor7 at 10:19:00 AM 0 Comments

Labels: none

* * *

Saturday, June 24th, 2023

Is anyone out there?

My name is Elizabeth Towner. I'm in the northern Utah area. I'll be at Temple Square in Salt Lake City today (24 June) between the hours of noon and 3:00 PM, Mountain West Time.

If there is anyone out there, please, let me know.

Posted by lonelysurvivor7 at 01:52:00 AM 0 Comments

Labels: none

does this work?

hello? does this work? testing, 1, 2, 3...

Posted by lonelysurvivor7 at 01:47:00 AM 0 Comments

Labels: none

BIO

Christopher Husberg grew up in Alaska and now lives in Utah, where he writes, reads, runs, hikes, games, builds Lego castles, and spends time with his wife, Rachel, and daughters, Buffy and Arya. He received an MFA in creative writing from BYU (where he studied under Brandon Sanderson), and an honorary PhD in *Buffy the Vampire Slayer* from himself.

He writes fantasy novels, of the epic and dark varieties, and has nearly finished his first series, the Chaos Queen Quintet, published by Titan Books. *Duskfall* (2016), *Dark Immolation* (2017), and *Blood Requiem* (2018) are available now, book four (*Fear the Stars*) will hit shelves in June 2019, and the final volume (*Dawn-rise*) will be available in June 2020.

3

THE DEAD WHO CARE

D.J. BUTLER

Hiram saw the man standing beside the road from a long distance away, first as a smudge of gray, but then as a tall fellow, thin like Hiram himself, in a frock coat and a short top hat.

It was odd that the man stood beside the road out here, in the dark deserts of eastern Utah. The nearest town was an hour's drive, and Hiram didn't see a car or a horse. The Model T's lights showed sagebrush, tall grass, and talus slopes, all chalked white by the spell of the electricity.

What the man wore was stranger still: he was dressed in a dark blue frock coat, such as would have looked old-fashioned, quaint, or overly formal before the war. Now it looked like an echo of a world long dead, as did his hat.

Hiram almost drove past, leaving the man to his fate; after his defeats in Cameron, he was in no mood to be company to anyone. But the stranger waved his arms to flag Hiram down and Hiram abruptly thought of the tale of the Good Samaritan.

Grandma Hettie hadn't raised Hiram to be a Levite.

Taking a deep breath, he stopped the car.

In the pocket of his army coat, Hiram had his service pistol.

Traveling these desert roads alone, it didn't pay to be defenseless. The stranger didn't look like a robber, anyway.

The man in the frock coat reached for the handle of the car door, then hesitated. His face was poorly illuminated standing beside the car, but he looked middle-aged, thin as Hiram himself. He was clean-shaven and pale, like a man who worked indoors, and had a long-bridged nose that ended in a bulb, like an onion. "Can you give me a ride?" the stranger asked.

"As long as you mean me no harm," Hiram said. His response was no trivial word game; the Model T was protected by a lamen, a paper talisman that Hiram himself had made and tacked to the floorboards underneath the seat, and Hiram didn't want to say anything that would lower his defenses.

"I mean no one any harm." The stranger smiled. "My name is Asael Johnson. I need a ride to the meadows."

"Asael. *God's healer*. That's an angel name."

Johnson's face brightened. "Do you know Hebrew, then? You don't look like a rabbi."

"I don't know any Hebrew. I barely know English." Hiram laughed. He wore denim overalls under his soldier's greatcoat, and a fedora on his head. "I'm Hiram Woolley. I'm a beet farmer now, I guess, and I'll take you to where you want to go."

Johnson stepped into the Model T. As Hiram put the motorcar into gear and lurched forward again over the gravel road, he had the uneasy sensation that he hadn't seen Asael Johnson either open or close the car's door.

"That's quite the coat you're wearing," Johnson said.

"I fought in the war," Hiram said.

"A lot of men died," Johnson said. "You're lucky you came home."

Hiram nodded. His best friend, Yas Yazzie, hadn't been so lucky. Hiram blinked away sudden tears and tried not to remember Yas's last moments, kicking his life out in a frozen ditch as the wolf-men on their trail howled for blood.

He tried not to remember his own failure, too. Yas had had a child on the way, and he had made Hiram promise that if he didn't make it home, Hiram would see to it the child was taken care of. That was what Hiram was doing down in Arizona—for two years, he'd kept on eye on Betty Yazzie, making sure she had work and enough money. With her death, Hiram and his wife Elmina were trying to adopt the boy.

Michael, a big-eyed, staring toddler.

Hiram had come down to talk to tribal elders as well as the judge. He'd thought he'd be able to bring the boy back with him, but the foster parents in Cameron were objecting, and trying to adopt the boy themselves. Goodman, that was their name. The Goodmans wanted to keep Michael. Hiram had appealed to the elders to intervene with the judge on his behalf, but they had been reluctant. What made one set of white Mormon adoptive parents better than another?

The elders hadn't intervened, the judge had sided with the Goodmans, and Hiram had driven north, empty-handed. He had tried. He had failed, but he had tried to keep his promise to Yas.

Wasn't that good enough?

"The best men died," was all he said. He cleared his throat, suddenly thick with phlegm.

"Good men died," Johnson agreed. "Good men lived, too."

"What town did you say you needed to go to?" Hiram asked. "Meadow?"

"It's not a town. Mountain Meadows."

Hiram's breath stuck in his chest. "The massacre site?" He hadn't realized this road passed the location of the 1857 mass murder. "Someone lives there?"

"One man."

Hiram's sense of unease grew. Keeping his right hand on the wheel, he sneaked his left under the loose collar of his shirt and gripped the iron of his chi-rho medallion. "You have to be careful at a place like that. There are dead who linger."

"The dead who care." Johnson smiled faintly.

"Unfinished business." Hiram wasn't sure why he was still talking. "Vengeance. Justice."

"Mercy."

Hiram took a deep breath and drove a few minutes in silence. "You're wearing quite the coat, yourself."

"I was a doctor," Johnson told him. "This was my coat for formal occasions. It was a common enough sort of coat at the time."

Asael Johnson was a ghost.

Hiram was giving a ghost a ride in his car. He took a deep breath.

"And is tonight a formal occasion?" Or had Asael Johnson died at a dinner party? If the man had been killed at Mountain Meadows, surely he wouldn't have died in evening wear.

"I suppose it is. I will need your help, of course."

Hiram nodded slowly. What help could the dead man need from him? "Because I was a soldier?"

"No, I don't need help for that."

The words didn't put Hiram's mind at ease. Could he say no to whatever the ghost wanted? Of course he *could*, and then he'd have to be prepared for the ghost's reaction. Some ghosts threw things. Others caused people to die of heart attacks, and pure fear. Could Asael Johnson grab the steering wheel and drive Hiram off the road?

Hiram slowed down, just a bit.

But ghosts lingered on earth because they had unfinished business. Business of a passionate nature, business important enough to stick around for, which often meant they were murder victims themselves, intent on avenging their deaths. Ghosts were the dead who still cared about what happened on earth, and needed to set something right.

Something the living *couldn't* fix or *hadn't* fixed.

Maybe Hiram could help Asael Johnson resolve his unfinished business in a way that would minimize the mischief.

"It's horrifying what was done to those people." Hiram offered. "They were innocent."

"There was a lot of fear in the air at the time." Johnson nodded. "The Mormons were polygamists who had tried to flee the country because they didn't quite fit in and talked about building their own kingdom in the Rocky Mountains. The federal government thought the Mormons were in revolt and the Mormons thought the federal government was out to get them. Then the Baker-Fancher wagon train came through, announcing that any Mormons who were sick of Brigham Young's rule could take refuge with them and be escorted safely out of the state. There were rumors that members of the Baker-Fancher party had poisoned Mormon wells, and that they had killed Mormons in Missouri, back in the 1830s."

Hiram's own father was a polygamist who had never quite fit in, taking additional wives even after the Church had publicly disavowed the practice. Hiram had only learned about his father's other families when Abner Woolley had abandoned him and his mother and gone to live in Mexico. "There were provocations, all right. Those don't justify murder."

Johnson smiled. "I was not killed at Mountain Meadows, if that's what you're guessing."

Hiram felt cold. "Am I guessing?"

"If this were an old riddle game," Johnson said, "or part of a fairy-story, you'd get three guesses. If you guessed the answer in three, you'd get a prize of some sort. A magical power, a wish granted, a secret treasure. And if you didn't get the answer in three guesses, something terrible would happen."

"I would lose the princess."

"Or you would die."

The Model T struck an unseen stone or root, leaping into the air and landing with a hard rattle. They rode in silence for a minute. Hiram's heart clubbed his lungs and he tried to control his breathing.

Hiram forced himself to think. The ghost of a dead man—a man not recently dead—was coming to Mountain Meadows, to meet another man. A living man, it seemed. The dead man hadn't been murdered in 1857, but had unfinished business with the living man.

Who could the ghost be?

The current year was 1921; sixty-four years had passed since the massacre. That meant that the living man could have been an adult at the time, now in his eighties or nineties. A perpetrator?

But Asael Johnson had said he hadn't died at the Meadows. Could Johnson be a relative of one of the victims, come to avenge the death of a loved one on an old murderer?

What consequences would Hiram suffer if he guessed wrong?

"I died of a heart attack," Johnson said.

"Unexpected?" Hiram asked.

Johnson nodded. "I was visiting a patient. My patient suffered from gout, and after giving the man his bottle of Haycock's Celebrated Gout and Rheumatic Pills, I stepped into St. George Boulevard and dropped dead without a word."

"There are worse ways to die."

"You have seen many, I expect."

Hiram nodded.

"I have seen quite a few, myself." Johnson paused for a moment. "William McKinley had just been elected president."

Hiram thought. "Nineteen hundred, then."

Johnson nodded. Jackrabbits hurled themselves across the street in the glare of the headlights. It occurred to Hiram that he couldn't smell the dead man at all—he smelled his own sweat, and the oil and exhaust odors of the Model T, but not another human being.

"You were forty years old?" Hiram wasn't sure that a ghost retained the last appearance it had had in life, but that seemed reasonable, especially in light of the fact that Asael Johnson was apparently wearing the clothes he had died in.

"Forty-four."

Forty-four. That would make the year of his birth 1856. That very nearly ruled out revenge for the murders as Asael Johnson's reason for continuing; he would have been an infant at the time of the massacre, so he would only have known any dead kin as stories told to him later.

Hiram doubted anyone could work up enough passion to continue as a ghost over the murder of someone they didn't personally know.

On the other hand, there had been small children in the wagon train.

"You know," he said, "Brother Brigham taught that a child under the age of eight isn't accountable yet for sin."

Asael Johnson laughed. There was wind in the sound, and a faint echo followed after it. "Yes. So did Joseph. But they got it from Mormon, you know. 'Behold, I came into the world not to call the righteous but sinners to repentance; the whole need no physician, but they that are sick; wherefore, little children are whole, for they are not capable of committing sin.'"

"You were raised Mormon," Hiram said.

"I feel a second guess coming on."

"Maybe." Hiram shrugged. "There were children in the wagon train. The Mormons and their Indian . . . allies . . . ?"

"Accomplices?"

"That's fair. The Mormons and Indians killed all the adults, but they let children live. Because Brigham taught that children weren't responsible, weren't guilty. And whatever the wagon train had done—if they had poisoned wells, if they had killed Mormons in Missouri, whatever—the children didn't deserve death."

"What are you saying, Mr. Woolley?"

Hiram was still formulating his thoughts. "The Mormons took those children home and adopted them. Or they tried to, anyway, but when the Army came through and heard that there were surviving children, they forced the Mormons to give them up."

"Are you suggesting I was one of those children?"

Hiram considered. No, that didn't make sense. Those children were returned to kin elsewhere, and would have been raised anything in the world other than Mormon. A one-year-old boy exposed to Mormons for a few weeks would not remember a passage from the Book of Mormon on child baptism decades later.

"There were rumors of other children. Jacob Hamblin had adopted Indian children . . ." Hiram suddenly found himself tearing up, thinking of Michael, Yas's and Betty's boy he and Elmina had tried to adopt. What had Hamblin's son been named? Albert, he thought. And if Hiram failed to keep his promise to Yas and abandoned Michael, would Yas return as a ghost to haunt him? Surely, Yas would have enough passion to be able to do that. And Yas had been one of the most spiritually powerful men Hiram had ever known.

"Yes?"

Hiram cleared his throat. "Not all the children were accounted for. There were rumors about why not. Some said that Jacob Hamblin's adopted Indian children killed some of the wagon train children, or some other Indians killed them. Others said that some of the Mormons simply hid the children from the Army and raised them as their own."

"This is your guess, then," Asael Johnson said. "That I was the child of one of the Baker-Fancher party. That my parents were killed in the massacre, and that I continue on the earth until I have my vengeance?"

Hiram gripped his chi-rho amulet. "Yes."

"Wrong."

Hiram exhaled slowly, his chest tight. What, then?

"But you are getting closer," Asael Johnson added. "Much closer."

The Model T knocked around the ragged edge of a gentle, oblong hill, and a single light drifted into view. It was yellow, the warm light of an oil lantern, and it was a short distance from the road.

"Is this Mountain Meadows?" Hiram asked. "Is that the man you've come to see?"

"Yes."

Lost in his thoughts, Hiram nearly missed the turnoff. Slowing and turning left from graded gravel onto rutted red clay, he startled a small herd of pronghorn antelope. Their white rumps bounded away into the darkness like bouncing balls in retreat.

Hiram parked at the house. It was a sagging, hand-built shack of red stone, with a bleached-white wooden porch slouching even further on one side. The shack was large enough to contain two rooms at most, and the light seemed to come from the back room. There was a hint of an outhouse beyond the structure. Hiram aimed his headlights at the front porch and set the hand brake.

What was the connection between Hiram's ghostly passenger and this rickety cabin?

"Is this man one of the murderers?" Hiram asked. "Did he pull the trigger at Mountain Meadows?"

"Is that a guess?" Asael Johnson's voice was hollow and gloomy.

Hiram shook his head. "Just a question."

"He wasn't," Johnson said. "He moved here later."

What kind of man moved to a massacre site? A morbid man? An obsessed man? A grieving man? An angry man?

A man who wanted never to forget?

"He's dying now," Johnson said. "Old age."

Who was Asael Johnson? The man in the cabin was old, but he wasn't one of the 1857 murderers. And nevertheless, the old man had moved to the massacre site to die here alone. And Johnson was the right age to be one of the wagon train's children, only he wasn't.

And now the two had unfinished business.

"If you have no more guesses to make," Asael Johnson suggested, "perhaps you'd like to knock on the door."

Hiram shut off the car and stepped out. Circling the Model T and stepping onto the porch, he felt cool sweat trickle down the small of his back. He thought of exorcism techniques, and prepared to shout the sacred names and secret words he knew that might chase the ghost away.

The door was a slab of bleached wood, hanging ill-fit in the roughly rectangular doorway. Hiram smelled the exhaust of the Model T and the crisp tang of sagebrush. He knocked.

There was no answer.

Hiram turned back to the Model T and found Asael Johnson standing beside him on the porch. The ghost had taken its hat into its hands, which prompted Hiram to do the same. His hair was beginning to thin on top, and the chill night on the sweat of his scalp was shockingly cold.

"This wasn't your home, was it?" Hiram asked.

"Never."

Hiram knocked again.

This time, he heard a groan within. Asael Johnson watched him intently. Hiram touched his chi-rho amulet through his shirt and overalls, but resisted putting his hand on the revolver in his pocket. The hammer was on an empty chamber, so he'd have to pull the trigger twice before the weapon would shoot.

Hopefully that would be unnecessary.

"I'm coming in," he called in a loud voice.

Then he opened the door and stepped into the cabin.

The front room held a three-legged table with a scarred and stained white linoleum surface, a cast iron stove throwing an ebbing wave of warmth against Hiram's legs and belly, and a small bookshelf. A rag tie rug lying in the center of the floor had been walked almost to ribbons. The light from the second room was strong enough for Hiram to see photographs in cheap frames standing in a row along the shelf, beside a small stack of books.

Lots of photographs.

"Hello?" Hiram called. There was no answer. He stepped into the center of the room; turning, he saw Asael Johnson, standing motionless on the porch outside. Johnson's face held no expression. Why was the ghost waiting?

Then Hiram saw a sheet of paper tacked over the doorway. The light was too dim to read the words, but stepping close, Hiram would make out the astrological signs and the columns of Hebrew characters that told him what the sheet was: a lamen, a paper talisman much like the one protecting Hiram's car.

Asael Johnson wasn't coming in because he *couldn't* come in. The lamen stopped him.

This was why Hiram had been brought to this place.

But he wasn't ready to play his assigned role quite yet. He wasn't sure he *should*.

He lingered to examine the photographs. They were family pictures, mostly, of different families, all old and yellowed with time. They wore nineteenth-century clothing, bonnets and corsets and frock coats and top hats.

The photographs were *almost* of different families. As he looked from one photograph to the next, Hiram realized that he was seeing seven different families, all headed by the same man.

The realization hit him like a punch to the stomach.

Was Hiram's own father living a shack like this, somewhere in Mexico, his bookshelf cluttered with portraits like these?

Hiram stepped away from the shelves to catch his breath.

"Hello?" he called again, and stepped into the second room.

This room was smaller and held nothing but a bed and a lamp. The lamp was a brass oil lamp, sitting on the wooden floor, its flame turned down low. The bed had once been a four-poster, but one of the posts and the canopy were gone, the bed sagged toward one corner, and it was heaped with ragged wool blankets and furs. For a moment, Hiram thought he was alone, but then he saw the face.

It protruded from one end of the pile of coverings, shrunken and shriveled like an old apple. The face was a man's, pitted and gaunt with age, and only a few wisps of hair clung to the mottled dome of his skull. The pile of blankets rose and fell slightly, and then the man opened his eyes. Blue irises swam in glistening rheumy pools. They wandered slightly, as if the man's attention was distracted.

This was clearly the same man sitting as the head of the family in each of the photographs.

And he had a long, onion-shaped nose.

And then Hiram understood.

"Are you a doctor?" the old man asked.

"No," Hiram admitted.

"I've been praying for a doctor."

The old man closed his eyes. Was he dead? But no, the heap of furs and wool rose and fell again.

He walked to the door and stood just inside it, meeting Asael Johnson's gaze. Johnson's eyes were full of tears, glittering like the old man's.

"Well?" Johnson asked.

"This is your father," Hiram said.

He paused, but Johnson said nothing.

"Your mother was one of his wives. Maybe his first or second, when he was a young man. And she didn't want to live in Utah anymore. Maybe she was the first wife, the wife of his youth, and when he proposed taking a second wife to her, she rebelled. Or maybe she found she no longer believed. Or she didn't believe enough to live in the desert, deprived of the conveniences of civilization. And she heard there was a wagon train coming through, offering asylum for Mormons who wanted to flee."

Asael Johnson was a mirror image of Hiram Woolley, in some ways.

Johnson looked down at his feet.

"She took you with her and joined the Baker-Fancher wagon train, heading to California and a new life. Only she was killed. And then you were taken in by a Mormon family and raised as one of their own. And when the Army came through looking for taken babies, they were looking for children who had been with the wagon train. They had a list, I guess, and you weren't on it, so you just disappeared. You were raised with the name Johnson, as a Mormon. Probably somewhere not too far from where your father lived."

"That's your guess?" Johnson looked up, face expressionless.

"At some point, the old man figured out what had happened,

because he moved back here. Maybe hoping to find you and your mother. Maybe afraid of your ghosts. Maybe just feeling guilty."

Johnson said nothing.

Reaching up, Hiram pried out the four tacks pinning the lamen to the wall and then took the written amulet down and folded it into quarters. "How did you find out? Did you know, in life?"

"Yes," Johnson said. "My dead mother came to me."

"In waking?"

"In dreams. I wore a Saturn ring, and it brought her to me."

"You never contacted your father in life?"

"She didn't want me to. She wouldn't tell me his name, and I couldn't discover it from the records."

Hiram thought of Yas, and his promise. He thought of Michael, staring up at him with big brown eyes. He thought of the Goodmans, who worked hard and meant well, but had known neither Betty nor Yas Yazzie.

"Will you stay?" Johnson asked.

"No." Hiram tucked the lamen into his pocket. "Whatever healing is going to happen here, you don't need me to witness it."

Johnson entered the shack and Hiram exited. His boots crunched loud on the sand and pebbles as he walked to the Model T, which started on the first try, still warm from being driven earlier.

He turned the car around and drove back to the main road. There he hesitated.

God's healer. The whole need no physician, but they that are sick.

Yas Yazzie would care. So would Betty.

Hiram took a deep breath, and turned the car back, toward Cameron, and the tribal elders, and Michael.

BIO

D.J. (Dave) Butler writes fantasy novels -- he's also been a lawyer, consultant, and corporate trainer. He travels to multiple comic cons every year to meet readers and talk about writing, but he spends as much time as he can at home in Utah, playing games with his three kids.

His epic flintlock fantasy novel Witchy Winter won the 2018 AML Award for Best Novel and the 2018 Whitney Award for Best Speculative Fiction. Both Witchy Eye and Witchy Winter were finalists for the Dragon Award in 2017 and 2018 (respectively), and Witchy Eye was a preliminary nominee for the Gemmell Morningstar Award.

His books are published Knopf (*The Kidnap Plot),* Baen Books (*Witchy Eye),* and WordFire Press (*City of Saints).* The character Hiram Wooley makes his novelistic appearance in the forthcoming book *The Cunning Man,* from Baen Books, co-written with Aaron Michael Ritchey

4

MYTH DEEDS

JODY LYNN NYE

BAMF!

"Peee-yew! What a stink!" Aahz bellowed, pinching his nose with a green-scaled hand. "Are you sure you got us to the right place?"

My eyes watered. I dashed the tears away with the back of my hand and peered around. Clouds of smoke covered everything more than a few yards away.

"I'm sure," I said, checking the settings on my D-hopper. I had set it to transport us from the dimension of Deva to Grizzle, although the elderly magik item had been known to go wrong on occasion. I glanced toward my four companions with a smile on my face. I had to sound confident even if I wasn't. We had company. "Really."

"And this is where I will find my destiny?" Havago asked, stepping forward and thumping his armored chest with a mailed fist.

"Yeah, yeah," Aahz said, dismissively. "Let's find out who's in charge here."

I'd been in Grizzle only once before. Dimension-hopping was a complicated business. Some dimensions required only one step, such as from my native Klah to Deva, where the Bazaar, where the M.Y.T.H., Inc. office, my home and place of employment, operated. To reach others, you had to go through one or more intermediate steps. Grizzle happened to be a low-magik, neutral location in the middle of a cluster of high-magik or high-technology dimensions. Aahz referred to it as a "rest stop." It had little to recommend a longer stay. No traveler really went there on purpose.

Except now. We were on an assignment. Hand-holding, Bunny had assured me and Aahz. Havago was a Titan –a denizen of the dimension of Titania. He stood head and shoulders above me, and his toned body in its custom-fitted silver armor was impressively muscled, unlike my slim, weedy form. Gazinda, his companion, or secretary, or "here," which is almost the only thing Havago ever said to her in my hearing, when he handed her something to keep for him, was a Titan, too, or so she said. If I had met her in the street, I would never have guessed that. Sure, she had the silver hair, golden skin, and the fanatic expression, but I could explain the latter from her utter devotion to Havago. Gazinda adored him, and let his careless comments slide. When he touched her hand by accident, I thought she was going to pass out from bliss. Not surprisingly, he had no idea she worshipped him, or maybe he took it as his due. She stood only two thirds of his height, and weighed maybe a sixth of what he did, which was to say half my weight. I had about two handspans on her, making her fairly small for a female of her type. Still, I had gone drinking with a bunch of Titans once [&], and I had to assume that she could take me out with a single punch. My partner, Aahz, would have been a tougher proposition, though he was shorter than me. His bat-winged ears, scaly green skin, four-inch pointed teeth, and yellow eyes identified him as a native of the dimension Perv. Titans, among others, had learned to regard Aahz and his compatriots with wariness. Klahds like me, with a slender build, blond hair, and innocent blue eyes, were considered largely harmless, even the butt of numerous jokes.

Havago had come to M.Y.T.H., Inc. to get help solidifying his reputation as a hero. He wanted the recognition that he was sure he deserved that had so far passed him by. The rest of us had been pretty skeptical about that aim, since most heroes are diagnosed post-mortem. The real people who do brave deeds to help others and just go on with their day afterwards don't want any special fanfare.

Havago wasn't willing to wait for fame to find him. From her tiny handbag, Gazinda had pulled a massive scrapbook full of smalltime exploits that he had performed in other dimensions. I had to admit those deeds were fairly impressive: princesses (and one prince) rescued from villains or monsters, treasure restored to its rightful owners, even a couple of cats retrieved from treetops. Havago had collected a few medals and some rewards in gratitude as well as quotes Gazinda had carefully recorded for posterity. None of that seemed to have satisfied his yen of being famous across the dimensions. Gazinda pleaded with Bunny to have M.Y.T.H., Inc. take him on as a client and find him some meaningful acclaim. More for her sake than his, Bunny agreed, and assigned us to help him.

In fact, the right job had turned up in our office almost the next minute. A Grizzly, who had mortgaged himself and half his dimension to a Deveel to get magikal passage to our office, asked for help. A monster was destroying their town, and the people were terrified. He and Bunny had negotiated a fee of one gold piece, which he swore was all that the town could afford.

Havago couldn't wait to set out. We had a tough time convincing him that we needed time to prepare. He fidgeted the whole time, hanging over my shoulder while I went out into town to buy necessities and helpful oddments.

I had already taken a pretty solid dislike to Havago. Aahz shared my opinion of the big blowhard. If it hadn't been part of my job, I wouldn't have escorted him to the corner inn, let alone a transdimensional jump in a bid to build up the fellow's resume of heroic derring-do. Neither would Markie, who had agreed to come along with us in case we needed backup magikal muscle. She was less than half my height and looked like an adorable little child from my dimension, dressed in a flouncy pink dress and matching shoes. Behind the precious exterior was a devious mind and some significant magikal firepower. *

What I really resented the most was letting Havago take on a job that one of us should have handled. I might not have been the greatest or most knowledgeable about interdimensional monsters, but building up someone else's fame on the back of ours burned me. Bunny assured me our reputation could take the hit. With the deepest of reservations, I promised I'd help Havago and the people of Grizzle at the same time.

I tried to remember all the details that Barstow, Grizzle's representative, had given Bunny, although it wasn't much. The day before we arrived, something big had appeared out of nowhere and started destroying the town, and no one knew why. No one had gotten a good look at the thing, because it caused explosions and plenty of smoke. That part I could now confirm.

On my previous visit, Grizzle's capital, Actinup, had looked like any town in any low-magik dimension. Practically all traffic moved at ground level, and people had to snoop into each other's business by straightforward means like eavesdropping and gossip. This time, thanks to the thick haze, I couldn't see more than twenty feet from the end of my nose. I could hear alarmed voices and the sound of wagons and dray animals retreating from our position.

"The force lines aren't much to write home about," Aahz said. That was my cue to scan the local source of magik and see what we had to work with. No one outside of M.Y.T.H., Inc. knew that Aahz had lost his powers #. As a Pervect, he was pretty formidable anyhow, but the illusion that he was still a fearsome master magician kept a lot of trouble at arm's reach.

"The red one under the main road isn't too great, but it'll do," I said, with a casual flip of my hand. I was glad I had filled up my internal batteries before we left Deva.

"I'll clear the air so we can see what we're dealing with," Aahz said. With theatrical passes for the benefit of Havago and Gazinda, he spread his arms out and rotated his hands in circles.

From the tips of his fingers, I extended visible cones of blue lightning. The base of each cone drew the smoke inward and sucked the ashes out of the air, trickling them into heaps on the ground. In moments, the street cleared.

"*Voila*," Aahz said, clapping his hands together. It was a Pervish term he sometimes used. As far as I knew, it meant "Admire my handiwork."

"Nice," Markie said, applying her sucker to her outstretched tongue for a lick. She tossed her head of golden curls. "Couldn't have done better myself."

"Crom's antlers!" Gazinda said, looking around us. "What a mess!"

Knots of Grizzlies and hairy gray animals clung to one another in what shelter they could find, in the corner of ruined houses, under bridges, or behind fallen blocks of stone. Half the buildings on the cold street were on fire, had chunks gouged out of them, or both. Not too far away, I could hear banging and crashing noises. Whatever had caused all the mayhem was still there.

"What happened?" I asked the nearest Grizzly, a tall female with a gold chain around her neck. The locals had long, thick, brown or black fur, prominent muzzles filled with sharp teeth, and little round ears.

"It came out of nowhere!" she said, pointing an impressive talon into the air. "Huge! Ugly! Blue! All of a sudden, it started thrashing and breaking things! We've been running away from it ever since."

Aahz's eyebrows went up. Grizzlies might be boring, but they had a reputation for being able to defend themselves. Something that scared them had to be formidable.

"What is it?" he asked. She turned wide brown eyes toward him.

"We don't know! We've never seen anything like it – or them. I... I can't tell you if it's one thing or a bunch of them!"

"An *it* or a *them*?" I asked. "What do you think it is?"

"I don't know," Aahz said, scratching his chin. "It could be a lot of things. None of them good. I'd like more data, preferably before that thing, or things, comes charging out here again."

"It doesn't matter what it is!" Havago proclaimed, stepping forward. He drew his sword with an audible clash of metal and held it up to the murky sky. "I, Havago, am here to save you!"

Then the Doodlebug hit him.

A long chain of brilliant electric blue, taller than me and almost half a block long, moving on tiny pairs of black legs, shot out of a nearby alley, hurtled past us, and bowled into the Titan. Havago went flying down the street. His sword went one way, his silver helmet another. The blue beast, or beasts – the Grizzly wasn't wrong – put a long, skinny black nose under Havago and flipped him over. The Titan bellowed, but couldn't get to his feet. The Doodlebug flipped him again, rolling him down the street like a hoop.

"Stop! That! You! Varlet!" Havago bellowed, one word per bounce. His cuirass fell off, followed by both gauntlets. "Let! Me! Up!"

"Oh, my!" Gazinda shrieked. She shot after Havago, picking up his discarded belongings along the way. "Oh, my! Oh, my! Havago!"

The Grizzlies rushed out into the street, watching the three of them disappear in a cloud of dust.

"*That's* not local. What's it doing here?" Aahz asked.

"How should I know?" the Grizzly bellowed, going nose to nose with my partner. She bared her teeth, which weren't as impressive as Aahz's, but still pretty fierce, and held up her claws. "I don't know where *you* came from, either!"

I pushed the two of them back with a thread of magik, just enough to get in between them. With Aahz growling over my shoulder, I turned to face the female.

"Okay, let's start over. I'm Skeeve. This is Aahz, and Markie.

We're from M.Y.T.H., Inc. We're here to help you. What's your name, ma'am?"

"Tedina," the Grizzly said, still glaring at Aahz. "I'm mayor of this city."

"Glad to meet you," I said, with a pleasant smile. "Your representative came to see us yesterday. You... you did send for us? Because of a destructive monster? *That* destructive monster?"

"Yes, we did! We thought you'd be able to handle it, until those two idiots got involved! Who are they?"

I glanced up the street, where the Titans and the blue monster had disappeared in a cloud of dust.

"Uh, well." I swallowed my misgivings, and held my chin up proudly. "We were fortunate to be able to bring the great hero Havago with us. He's defeated monsters in sev—um, a few other dimensions."

"Well, he looks like an idiot," Tedina said. "We thought M.Y.T.H., Inc. would be more effective!"

I felt a pang. Our reputation had already taken a hit. I cleared my throat.

"Havago will take care of it for you," I said. "And his assistant Gazinda. Have no fear."

The Doodlebug hurtled past again, knocking us all off our feet. Havago thundered behind, waving his sword. His shiny silver helmet had a visible dent in the side.

"Come back, foul knave!" he bellowed. "Come back and let me chop you into pieces!"

"Yeah, right," Tedina said, her furry face a mask of skepticism. I couldn't disagree with her.

Gazinda puffed in his wake, her handbag slung over her wrist, her short legs threshing as she did her best to keep up with him.

"Oh, dear! Oh, my!"

I heaved myself to my feet and took off running after them. Markie lifted herself on a carpet of magik. I grabbed up Aahz in an envelope of force so he looked as if he was floating by himself. He swam through the air to catch up with me.

"How can we get rid of it?" I asked. "Brute force doesn't seem to have much of an effect on it."

"You have to trap it in a place where it can't split up," Markie said. "That big idiot is doing it all wrong. If you attack it in the open, it will just divide into segments. If we're really unlucky, it'll spawn more of them. Watch!"

Just as she predicted, the Doodlebug headed straight for a wrought iron gazebo in the middle a garden in the town square. The round structure had only one entrance. It looked almost strong enough to hold the creature in place.

"Aha!" Havago chortled, bearing down upon it, sword held high. "I have you now!"

But instead of plunging into the metal cage, the bright blue streak divided into a dozen smaller pieces that raced off in all directions. Two of them came around the far side of the gazebo and charged each other.

"Uh-oh. Down!" Markie yelled.

"Drop us," Aahz commanded.

I dropped us into the scorched grass on the edge of the garden. Aahz threw his arms over his head. The Titans stood watching the pieces of Doodlebug hurtling toward one another.

"Havago, move!" I shouted.

A deafening boom split the air. A blast of flame shot toward us, melting the ironwork into red-hot slag. The big warrior stood as if stunned. Gazinda leaped on him, knocking him sideways. The tongue of fire missed her by inches. The two of them went rolling over and over into a flowerbed. She lay on the ground coughing, a wreath of daisies festooning her hair. Havago sprang up and brushed down his armor, ignoring her. Masses of smoke rose around us, obscuring the buildings on either side. The Doodlebug had used it to make a complete getaway.

"Does the phrase 'doesn't know what he's doing' start to make sense?" Aahz asked. I pulled us both to our feet.

"I vote for 'complete lunkhead,'" Markie said, clearing the air without ceremony. "And 'inconsiderate jerk.' But he is the client."

"One of them," I said. "We're making it worse for our other client."

"Where did it go?" Havago asked, looking around in puzzlement. Gazinda climbed to her feet, the smile on her face as undimmed as if he had rescued *her*. He took his helmet off and shoved it into her arms. "Here."

"It split," Aahz said. "Let's take the timeout to hear from the locals what's been going on."

"Barstow didn't exactly give us a lot of information," Aahz said, to the gathering of Grizzlies who met with us in what remained of a sports center. Springs and weights still clung to the broken walls, and sunlight filtered through holes in the ceiling. Everything was covered with dust. "We came into this flying blind. When did the Doodlebug first show up?"

"You know what that thing is?" Tedina blurted, over the murmurs and complaints of her citizens.

"I've seen one in a book," I explained. "I didn't think they were from around here."

"They're not! We never have anything like that, except when you people come charging through Grizzle on your way to somewhere else!"

"Cool your jets, lady," Aahz said, the veins in his yellow eyes turning ochre. "*We* didn't dump it here."

Tedina sighed and backed away. "No. I know that. It was those BEASTA people."

I felt my ears prick up, not in a good way. "BEASTA? They were here? Why?"

The Grizzly patted the shaggy animal at her side with an affectionate paw. It drooled and leaned against her leg.

"They don't like our pets," she said. "We're good to our grizzhounds! They eat the same food we do, sleep in our dens, go to school and work with us! Setting them loose to fend for themselves would kill them! But the BEASTA people wouldn't listen."

BEASTA. I groaned. We had run into the Beings who Enjoy Altruistically Starting Trouble over Animals more than once. They caused a near riot in the Bazaar on the one time they made it through into Deva. They were known to be sneaky about promoting their agenda. The details of that agenda weren't really clear to me. I only knew some fast-talking individuals tried to take Gleep away, citing his right to be free to be a dragon. Fortunately, my dragon is smarter than he looks, and led them all over the Bazaar before dumping them in the dungheap behind the dragon lot. The Merchants' Association had kicked them out and put a bounty on their heads, so they never tried to come back.

"Doodlebugs come from Boozen," Markie said. "They'd be at the top of the food chain anywhere else. Except maybe Draco. Or Cupy. Import is outlawed anywhere else. They're too dangerous."

"Get it out of here!" Tedina exclaimed. "That's what we're paying you for!"

"It shouldn't be that serious," I said, alarmed. "Look, it's one monster – "

"Or group of monsters," Markie interrupted.

"Right. We're going to…." I began.

"Good people of Grizzle," Havago announced, spreading his arms wide. Gazinda had pulled a polishing cloth from her tiny handbag and was shining the big Titan's silver armor to a gleaming finish. "I have defeated innumerable creatures and brought justice to legions. Let me assure you that it will be my pleasure to free Actinup from the toils of the treacherous Doodlebug! It will trouble you no longer. I would give my life to defeat the monster in your midst!"

"If there's anything left of the town once you're done with it!" one of the Grizzlies said. "It blew up the town square!"

"How was I to know it was that fiendishly clever?" Havago asked, with a majestic frown.

"You're supposed to be experts!" another Grizzly said.

"And we are," Aahz said, moving over to crush Havago in one

arm. The Titan grimaced. "He's just a little exuberant. He was testing the monster's reflexes, that's all."

"My intent was to slash its head off! I will rend it into quivering ribbons. I will…!"

"Havago," I said, taking the Titan's other arm. "We need your guidance. Folks, let us confer with our, uh, hero, and come up with a plan."

Over his protests, Aahz and I steered him away from the crowd. The Grizzlies gave us baleful looks as we moved into a corner.

"Why did you stop me?" Havago said, looking back at the locals. "I was gaining their confidence!"

"Any more confidence, and they'd run us out of town on a rail," Aahz said through a fixed smile that showed all his teeth.

"They do not know what true heroism is," Havago said. "I will show them. I repelled a Kraken from a seaside town! The Ferdalump that threatened Gurnie is now a trophy on the Gurnica king's wall! I shall go up against this Doodlebug in single combat and defeat it."

"Look, Havago," I said, keeping my voice as reasonable as I could. "This one doesn't behave like those other monsters."

"All monsters are the same," Havago said, with impervious confidence. I felt my temper rising. I wanted to take him back to Deva and leave him there until someone asked us to save a cat from a tree.

As if she could sense my mood, Gazinda fluttered in between us. From her handbag, she had drawn a silver tray. On it sat half a dozen silver cups frosted with condensation. They were filled with pink liquid.

"Strawberry cordial?" she said, with a brilliant smile at me. "Havago likes to have a cold drink at this time of the morning. It helps brighten the day!"

"Uh, thanks," I said. I sipped the beverage. It actually did make me feel more relaxed. I made my ire retreat.

"My cordial!" Havago said, raising the small beaker to the others in the room. "To the success of our enterprise!"

"You have anything bigger than a thimble?" Aahz said, tossing back the contents.

"Of course!" She pulled the purse open and felt around inside it. "Ooh, it's cold!" She handed Aahz a chilled silver jug that must have held a gallon. Aahz grinned and took a solid slug from the lip.

I was accustomed to extradimensional spaces, so the idea of a handbag that was a lot bigger inside than outside didn't surprise me. The contents did, however. I caught a glimpse of several pieces of armor, a wall of weapons, and a formal portrait of Havago that was even larger than the oversized original standing beside me. She noticed me looking, and gave me a conspiratorial smile before she closed the clasp.

"Why do you let him treat you that way?" I asked her.

"He's wonderful!" Gazinda gushed, hugging the purse to her. "You just aren't seeing him at his best."

"He has a best?" Aahz asked.

"Oh, he does! In the end, he manages to make everything go right!"

He didn't seem to live up to her ideal, no matter how I stretched the definition. She spent the next hour helping him to tidy his armor, fussing over him, and feeding him small delicacies from her handbag.

"Just keep your mind on the job, partner," Aahz said.

Markie popped out of Grizzle and come back with a massive bestiary.

"I borrowed it from the Library at Mesozandria. I have to get it back before night, but there's a comprehensive article about Doodlebugs. Did you know this dimension doesn't even have a decent library?" She set the huge scroll hovering in the air. It unwound, passing through one fascinating-looking illumination to another, until it stopped on an ornamental letter D. "Doodlebug." The scroll obediently burped up the appropriate page and folded back on itself so we could all read the hand-limned text.

"They start out as single pups," Aahz read aloud. "Their natural habitat is caverns and closed places, kind of the opposite of claustrophobia. Hey, Havago, are you listening? This is important stuff."

The Titan looked up from sharpening his sword on a grinding wheel that Gazinda kept for him.

"I care not for unimportant details. I will follow my instincts. I only care about slaying the beast and freeing the people of Grizzle from its turmoil."

"How about doing it with the least disruption for the local population?" I asked.

"Collateral damage happens, my Klahdish friend," Havago said. He tried the edge out on his thumb and shaved off a translucent slice of fingerprint. "What care I for such petty considerations when a great task is at hand?"

"Maybe you should listen to them, Havago," Gazinda suggested humbly. "They have a lot of experience."

He didn't even look at her.

"Not as great as mine. Don't try to tell me how to manage great deeds!"

I wasn't the most polite being in the world, but I found myself speechless at his rudeness. I started forward, my hands balled into fists at my side. I was ready to let him fall on his face, reputation or no reputation, and take care of the matter by myself. Aahz dropped a heavy hand on my shoulder.

"Hey, Havago, c'mere a minute," he said. He threw a companionable arm around the Titan and dragged him off the grinder stool. I followed until we were out of Gazinda's hearing.

"Why do you behave like that?" I demanded. "Why do you treat her like she's not there?"

The Titan peered down at me from his lofty height. "Who do you mean?"

"Gazinda," I sputtered. "The woman you can't even seem to address politely, let alone thank for running damage control for you."

"Do not dare to sully her name with your foul tongue, Klahd!"

"The name's Skeeve," I said, "and if anyone's doing the sullying, it's you. We're here to do a job. Two jobs. She's trying to help, and you don't pay attention to anything anyone says, especially her!"

"It's like you don't want to succeed," Aahz said. "If you want to die gloriously, you can do it other places, without inconveniencing a lot of innocent people."

"I will succeed here despite what you say, Pervert!" Havago said.

Aahz snarled. "That's PerVECT, and what's your problem? Why do you want to be a hero so badly? They end up dead more often than not. This goes way beyond common sense. Throwing yourself into the path of a monster that can melt metal isn't heroism, it's suicide."

Havago sat down on the nearest chunk of broken wall and let out a huge sigh. He glanced up at Gazinda, then turned his eyes away before she noticed.

"She is my problem, good Pervect. She is the most perfect Titan who ever lived. I want to live up to the image of the hero that she thinks I am. Every time I try to speak her name, my throat closes up. I can barely even think of her without my heart pounding as if it would leap out of my chest and fling itself at her feet."

"Yuck," I said.

My eyes met Aahz's. He grinned, and I couldn't help but let a smile spread across my face. All my resentment for Havago dried up. He was in love. Even the smartest people in the world lost their minds when they were in love.

The Titan turned up his hands in a helpless gesture. "All I want to do is perform great deeds so she will think I am worthy of her."

"That's sweet," Aahz said. "But she's going to think you're a total loser if you keep letting the Doodlebug wreck everything here."

"Then what should I do?"

"I've got a plan," Aahz said. "We surround it, herd it into the nearest closed room, then blast it back to Boozen. It'll take all of us to get it confined, but after that we shouldn't have any trouble with it. It might even go dormant."

Havago straightened up, indignant. "But what about my reputation? I need to be seen as the one who defended Grizzle! For *her*."

"We'll give you all the credit," I said. "You don't have to mention us at all."

With a patronizing smile, Havago threw his massive arms around our shoulders. "I will do better than that. I will give you a shout-out. After all, you will have assisted me a bit in my great effort." He strode back to his workbench and bent over the grinding wheel.

"I still don't like him," Aahz said, shaking his head, "but I understand him."

"The last major building still standing is the primary school," Tedina said. "You can use the kindergarten room."

"Will that be strong enough to contain a monster like the Doodlebug?" I asked.

"Are you kidding? It's strong enough to hold thirty five-year-olds!"

"That'll do," Aahz said. "Get everyone off the street but the grizzhounds. I want them to help us herd the Doodlebug inside."

Markie and I topped up our magik from the red force line for the illusions that I planned for us to cast.

"That's one sluggish source," Markie said, dusting her little hands together. Tedina looked embarrassed.

"We don't have a lot of magik in Grizzle. That's one of the reasons people never visit us. No sights to see worth mentioning. No attractions. No hot spots or night clubs. We're just a stop on the way to somewhere else." She chuckled ruefully. "The Doodlebug is the biggest thing that has happened to us in ages."

Havago stood in the middle of the street, the sword held high in his hand as if he was posing for a Shutterbug. Beside me, Gazinda sighed. Havago carefully did not meet her eyes. It was ridiculous. Each of them was in love with the other, but neither of them could say so. If we weren't about to get attacked by a monster that could make buildings explode, I would have thought it was funny.

"I feel like a gunslinger waiting for high noon," Aahz said. I frowned.

"Why would you sling a gun at something?" I asked. "Isn't the idea to shoot it?"

"I… never mind," Aahz said. He pointed up the street. "Here it comes! Get those spells working!"

Sections of the blue monster trundled out of different pieces of wrecked architecture and assembled in a line. Once I counted twelve segments, that was my cue. I pictured the illusion I wanted in my mind, and cast it around the Doodlebug. I couldn't see the spell I cast, but the gasps from Tedina and Gazinda, it must have been effective.

"Giant Doodlebugs!" the Grizzly mayor exclaimed. "Where did those come from?"

"A little illusion of mine," Aahz said, buffing his claws on the breast of his jumpsuit. "We want it to feel threatened and start looking for shelter."

It began running around in circles. Everywhere it went, though, grizzhounds disguised as bigger and meaner Doodlebugs met it. They chased it, baying, down the street toward us.

Markie and I kept the illusions closing in on the Doodlebug, steering it out of alleyways and . The only place it could run to was into the primary school, and the kindergarten room. As soon as it hurtled through the door, Havago dashed after it.

"On to glory!" he bellowed.

The rest of us followed him.

Within the kindergarten, the Doodlebug raced around in a frantic fit. The room was too small for it to break apart into sections, so it recoiled when Havago charged it. To my horror, it coiled into a small spiral, and whimpered.

"Oh, no!" Gazinda said. "It's scared!"

"Stand back, woman!" Havago shouted. "You are in terrible danger!"

"From this?" The Titan female moved forward with her hand outstretched. Several of the Doodlebug sections put their elongated noses into her palm. "It's not dangerous."

Aahz, Markie, and I looked at each other.

"It's not wild," I said. "I bet those BEASTA people stole a pet, or a zoo animal, and left it here to cause trouble. It's setting fires and causing havoc because it wants to go home, but no one can understand it."

"Oh, we'll find your home," Gazinda cooed, petting as many of the noses as she could reach. The Doodlebug cooed back. It shifted its coils until it surrounded her in a massive circle of blue and stared at her with the same adoring gaze as Havago.

Pounding came at the door. We all jumped, and the Doodlebug hissed.

"Have you killed it yet?" Tedina shouted. Gazinda's eyes went wide.

"You can't kill it! It's innocent."

"The beast is harmless!" Havago shouted back. "We will not kill it!"

That wasn't a good enough answer for the Grizzlies. As we watched in horror, the door splintered, and a crowd of angry townsfolk poured over the threshold.

"Get out of the way, Havago," Tedina said, baring her teeth.

"I will not," he said. "This creature was brought here against its will. Stay back! It is harmless."

"Harmless?" a plump Grizzly holding a hay fork growled. "It burned down my store!"

A dignified Grizzly with silver fur exclaimed, "The high school blew up! And right before final exams!

"Our Grizzle diorama is in pieces! Now what will we use to attract tourists?"

"Now, come on, everyone," I said, trying to be reasonable. A rock came flying toward me. I fielded it easily with a thread of magik, but it was the beginning of an onslaught by the angry villagers. All of them fought to get past the Titan with their makeshift weapons.

"Havago, stop them!" Gazinda insisted.

"As my lady insists!" Havago flipped his sword into the air until it came down pommel first. He brought it down on the wrist of the first attacker, then skillfully knocked the next Grizzly into the three coming up behind. He spun, pushing the next Grizzly with a kick to the midsection that made it sit down with an "oof!" I was dumbfounded, but Aahz watched him with a critical eye.

"Damn, he's good!" Aahz said. "Maybe he deserves the reputation he's trying to promote."

"Aren't you going to help him?" I asked, as another half dozen Grizzlies joined the fray.

"Naw, I'm going to enjoy the show. I'm just sorry I didn't bring any popcorn." Aahz leaned against the wall with his arms folded, a big grin on his face. "He's that good. If he wasn't such a jerk, he could go down in history as one of the real heroes."

Two Grizzlies started to charge Havago with a heavy board between them. Havago fell to his back, rolled over in a reverse somersault, then sent both Grizzlies sprawling each with a kick to the backside. He sprang to his feet.

"Who's next?" he bellowed.

"I... I think we should...." I started forward, wondering what I *could* do. I was no fighter, but the odds against Havago were tremendous. I felt a belt of magik hold me back. Markie grinned up at me.

"Let him take care of it, Skeeve. He's doing fine."

Before I knew it, Havago had repelled all the Grizzlies, and driven them back beyond the broken door. He stood on the threshold, snarling. None of the Grizzlies came forward to challenge him again.

"Look, Gazinda cooed, leading the Doodlebug forward. It licked her palm with a long black tongue. "You see? It just wants to be friends."

"But the whole town is ruined!" Tedina cried. "We don't have the budget to rebuild all of this... this catastrophe!"

The idea that had been percolating in my mind since the melee erupted came into full focus.

"I think I know how you can make it back," I said. Havago looked upset. I was stealing his thunder. I held up a hand "Hear me out! Look, you didn't know this creature was harmless – all right, relatively harmless. But you have a *genuine hero* here. He could have chopped you all to pieces, but he didn't! In fact, he defeated you all without hurting any of you."

"Much," one of the Grizzlies muttered, holding his wrist.

Havago looked mollified. I went on, talking faster as the idea pressed at my imagination. "What if... what if you advertised that you had a champion who would take on all comers in non-magikal combat? I mean, not that you would want to make side wagers about the outcome. Havago would never throw a match."

"Never!" Havago bellowed. "My integrity is matched only by my prowess!"

A few of the Grizzlies shared private glances. I could see the beginning of an underground betting ring forming. I didn't mind. The organizers would work hard to support Havago if he was going to make them money.

"It sounds like an interesting idea," Tedina said, stroking her chin. I could tell she was half convinced. I pressed to push her the rest of the way.

"Grizzle won't be just a stopping off point on the way to somewhere else. You'll have your *very own hero:* the Champion of Grizzle. People would come from all around just to watch matches against him. Look at him." Havago struck a pose as I gestured at him. "He's the biggest, strongest person here, but he knows how to hold back on that strength when it's appropriate. The more spectators you have, the wider his fame will spread."

Enlightenment dawned on face after face. Gazinda beamed with pride.

"I like it!" Havago said, sheathing his sword. "Will you have me, good Grizzlies? I would be proud to be your hero."

"He could make you all rich," Aahz added. "If you promote it right."

"But we don't know how to organize that kind of publicity," Tedina said.

"Oh, I do," Gazinda said, waving a casual hand. "I've been doing it for Havago for years. I can put advertisements on the Crystal Ethernet, and cross-publicize with popular acts in a hundred different dimensions, sponsor contests, all the usual things. But we never had a place that we could call our own, you know, that people knew where to find us. This would… this would be wonderful!"

"What about the Doodlebug?" Markie asked.

"I'm going to keep him," Gazinda said, firmly. "He can live in my handbag! He's so insecure out in the open."

"I don't like it," the silver Grizzly said. "What if he gets loose and wants to blow something up?"

"He can do demolition work for you free of charge," Markie said. "Or you can set something up for him to destroy. And," she added temptingly, "sell tickets."

That certainly got their attention, as did the scrapbook Gazinda pulled out of her handbag. The Grizzlies moved in to ooh and aah over the clippings. Havago pulled poses and signed autographs for some of the enterprising locals who foresaw a market for them in the not too distant future.

I patted the Doodlebug one more time and turned to leave.

"Wait!" Havago shouted, shaking the room with the power of his voice. "I promised a shout-out to my friends! My heroes! Aahz, Markie, and Skeeve, for assisting me – a trifle – in starting my new life here in Grizzle."

I chuckled. He couldn't make me angry any longer.

Tedina pressed the gold coin for our fee into my palm and shook hands with all of us. We left the Grizzlies and the Titans sitting around tiny tables in the very crowded schoolroom, talking over plans. Night had fallen when we emerged.

"Well, I need a drink," Aahz said.

"Strawberry milkshakes on me at the Yellow Crescent Inn," I offered, taking the D-hopper out of my belt pouch.

"That was a good deed you did back there," Markie said. "That was one heck of a good idea, and it solved all of their problems in one swoop."

"Me? I didn't do anything," I said, my eyes wide with innocence, as I pushed the button. "I'm no hero."

BAMF!

** You can read about this semi-heroic exploit in **Myth-Fits**, available from bookslingers and other smugglers of literature.

* Anyone who would like to discover the range of Markie's talents is invited to delve into the marvelous recounting in **Little Myth Marker**, available from your physical and ethernet purveyors of literature.

Thanks to a practical joke. The record of Aahz's deprivation can be found in **Another Fine Myth**, enshrined in libraries and for sale elsewhere for a few simoleons.

BIO

Jody Lynn Nye lists her main career activity as "spoiling cats." She lives northwest of Chicago with three feline overlords, Athena, Minx, and Marmalade, and her husband, author and packager Bill Fawcett. She has written over fifty books, most of them with a humorous bent, and over 165 short stories.

Jody has been fortunate enough to have collaborated with some of the greats in the field of science fiction and fantasy. She wrote several books with Anne McCaffrey or set in Anne's many worlds, including **The Death of Sleep**, **The Ship Who Won, Crisis on Doona** (a *New York Times* and *USA Today* bestseller), and **The Dragonlover's Guide to Pern**. She wrote eight books with Robert Asprin and has since his death continued two of his series, the *Myth-Adventures* and *Dragons*. She edited a humorous anthology about mothers, **Don't Forget Your Spacesuit, Dear!**

Her latest books are **Rhythm of the Imperium** (Baen Books), **Moon Tracks** (with Travis S. Taylor, Baen Books) and **Myth-Fits** (Ace). She is one of the judges for the Writers of the Future fiction contest, the largest speculative fiction contest in the world. Jody also teaches the intensive two-day writers' workshop at DragonCon.

5
THE SHADOW OF MARKHAM

R.R. VIRDI

The only lives to pass this night would be those taken by my hand.

I resolved to make that the case as I raced over the flat rooftop, cold and porous stone leeching the warmth from my bare feet. But the city always took her toll out of my nightly exploits.

Markham, my new home, collected her tax for living within the walls in other ways at times.

Like the occasional child going missing.

It wasn't unheard of in a place like this.

One or two through the months was as normal as alleyway attacks.

But a dozen children vanishing in the span of ten days was too much even for this place, harsh and hard as she was.

I'd find them, though.

My feet beat against the roof with a sound like wood on stone. Old callouses had long since formed over themselves and made the skin as tough as anything I ran over. I neared the edge of the structure and sped up towards the lip.

My cloak billowed behind me, a train of spun shadow darker than ink smeared with coal. Yet still shades lighter than obsidian of my skin. The multiple layers of fabric flapped wildly as my feet hit the end and I sprang forwards. I shot through the city tops like an arrow—a wraith of black, passing overhead too fast to be seen.

The edge of the next building closed in quicker than I'd expected. I angled myself properly, touching down on the balls of my feet and tucking downward. Momentum carried me forwards as I rolled to take the brunt of the impact across my back and shoulders. The maneuver brought me back full circle to my feet, and I sprang, pushing myself back to a sprint.

A gust of wind threatened to rip away the cowl obscuring my face. I reached up absentmindedly, cinching it tight with a tug against the ties. My pace quickened and I barreled towards the next edge.

Time slipped away, and the night here was unkind to those who dallied. Another child would go missing tonight. But if I played my part right, I'd be able to follow the people behind it back to wherever they took the little ones. A dangerous game.

The only kind the city of Markham played.

A shrill scream cut through the blanketing silence of the night.

I snarled, looking ahead at the next jump, then to where the noise had come from. An alleyway sat between the buildings, nestled low and long right below me. Stopping to investigate would only hamper my chase.

The weight of one person's suffering versus that of many children.

It all weighs the same in the end. Failing to stop one leads to a ripple like a stone thrown into water. One action—endless possible consequences.

People harmed by Markham's late night side tended to spiral down terrible paths. An ill turn following another leading to a dark road with no end in sight.

And I could stop it.

I exhaled, tucking my weight and diving towards the ledge. The roof banged against the dark leather around my waist, promising bruises in the morning despite the padding. I ignored the aches and closed my fingers around the wall's lip. My body sailed past the edge as momentum carried me onward. I grimaced as my battered torso stretched for a brief moment before I twisted and arced down. The balls of my feet touched down against the building's side as I hung in place.

The scene below was one all too common for the city. A woman—human—scurried through the narrow passage of worn stone and remnants of evening's rain. Her feet beat like mine had across the ground, drawing the occasional sharp *snap* as she hammered her away ahead. The green cloak over her shoulders looked to be of an expensive make. It was good wool that the tailor had somehow found a way to dye the color and depths of a rich forest.

Wealthy. The thought echoed through my mind as I took in the rest of her.

Something flickered along her neck, catching the scant bits of candle lights lining the odd balcony through the way. A garland of white stones, each just a fraction smaller than a man's eye, ran along her throat. *Gemstones.* I confess I didn't know what sort.

Two men trawled at the beginning of the alley, unperturbed their quarry had gotten so far ahead of them.

A look down the way revealed why. The passage stopped. *Dead end. Aptly named.*

The woman stopped, exhaling loud enough in frustration and panic to course through the alley. She turned and whipped her head to stare at the slowly approaching duo. Another look over her shoulder, more out of fear than logic, reminded her of her predicament.

The men quickened their pace, tired of simple pleasure in watching her run herself into an inescapable situation. One of the man had made a habit of not skipping any meals, plump and squat. He reminded me of wooden dolls with wide bases that wobbled back and forth. He had a nose that had been blunted several times by no accident. His lips were thick and fleshy, pulling awkwardly to one side as he chewed on something. A toad of a man.

His partner strolled alongside him as an antithesis to him. Long of limb and face, grizzled and carved of driftwood. He reminded me of the underfed and feral dogs lurking through parts of the city. Dark featured with narrow and intelligent eyes. Scraggly patches of hair grew at the sides of his face with no hope of properly filling in. A long tail of hair hung from the back of his head, thinning like the rest along his skull. Someone had pulled and pinched his face at birth it seemed. The reedy man took a pair of lengthy strides, putting him paces ahead of his companion.

I released my hold and sank soundlessly through the air. Another lip, this one belonging to the base of a window, crossed my path. I clung to it, tightening the muscles through my legs and back as I tried to hold myself in place without slamming into the wall.

A sliver of metal flicked into view with a metallic *snap,* glinting for a moment.

The knife wouldn't be much threat. That all depended on the man wielding it.

The dog-faced thug carried his weight more to one side than normal. His left seemed to absorb more of the impact behind each step.

The toad's face scrunched up and he turned to the side, racking his throat to spit hard. He made the sound again as he snuffled. His color paled for the briefest of instances. He breathed laboriously.

I smiled. This would be over soon enough.

My fingers loosened and I sank again, grabbing hold of an aged wooden poll. I held to it with all the strength I could. Fatigue and pain gnawed at the small muscles in my hands. I banished them both, setting my jaw hard to take my attention away from the sensations. Another wooden beam stood across the alley from me, closer to the where the men would pass under.

I waited, stilling my breath.

Patience—a skill, a virtue that one needed to truly thrive in the city. But it was part a lie. Waiting, deliberating instead of acting could get one killed here. Sometimes you needed to act faster than you could think.

I gritted my teeth and swallowed the urge to swoop down and throttle the men.

Their pace quickened and they passed under me.

I sprang again, my lithe form and dense muscles shooting me towards the beam with ease. My surge brought me to it in an instant. I wrapped my arms around it, momentum driving me into a dervish as I whirled to reposition myself. The leather and cloth over my hands allowed me to slip down a few hand lengths with ease.

The woman at the end of the alley didn't linger in place. She must have decided it wiser—safer—to walk towards the men in hopes of slipping by. To distract them for long enough to let her get past and break into a run.

I'd seen it before.

And I'd watched it fail every time.

I readied myself for what had become second nature by now, tensing against the poll.

The woman made it several feet before the pair of men. She clutched her hands to her chest as she stepped faster.

The men moved a pace apart from each other, giving her the ability to pass between them. That's when it'd happen.

I leapt, crashing into the slender hound of a man. The collision knocked him off balance and buckled his weak leg. He fell flat, flailing as I bounced back to a stand. No wasted movements. My fist snapped out, connecting with the toad-faced cretin's throat.

The woman screamed.

It rattled me, worming through my sensitive ears like thunder and breaking glass—metal dragged against rough stone. I winced through it and shoved my palms into the portly man's eyes. He staggered back, hacking violently as he pawed at his face. I didn't relent and stormed forwards to drive the heel of a boot into his sternum.

The blow struck with a heavy *whoompf* that drove him back until he stumbled head over heels.

I spun and dove. My body crashed with the reedy cutthroat's, limbs tangling as we wrestled for control. He carried more strength than I would have guessed for someone with his lanky build. My cloak spread wide as I took his wrists in my hands, bearing down on him. As my weight brought his arms closer to his chest, I released the hold, twisting to drive the edge of my elbow into his skull.

His head snapped back. The crown of his skull struck the concrete, his eyes losing clarity as the strength left his arms.

I pushed off him, bounding back to my feet as the squat toad of a man barreled into me. Dull aches built in my ribs from where he bashed his fists. He swung wildly, letting his bulk and charge do the work in forcing me back. I spread my feet and leaned into him, using all of my body to keep from toppling. He pushed me back another foot until I pivoted, upsetting his balance. He stumbled past me as I lunged to snap my knee towards the side of his skull. The blow connected with the force of a hammer, sending him staggering to the side. I leapt and brought my elbow overhead.

He turned in time to see me, eyes going wide as I brought the joint down against his temple. The strength left his legs. He crumpled into a heap like his friend.

The temptation to slit his throat and be done welled inside me. It morphed into the heat of a bed of coals, resting deep within the hollow of my stomach, threatening to set me afire and burn their way out of me. But that wasn't my place.

I am no man's judge.

They did that enough to my kind.

And I wasn't their executioner.

I turned to face the young woman.

Our eyes met and she sucked in a breath. One of her hands went to her mouth, covering it as she recoiled.

I knew why. The hard yellow-gold of my eyes marked me plain and clear as the sort of creature most unwelcome in Markham. Even in the darkest of nights.

"Your mouth…your teeth." She bared her own canines in what looked like an unconscious gesture. Catching herself in the act, she promptly shut her mouth. The woman reached out to me gingerly with a hand, pausing an inch from my face as if close contact would burn her.

I reached up and unfastened my cowl. It fell, bringing my full features into clarity for her to see. My visage didn't inspire calmness and reassurance to those inhabiting Markham. The tapered ears, long and coming to a point like knives, and my elongated incisors marked me well as an elf. The fact my skin brought a truer definition to the word, "dark," was the last and most obvious piece anyone needed to know to label me.

Umbra elves were the lowest class of inhabitants in the city—most of the "civilized" world in fact.

She finally brought her fingers against the flesh of my cheeks, brushing them gently before pulling back. Her mouth worked soundlessly for the space of several breaths. "You saved me."

A simple statement, carrying no end of weight behind it however. I knew the question that lingered under what she had said. She was silently asking, "Why?"

A question of three parts in truth: Why did I save her? Why would an elf, my kind in particular, bother at all? And what would happen now that I had?

Two words were all it took to put her concerns to rest. "Why not?" I turned, drawing my hood overhead as I moved away from her.

"Because," she said. It was a good point. None of my kind should have made the effort given the treatment we'd received among the human population. She knew it as well. My actions had shaken some her beliefs, and now caught in the midst of sorting through them, she needed a clarity I couldn't offer.

I ignored the comment, listening to the sounds of something hard and flat against stone. *Footsteps. Hard-soled boots.* The constabulary were on their way. My eyes turned to the windows lining the alley. Someone had taken note of the altercation and sent word to the authorities. I had an idea of who would round the corner at the alley's opening.

"The man coming ahead is a good one. A member of the constabulary I happen to trust. His name is Inspector Cardinane. Tell him what happened...leaving out the finer details about me, if you'd be so kind." I didn't need to turn around to know she was nodding along.

"I will."

"Good. Now turn around to make sure our sleeping friends aren't close to waking back up. I'm sure you'd rather not have to deal with that again." I knew the effect my words would have on her and broke into a run as she shifted away from me.

"What?"

I disregarded her absent comment, throwing myself at the beam I'd jumped from earlier, mantling it to spring to the nearest window sill. Hauling my body up from there was trivial and second nature by now. I'd made my way to the roof of the building opposite from where I'd first spotted the scene unfolding. A last look down showed me the young woman eyeing the spot I'd been before she'd turned around.

Her attention moved to scanning the rooftops.

I melted away into the shadows before her eyes could fix on me. My mind turned back to the issue I'd buried to help her, the children. It had taken me longer than I would have liked to deal with the thugs, but if I hurried, I could make it to where I needed to be before losing my opportunity.

I burst into a full sprint, spurred by the thought. The edge of roof offered a better lip for me to jump off in my effort to reach the next building. I repeated the process for several buildings, falling into the act with a cold and practiced familiarity.

A faint row of shimmering pulled my attention, drawing it to the Emthe River. Its surface carried motes of crystalline light, almost as if it had been littered with thousands of flecks of glass, each catching scant bits of the moon's own radiance. Though, knowing the locale and the area's history, it was likely the case.

Markham had no need of a shining veneer. She wore herself open and proud of every scar, gritty mark, and whatever stains had marred her. The city made no false illusions as to what you'd find inside her. A place of unvarnished truth from the moment you entered.

Well, some truths at least. Every place like this carried its fair share of lies. Though, it was obvious it would from the beginning as well. The problem rested in knowing what those falsehoods were, and who they belonged to.

A difficult thing. And equally dangerous.

But then, so was I.

I moved my way to the edge of the last building on the dock and kept my eyes to the walkway below.

The usual sort of men and women moved about: Shirtless deck hands and laborers, thick with slabs of muscle built up from years of heavy toiling. A few strumpets, clothed in old pieces, all artfully arranged to show the most enticing bits of their curves and skin. Their swaying walk only served to accentuate their best features. Late night merchants, wearing ensembles of total black, lined with silver cords over their left shoulders.

The latter signified their certifications and license to trade under the rules and protection of the guilds within Markham and the wider world.

An ordinary crowd for my city. At least at first glance. Several buildings down, something else happened far out of the norm.

A trio of men, working noticeably too hard not to be seen, wrestled with a fourth figure within their collective grips. The last of the people fought back from under a black tarp. They barely came up past the mens' abdomens.

A child. It explained the ease with which the trio handled the diminutive person.

The group dragged and shoved the smaller form along, heading toward a warehouse half a dozen buildings from where I sat perched.

I raced into action, taking a short leap onto the roof of the next structure, giving thanks at the close proximity the constructions shared along the dock. The low lighting through the area was a boon. I made my way over to the top of the storage house with ease, skulking over to the nearest lip to peer over.

The men passed below, pulling open the large wooden doors and entering.

I exhaled and turned to scan the roof. The rough and corrugated tiling gave me firm purchase to walk, but a single misstep could crack one of the pieces, generating a loud enough sound to draw unwanted attention in the quiet night. I positioned my feet with my toes pointing out toward my shoulders and walked in an odd gait. It muffled the noise of my steps and helped me realign where and how the bulk of my weight would come down.

My search along the roof revealed a balcony hanging ten feet below me, running most of the length of the warehouse's right side. No lights shone through the glass windows set into the mortared and irregular stones comprising the wall beneath me. I eased myself down, taking care not to hang too long before the clear panes. No raucous *thud* emanated from my impact as I landed on the wooden platform. One board did creak under the pressure, letting up as fast as it had made the noise.

I sucked in a breath through my teeth. No disgruntled sounds came from within the building. I remained undetected…for now. My face pressed against the panes of glass as I looked inside.

Torches burned from holders throughout the area. A variety of barrels and crates filled the place, stacked high enough to obscure sections of the room.

Good. Plenty to work with. As always, my city provided.

I brushed aside my cloak and reached into one of the small leather pouches fastened tight to my body. My fingers slipped into it, retrieving a slender sliver of braided steel wire. Threading it through the space between the window and where it met the wooden lip was simple. I pulled the flexible strip of metal along until it caught the latch. Another series of short tugs and twists forced a satisfying *click.*

I pried the window open, taking care to not elicit the odd *squeak* old and ill-cared for hinges and joints made at times. It slipped upward in silence. The pane's weight rested on one of my shoulders as I propped it in place, sliding through the space. I let the glass come back to a gentle close, knowing that should a gust of wind kick up, it would betray my entry and roll through the open room.

The closest stack of crates towered high enough to reach a few feet below the wooden platform I stood on.

Voices grumbled through the warehouse loud enough to catch my attention.

I shut my eyes, tuning myself to the words with as much care as I could muster.

"—do with these pissants?"

"Not our worry. We get paid and—"

"That's all, honestly. Coin spends the same no matter what ya do for it."

"Kids'll start talking with others. Take note their chums go missing."

One of the speakers snorted. "Mine doesn't take note for anything but when supper's on and when to shit. Even forgets that last one proper at times."

The trio laughed in unison.

"This feller will fetch us something decent. That's all—hey, stop it you little pisser!"

A pained whimper sounded through the warehouse.

I hadn't heard the strike. But a noise like that only came from a young one being beaten. My teeth grated against each other as I descended onto the topmost create and worked my way down.

"Just gag the kid and be done with it. Bind and leave him here. They'll come and take him how and where they do. Not for us to bother with."

A pair of voices murmured something that sounded like agreement.

The child screamed incoherently, grunts of exertion peppering the shout. His clamor cut off suddenly as if the trio's threat had been carried out.

My ears picked up nothing in the way of the mumbling associated with a gagged man. Had they rendered the child unconscious?

"Stuff'll drop an ox with a whiff. Shitter will be out for set of days," said one of the voices.

I grimaced at that. I'd suspected the kidnappers had been drugging children with a sedative to keep them quiet. Moving about with reluctant children was no quiet task, especially if you were not their parents. One of my hands went instinctually to a pouch along my waist, fingering the flap. A possible counter to the solution rested inside. That all depended on if my guesses were correct on what substance was being used.

I made my way closer to the ground, staying a dozen feet above it on a row of poorly stacked crates. A single improper shift of weight would bring the whole set crashing down with thunderous noise I couldn't afford. My hand moved to another pouch, and I thumbed it open. Cold spears of metal pressed against my fingertips. I plucked several free, looking to the space between where I crouched and another formation of crated. A flick of my wrist sent the nails clattering against the nearest box before tumbling to the ground.

They *clinked* like small stones striking glass. An inaudible sound in most scenarios, but given the hushed state in the warehouse, it was like the breaking of a bottle.

"S'what was that?" The voice belonged to the man who'd first spoken earlier.

"Dunno. Probably a shiking rat or summing."

A loud and fleshy impact rang out, like an open-handed blow across someone's face. "That sound like a rat to you?"

"I'll take a look." The third speaker sounded resigned, but more so with his companion's bickering and stupidity. "I'll holler if I see something. If I go quiet, it's me taking a piss."

Snickering filled the warehouse tinged with a single snort from one of the men.

For as much noise as they made, I made equal effort in silencing the space around me. My breath stilled and body followed. I ignored the burning sinews within me from the effort of being crouched. My tendons ached, promising to crack slightly to relieve some of the tension. I shut my eyes and became the stone and mortar of the building itself, strong—rooted—immovable.

My pains dulled and grew distance. The throbbing in my chest, lungs asking for air, quieted as I banished the concern. I needed only to listen.

The sound of feet over hard stone reached my ears. They slowed and grew muted. My quarry had stopped, grumbling something only they could hear. A soft tinkling, like falling coins, came from nearby.

"There's a bunch of…nails lying about?" The thug coughed. Another chime as one of the slivers of metal bounced off the ground. He'd likely kicked one of them away from himself. "Gonna take a bit more of a look."

His companions grunted noncommittally from farther ahead.

His footsteps grew louder—closer.

I waited until their sounds emanated below me. My eyes flitted open and I moved with sinuous grace, like the first bands of night encroaching across the sky. I slipped down and behind the brute.

He stood a head taller than me with the broad back and muscles of someone who work tirelessly through the days in hard labor. The man dressed similarly to the men in the alleyway: nothing but simple pants and a shirt of homespun.

I made no sound as I moved, rushing to close the distance between us as he walked on obliviously. A quick leap sent me to the air and allowed me to kick off one of the crates lightly as I passed by. I soared overhead the thug, drawing his attention at the last moment.

He craned his head up, blinking—stupefied.

I grabbed hold of the sides of his skull as I arced by. My weight brought us down, his head crashing into my knee with an impact reserved for a hammer on stone. His body went limp in my grip. No pained sounds escaped his lips. The confrontation had happened in perfect silence. *Two more to go.*

I grabbed hold of the unconscious man under his shoulders, wincing as the muscles in my back went taught under his weight. Hauling him around the corner took more effort than I would have liked to have exerted. Content he was out of sight, I mantled the next row of crates, skulking along their tops to the where the nearest of the torches burned. My fingers went into one of the pouches over my many belts. I retrieved a pouch, no thicker than the bulb of a man's nose. A quick snap of my wrist sent it hurtling toward one of the flames.

It burst on impact with a barely audible *pfft*. A cloud of white dust plumed to life, smothering the fire. I repeated the process in quick succession. Each flick of my hand sent more pouches into the torches, extinguishing them. The room plunged into darkness.

Screaming followed. One of the man hollered, whipping about in the blackness. "What's going on? Skreet, you there? What'd you find? Oi, answer me?"

I could make him out almost as if it were a dim evening, but his incessant shouting only made my work easier.

"Clep, go check on Skreet."

"Like hell. I'm not—"

I crashed into the second speaker, taking him by the waist and pulling us both to the ground.

The standing man hadn't adjusted to the lightless situation. "What was that? Clep."

I jumped to my feet, putting my weight behind my right fist as it snapped out. It struck the man squarely on his nose, deforming it with a wet crunch like a foot over hard snow. My other hand followed and slammed into his throat.

He pawed at the spot I'd struck, gagging.

I sank to my haunches, grabbing hold of his ankles and wrenching upward.

The man fell to his back. His head struck the unforgiving ground with a noise that made it clear he wouldn't wake any time soon.

My cloak whirled about as I spun to tackle the last man. He had pushed himself to a shaky stand, hands up. I took him at the knees, delivering a series of short punches that caused the joints to buckle. My heel hurtled into the side of his face as he fell, concluding the fight. I turned my attention to the young child.

The darkness didn't keep me from making out his features. He had hair the color of sand under sunlight, thin and wispy. His body rested against the ground and curled tight into a ball. The child had a tan around where his shirt failed to cover, indicating he'd spent a good deal of time out along the docks. His bare feet told me he wasn't one of the better off children running about on little adventures along the waterfront, dreaming of pirates and sailor's tails. He ran errands for merchants and the like, delivering letters between ships and crews.

Someone unknown. An impoverished child with likely no one of consequence to come looking after them. If anyone bothered at all.

I traced the tip of an index finger along the mouth of another pouch, reaching in to pinch a bit of white powder from it. The small clumps broke easily in my grip as I sprinkled it over the child's nose.

A second passed and a stench like discarded boiled eggs and rancid fish tickled my nostrils. My acute sense of smell only served to worsen the odor, causing faint pinpricks to blossom within my nose and eyes.

The child coughed, shivering once before snapping upright. He wheezed and sputtered, wincing as if he could blot the problem away. "Yuck. Foulest"—he coughed again—"what's it?"

"Magic." The word came out harsher than I had intended. But bothering to explain the chemistry behind the simple concoction would have been a waste of both our time.

The boy's eyes widened and he recoiled from me.

I gave thanks he couldn't make out my features in the dark. He'd have likely thrown a manic fit and been impossible to deal with. I didn't bother with niceties, having looked him over enough to know he was fine. "Leave the same way you were brought in. Head right alongside the dock and flag down any of the merchants.

Tell them of the bounty for aiding in dockside crime. Make sure they alert the constabulary and get Inspector Cardinane down here to investigate."

The boy opened his mouth to likely protest, but I growled and waved him off.

"Repeat it back to me."

The boy did, struggling to get to his feet.

I placed a hand at his side and helped ease him. "Now go."

He didn't waste a moment, scampering off at a full run, leaving me behind with the unconscious men.

The temptation to string them up and wait for them to rouse built inside me by the moment. I could wheedle whatever information I deemed necessary out of them, but it would come at the expense of time—the other missing children. My options whittled down into two: interrogate one of the men or forge ahead on my own, hoping the extra minutes I saved would lend to my search.

I thought back to the conversation the trio of kidnappers had. They'd alluded to another party coming to take the children. Given that they hadn't bothered to deliver the boy elsewhere, it meant the warehouse was the final destination as far as they were concerned. Those who meant to take the boy would be doing so from here. The lingering question was: where?

Waiting for the inevitable persons to come take the child meant risking all those already in their grasp. I scowled and set to the task of combing my surroundings.

The crates revealed nothing but various kitchenware and pottery. I circled the area again, stopping as the hollow clang of metal sounded beneath me. Looking down revealed a drainage grate wide enough across to swallow my body hole were it not for the bars running between it. No water leaked into the building, nor was there any sign of interior works that moved liquid about and would require the dumping point.

I frowned, looking down into the passage. It led into the sewers, likely flowing back out into the walls along the dock to pour waste. *But with no use for it...* I kneeled, gripping two of the bars and wrenching on the grate. The metal didn't groan or creak along the edges in protest. It popped free as if it hadn't been properly fastened at all, resting in place only by its weight.

I let the piece clatter to the ground beside me and grabbed hold of one the edges of the opening. *What better way to come in and out undetected than through the sewers.* All I needed to know is where my city's underworks led—and to whom. I slipped through the opening, falling

more than a dozen feet. The muscles in my legs quivered for the span of a quick breath as I sank to my knees to mitigate some of the impact.

The ground below me was drier than autumn's last leaves. Enough evidence that the grate had never been used for its actual purpose. My suspicion had been correct, and I decided to follow it through Markham's hidden veins.

The tunnel was another shade of darkness that would have made the unlit warehouse above seem truly bright in comparison. My eyes took longer than I would have liked to adjust, bringing the world before me into a hazy grey clarity.

A fist-sized orb of light pulsated ahead, jarring my sight and tinging everything a hellish orange. I winced, bringing up a hand to shield against the torch light. *That means someone bothers to keep them lit. This passage is well-traveled enough.* But that meant someone could just as easily be waiting around the next bend on their way to retrieve the boy.

I leapt over the channel running between and carrying water out of the sewers. Putting myself against the other wall ensured I could close in against the corner without the corona of the light revealing me. Should anyone be lurking there, I wanted to see them before they could put their eyes on me.

My instincts proved right as I rounded the turn.

A slender figure stood in the way, garbed in loose-fitting robes the color of freshly turned earth. A cowl of the same material and shade did little to obscure his face. He had a pinched face, unnaturally pale, likely from his time spent in the sewers. Strands of wispy thin straw hair fell to just above his brows. He didn't seem perturbed by my sudden appearance. "Are you lost?"

I shook my head, surveying him without moving my head. The man likely didn't see many strangers wandering through the passages. But given the nature of his work, I believed he had no problem dispatching any who poked too far into his business. This was nothing but a kind and simple way to deter people from snooping. "On some things, yes."

The man's mouth spread into a slit of a smile, pulling far more to one side than the other. "Then that is the easiest thing to fix. Turn around. Go back the way you came." He raised his hands to his sides, making a little flourish. "Then you're no longer lost."

I matched his lopsided and thin smile. "Lost on something else, I fear."

He arched a brow.

"Children have gone missing above. I've followed them this far"—I narrowed my eyes, spreading my mouth wider to reveal my teeth—"and I intend to follow them farther." I inclined my head to the way behind him. "What do you think I'll find if I go past you?"

"Trouble." His voice had become something like coarse stones sifting through roug sand. He moved his hand, blurring as he reached for a knife strapped to his waist.

I lunged. The fingers of my right hand stiffened as I formed them into a shape like a crude shovel, striking the hollow of the man's throat as hard as I could.

His eyes bulged as he leaned forward, dropping the knife to paw at his throat. He racked hacked and released a guttural sound.

I grabbed hold him by his hair, twisting to slam his skill into the brick lining Markham's underbelly. She was as hard and unforgiving here as she was above.

His eyes lost their focus, but not dimming completely.

"Answer me if you don't want to end up a floater." I nodded to the slow moving waters in the channel.

His smile widened, making his choice clear before he spoke. "I float well as any man—"

I slammed his head back into the wall, taking care not to dash his brains out. Cloudiness filled his eyes as I leaned him toward the channel. My grip slackened and he fell into the water, unconscious and drifting away. Taking the time to make him talk wouldn't have been worth it at this point.

I trudged forward, rounding more twists and turns for close an hour until I came to the only point that looked promising.

A long recess sat in the wall before me. Sconces on either side illuminated it with a golden-orange tinge from torches. Rungs of steel, no thicker than my thumb, ran upward like a crude ladder. A hatch sat dozens of feet above.

Lack of a grate and the way up indicated one thing as far as I was concerned: this was where the children were brought.

I grasped a rung and climbed up, taking care to muffle the sounds of my boots impacting the metal. Thoughts on what was to come flooded me. Every possibility of what I could find, every threat to go in hand with it. I buried them all knowing that no matter what, Markham would provide for me.

She always did.

I climbed up the makeshift ladder, reaching the hatch. If my instincts were right—and they always were—I'd find the children in the room above. And whoever took them. I sucked in a short breath, holding it in my chest as I pushed against the wooden board above me. It inched open, faint bands of torchlight seeping through the crack.

It took me the span of a few breaths to adjust to the lighting and make out the room properly.

Spacious, and a great deal of visible effort went to keeping it that way. The only objects in view were the wooden altar, solid in construction, and iron cages.

My teeth ground as I made out what occupied the metal structures: Children. Each of them lay slumped against the thin bars of the iron frame. *Sedated.*

I counted half a dozen. A longer look revealed pairs of slippers, rich in material and earthy brown in color. I tallied up the number of shuffling feet, putting the number at one person per trapped child. It could have been nothing more than coincidence.

But Markham wasn't a city for that sort of thing. No. She always had something at work, whether it was nefarious in nature or not. The secluded area, far below ground and out of the way, pointed me to one thought. Everything else from the numbers, the presences of the altar, and the hems of rippling robes, solidified my theory.

A ritual. And Markham exacted a heavy toll when it came to those. She didn't have a reputation for light and ethereal sort of magical practices. She was the home to dark and macabre things. And those children wouldn't be walking away from the end of this if I didn't intervene.

Easing into the room soundlessly wasn't an option. My limited view showed enough to make it clear all eyes would fix on me the instant I entered fully.

Then I should do my best to give them something to truly see and remember. Something to haunt them. Show them what else prowls the dark.

I reached into another pouch, pulling free several beads of fragile glass the shape and size of apple seeds. Another breath stilled me for what was to come. I released my hold on the metal rungs, thrusting a palm into the hatch with thunderous force. Wood splintered, showering the room with slivers as I pushed off the ladder with all the might I could muster in my legs. I sprang onto the floor and snapped my wrist before the occupants could register what happened.

The beads cracked onto the ground, sounding like hailstorm on glass windows. Plumes of thick smoke billowed from each of the artificial seeds. A sulfurous odor filled the room, forcing the robed and cowl-covered figures to raise their hands to their mouths as they hacked.

I used the spare moment to assess the contents littering the altar: a silver bowl, stained red around the lip. A curved knife, more ornamental in design than for function by the looks of it. It still carried a visibly wicked edge. Clumps of hair in varying colors sat across the end of the wooden surface, each fistful of hair bound tight in a leather thong.

It was enough to know what had been done to children prior. And I was going make sure it would stop here tonight.

A primal scream left me, echoing through the room as I rushed toward the closest of the robed figures. My hands closed around the outermost edge of their cowl, balling tight around the fabric. I pulled down and launched my knee into where their forehead would be. The blow cut their legs out from under them as if they were lifeless. The figure slumped, cowl slipping from their face.

The woman could have been in her thirties by looks alone. Fair skinned without a hint of crease and weathering to her face. Her hair held all of its dark color, showing no signs of gray. But I recognized her. And the woman should have been well into the latter half of her life—visibly so.

The Lady Mayorca had turned to something else to restore her youth. Not the bottles and cure-alls hawked about in the marketplace. Those trinkets all promised to ward off age and bring about a new lease of beauty. No. She'd turned to stealing the years from elsewhere.

I glanced at the children, then the altar. None of those missing folk had been rumored to have been found or returned home. That left only one outcome.

The thought galvanized me into action. I surged forward, leaping to one side as a robed figure swiped blindly at me. My foot snapped out and struck the base of their jaw. Their head rocked back, letting me take advantage of his upset balance. I closed in, grabbing their collar and twisting, my hips bracing against theirs. The cultist flipped over my side to crash hard against the legs of another figure, taking them to the ground as well.

"Wait!" The robed man's voice rung with wavering authority. A clear sign he was in command, but my performance had left him shaken. He held out a hand as if to stay me while he lowered his cowl.

He had the features of a razor: cold, straight-edged, and mercilessly sharp. I'd seen warmer looking stones in the night of Markham than sort of gray I found in his eyes. His skin was without flaw, much like the baroness. No flecks of gray stood out amidst the wash of wheat-colored hair lining his face and atop his head. A faint glint along his throat drew my eyes to a gold chain. Emeralds the size of my thumbnails studded the necklace.

I arched a brow, regarding him and the still standing cultists. "Baron Coldwater."

He said nothing.

"This isn't the sort of thing high ranking lords and ladies of Markham should be up to in the late of night. It's bad for one's reputation."

The man's mouth spread into a smile as thin and severe as the rest of his features. "*Our* reputations are what hold this broken and perverse city in check—stable. We are Markham's backbone."

I matched the baron's smile. "Her back's strong enough without you sort. And"—I gave the altar and children another look before settling on him again—"the only broken and perverse things I see are you." I gestured to some of his companions. "Let me guess: Lady Viean, Lord Prevek, Lord Vocle."

The figures bristled in unison but made no further move.

"Every city needs their caretakers." The baron pointed toward the caged children. "We're cleaning some of the rabble from Markham and, in turn, we're restored so we can continue doing our good work."

"I'm in a similar line of work myself." I bared my teeth. "Removing the filth." My fingers dug into the flesh of my palms, small bones cracking as I balled my fists.

The baron's eyes widened at this. "And what do you think you'll do here tonight?" He let out a short bark of laughter. "Save them? From whom? What do you think happens if you succeed? Who will the constabulary believe?" Baron Coldwater touched a hand to his chest before waving to his group. "You're an umbra elf—the sort of thing people know all-too-well for stealing children away in the night and doing dark things with them." His smile managed to grow thinner—colder.

"It's not about what I believe." I nodded to the children. "They would know the truth. They would be alive to appreciate it. And that's enough. And maybe one day there'll come a day people won't fear someone like me simply because of this." I waved a hand to my face.

"We'll see to it that you're seen as nothing but a monster. That, should you survive this, you're branded as the fiend that took these children. The city will hate you. Fear you. They'll hunt you when and where they can." The baron's hand slipped into the folds of his robes.

"They already do. It won't stop what I have to do." I took in the subtle motions made by the remaining cultists. Each of them shifted slightly, brushing aside their robes so they could easily reach within. *Daggers. Not much else they can have in there.* I braced myself for the possible exchanges to follow.

"And what's that?" Coldwater sneered, pulling free a slender blade—curved and serrated like the one on that altar. He lunged, blade arcing toward my throat.

The cowl slipped from Lady Viean's face, revealing a woman sharing enough of the baron's sharp features they could have passed for relatives. She closed in with a similar knife. Another of the robed figures drew a hooked blade that looked more suited to gutting fish than combat.

I rushed to meet them, slamming the side of a wrist against the inside of Coldwater's. His fingers loosened over the knife and let it clatter to the floor. Lady Viean's blade closed in, threatening to sink into the meat between my ribs. I shifted, clapping my open hands against her forearm in quick succession, managing to bat the knife out of her grip. A snap of my foot caught her behind one of her knees. She buckled, letting me turn in time to catch the hook-blade in the muscles of my left shoulder. I gritted my teeth, silencing the mounting scream.

The cultist snarled as they twisted.

I moved with them, lashing out with my fingers toward their eyes. Markham's luck was on my side. I struck one of the organs, causing the robed figure to break their hold before they could tear the tissue in my arm any further. My weight shifted and I pivoted, twisting to thrust an open hand into the base of the figure's chin.

Their feet left the ground by an inch. They landed shakily, rocking once before collapsing against the unyielding body of the altar.

Coldwater eyed me, unmoving. Lady Viean's attention turned to one of the fallen blades. The intent sat clear on her face.

I kicked out, sending a heel crashing into her face. Cartilage cracked with a sharp wet sound that stirred some of the drowsy children. The woman slumped unconscious from the blow, leaving me to face the baron and the remaining cultist by his side. "This isn't going to go the way you think, Coldwater."

He managed to keep a thin smile on his face. "I was going to say the same to you." The baron held up a hand in an effort to stay me. "If we don't return, people will look into our disappearances. It won't be so hard to make it look like you were behind it all. It won't be merely blame. It will be worse. Umbra elves through the city will be hunted down and executed. Or..." Baron Coldwater trailed off, giving me a sideways and knowing look.

The words were nothing more than a ploy. I knew that much. But every moment he spoke meant the children were safe from harm. It was another second for them to rouse from their stupor. I arched a brow, keeping my face an impassive mask. "Or?"

"Or you could leave"—his smile widened—"with something in tow, of course."

Of course. A bribe.

The baron gestured to caged children. "Take them."

I inhaled, slowly turning my attention away from the cultists. A chance to take the little ones away. And all without bringing down everything the nobility could muster against my people. I cared little for their threats against me. But other elves wouldn't be able to bear the repercussions. Sparing my kind now meant leaving more children to suffer later. That decided the matter for me.

"I'll take them—"

"Perfect." The baron's mouth curved into a smile of self-satisfaction.

I waved him off. "I'm taking them, and I'm bringing *you* in as well." His smile faded as I rushed him.

The remaining cultist stepped before the baron and acted as a shield. His cowl slipped from his head, revealing a pinched face more suited to a rat than a man. Thin hair, ruddy brown in color, clung tightly to his skull mostly from sweat. His eyes were the same color and narrowed as his face pulled into a mask of rage. He drew a short knife, lunging toward me.

A cloud of white powder filled the space between my face and my assailants. A point of hot pressure exploded between my ribs, acute and the size of a pin-head. I winced and brought a hand to the spot as the knife pulled out from the hardened leather around my torso. The weapon had pierced the piece of armor, burying itself into the barest bit of my flesh. It wasn't lethal, but the suddenness of it pulled all of my focus from my surroundings.

The assailant brought the hilt of the knife down on my skull like a makeshift club.

A streak of brightness, unlike any light I've ever seen, lanced my vision. I staggered, lashing out on instinct and training to where the blow had come from. My fist collided with the soft mass of his belly and drove him to double over. A kick struck my right shoulder, throwing me off-balance. The baron's strike had been halfhearted, more an attempt to gauge my condition after the paltry stabbing and clubbing. I recovered, reaching out to grab Coldwater's collar. I hauled and sent him staggering past me. The break in the fight gave me the moment to capitalize on the winded cultist. I grabbed his wispy hair, pulling tight enough to draw a sharp yelp from him. A twist and launch of my knee brought tough bone to the side of his skull.

He collapsed.

I turned to face Coldwater just time.

The baron charged me, a manic light filling his eyes that brought iron hardness to them. His shoulder crashed into my sternum and renewed the minor heat throbbing from my knife wound. The baron's momentum drove me back until the altar slammed into my spine, drawing a pained breath from me. Coldwater didn't relent in his bullish action, pushing harder against me as if trying to crack my between his own mass and the solid table behind me.

I gritted my teeth with enough force to threaten chipping a few. My knees worked like a pump, moving with mechanical effort as they slammed into his waist and gut. I met resistance in the form of flexible metal—chain or scale mail—keeping the blows from felling him.

Coldwater launched a fist into my side, hammering away without any signs of relenting. The briefest of pauses came—not long enough for me to take advantage of—and the baron drew a makeshift weapon from another fold of clothing. He held it between his first two fingers, its base resting comfortably in the seat of his palm. The tip of the weapons might as well have been an arrowhead, broadened a bit and clearly thickened to aid it in puncturing hide and leather.

I grimaced and took a fistful of the baron's hair in hand. The weapon sank into the meat between my ribs effortlessly, parting my cloak and leather like they were nothing but wet parchment. I swallowed the mounting scream, tearing free a chunk of hair at the root from the baron's head.

He yowled and retaliated in kind. Coldwater drove the arrowhead into my flank like a child poking holes in the dirt—frantic and thoughtlessly.

Each stab threaded my side with strings of fire—searing and all-consuming. I shut my eyes, picturing the children not too far from me. The thought pushed me. I let loose the scream I'd buried earlier, seizing the baron's shoulders. My ribs followed suit in mimicking my pained cry as I wrenched. Our positions switched,

Coldwater slamming mercilessly into the altar with a jarring *crack* at his shoulder. I plucked the weapon from his slackened grip and sent it into a shallow across the baron's face.

The sliver of metal split his lip at a harsh angle, clipping the edge of a nostril, and stopping just below his left eye.

He screamed, choking off as he pawed gingerly at the gash.

I seized hold of his neck with one hand, bringing the tip of the weapon to the side of his throat. "One more cut. *One.* That's all it takes to end you—end *this.*" I nodded to the children. Some of them had awakened in full, eyes widening as they took in their surroundings. The faint beginnings of words filled the mouth of one youngling, not quiet making their way into anything coherent. I looked away from them, placing a bit of pressure on the edge of the blade.

A thin red line beaded into life along Coldwater's throat. His lips quivered out of control, blood tinging his teeth as he flashed me a macabre smile. "Do it." He coughed, red spittle flecking my cloak and sleeve. The tissue of his lips split further under the strain. "It's the only way to stop this." Coldwater winced once, regaining a hint of his composure. "We won't stop. Tonight, tomorrow, a month from now, I'll be free of this. We are Markham. It's our blood and sacrifice that keeps it going." More blood pooled into his mouth, leaving just as quickly as he sputtered. "There is only one way to spare yourself, the children, and your people." He managed to give me a knowing smile, devoid none of the cruelty he'd shown earlier. Quite the feat considering the state of his face.

I held the weapon firm, but my hand shook almost imperceptibly. "My people know suffering. Anything you can do, we will bear—proudly, without complaint—knowing it's for a reason." I tilted my head back toward the children. "I'll make sure the word spreads. Every child you try to take, I will find. I will stop it. Tonight. Tomorrow. A month from now. *Always.* And I will do it my way." I snarled, tossing the weapon aside.

It clattered against the far edge of the altar before tipping over onto the ground.

I pulled the baron close enough to feel my breath—to look into the yellows of my eyes. "I am *nothing* like you. I have the face of a monster, but it's a mask. The same can't be said of you. A man with something far worse inside him." I pulled him by the hair again, dashing his head against the wood of the altar until the coldness faded from his eyes, leaving nothing but fog and cloudiness.

I released my hold and let the man slump to the ground. The following moments passed in a blur of anguish and weariness coloring my movements. I searched Coldwater's unconscious form for a key to the cells. Finding that, I took the time to bind each of the cultists with torn strips of their own clothing, going as far as braiding the lengths of fabric to ensure they wouldn't free themselves.

My hand twitched, almost as if regretting not slitting Coldwater's throat. One action could have spared me and the children from reliving this. One action would have set me down a path no different than the baron's though. It always starts with one choice.

I looked to the children, closing in on their cages to free them.

As I did, I knew I'd made the right choice.

I could live with it.

I unlocked the first of the cells, wincing as a child threw the whole of their weight against me, lighting up my wounds again. They held me tight in a hug, exhibiting the unrestrained strength only a little one could. I returned the gesture, relieved my appearance and state hadn't frightened them. "Are you fine?"

The child nodded, mucus and a hint of drool streaming down one side of their face. A likely result from the substance used to subdue them.

"Let's get the rest of you free and take you home." I smiled.

The child returned it and help me set about releasing the rest of taken.

Markham would see they were taken care of, just like she did for me. And she'd see the wicked punished. I'd make sure of that.

BIO

R.R. Virdi is a two-time Dragon Award finalist and a Nebula Award finalist. He is the author of two urban fantasy series, The Grave Report, and The Books of Winter. The author of the LitRPG/portal fantasy series, Monster Slayer Online. And the author of a space western/sci fi series, Shepherd of Light. He has worked in the automotive industry as a mechanic, retail, and in the custom gaming computer world. He's an avid car nut with a special love for American classics.

The hardest challenge for him up to this point has been fooling most of society into believing he's a completely sane member of the general public.

A story from his award-nominated urban fantasy series, The Grave Report, is scheduled to be in Jim Butcher's upcoming urban fantasy anthology, Heroic Hearts. TBA.

6

DAVY CROCKETT VS. THE SAUCER MEN

DAVID AFSHARIRAD

I heard Mom call me from the kitchen the first three times, but I didn't come to the table, much as I wanted to. I could smell pancakes, my favorite, and my stomach was rumbling, but I had to hold strong.

"David, I'm not going to—" Finally, it clicked with her, what she was doing wrong. "*Davy*, breakfast is ready."

Like a runner at the starting gun, I was off, my sneakers slapping the wooden floor of the hallway, skidding to a halt just outside the kitchen. I pushed through the swinging door and walked in at a respectful, indoor pace, but Dad still muttered something about no running in the house, from behind the paper. I sat down at the table in my usual spot. Mom brought over a plate of pancakes and a glass of milk, and I dug in, trying to keep from watching Ronnie, my little brother, in his baby chair. He was learning to feed himself and his face was covered in drool and bits of pancake. Disgusting. Other kids' moms spoon-fed their little brothers and sisters mush, but Mom and Dad said it was better that babies learned to do it themselves. Better for the babies maybe, but it was a sickening display to anyone trying to eat in the same room.

I was halfway through my short stack when Dad set the paper

aside and got up from the table. He taught English at the high school and was out for the summer same as me but was picking up some extra work teaching driver's ed. He kissed Mom, then gave Ronnie a peck on the top of his head. Ronnie just gurgled the way he always did.

Dad ruffled my hair. "See you tonight, David," he said.

I cleared my throat real loud.

"Sorry. Davy." He winked at Mom and she smiled. "So, what's it going to be tonight, do you think?"

I knew he was talking about *Disneyland*, my favorite television program. Since it'd first come on last year, my whole week revolved around Wednesdays at 7:30. It wasn't like other shows, where they had the same characters doing the same thing week to week. It changed up all the time, but it was always something good.

Best of all had been the three programs about Davy Crockett. I'd never heard of the frontiersman before—they never teach you anything good in school—but after "Davy Crockett, Indian Fighter" came on *Disneyland*, he'd replaced the Lone Ranger as my role model. For Christmas, Santa had left me a coonskin cap, same as Davy's, and Mom and Dad had bought me Ol' Betsy, Davy's gun. Ol' Betsy was just a toy, didn't shoot, not even b.b.s, but that was all right with me. She was a real beaut. Since then, I'd saved up my allowance and bought a Davy Crockett folding knife, and Mom had made me a genuine buckskin shirt, with fringe and everything, out of an old flour sack. I'd taken to only answering to "Davy" around the house, though I couldn't get any of the guys to go along with it.

"I don't know," I said, answering Dad's question. "Maybe a cartoon or something."

"Guess we'll see," Dad said. He knew I'd been disappointed when Davy died at the Alamo in the last show. I'd asked him why they couldn't just let Davy live. Seemed to me that Santa Anna's men shouldn't have been any match for the King of the Wild Frontier. Dad had kind of laughed and said that Walt had taken too many liberties with history as it was, that they couldn't very well rewrite Davy's death. I didn't see why not, but I didn't argue.

After Dad left, Mom cleared the dishes and cleaned up Ronnie's mess.

"I'm going to put him down for his nap," she said. "Have fun today. I'll see you at lunch."

She leaned her cheek toward me and I gave her a quick kiss, then put my dishes in the sink and went to grab my baseball glove, which I found under my bed. I paused on the way out of my room, wondering if I should wear the coonskin cap. I *wanted* to, but the other guys sometimes ribbed me about it if I was wearing it when we weren't playing Davy Crockett or cowboys and Indians, so I left it hanging on the bedpost and wore my baseball cap instead.

The screen banged shut behind me as I ran out the back door. It was already hot. It'd probably get up to a hundred again, Dad had said at breakfast, and he wasn't looking forward to sitting inside a car all day while some teen-ager rode the brake. I didn't blame him. I couldn't figure how he and Mom could stand to be inside on these hot summer days.

As I made my way over to the lot where me and the guys played ball, I made a game of trying to walk only in the shadows, running fast as I could through the sunny patches when they were unavoidable, pretending the soles of my shoes would melt if I tarried too long. When I got there, Pete Blockburger and Ricky Boehner were practicing catching grounders. Steve Hurley was out of town, visiting his grandmother in Marquez for the month, which meant that only Billy Hughes was missing from our group. There were other guys we sometimes hung around with, but the five of us were the main ones.

"How's it going?" Pete called as I slid to a stop near the bare patch of earth we had designated home plate, my sneakers kicking up a cloud of dust.

"Where's Billy?" I asked.

Pete shrugged. "No idea."

That wasn't so unusual. Billy was a year older than us, though he'd been in our class since the second grade. He'd failed out the first time through on account of missing too many days and had been held back. We sometimes teased each other about being so dumb we failed Sandbox, but never Billy. It was a sore subject with him. Billy's dad wasn't around and his mom...well, I'm just glad Mom was my mom and not Mrs. Hughes. Mostly, Billy's older brother took care of him. He was a senior at the high school and in Dad's American Literature class. Dad had talked the principal into letting Ray Hughes take the class, though for all the other subjects, he was on the vocational track. He even got off early every day to go work on the oil rigs outside town, which sounded great to me, but when I'd said as much to Dad he got real serious and told me I'd think differently if I knew what Ray's life was really like.

When Billy was around, he was sort of the leader of our group, and it always felt a little weird without him.

"He'll probably show up later," I said.

I slipped my glove on and gave it a good smack. There weren't enough of us to get up a game, not even close, so we just tossed the ball back and forth and took turns batting. It was an all right way to spend the morning, but I'd rather have been playing Davy Crockett, shooting Indians with Ol' Betsy and defending the Alamo against the Mexican Army—and you can bet Davy and Travis and Jim Bowie would win in our version. They always did.

I lobbed a slowball and Ricky knocked it out of the park. Of the five of us, he was by far the best ball player, though he was also the smallest. We watched as the ball sailed clear out of the lot, landing in a patch of scrubby bushes.

"You hit it, you get it!" me and Pete shouted together. Ricky sighed and went after the ball. It was a job he was used to. I guess it was sort of a punishment for him being too good at bat, but I sure didn't want to dig around in the thorns for the ball.

As we waited for Ricky to find the ball, Pete and me dug up our stash of candy. We kept it buried by an old broken-off fence post on the edge of the lot. Our Moms would've taken it away if we'd tried to bring it in the house and anyway, this way we didn't have to tote it around with us.

"Pickin's are getting kinda slim," Pete said, opening the cigar box. "Gonna have to make a run down to the trading post to fortify our larder." He said this in a cowboy accent, and I laughed.

"What's left?"

Pete tipped the box so I could see. Inside were a couple of Tootsie Rolls, a few sticks of Wrigley's, and a wadded paper sack I knew contained jawbreakers.

"Give me a jawbreaker."

Pete did, then unwrapped a Tootsie Roll. He was really the only one of us who liked the things, which worked to his advantage.

"Find it yet?" he yelled at Ricky.

Ricky said something unkind about Pete's mom, and then went back to looking. We helped ourselves to more candy, then dropped the cigar box into the hole and kicked dirt back over it.

When we turned around, we saw Billy riding up on his bike. He was pedaling fast enough to beat the band and had a sort of wild look in his eyes that spelled trouble. First thing we figured was some big kids were after him and that we'd better hoof it on out of there in a hurry, but no one was on his heels. He jumped off the bike without coming to a stop, let it roll off on its own before it tipped over.

"You guys!" he said. He was panting and couldn't get out much. "You've gotta—see—this. Right now."

"What?" Pete asked.

"Seriously—it's crazy!" Billy put his hands on his knees, bent over, trying to catch his breath.

Ricky gave up looking for the ball—looked like we'd have to take up a collection for a new one; so much for buying more candy —and came over to where we stood.

"Hey, Billy," he said. "What's going on?"

"It's—it's—"

Billy was struggling to get it out, whether because he was so winded or…I didn't know what.

Pete gave Billy a friendly punch in the arm. "Come on, Big Bill," he said. "It's what?"

"It's a flying saucer, is what it is!"

None of us said anything for a while. The sun beat down, and I could feel the back of my neck getting red. A wind had kicked up, blowing dirt around the empty lot. The only sound was Billy's heavy breathing.

Then Pete started laughing. It was just a chuckle at first, but it grew into full-blown hysterics. It didn't take long until Ricky was laughing too. He was never the first in on a joke, was kinda slow when it came to picking up on things like that, so to make up for it, if someone else was laughing, he'd join in—louder and harder—even if he didn't know what was supposed to be funny.

I wasn't laughing, though. I was looking at Billy's face, and I could tell this wasn't a joke, at least not to him.

"Come on, guys," he said. "Cut it out."

Pete and Ricky just kept on. It was a real knee-slapper.

"I said cut it *out!*"

Billy shoved Pete, not too hard, but hard enough. Pete lost his balance and landed on his rear. Ricky clammed up quick and of course Pete wasn't laughing anymore. He jumped back up and brushed the dirt from his blue jeans, then went to shove Billy. But Billy was ready for it, and as Pete stepped in, Billy hit him in the stomach. The two of them would have gone at it—we'd all been in fights with each other over the years, but Billy and Pete most of all—but me and Ricky got between them and kept them apart until they'd cooled off. The two of them shook hands, then Billy launched back into his flying saucer story.

"I'm not kidding," he said. "It's an honest-to-God flying saucer."

"Oh yeah?" Pete said. He still thought this was some sort of a joke—and Pete *hated* to be the butt of the joke.

"Yeah," Billy said.

Pete crossed his arms. "And where is this flying saucer? On the courthouse lawn? Come to talk to our leaders?"

It looked like Billy was gonna give Pete another hard shove. If he did, they'd go at it and me and Ricky getting between them wouldn't help this time. They'd fight until one of them cried uncle. Instead, he said, "Nah, not at the courthouse. In the woods. It must've landed last night."

"The woods" weren't really woods, just a medium-sized grove of trees with a creek running through it on the other side of town, just outside the city limits. It was kinda far from where most of us lived, but close enough to Billy's place that we sometimes played there, even though our parents would have had fits if they'd found out. The train tracks cut through a corner of the woods, and a couple of times we'd found evidence of hobos having camped out there. It was a great place for playing all sorts of games, especially Davy Crockett. The scraggly patch of mesquite and live oak didn't compare to the mountaintops of Tennessee, but it was the closest we had.

"How do you know it was last night?" Ricky asked. "That they landed?"

"I was out there after supper yesterday and it wasn't there," Billy explained. "Then this morning, it was." He went and picked up his bike, walked it back over. "So come on! You gotta see it!"

The three of us—Pete, Ricky, and me—all looked at each other, none of us wanting to be the first to agree in case this was a joke, after all.

"*Come on!*"

Pete sighed, picked up his glove and the bat and slung it over his shoulder.

"This better not be horse hockey, Billy," he said.

It took us most of an hour to walk there. The saucer, Billy said, was down in the gully where the creek bed widened. We all knew the spot. We'd occasionally strip down and go swimming there if the creek was high enough, which it usually wasn't. I thought it was a pretty smart place for the saucer men to park their craft. If you were walking through the woods, you wouldn't be able to see it unless you were looking for it, could walk right past it and not notice it.

Billy left his bike propped against a tree and we followed him through the tangle of trees, bushes, and dead branches. As we got close to the spot, Billy told us to be real quiet. We got down and Army-crawled the last few yards up to the edge of the gully and poked our heads over.

"Holy smoke!" Ricky said.

Billy slapped him in the arm, put a finger over his lips.

"Holy smoke," Ricky repeated, in a whisper.

"'Holy smokes' is right," Pete said.

Billy mouthed the words *Told ya!*

I couldn't say anything. Couldn't even *think* anything! Down below us, a few yards up-stream, sat a silver saucer. It shone in the late-morning light. So far as I could see, there wasn't a single rivet or seam in the whole thing. It looked cast from a mold. It wasn't big, about the size of three cars put together and just tall enough that it looked like I might be able to stand up inside. It stood on spindly legs that made me think of a spider. A sound like television static only more low-pitched filled the air. It came from the saucer.

Billy motioned for us to move back. We slid on our bellies until we were a good distance from the edge of the gully, then got up into a crouch and walked even farther away. When we figured we'd gone a safe distance, we stood.

"Holy smoke!" Ricky said again.

"Where do you reckon it came from?" Pete asked.

"From outer space," Billy said. "Where else?"

"Mars?"

Billy shrugged. "Maybe. Maybe Venus. Or heck, it might not even be from our solar system. Who knows?"

"What do you think they want?" I asked. I'd had a bad feeling ever since Billy rode up on his bike. Seeing the saucer, it was like I'd been punched in the stomach. This wasn't good. Not at all.

"What else?" Billy said. "They're tryin' to take over."

Ricky's eyes got wide. "*What?*"

"Sure," Billy said.

"We don't know that," Pete said, sounding more sure than he looked. "Could be this is just a what-cha-ma-call-it, a *probe*. Sure. There's probably not even any spacemen in there at all. Just a probe."

"Baloney," Billy said. "That's not what a probe looks like. They're long and pointy and have transmitters on them and stuff. This is a ship, for sure."

We were all experts on extraterrestrials. Ray Hughes let Billy have his old comics when he was done reading them, and Billy was always willing to share them around. Stuff Mom would *never* have let me buy, even with my own allowance money. *True War Stories* and *Vault of Horror* and *Tales from the Crypt*. I liked the war comics the best, along with the cowboy ones. Though I watched *Captain Video* and *Tom Corbett, Space Cadet* back when they'd still been on television, I didn't really like science fiction. Give me the Lone Ranger over Buck Rogers any day. But the other guys—Billy especially—*loved* the stuff, the scarier and bloodier the better.

Pete mulled over what Billy had said, about the saucer being a ship and not a probe based on how it looked. Finally, he said, "Okay, so it's a ship. So what do we do?"

"We gotta tell someone," I said. "The police or—"

"Are you out of your mind, David?" Billy said. "That's the dumbest thing I've ever heard. We can't trust anyone!"

"He's right," Pete said. "Don't you remember Billy telling us about *It Came from Outer Space*?"

Boy, did I remember! We'd been camped out in Steve's backyard, over spring break. Billy hadn't seen the movie, we'd all been little kids when it came out, but Ray had seen it at the drive-in and had told Billy all about it. Billy held a flashlight under his face and laid the whole thing out for us, even doing different voices for the different parts. It was about an alien ship that crash lands out in the desert. In the movie, the aliens can take on the form of whoever they want, which was what Pete was getting at now.

"The police could all be aliens by now, for all we know," Billy said.

"Heck," Pete said, "We can't even trust our parents."

"What? Nu-uh," Ricky said. He was sort of a mama's boy.

"It's true," Billy said. "In fact, *anyone in town* might actually be an alien."

We took a second to let that to sink in. Ricky looked a little like he might cry. He did a lot, and we all gave him a hard time about it.

Pete's eyes fell on Billy. "Wait a second," he said. "How do we know… We're supposed to believe you found this saucer and the aliens just let you come blab to us about it?"

"Yeah. I mean, they're still inside the ship. They didn't see me or anything."

"Or did they?" Pete cocked an eyebrow. I loved when he did that. I'd tried in the mirror for hours to learn how, but never could.

"What's that supposed to mean?" Billy asked.

"It means, how do we know you're you?"

"Of course I'm me! We got a problem here. Let's not waste time arguing over stupid stuff."

"That's what an alien would say," Pete said.

Billy looked to me and Ricky for help. I couldn't look him in the eye, pretended to scrape some mud off my shoe onto a fallen log.

"You gotta prove it," Pete said. "Prove you're you."

"How am I supposed to do that?" Billy said.

This stumped us all, until Ricky spoke up. "The handshake!"

"Yeah," I said. "That's it. No way an alien would know that."

Pete thought it over, decided we were right. He held out his hand. "Come on," he said. "If you're really Billy, do the secret handshake."

Billy rolled his eyes, walked over and did the complicated

gestures of our secret handshake—the one we'd spent months perfecting—without a hitch.

"Satisfied I'm not a spaceman?" he said after the finishing double-snap.

"Sure, Billy," I said.

"We knew you weren't really an alien," Ricky said.

"We just had to make sure," Pete said. "You understand."

"Sure, I understand. Now can we get down to business? We gotta *do* something."

We all agreed with Billy that something had to be done, but none of us knew what. After arguing about it for a while, I said, "Let's take another look at it," though I really didn't want to. If it was up to me, we would have gone back to the lot and finished playing ball, left the saucer and its crew for someone else to find. It was cowardly, I knew, not at all how Davy would have handled things, but I was scared. I thought maybe if we looked again, we'd find that the ship had taken off silently or that we'd been wrong and that it really was just an unmanned probe or…well, I didn't really know.

"Yeah, all right," Billy said. "Let's take another look."

We Army-crawled back to the edge of the gully and peeked over.

My eyes just about bugged out of my head.

A section of the saucer had opened up and a ramp was extended that reached to the ground. Three saucer men were milling about. They looked to be about our same height, but they were hairless and gray-skinned. Their huge eyes looked like the eyes of a fly, shiny and silver. They had two fingers and a thumb on each hand and wore some sort of skin-tight jumpsuits and carried strange instruments. One of them knelt down by the creek and dipped a long metal tube into the water. Another waved a wand over the base of a nearby live oak, while the third just sort of walked around in circles. He had something in his hand. It didn't look like any ray gun I'd seen in Ray Hughes's comics, but somehow I knew that's just what it was.

I felt a tap on my shoulder and looked over at Billy. He motioned for me to follow him back into the woods. Pete and Ricky were already gone. I hadn't even noticed.

We found them all the way back at the edge of the woods. Ricky was concentrating really hard on the ground, his upper lip tucked into his lower teeth, trying not to cry. I wouldn't've made fun of him if he had, and I don't think Pete and Billy would have either. Pete looked as pale as milk and Billy's cheeks blazed red. I don't know what I looked like, but it was all I could do to keep from shaking.

"What do we do?" I asked. "Billy, we gotta tell someone. *We got to!*"

Billy swatted the back of my head. It smarted, which helped.

"We already been over that, David!" he said. "We can't!"

"Let's just go," Ricky said, a quiver in his voice.

"And let them take over the town? You saw what they were doing, poisoning the creek. They probably think that's the town's water supply. When they figure out it's not, they'll come in both guns blazing."

"He's right," Pete said. "We gotta stop them."

"How?"

"Just let me think a minute," Billy said. He took to pacing back and forth. We all held our breath, waiting to hear what he'd come up with.

After a couple minutes, he stopped with a snap of his fingers. "Any of you bring your slingshots?" he asked.

The slingshots had been a project the summer before. After some serious hunting, we'd found five perfectly forked branches out in the woods. We'd pooled our allowances and bought some surgical tubing from the drugstore, which Billy had said was much better than regular old rubber bands. For the sling part that held the rock, we cut the tongues out of some old work boots Ray had let us have. For a while, we'd carried the slingshots around with us *everywhere* and were always on the lookout for rocks the right shape and size to use. But that had been last summer. You couldn't take a slingshot with you to school, and most of us had gotten out of the habit of carrying them around and hadn't picked it back up when school let out this year. Mine was in the bottom drawer of the bureau in my room.

I told Billy that no, I didn't have mine with me. Ricky didn't either, but Pete did. He pulled it out of his back pocket.

"Only one of us?" Billy asked. "Jeez! Well, I guess it's better than nothing." He held out his hand. "Lemme have it."

"Why should you get to have it? It's mine," Pete said.

"'Cuz I'm the best shot."

"Are not."

"Am too."

"Are not, and anyway I ain't giving it to you, even if you are, which you ain't."

"Fine, then, " Billy said. "But don't miss!"

"I won't miss!"

We all four of us searched around for good rocks. When we had a decent handful, me and Billy and Pete crawled back to the edge of the gully. Ricky didn't want to look at the saucer men again. Truth was, I didn't much want to either, but I didn't like not knowing what was going on. And Davy would have looked, I reminded myself.

The saucer men were more or less doing the same as they they'd been before, only the one who was waving the wand was now waving it over some dead leaves instead of the trunk of the live oak.

Pete slipped a rock into the slingshot and pulled back on the tubing. Squinting one eye, he took aim and released. The bands snapped and the rock whizzed through the air and splashed into the creek with a *plunk*. The alien with the ray gun whipped around at the sound and fired. An electric crackle sounded and section of the creek bank glowed bright purple for a split-second—and then it was just…gone. Disintegrated.

Seeing that made me dizzy. My heart pounded in my ears and my mouth went totally dry. There was a hollow feeling in the pit of my stomach and in the palms of my hands, the kind you get on a carnival roller coaster.

Billy gave Pete a dirty look for missing. Pete ignored him and fitted another rock into the sling, took aim and shot. This time he didn't miss. The rock sailed through the air and hit the saucer man who was poisoning the water square on the back of the head. He fell over, hurt but evidently not dead. He was still moving and making angry sounds. The one with the ray gun ran to his side.

The three of us ducked out of sight and made for the edge of the woods. Ricky was gone when we got there. He'd decided to chance his parents not actually being aliens and had run for the safety of home. Billy and Pete didn't seem to notice he was gone.

"You got one!" Billy said.

"Sure did." Pete was standing eleven feet tall.

"Got him right in the old bean!"

"But they're still here," I said. "You didn't kill that one, just hurt him. And you saw what that ray gun can do."

"Don't be a wet blanket," Billy said. "Sure we didn't chase 'em off, but they're not invincible. I was sort of afraid they might have some sort of protection ray, but they don't! We can get 'em, guys!"

"We can't," I said. "We're just kids! All we got is one slingshot. They got a ray gun that can vaporize rocks. We gotta tell. We *gotta.*" I bit my tongue. I could feel a lump rising up in my throat. I thought about Davy facing down all those Mexican soldiers at the Alamo. He hadn't cried. No, sir.

"Don't be a baby, David," Pete said. "We can get other stuff to use against 'em. It's almost lunch and my dad'll tan my hide if I don't show. I'll grab my b.b. gun while I'm there."

"Yeah," Billy said. "David, you do the same thing. Bring whatever you can think of. I'll stay here and make sure the saucer men don't move in on the town. If they make like they're going to, I'll jump on my bike and beat them there."

"We gotta tell," I said, quietly.

Billy stepped up close to me. "We can't, David. Anyone in

town might be one of them. We got to handle this. Us. It's the only way."

"But..."

"But nothing." He laid a friendly hand on my shoulder. "This is the line in the sand," he said. "I'm Travis and this is the Alamo and we got to defend it. Can I count on you or not?"

Well, how could I say no to that?

"Sure," I said, forcing a smile. "We'll lick 'em!"

I almost believed it was true.

Billy slapped me on the back. "Good. Now get going and get back here fast as you can! Skip lunch if your moms'll let ya."

Me and Pete all the way back into town, breathing too heavy to do any talking. I could tell he thought I was being a sissy, though, just by the way he kept trying to leave me behind. He was taller than me and faster, but I wasn't gonna let that happen. It felt like my chest was on fire, but I kept up with him the whole way, until he turned off Lemmon to go to his house and I kept on straight to get to mine. Once he was out of sight, I slowed down, but I kept running all the way up the back porch and into the kitchen where Mom was making sandwiches and coleslaw for lunch.

I blew past her with a "Hi, Mom," and went to my room. I heard her tell me not to run in the house, but I couldn't make my feet stop. I got my slingshot out from the bureau and then went to my closet, where Ol' Betsy was stored. I tossed her on the bed with the slingshot, then stripped to the waist and put on the buckskin shirt Mom had made me. I grabbed the coonskin cap off the bedpost and slammed it on my head.

Putting that stuff on, with Ol' Betsy in the crook of my arm, I felt better. I was ready. Just let those saucer men try and take our town!

I was halfway down the hall when I remembered the folding knife. I hoped it wouldn't come to close-quarters combat with the saucer men, but you can bet Davy Crockett was always prepared. I got it from the shoe box in back of the closet where I kept it, along with some firecrackers and other stuff Mom wouldn't have been too happy to know I had, and slipped it into the pocket of my bluejeans.

When I came back into the kitchen Mom was just setting out a plate of sandwiches.

"Gotta go, Mom," I said. "We're playing the Alamo and it's real serious."

Mom gave me a look. "Not more serious than lunch." She pulled out my chair and made a motion for me to sit.

"Aw, come on," I said. "Can't I take it with me? I'll eat it on the way. Promise."

"David."

"Please? It's just sandwiches. Dad takes his in a paper sack all the time."

"Your father is a grown man."

I thought about the aliens in *It Came from Outer Space*. Had Mom been replaced by one of the saucer men? Was she trying to keep me here so I couldn't get back to help Billy stop them?

"*Pleeeaaaaseee???*"

Mom sighed. "Oh, all right." She went to get a paper bag and wax paper out of the cupboard. "Drink your milk while I get this together."

"Thanks, Mom!" I threw my arms around her waist, trying not to recoil at the thought that I might be hugging a saucer man. It didn't seem likely though. I was pretty sure Mom was Mom. We didn't have a secret handshake I could use to test her, but she didn't feel any different—and begging always worked pretty well on the *real* Mom, so I was reasonably certain.

It took me only three gulps to empty my glass of milk. Mom handed me the bag of sandwiches and I was out the door. I ate them on the run, tossing the bag into a storm drain when I'd finished with it.

Billy was right where we'd left him at the edge of the woods. He had one hand on the handlebars of his bike and a foot up on the pedal, ready to jump on and ride through town, yelling that the aliens were coming like Paul Revere. Pete wasn't back yet.

"Anything happen while I was gone?" I asked.

"Nah," Billy said. "I went in and took a look a few minutes ago. They're back at whatever it is they're up to. The one Pete hit seems fine now. They might have some sort of rejuvenation powers. This may be tougher than we thought."

I'd sort of talked myself into thinking this was all a game. It was easy, away from the woods. But now that I was back, I was starting to get scared again. I tried to think of Davy, but it didn't seem to help much.

"What you bring?" Billy asked. I showed the slingshot and Ol' Betsy, pulled the folding knife out of my pocket.

"Hey neat!" he said, grabbing it out of my hand. "Didn't know you had this."

"Sure," I said. "Bought it with my allowance."

Billy looked at the knife a little longer then reluctantly handed it back.

"That thing shoot?" he asked, nodding at Ol' Betsy.

I felt my face flush. "Nah," I said. "It's just a—" I didn't want to say the word *toy* "—just a replica."

"So what good is it?"

"I figure the aliens don't know that," I said. "Might scare 'em."

Billy thought on this then nodded. "Reckon so," he said.

We looked for more slingshot rocks while we waited for Pete to show up. We had a good two dozen by the time he rode up on his bike.

"Sorry," he said. "My old man was late and Ma wouldn't let me leave until he got home and ate."

Pete laid out what all he'd brought—his b.b. gun and slingshot and a strand of firecrackers. I kicked myself for not thinking to bring mine. Billy picked them up.

"This is great," he said. "We can distract 'em with these."

Only it turned out Pete hadn't thought to bring matches, so that was out.

"Okay," Billy said. "I been thinking on the plan. Me and David'll use the slingshots. Pete you use your gun. We'll crawl up to the side of the gully and on 'three' we all open fire. Take 'em by surprise."

It wasn't much of a plan, but sounded as good any. We made our way to the gully. I brought along Ol' Betsy, though I didn't really think she'd scare the aliens any. I just hadn't wanted to tell Billy the truth, that having her with me made me feel a little more like Davy, a little braver.

The aliens were still up to whatever bad business they'd been at before, waving their strange instruments around. I set the pile of rocks in easy reach. Pete had already loaded his gun and pumped the action.

We were on our stomachs now, but when Billy counted three, we'd leap up and start firing. He held up a hand, counted it off silently

One.

Two.

Three.

I stood and let the rock fly. I'd taken pretty good aim at the alien with the ray gun. It was sailing straight for him. A direct hit!

Only it wasn't.

The rock stopped three feet from the saucer man's face, like it had hit a wall, only there was no wall. Same with Billy's, which had been aimed at the same saucer man. Pete's b.b. was too small to see, but I guessed that whatever it was had blocked our rocks had blocked his b.b., too.

"Protection ray!" Billy said. He shot another rock and the saucer men for good measure, but it bounced off the invisible wall same as the others.

The saucer men stopped what they were doing and looked up at us with their silvery eyes. There was no way to tell what they were thinking, but I knew it wasn't warm thoughts about us Earthlings.

"Get down!" I yelled just as the saucer man raised his ray gun and took aim.

We all hit the ground. The air crackled with electricity. Behind us, the top of a tree glowed purple for an instant and then was gone.

"Run for it!" Pete said.

Billy threw his weight on top of him. "We can't stand up," he said. "He'll hit us for sure!"

Another crackle and this time a section of the ground not a yard in front of us vanished into thin air.

"We gotta go!" Pete said. There was a panic in his voice like I'd never heard.

Another crackle. This time a rock to our left got hit and was gone.

"Crawl back," Billy said. "Don't put your head up."

We all did, as pieces of the woods vanished around us. I'd gone maybe ten yards when I realized I'd left Ol' Betsy behind.

I had to go back. No way I could leave her. Not only would I be in trouble with Mom and Dad for not looking after my things, it just didn't feel *right*.

I turned around and crawled back the way we'd come.

"What are you doing?" Billy said. He was crying now, scared half to death. So was Pete. I would have been crying too, only I was too sick with worry about leaving Ol' Betsy.

She was propped up against a fallen log, just where I'd left her. I closed my fist around her stock. Soon as my hand felt that polished wood and cold iron, a calm came over me.

I hadn't wanted to fight the saucer men, but they'd come to take over our town. You didn't run from fights, not even fights you knew you were going to lose.

Instead of crawling after Billy and Pete, I stood and walked toward the edge of the gully. I was scared. But being scared don't make you a coward. Not doing the right thing because you were scared did.

Two of the saucer men had retreated to the base of the ramp that led to their spaceship, the third, the one with the ray gun, was standing in front of them. When he saw me, he aimed and fired.

I jumped out into nothingness, fell for what seemed like

minutes. My knees buckled as I landed, and I had to put my hands out to keep from falling face-first into the dirt. But I kept ahold of Ol' Betsy. I'd fallen not more than a dozen feet in front of the lead saucer man. The ledge on which I'd just stood had vanished. If I hadn't jumped when I did, I'd have been disintegrated, too.

I got to me feet quick as I could, Ol' Betsy still in my hand. She was just a toy—not even a b.b. gun—but she was made out of good, sturdy wood. I thought of Davy at the Alamo, swinging Ol' Betsy like a club, taking down as many of Santa Anna's men as he could.

I raised Ol' Betsy. The alien leveled his ray gun at me.

I reared back.

Only I didn't take a swing at the saucer man. Instead, I held Ol' Betsy out front of me, then, just as the alien was about to fire, I tossed her aside. Ol' Betsy spun like a tomahawk and landed somewhere in the brush to my right.

The saucer man flinched, looked from me to where I'd thrown the gun and back. He seemed confused.

I dug into my pocket, pulled out the Davy Crockett folding knife. I held it up for the saucer man to see.

From behind and above me, I heard Billy say, "What's he doing?" and Pete say, "He's crazy!" I guess they'd come back to watch me get killed.

I opened the knife. The saucer man stared at it for a long few seconds, then I threw it away, too.

"Davy Crockett at the Alamo" was by far our favorite of the three *Disneyland* programs. We'd played it so many times, it was easy to forget the other two shows about Davy. I'd been thinking of this showdown with the saucer men like Davy at the Alamo, like his last stand—*my* last stand.

Only it didn't have to be that way. There was something else just might work. It was worth a try.

I took two long strides forward, until I was not more than five feet from the saucer man. I planted my feet, set my fists on my hips...

...and grinned. Grinned the biggest, widest, brightest, *Daviest* grin I could muster.

"What in the world!" It was Pete. "He's gonna get killed! He's gonna—"

"*Shhhh!*" Billy cut him off. "Don't break his concentration."

The saucer man just stared. Slowly, he lowered his weapon, slipped it into a loop on his belt.

I kept on grinning.

The story went that Davy got his coonskin cap by grinning a raccoon out of a tree. He'd grinned down a bear the same way. The saucer man wasn't a raccoon or a bear, but I figured the principle was the same.

I grinned and grinned and grinned.

The saucer man's fly-eyes darted from side to side, not sure what to make of me.

I just kept on grinning.

He removed his ray gun from his belt, waved it around, shouted something in a language I couldn't understand. He pointed the ray gun at me.

I didn't flinch, and I never let that grin fall from my face.

I don't know how long we stayed like that. Felt like hours. Flies landed on my nose and mosquitoes bit my neck and face. I swatted them away best I could, but I made sure never to let that grin drop.

I grinned. I grinned so big and so hard and so long that my jaw ached. My face cramped up.

There was another story about Davy that said one time in the dark he confused two knots on a tree for the eyes of a racoon. He tried grinning it down all night long, and when the sun came up, he'd seen his mistake. But he'd grinned so hard he'd grinned the bark right off the tree.

I thought about that. If Davy could stay up all night grinning down a tree, then I'd grin down this saucer man, no matter how long it took.

After a while, the saucer men began retreating back into their spaceship. They backed up slowly, the leader keeping that ray gun aimed square at my chest until they were all three on the ramp. Then one of them gave a command and the ramp closed back up into the ship. The static sound got louder and louder until it was all I could do to keep from covering my ears. Then, with a pop like the cork out of a bottle, the ship was gone.

Billy and Pete let out a whoop from the top of the gully where they'd been watching.

"You grinned 'em down!" Billy yelled, jumping up and down and pumping his fist in the air.

I turned to face my friends. They were smiling ear-to-ear. I took off my coonskin cap and bowed, real formal-like.

"You did it, Davy!" Billy cheered.

I tried to relax my face, it was sure sore—but I couldn't. I'd saved the town—the Earth—from the saucer men, and that was something to grin about.

BIO

David Afsharirad is the editor of The Year's Best Military and Adventure SF series and the anthology *The Chronicles of Davids*. His short stories have appeared in various mystery and science fiction magazines and anthologies. He lives in Austin, Texas with his wife and sons.

7
DEAD RUN

AARON MICHAEL RITCHEY

Jake Koum showed his unconscious sister the turquoise eMuse phone with the case cracked open.

"This should have enough memory to handle the download, Talitha," he said.

The disease chewed pink holes into his sister's gray skin. She didn't cough; she rattled with every breath. Sweat trickled down her face to drip on the bare mattress resting on the scraped wood floor of what had been the master bedroom in better times. Now, the place stank of the mold in the carpet and the mildew in the drywall. And his sister's failing body.

"It'll be all right," Jake said. "I was at the door of the storage unit trying to download the security hacks. I heard babies yesterday." His old phone had maxed out only a few gigs away from finishing the download. That forced him to steal the eMuse from Harper, though it didn't feel like stealing. Not when the buttsucker had five of them lying around his West Colfax apartment.

"Tonight is my last chance to get one of the babies," Jake whispered. "They grow so fast."

On the other side of the unpainted drywall, the Jaya family murmured and creaked around. A century ago, only one family had lived in the Denver suburban house. After the dollar fell to zero and the corporations guzzled the last pints of oil, the Littleton neighborhood had been converted into low-income housing.

MBiti, their landlord, had used sheetrock to convert the whole place into little ratholes where Jake and his family lived, where the Jaya family lived, the Ling family, the Winters, and old MBiti himself, downstairs because he was too fat to climb steps. The rich man's AC chugged and whirred.

On the other side of the wall, a toddler whined, and Grandpa Jaya coughed—a real cough, harsh, yet so much better than Talitha's rattle. First you got the big capital-letter disease. Then you got the pneumonia. Then you died.

"But you won't die, Talitha" Jake said. He dipped a Hello Kitty t-shirt into a clean bowl of water, brought directly from the hydrant, and wiped the sweat off his sister's gray skin. His own hand seemed so dark in comparison.

Before the disease, she had been beautiful, his beautiful older sister, seventeen-years-old and white teeth and shining hair and skin so dark it looked like her shadow. She had been full-faced despite the thin oatmeal they ate. But that was before. Before his father gave her the disease. A four-letter word that spelled death.

"I'll sell the baby, and we can get those retro-drugs I've read about online at school. It's not a cure, but you'll feel better. As long as you take a pill every day, you'll be able to live longer than me." Jake stood up abruptly. Below, old MBiti's TV blared. He probably had it split-screened so he could watch a hundred shows at once, stuffing his face, sitting on his sofa, in the comfort of his air conditioning.

Jake rubbed sweat off his forehead with his arm. Once he sold the baby on the black market, if there was enough money left, he'd get an AC for their room. In his fantasies, the scientists gave him enough cash to buy out MBiti completely. He'd find homes for the other families, and then he and his sister would live in the huge house like people had done before. But those were just dreams.

Heavy footsteps shook the outside staircase.

The patio door to the balcony slid open, and Jake moved away from Talitha.

Jake did not want to face his father, not on the most important night of his life.

But it was too late. His dad stood in the patio door, blocking his way. His dad's yellowed eyes squinted from an acne-chopped face, thinned from the disease. He swayed.

"Where're you going?" his father slurred.

Jake grabbed his torn backpack off a folding chair. He shuffled through the contents: computer parts, tablet, and cables. He placed the eMuse on top of the pile. He was ready. But his father blocked the door.

"You can't go. I'm in no shape to take care of your sister."

"I'm going," Jake said, glaring.

"She's…she's…dying." His father's mouth stumbled. His feet stayed planted on the chipped wood.

"Because of you…" Jake knew what the words would do. Like the dominos he and his sister would arrange on the floor of their room. You set them up, and then you tapped just the first one, and the rest rattled down. Rattled, like his sister's lungs.

His father reached for him but was too slow, too drunk. Jake slipped past him and onto the balcony and then ran down the stairs. The old nails holding the staircase to the siding squeaked and strained. Some pulled loose.

His father shouted down the landing. "It wasn't me, Jake. I never touched her like that."

"First you get sick, then she gets sick. I'm not stupid. Why aren't you dying instead of her?" Jake called up from the garbage in the yard. He saw the windows fill with people. He didn't blame them. When they fought, he listened. It was better than TV.

"Jake, please. It wasn't me. There was another woman. After your mother got burned during her shift—"

"You're a liar!" Jake roared. He tore off through the trash-thick weeds in the backyard and ran through the shanties built on, around, between the old suburban houses. Cardboard flapped in the light breeze, mothers with the disease held babies with the disease, all eyes on Jake.

The sweat slid off him like rainwater, dripping onto his white t-shirt and green canvas shorts. He dashed through the plywood maze and found the chipped asphalt of Ammons Avenue, glittering with broken glass, littered with papers and wrappers, cans, sofa stuffing, electronic parts, a few dead monitors beyond repair. The hulking wrecks of cars lay surrounded by a penumbra of tubes, gears, wires, hoses, and tires. Families were always working on their cars, and stealing parts was as popular as swapping them.

Jake had just started to breathe normally when he saw the group of boys coming down the street, four of them. Including Harper. All had pink hair, bright red lips, and black-and-white metallic shirts. And the tight jeans poor *tueet* boys wore when they wanted men with money to notice.

Harper didn't need to point. His eyes ripped through Jake.

Harper and his gang took off in a sprint, fanning out, as if they owned the street.

Jake whirled and ran

* * *

The chemicals in the air left orange and purple claw marks across the sky. It never got dark. At night, the orange left and only the purple remained, cooked darker by the heat.

Jake sped away. The loose plastic on his shoes flapped with every step. He ran towards Rudyard, where the third-shift workers would be bicycling home.

Bicycles packed the four lanes of Rudyard, holding back a big truck and an ancient Toyota Prius. He had to get across the wide street, down into the culvert, up the other side, across the carrier tracks, and then to the storage units. Where the babies were.

Harper screamed, "I'm coming for my eMuse, Jake. You thief. You dirty thief."

"We're gonna hurt you bad, thief." One of Harper's friends added, a big kid marked by scabs and scars.

Jake rushed into the swarm of bicycles. They swerved, not to save Jake's skin, but to save their wheels.

A truck, belching smog into the heat, jerked forward. Jack put up a hand to shove himself away, and that one second was all it took to scorch his palm. Jake hissed in pain.

More yells from Harper and his gang. The commuters had closed ranks, stopping them from busting through, which gave Jake time to get to the other side of Rudyard. He dropped down into the culvert swimming in more garbage, splashing through slimy puddles. He slipped and fell. The mossy scum soothed the burn on his hand—probably infected it as well.

Infection. Not the big capital-letter disease, but some other bug had crawled into his mother through her burn and killed her.

Harper and his friends might not have seen him drop into the culvert. They might think he was heading over to the school. But then again, maybe not.

The storage units were just across the carrier tracks, not steel train tracks, nothing so ancient, but frictionless magnetic tracks glowing blue. Jake's dad said the destruction equipment had bulldozed through houses to lay the tracks. The people had leapt from their shanties, shacks and mouse holes like ticks off a drowning dog. Nuclear-powered carriers, massive, hulking buckets, carried chunks of re-processed material to Optimum's recycling plant. Optimum took hundreds of years of trash and turned it into shit that fifteen minutes later the rich people would throw away. Trash into shit and right back into trash.

Jake clambered up the cement bank, and he was slim enough to slip under the bottom of the razor wire. He turned and saw Harper and his gang in the culvert. He ducked behind a big cement post. He hid for a moment in the shadows of the purple night. Then he risked a glance.

Harper and his gang jogged toward him, going south. Jake realized they knew where he was going.

His hand hurt. Bright red grill marks crisscrossed his palm. However bad the pain, it wasn't going to hinder him from getting a baby, not when he had a chance to save his sister's life. A burn. So what? Burns had almost become a family tradition.

A carrier rumbled from the west, fifty feet high, shaking the ground. Hissing and shaking, a metal dinosaur, it moved slowly but steadily down the eerie blue of the magnetic tracks. Jake had to get across the tracks before the carrier came.

Even if it meant Harper and his gang would see him.

Jake fled.

The yells erupted.

He darted in front of the carrier. The radiation and power of the thing made his skin crawl. He leapt over the glowing magnetic track, then climbed a dirt slope and slid under another razor-wire fence. He rose, facing the storage units—rows and rows of garages with their orange doors closed tight.

Harper knew where Jake was going. Harper had read the same books, and maybe had the same ideas.

After all, Jake and Harper had been brothers not too long ago. Before Harper went insane.

Jake raced down the alley on the north side of the storage units, thirteen aisles, running north to south. The north alley lay between the storage units and a big Optimum warehouse—new concrete, nice steel, bright flex-glass windows. The storage units next to it looked like they thousands of years old, something from ancient Egypt. The concrete was flecked, the sliding doors were made of cheap aluminum doors, and the shingles on the flat roofs were decaying.

Aisle thirteen had the big storage units. The smugglers would need the big ones to hold the mama and her babies.

Denver gleamed in the distance. The running lights of flying cars floated around the glowing skyscrapers. Real sci-fi stuff, his dad always said. Jake didn't get it, but his dad would laugh. Every time his dad laughed, Jake hated him more.

Jake's mom, her body blackened, had shrieked herself into silence. Jake joined her in the silence and hadn't laughed since.

Not his dad. A few months later, he hooks up with some woman. Then he gets sick. Then he gives the capital-letter disease to his daughter. His own daughter.

Unit 13E was all the way at the end of the corridor next to the southern alley. Jake sped to the garage door and retrieved the legacy tablet from his backpack. He heard a growl come from inside unit 13E. He froze and listened for a long time but heard nothing more. Maybe he'd imagined it. He hoped he had. An adult would tear him apart and slurp up his bloody bones.

The mama and her babies should still be sleeping after coming through the portal. If the internet was right about them.

The full-grown ones were cheap. The scientists wanted the young ones, the babies.

Two days ago, while dawdling on his way home from school, Jake had seen the rough-necked traders lock them up in the storage unit. Probably got greedy. Didn't go with the first buyers. Like Kino from The Pearl, which Jake was reading in school.

Jake wouldn't make that mistake.

The tablet sparked on, the battery light steady. The link to the wireless connection was weak, but not weak enough to drop. Couldn't drop. It was a dynamic download, which meant the security hacks code would need to run continuously while connected to the internet.

Jake plugged in the eMuse, then used the custom cable to link the tablet to the security lock on the door. The light on the pad glowed a defiant red.

Harper's cursing drifted through the air from somewhere in the storage unit facility.

Jake would start the download and then keep them away from the door.

The thing shifted inside, a huge weight, its lungs inhaling and exhaling huge gusts of air. The adults were the size of elephants.

He found the hacking website and started downloading all possible combinations for all possible storage containers across the west into the eMuse's memory. Couldn't use the tablet's memory, too small. Only a couple terabytes. Tiny. Worthless. The eMuse was newer, tons of space.

Jake sprinted down the southern alley, making noise as he went, until he got to aisle six. He climbed up onto the roof and hoped he was far enough away from the tablet so they wouldn't find it or Harper's eMuse. A cinderblock lay on the roof. He scooped it up and winced. His hand, the burn.

Chatter below made him freeze.

Harper and his boys were right under him.

"Do you think he found one?" the big scabby kid asked.

"Why else would he come to the storage units?" Harper asked. "The BRSM smugglers use these storage units for xeno biological contraband. And I know, Jake. I know how he thinks. He loved those books and movies."

"Xenobiology? Like from outer space?" one of the others asked.

"No, from an alternate reality," Harper said. "I guess scientists can visit other dimensions or whatever. Even storybook worlds."

Jake listened, a grim panic nipping at his guts. If he could drop the cinderblock on Harper, kill him, the other gangers would scurry away.

But could he do that to his own brother?

A brother's life for a sister's. Talitha had been brilliant in school, funny, so quick to laugh. Harper was just another *tueet* who left his family for a nice apartment and hamburgers. Never sent a single dollar home.

Jake never had the chance to use the cinderblock. Harper and his boys moved down aisle six, turned and headed down the southern alley toward aisle thirteen. Unit 13E. They would see his tablet and the eMuse.

Jake hefted the cinderblock onto his shoulder and threw it into aisle six. The cinderblock shattered.

"Hey, Harper!" Jake yelled. "Mom said she liked me the best. She said she didn't even know if you came from Dad."

That would hurt Harper. A bad thing to say about his mom, but she was already dead. His sister was alive.

"Why do you want us to chase you, baby brother? What have you got going here?"

Jake dropped to the ground and ran to the north alley to aisle nine. "You're a coward, Harper. Leaving us like that. Just for the money. Just for better food. You broke mom's heart. That's why she died. You like being a *tueet*, Harper?"

Silence, for a minute. Then Harper's voice carried over the units. "Mom died 'cause she got burned working for Optimum. Just another way of being a *tueet*, if you ask me. That had nothing to do with me."

Whispers in the purple night. Jake knew they were planning something, but what?

He had to keep them distracted, to give the download time to finish. "You didn't answer my question, Harper. You like selling your butt on Colfax, huh?"

"Why'd you stay with the old man? You know he don't care nothing about you now that Mom's dead." Harper was breathing hard.

"For Talitha." Jake said.

"She's as good as dead."

"No, she's not!"

Two boys appeared from down on aisle six. "We got him, Harper!"

Jake bolted down the alley, headed toward aisle thirteen.

Jake would have to be fast—faster than the thing in the storage unit.

Faster than Harper, wherever he was.

* * *

Even halfway down aisle thirteen, Jake saw something was wrong. The light on the security pad was still red.

Jake made it to the tablet. The download was stuck at 99%, which was why the light wasn't green.

Harper swung into aisle thirteen from the southern alley. Right in front of Jake.

Jake only had seconds. Key strokes, pad clicks, the eMuse's memory was nearly full. But it still had enough space, easily enough space for another 1% of data.

He couldn't start the download again.

Harper was close enough for Jake to smell his stink and expensive cologne.

Too late.

Jake flicked down through the files on the eMuse, found the unlock executable, and clicked it. He had to pray the 99% was enough, that the program didn't need the full 100%.

Harper kicked the tablet away and it skittered down the concrete. The screen flew loose, plastic components spraying like intestines. Two boys charged from the north. From the south, behind Harper, stormed the scabby boy.

Jake threw a punch, but Harper grabbed his fist and threw him against the door of the storage unit. The adult inside let out a growl, a very awake, very angry growl.

"Jesus, there really is one of those things inside," Harper said, awe in his voice.

The other three boys ran up, panting. They stood around him in a semicircle; their cologne was stifling.

Jake saw Harper's eMuse on the ground. He bent and lifted it up weakly. The case was off, and the circuit board was cracked.

"Here's your eMuse back," Jake said. "Part of it anyway."

Harper punched him the face.

Jake heard his nose snap. Blood gushed down his face, and he spit blood and mucous onto the asphalt. His face burned, part pain, part numb swell.

Harper plucked the eMuse out of Jake's hand and threw it

against the door of 13E. "I don't give a shit about an eMuse. I have five of them."

He slugged Jake in the stomach, and Jake went to his knees. The air felt like sludge in his lungs.

Dimly, Harper laughed. "You like talking about *tueets*? We're going to treat you like one." Harper's belt jingled. He started unbuttoning his jeans. "And it wasn't dad. It was me that gave it to Talitha. I didn't know I had it when I did her, but I know I have it now."

Jake looked up, pain smearing his vision. Harper's face was a leer, a mask, a horror show, painted green.

Green. Because the light on the security pad of 13E was green.

Harper's grinned. "I'm dying. And soon you will be too."

Jake lurched forward and slammed his burned hand on the button to open the door. The blisters on his palm burst.

The aluminum door wheezed open. The smell rolled out of unit 13E like a fog. Excrement and sleep and something completely other, completely alien. Then, the purple light revealed a feline shape, tawny fur, multiple legs ending in massive paws, hooked claws reaching from black pads.

The adult launched herself out of the unit taking Harper's head in her jaws.

Jake saw a kit the size of a small dog, scooped it up into his hands, and ran.

And ran.

And ran.

He breathed through his mouth because blood and snot packed his nose.

The howls of pain and the splatter of blood disappeared behind him. The roar of the adult echoed through the aisles and alleys of the storage units.

* * *

Jogging down Rudyard, Jake saw the lights of the police cars charging through the bicycles. Black vans followed. And then, finally, the floating cars carrying men who possessed more wealth than he could imagine.

He didn't know if the adult would retreat into the storage unit, or if it would pursue him in search of its lost kit. Either way, the government men and their guns would capture the mama, seize the kits, and study them. The offworld traders wouldn't get a dollar.

Jake kept the kit wrapped in his shirt. He expected the animal to scratch him, but it didn't. It probably thought it was safe with Jake.

Wearily, Jake climbed up the steps to their room. His father was asleep in the folding chair, but Talitha was awake on the mattress.

Her eyes were bright for once.

"Where were you?" she asked.

Her question woke up their father.

Jake took the kit out of his shirt and put him down on Talitha's bed. The kit was a boy.

"We can sell it to the scientists for the retro-drugs," he said. His hand throbbed, but he'd take care of the burn in a minute.

"Where did you get him?" his father asked.

Jake shrugged.

The kit had the same tawny coat of a lion, but instead of four legs, he had ten. His eyes were a reptilian green. A pink tongue licked his sister's gray skin.

"Can we keep him?" Talitha asked, giggling as the little guy toyed with her hand. Five paws held its lithe body on the bed while the other five wrestled with his sister's hand.

Jake watched the baby. What kind of life would the kit have in a lab? How long before some scientist split him open to study his guts? Or would they let him grow and put him in a zoo? Jake couldn't think about that.

"No, Talitha, we have to sell him. You need medicine."

His sister's eyes dimmed, a frown bowed her lips, as the kit playfully nipped at her hand.

"You did good," his father said.

"Maybe," Jake said, thinking of Harper, thinking of the animal.

"It'll be okay," his father said.

"Maybe." Jake lifted his eyes and looked into his father's face. "I'm sorry, for what I said before. I know the truth now."

Jake and his father gazed at one another for a long time. With an understanding that had not been there before. Jake's burned hand throbbed.

Talitha continued to play with the animal that would save her life at the cost of its own.

BIO

Aaron Michael Ritchey is the author of seven young adult novels and his short fiction has appeared in various anthologies and online magazines. He is also a dynamic speaker, having taught classes all around the country on all aspects of writing fiction.

His series, *The Juniper Wars*, is about three sisters on a post-apocalyptic cattle drive. Aaron lives in Colorado with his cactus flower of a wife and two stormy daughters. Visit his website at aaronmritchey.com or find him on Facebook.

8

UNNAMED

GAMA RAY MARTINEZ

Thomas tapped his Bluetooth earpiece to mute the call just as the ball of lighting zipped over his shoulder and crackled into the steel girder behind him. The gremlin who'd thrown it growled a series of incomprehensible sounds. Its two companions leaped from window to unfinished wall and back again while some middle manager blathered on about quarterly earnings not being as high as they should.

One of the creatures launched itself at him, but Thomas twisted out of the way and slashed with his sword. The light blade barely slowed as it sheered through the creature's wrist. A leathery hand fell to the ground and evaporated in a puff of green smoke. The creatures shouted at him in unison. Thomas resisted the urge to laugh. They weren't much bigger than rats, and their ears, each as big as his palm, flapped as they jumped up and down. They had a penchant for messing with technology, and they had driven the workers to abandon this site. Fortunately, no one had been killed. Yet.

Thomas stepped forward and swung his sword at one standing on a pile of bricks. It danced out of the way, avoiding his strike easily. It didn't, however, see the heavy dagger in his left hand.

The weapon slammed into the creature's face, and Thomas pulled it out just as the gremlin disappeared into mist. A question buzzed in his ear. Thomas ducked under a gremlin's leaping attack and unmuted his headset.

"I didn't get the reports until late last night. I'll get-ow!"

The one-handed gremlin slashed across his arm, tearing his sleeve and leaving three lines of blood. His dagger clattered to the floor.

"What was that, Thomas?" his boss asked.

"Sorry, Mike, paper cut. I'll get to them this afternoon."

He hurriedly muted his phone before slamming his fist into the one that had wounded him. It flew back and crashed into its companion. Pain shot up his arm, but the creatures tumbled back. He took a step forward and thrust before they could untangle from each other. His blade pierced them both. One growled something before they both vanished.

"Thanks everybody," Mike said. "Thomas, are you going to make it for the 11:00 status meeting?"

Thomas rolled his eyes and pulled his phone out of his pocket to check the time. 9:30. He sighed and tapped his headset again. "Yeah, I should be getting into the office in about an hour."

"All right. See you then."

There was a round of goodbyes as the conference call ended. Thomas pulled off his ear piece and stuffed it into his pocket. He looked at his wound. The cuts weren't deep and had already started to heal, as spirit wounds tended to do. Still, it could've been a lot worse. He must be getting old. It had been years since anything as minor as a gremlin had scored a hit on him, even while he was on the phone. He shrugged.

"It happens to the best of us," he said under his breath.

He reached into his pocket and pulled out a crystal hanging from a silver chain. He stared into it, but it remained clear and motionless, and indication that there were no other supernaturals nearby. It was only then that he allowed himself to relax.

He walked to the nearby alley and got into the sedan parked toward the back. He pulled a first aid kit out of the glove box and sterilized the wound before wrapping it. That done, he got his phone out of his pocket and spent the next few minutes disabling his GPS, his data, and every other app that could be used to track him. Then, he pulled out the false patch in his jacket and retrieved his other SIM card. He switched it out with the one in his phone and dialed. It rang twice before someone picked up, though no one spoke.

"Conundrum," Thomas said. "Omega three-two-seven."

"Who is this?" a distorted voice said.

"I have no name."

"Confirmed Unnamed. Status?"

"Just a couple of gremlins. They've been dispatched."

"That's the eighth incursion this week."

"Eighth?"

There was a pause. "We had one in London a few hours ago and another in Sydney just before that."

The line remained silent, but Thomas could guess at what they were thinking. Ever since the Unnamed had prevented the Mayan apocalypse of 2012, supernaturals had been coming into the world at an alarming rate, and not all of them could be vanquished as easily as gremlins. They wouldn't be able to keep them secret much longer.

"I'll log it with the others," the voice said. "Keep in touch."

He hung up and switched out his SIM card again. His phone chirped when he turned it back on. He groaned. Someone had scheduled another meeting for noon. It was going to be one of those days.

* * *

Thomas just barely had time to shower, clean his wound again (you could never be too careful with gremlins), and put on a fresh set of clothes. He sped to work and arrived just in time, as everyone was taking a seat around a large conference table. He sank into a chair and made a show of paying attention.

The status meeting, like many others of its kind, was filled with people who didn't really need to be there. Of the fifteen people, maybe five had something relevant to say. The rest, including Thomas himself, would've better spent their time actually doing their jobs. To make matters worse, the air conditioning had gone out again, and the windowless room was quickly becoming unbearable. Mike seemed oblivious to their discomfort and just went on with the pointless meeting. Thomas let out a long breath. In his experience, giving up your common sense seemed to be a prerequisite for going into middle-management.

That and gaining a few pounds, he thought as Mike waved his pudgy hands at a chart projected on the wall.

The meeting droned on. A few people started playing on their phones while others gave pointless reports. He found himself nodding off and decided that a game was better than the attention he would draw if he started snoring. As he reached for his pocket, he felt a vibration. Assuming it was another meeting request, he pulled out his phone, but he didn't have any new notification. He shrugged and opened a puzzle game he'd been working on.

He had just started when his pocket vibrated again. A sharp point poked at his leg, and his blood went cold. It was the crystal. He glanced down and saw a flash of bright green light. He reached into his pocket and closed his fingers around it before he could make out a pattern. It felt warm, and he cursed under his breath. Vibration, light, and heat. Three signs. This was no gremlin. He had to get out of here. He stumbled back and every eye turned to him.

"Sorry," he stammered. "I have to go."

"Thomas?" Mike asked.

Thomas got up and rushed to the door. The crystal was getting hot in his pocket. Mike got up, but Thomas didn't wait for him. He left the conference room and half jogged past the receptionist. He had just pushed the button on the elevator when Mike poked his head out of the conference room.

"What's going on?"

"Sorry, it's a message from my doctor." Thomas spouted the first thing that came to mind. "I have to go."

For a moment, Thomas thought Mike would insist he come back. He wouldn't, of course. It wouldn't be the first time he'd lost a job for his duties as an Unnamed, but Mike gave him a slow nod. "I hope everything is all right."

"Thanks," he said. "I'll try to get back this afternoon."

The elevator dinged and Thomas stepped through the door, wondering if he had misjudged Mike. As soon as the door closed, he pulled out his crystal. He had to hold it by the chain to avoid being burned. It glowed bright green. Every few seconds it flickered red, and once there was a flash of white. He searched his memory for what kind of creature that could be, but he came up empty. The elevator reached the ground floor, and Thomas shoved the crystal into his pocket, gritting his teeth against its heat. He nodded at the security guard in the lobby and rushed out to his car. Once inside, he replaced his SIM card and called in. They went through the same security measure, and the voice on the other side asked for a report.

"I've detected a major supernatural," he said.

"Signs?"

"Light, vibration, and heat. A lot of heat. I can't hold the crystal without being burned." Suddenly the crystal began to hum. "Do you hear that?"

The voice sputtered for a second. When it spoke again, there was fear in its words. "Sound?"

"Yes."

"Elements?"

Thomas waited until the pattered of lights repeated themselves. "Earth mostly, but there's a little fire and a touch of air."

Muffled voices came from the speaker as Thomas hung the crystal over his rearview mirror. It drifted to one side and he pulled out of the parking lot, following its direction. It only pointed to the source. It didn't tell him how to get there, and he wound through the streets. They were relatively empty, it being before the lunch rush. He was so focused on the crystal that he missed the red light. A car missed him by inches, honking and giving Thomas rude gestures. Finally, the voice came back over the phone.

"We think it's an earth dragon."

"What?" Thomas swerved in his lane, but managed to control his vehicle. "There hasn't been a dragon in fifteen hundred years."

"That's what the signs point to."

Thomas took several deep breaths to calm himself. It didn't work. "If I'm going to be fighting a flying fire breathing lizard, I'm going to need backup."

"Earth dragons don't fly, Unnamed."

"Does it still breathe fire?"

"Yes."

"Then, I'm going to need some backup."

There was the sound of rustling pages. "Nine-five-seven is in town."

Thomas cursed. "Anyone else?"

"How long?"

Thomas stared at the crystal a few seconds, timing its pulses. "Under an hour."

"No one else can get there in time."

"Fine. Give me a minute, and I'll get you a location."

The crystal led him across a series of turns before finally ending up at an abandoned warehouse. Graffiti decorated one wall, but no one seemed to be around. He gave the voice the address and waited. Unnamed nine-five-seven took less than ten minutes to arrive. He parked a beat-up old pickup next to Thomas and glared. Both men got out of their cars, and Thomas stood face to face with a man tall enough that he could've stood next to a professional basketball team and not stuck out. He spoke with a heavy Greek accent and wore a long trench coat, the kind that would immediately attract the attention of any police officer who saw it and make them worry that it hid all sorts of deadly surprises. Of course, in this case, it did.

"Dmitri," Thomas said, inclining his head.

"Thomas. What's this about?"

"Didn't command tell you?"

Dmitri shrugged. "Something about a prime supernatural."

"Haven't you checked your crystal?"

"I lost that in Moscow fighting against those vampires. Haven't had time to get a new one made."

Thomas pulled out his crystal and showed it to the other man. Dmitri blanched and took a step back, tripping over a beggar neither had seen. Dmitri retained his balance, but the other man fell to the ground. Dmitri reached into his coat, but Thomas grabbed his wrist.

"Leave him alone. We have other things to worry about."

The beggar looked from Thomas to Dmitri, apparently unaware of the danger he had been in. Thomas's eyes seemed to slide off of him, and indication that he probably had some sort of supernatural ancestry. Of course, so did about a quarter of humanity. Thomas glanced at the crystal, but this man was nothing special. The beggar picked himself off the ground and dusted off some of the gravel that had gotten onto his oversized coat.

"Mer's not here," he said in a raspy voice. "He's not here yet. He was supposed to be here when I woke up, but he's not here."

He shambled away, and his voice faded to mumbles. Dmitri sniffled, but Thomas quirked an eyebrow.

"You really shouldn't act that way toward the people we're defending."

"We're not defending him. His kind are a drain on society." Dmitri reached into his coat and pulled out a shotgun. "Did they say what kind of creature it is?"

"Where's your sword?"

Dmitri groaned. "You guys really need to come into the twenty-first century." He opened his coat and revealed a long thin blade. Like Thomas's weapon, it gleamed slightly blue from the fairy magic used to enchant it.

"Actually, I was thinking it would probably be a bad idea to fire that in the middle of the day inside the city limits. The police get a little annoyed at that."

Dmitri smirked. "Whatever is necessary."

"They think it's an earth dragon."

Dmitri laughed. "That'll be a story to tell. The legends are awakening, it seems."

"Do they always have to wake up grumpy?"

Dmitri kept chuckling as he put away the gun and drew his sword. The crystal pulled Thomas to an aluminum door. It wasn't locked. A pentagram had been spray-painted on. Thomas got close and sniffed at it, but it was only paint, probably from some fool who didn't realize how much power that symbol could have if done correctly. Of course no one who knew how to do it right would waste their time drawing it with paint so far from ley lines or other sources of power. He drew back and stepped into the warehouse.

It was little more than a large room with a bare concrete floor. A couple of worn boxes sat in the corner with assorted odds and ends scattered around, the sorts of things a homeless man not entirely right in the head might collect. They probably belonged to that poor fool outside.

The crystal took on a vague gold outline. The creature wasn't here yet, but it would be appearing soon. Thomas wiggled his fingers in a simple ritual, and the crystal dimmed and cooled. He stuck it in his pocket and drew his own sword. All they could do was wait. As the seconds stretched to minutes and then to half an hour, Thomas found it difficult to retain a full state of alertness. Dmitri's stance never wavered, though, and his eyes continually scanned the warehouse. Though he never would've admitted it, Thomas admired the other man. Of all the Unnamed, he was probably the rudest and least likeable, but few would deny that he was one of their best.

The ground trembled, sending adrenaline through Thomas. He tried to force down the fear forming in his throat. Cracks spidered through the concrete, and the middle of the warehouse floor bulged upward. Dmitri motioned to him, and they got on opposite sides, prepared to come at the dragon from two directions as soon as it appeared.

The stone exploded upward in a shower of dust and rocks. A growl that sounded more like a dog than a dragon came from the rubble. When the dust cleared, a reptilian head was rising out of the hole, swiveling back and forth to take in the room. Thomas and Dmitri charged, each swinging in a wide arc. The creature's slitted eyes looked at Thomas just as he drove his blade at its head. The monster didn't even blink as Thomas hit it. The force of the impact sent pain shooting through his arms. He drew back and gaped. The creature didn't have a mark on it. Dmitri delivered two other slashes in quick succession, but each strike was just as ineffective as the first.

The thing lashed out at Thomas, but he was already out of the way. Thomas gasped as it climbed the rest of the way out of the hole. Its serpentine head was about five feet long. Then, its scales gave way to orange fur dotted with black spots and a lean feline body. Its legs ended in cloven hooves. Thomas cursed. Dmitri kept his sword between him and the creature while he slowly circled around it.

"That's no dragon," Dmitri said.

It was a hundred times worse than a dragon. A thousand times worse. Dragons had been fought and killed by heroes throughout the ages. It was never easy, but it could be done. This thing, on the other hand...

"That's a questing beast."

"I thought they killed that thing at Camelot a thousand years ago."

"They tried."

Its head shot at Thomas, but he caught its long teeth on his blade. A clear liquid dripped off its fangs and splashed on the ground. Its rotting breath almost made him gag. Thomas forced his sword up hoping that he'd be able to cut into the soft flesh inside its mouth, but even that was too strong. Dmitri dashed in and thrust at its body but succeeded only in cutting away a thick tuft of fur. Both men backed away, and the creature hissed.

"How do we kill this thing?"

"The eyes?" Thomas ducked under another attack.

"Are you sure?"

"Not even a little bit."

"Right. I'll be the bait."

Before Thomas could respond, Dmitri charged with a battle cry on his lips. The beast's head turned to him. Thomas drew his dagger and stabbed in the same motion. It sunk into the creature's left eye. His dagger steamed. Blood spattered on his hand, and his skin sizzled.

The creature roared so loud Thomas thought his head would explode. He pulled back, leaving the dagger embedded in its face. He tried to shake the blood free of his hand, but it ate a small pit into his flesh, cauterizing the wound as it sank in. A second later, the dagger's hilt fell free. The blade had melted. The beast turned its lone eye to Thomas. He could practically hear its teeth grinding. It started to move, but Dmitri ran up behind it. He held his sword in both hands and thrust downward as hard as he could. The blade didn't go in, but a patch of blood no bigger than a fingernail spread from the point if impact.

"So you're not invincible," Thomas said under his breath.

The creature turned around and reared. It slammed its hooves into Dmitri, sending him to the ground. His sword slid across the floor and clattered against the wall. Thomas moved to help, but the beast anticipated his maneuver and rounded on him just in time to catch his sword in its teeth. It twisted its head, and the blade was torn from Thomas's grasp. Its jaw shifted, and the sword broke in half, releasing a dim flash as its magic dissipated.

"No!"

A loud boom drowned out Thomas' shout. He looked up and

saw the shotgun in Dmitri's hands. The other man pumped it and fired again. The creature twitched and looked at him. It roared and charged. Thomas could only watch as it barreled into Dmitri. It brought its hooves down on him, and Thomas heard a sickening crack.

"What's going on here?" an unsteady voice asked.

Thomas turned to the door. The beggar stood there, leaning against a wall and breathing heavily. The beast looked up. It roared even louder than it had when Thomas stabbed it. It thundered toward the beggar. Thomas cursed and threw himself at the creature as it passed, but he bounced off it with no effect. He picked himself off the ground and ran to Dmitri's sword, but it was too far. In horror he watched as the questing beast neared its new prey.

The beggar reached into his beer-stained jacket and pulled out a shining sword with a jeweled hilt. His legs were spread wide, and he held the sword steady like a man who knew well how to use it. Thomas froze and stared as the man sidestepped the creature's charge, slashing as it passed. His sword cut a long line down the monster's flank. It reared, but with a quick slash, its front legs came off. The beast tried to stand, but the stumps couldn't bear its weight, and it crashed to the ground. It lashed out, but the beggar moved like a cat and had no trouble avoiding its attacks. He let out a long breath and shook his head.

"You never fought with me last time," he said. "Just with Pellinore, Palamedes, and Percival. I always wondered what would happen."

The monster growled and tried to bite him, but the beggar flicked his blade in an almost casual fashion. Its head came free of his body, a pool of blood spreading on the ground. The man sheathed his sword and looked at Thomas. For a second his gray eyes and sharp features made him look like a soldier in his prime, but then it was gone, and only the beggar remained. His gaze wandered to Dmitri. The other Unnamed was a bloody mess. Thomas was sure he was dead until he groaned. Thomas rushed to his side. He knelt down and looked at the beggar, but the man had already turned and was heading for the door.

"Mer's not here yet."

Dmitri coughed. "What did I tell you? Legends are awakening."

He continued to mumbled, but Thomas couldn't make anything out. Suddenly, it all came together in his head. The questing beast. That sword. Pellinore, Palamedes, and Percival: the names of knights who had been dead for over a thousand years.

"Mer," Thomas said, not daring to believe what he was about to say. He spoke louder. "Merlin? You mean Merlin? Arthur?"

Arthur looked over his shoulder. "Mer's not here yet. He was supposed to be here when I woke up, but he's not."

Dmitri groaned, drawing Thomas' attention. He tore his shirt to make makeshift bandages and called to command.

"It wasn't a dragon," he said after he'd gotten through security and requested aid for Dmitri. "It was a questing beast."

There was a stunned silence on the line. "You killed a questing beast?"

"Negative, it was some guy off the street. I think-" his words caught in his throat. "I think it was Arthur. King Arthur."

The voice on the end of the line sputtered. "Say again."

"We were saved by Arthur Pendragon."

"Is he there with you?"

Thomas looked around, but the factory was empty. "No, he's gone."

"You have to go after him."

"Nine-five-seven is..."

"Go," Dmitri said between labored breaths.

Thomas looked into Dmitri's eyes. The fallen man was obviously in pain but just as obviously meant what he had said.

Thomas nodded at his wounded companion. All Unnamed had sworn to give their lives if need be. Arthur had built a shining bastion against the darkness once. Maybe he could do so again.

Thomas rushed out of the door just as the response team had

arrived. He uttered a silent thanks that Dmitri would survive. He scanned the area but saw no sign. In desperation, he ran around the warehouse, peaking into every nook and cranny he could find.

By the time he was done, others had started to arrive. Though Dmitri had been the only other soldier nearby when Thomas had made the call, the Unnamed had dozens of other agents in the area, and they spread out through the city like a flood. It was well after midnight before the search was called off. King Arthur was gone.

"But you're out there," he said to the night, "and we'll find you."

BIO

Gama Ray Martinez lives near Salt Lake City, Utah. He moved there solely because he likes mountains. He collects weapons in case he ever needs to supply a medieval battalion, and he greatly resents when work or other real life things get in the way of writing. He secretly hopes to one day slay a dragon in single combat and doesn't believe in letting pesky little things like reality stand in the way of dreams.

9

PRISONER 141

L. J. HACHMEISTER

Red lights flashed on the smooth black surface of the bomb, but 141 didn't pay attention, concentrating on exposing the sensitive innards. Wires spilled out, but she batted them aside, crawling underneath and flipping onto her back to get a better look.

Twin suns, bright enough to penetrate through the swollen brown clouds, afforded her enough light to see the alien inscriptions on the internal circuit boards, but she couldn't tell the difference between the routing wires. Once triggered, Pri'al bombs had to be disarmed in under ten seconds, a feat few Sentients—let alone humans—could accomplish, especially in the hazardous wastelands of Torrus Prime.

Seven seconds, she thought, her internal clock counting down. She wiggled her gloved hand inside the exposed underbelly of the explosive, feeling for the subtle texture variations in the energy chambers.

Five—

The red warning lights stayed on, growing brighter as she fumbled to identify the corrugated edging to the transfer conduit.

Damn these biohazard suits, she thought, frustrated by the thick gloves that blocked her sensitive touch.

Four—

141 ripped out her arm, tossed aside the glove, and shoved her hand back in. Even inside the bomb her skin burned from the polluted desert air.

Three, two—

Fingers grazing the ribbed lining, she thrust upwards, pushing her head and shoulder into the bomb to reach her target. Not that it mattered much. If she failed, everything in a fifty-kilometer radius without an active shield would be blown sky high.

One—

"Ahhh," she cried, grabbing the fragile transfer conduit connector and yanking as hard as she could.

Red lights sputtered, then shut off.

One down, she thought, removing her abraded fist. Red oil and serum mixed with her blood, giving it an iridescent sheen. *Two hundred more to go.*

Chucking the connector aside, she wiped her hand on her biohazard suit and thought about whether to even bother putting her glove back on. None of the other two hundred organic-tech bombs would be any easier, and with the cheap suits issued by her employer, the venerable Intergalactic Corrections and Containment Coalition, or IC3, she doubted that asking for better equipment would get her anything more than some quality time in an isolation cell.

The thought made her stomach knot. Being alone didn't bother her, nor did any physical punishment, but a night without sleep medicine did.

Movement near the bomb's gutted innards caught her eye. Nothing could have survived the attack on the planet. Still, she couldn't help herself, and carefully moved aside one of the broken tubes.

Where'd you come from? A rodent of some sort, small and emaciated, shivered under the wires, staring at her with beady pink eyes and a coat covered in red sand. It ducked when she brushed away the wires, but didn't run when she offered her injured hand for a smell.

You look like a chibi mouse.

Tiny whiskers tickled her finger. The delicate touch surprised her, made her forget herself for a moment, as if something important—something forgotten—tried to draw her into the sensation.

It's not like it's going to make it out here, she tried to tell herself. Not with the pollution, the radiation hazards, and God knew what else. And the Warden certainly wouldn't allow a rescue onboard. Still, she couldn't bear the hungry look in its eyes, or the way it trusted her not to swipe it up for an easy meal.

Stupid mouse, she thought, anger and frustration eclipsing her mind as it sniffed her bloodied fingers. What was this rodent to her? Besides, it's not like she had anything to spare. Her crappy protein bar ration wouldn't even last her the long hours ahead.

"Screw it," she whispered. She produced the bar from one of the pouches on her belt and offered the creature a chunk. The little rodent took it without hesitation, cramming it into his cheeks.

It won't live, her rational voice reminded. Not here, on this forgotten wasteland. Or would it? Maybe her sacrifice gave it the chance it needed.

Sacrifice. Chance.

Another more dangerous word lingered in the back of her mind, but a gruff voice, drowning in static, rang into the bud implanted into her ear: "Prisoner 141, come in."

The rodent scampered off as she scooted back on her elbow. Already dreading what the Warden wanted, she responded with a grunt.

No answer.

Crawling out from underneath the disarmed bomb, she faced north toward the skeletal remains of a city, hoping to get a better signal to the dropship two kilometers away.

What's that? she thought, wiping sand from her helmet's visor.

A sleek, gray ship, three times the size of the prison carrier orbiting above, hovered near the drop site.

That's probably the source of interference, she inferred.

Not recognizing the curved wings and seamless design, or the glyphs on the hull, 141 braced herself for the only two possibilities: an alien attack, or Warden Cooley making another unsanctioned deal.

She wished for the attack.

Looking over the ruined landscape of broken steel and consuming desert, she spied a dozen more bombs poking out from the canted slabs of broken street in her immediate radius. If she returned to the dropship to reestablish contact, she'd get in trouble for leaving her assignment, but if she continued without acknowledging the call, she'd be accused of disobedience.

She regarded her injuries with a distant loathing. The pain didn't bother her, nor the skin hanging off in ribbons. Staring at the mix of blood and oil brought heat to her chest, an agitation she could not acknowledge, one that wouldn't allow her to quit without disarming all two hundred or more bombs in the desolate city before returning, even if it took all day, at the cost of her hand, or her life.

She moved on.

As the first sun slid behind the muddied southern horizon, she heard a battlefield drone buzzing through the wreckage. Without pausing, she pulled out the innards of her ninety-seventh bomb and went through the disarming process, disregarding the chirps from the drone.

"A hundred and three to go..." she muttered, rolling out from underneath the dead bomb. As she stood, she held her shredded hand to her chest, not wanting to look at the white bone peeking out from the lacerations across the wrist. Exhaustion weighed down her movements, but she paid no attention to the aching protests of her body.

Finish the job.

Then, maybe relief. Or so she had told herself for the last nine years.

The drone, waiting a good distance away until she completed

her task, zipped toward her, antennae zeroing in on her position. Why its designer made it look like the upper half of a human with an insect head always incited conversation amongst the other duds, but not her. The drones did their job, and that's all the mattered.

Hovering above the ground to meet her at eye-level, the drone stuck out its three-fingered hand and projected a green-lit, holographic message from its palm. Warden Cooley's ugly mug appeared in three dimensions, greedy excitement in his eyes.

"Prisoner 141, return to the dropship immediately, priority 1."

Another job, she thought, gazing out to the setting red suns. Of course it would be dangerous, illegal, and fatten the Warden's pockets with more cash than she could know in a lifetime. If he lost prisoners in the process, he'd falsify a report, just like he'd done a thousand times before. After all, disarming bombs on war-ravaged worlds was hazardous, and there was plenty of opportunity for an unfortunate event to take the life of one of his many unwanted charges.

Maybe this will be the last one.

She bristled, uncomfortable with the idea, but drawn to it all the same.

The drone withdrew its hand and whistled as a small platform lowered out from the base of its glowing anti-grav pods.

He must really want this, she thought, surprised he sent a drone with transport capabilities. Under normal circumstances, Warden Cooley didn't care if she worked ten days straight without returning to the dropship, nor would he send out a drone to bring her back after a long slog.

Hugging her exposed hand to her chest, she climbed onto the platform and held on tight to the handhold on its back. As the drone whisked her away, she took one last look to the south, to the last light bleeding away into the encroaching darkness, imagining the ghosts of a past she could not remember rising from the tombs of the ruined city.

* * *

As Prisoner 141 stepped out of decontamination, she got a glimpse of four strangers before Warden Cooley slapped his sweaty palm down on her shoulder and redirected her toward the dropship prisoner cells.

"Removing a biohazard suit in the middle of a containment run is a violation of code 12 of the IC3's policy," he declared as he shoved her along, his squat legs pumping furiously.

The rest didn't matter. She knew the drill. Cooley wanted to appear dominant, controlling of his wards in front of potential clients, especially if he hungered after a big contract. Any other day he wouldn't give her sacrifice or injuries a second thought.

The strangers, dressed in exquisite garments made of shimmering fibers and projected light, didn't look like the Warden's usual band of seedy clientele wanting to purchase dangerous parts and equipment salvaged from their runs. Although humanoid in shape, their rich blue skin and yellow eyes spoke of outerworld origins, but she didn't know where.

They're wealthy, she thought as the Warden continued to spout policy violation punishments. *Probably want an extraction.*

Rich investors and warlords loved to get their hands on illegal power sources dug up from bombs and downed warship reactors. Though the last intergalactic war happened ten years ago, prisoners, or "duds", like her still worked every day to clean up massacred worlds, under the slick promise from the Starways' president that refugees could one day return home.

Not that she believed disarming bombs could salvage any of the dead worlds.

One of the strangers caught her eye. The alien's gaze, confident and knowing, as if recognizing an old friend, made her pause, but the Warden pushed her forward.

"No," she mumbled, resisting as he forced her past her designated cell and toward the red-marked door at the end of the row.

He pressed a stun gun into her back and pointed to the isolation cell. "Get in."

A jolt of electricity sent her sprawling into the dark prison. She wheeled around just in time to see the Warden slamming the door shut, a delighted smile upon his pudgy face.

How long will he leave me in here?

141 took a few deep breaths of the poorly circulated air. The isolation cell, light-free and sound proof, would make minutes stretch into days. Even if he only kept her in here for an hour, she didn't know if she could fight off the hallucinogenic effects, or worse yet, not succumb to exhaustion.

Don't fall asleep. Not without meds to stifle her dreams. Nausea squeezed down on her stomach at the thought of her last trip into hell.

Focus on the pain, she told herself, clutching her damaged hand.

But the darkness, patient and silent, waited her out, pulling down her consciousness piece by piece, and blanketing her pain in the promise of relief.

Don't...

Yellow eyes appeared in the distance as the darkness seized the last of her, watching as she spiraled away and into herself, into the nightmarish fold of her own subconscious.

* * *

The chorus of agonized voices called out from the shifting shadows. Stretched out and distorted faces appeared, then shattered, bleeding back into the restive gray sea. Her own panicked breath and heartbeat rose above the din as a cloud formed at her feet, then mushroomed upward, dwarfing her in its massive size.

One voice, cold and heartless, whispered in her ear as flames consumed the world around her: "141..."

"Wake up." A rough set of knuckles ground into her sternum, followed by a stinging slap to her cheek. "Get up!"

141 peeled back crusted eyelids. Blurry figures hovered over her as the dark images of her nightmare decomposed in the sting of the ceiling lights. Tight restraints held her down against a cold

metal table, not allowing her much movement beyond the turn of her head.

"Thank you, Warden. Allow us to take it from here," a feminine voice said.

"You don't have to coddle her; you know who this is, don't you?"

141 closed her eyes again, not wanting to hear the response. Even with a wiped mind, her body still reacted, as if the horrors of her past crimes had been indelibly etched into some kind of cellular memory.

"We are aware."

"For punishment and control purposes, IC3 protocol mandates that prisoners cannot learn of their former identities. Blow her up, kill her—I don't care; just don't give her back her name. Agreed?"

"We understand, Warden."

Hot breath blew against her cheek. An acrid stench, doused in antacids, filled her nose as the Warden whispered into her ear: "Do this job, dud, or you'll rot in isolation—*forever.*"

The sound of his pant legs brushing against each other grew more distant, followed by the *clank* of the infirmary door.

"Open your eyes," the feminine voice said, her tone soothing and melodic. Fingers grazed against the exposed skin on her forearm, stirring feelings that she simultaneously invited and repelled.

141 dared to open her eyes, this time adjusting much faster to the light. One of the aliens sat at her side, the other three fanning out in the small infirmary, interacting with specialized holographic modules attached to their sleeves. She'd never seen such advanced tech before, not even in the heart of the Starways.

"I am Raza," the alien besides her said, still touching her forearm. A faint smile touched her dark lips, transforming her already alluring face. Even if she could access all her memories, 141 didn't think she had encountered any other beauty that compared. "I've come a long way to find you."

Confused and transfixed, 141 could not look away as the alien continued to examine her forearm and injured hand with her blue fingers.

"You volunteer for the most dangerous containment and salvage missions, yes?"

141 kept her eyes on the alien as the tips of her blue fingers lit up. Deep warmth, followed by a pins and needles sensation, coursed up her arm as the alien pieced her injured hand back together.

"My people need your help. Long ago, in darker times, we built the sh'nar, a weapon that would end all wars, not realizing the magnitude of its destructive capabilities."

Echoes of battle, of great machines blazing over ruined landscapes and bombs screaming down from the skies, jerked across her mind, but she held her breath until the ghosted images passed.

Were those my memories? she wondered, looking down at the alien's glowing fingers.

Still holding, fast, the alien continued, her voice hardening. "We have since found peace, and are trying to move forward and rebuild, just as your species has done…"

The pause in her voice made 141 look up. Yellow eyes gazed back, wide and full of sorrow. "But we cannot. Not with the remnants of our darkest hour still haunting our dreams. Despite who we are now, we fear the sh'nar's invitation, and the call of its power to the other Sentients of this galaxy."

141 perked to the inflection in the alien's words. *Call of its power...*

Whispers of a new war, one that would destroy the fragile alliance forged between humans and aliens across the galaxy, had circulated for years amongst the duds, but she noticed a change a few months ago. Her bomb disarming runs on war-ravaged planets hadn't abated, but the Warden's illegal salvaging missions had increased tenfold, as if old enemies felt the need to stockpile the last war's most devastating weapons.

"I've studied your species for decades," Raza said. "Humans are remarkable; you can adapt to almost any environment, bond with anything or anyone, and thrive in the worst conditions. And above all, you are strong in your convictions. That is why I've chosen a human for this task."

Why me? Only the most notorious intergalactic criminals had their memories wiped and sentenced to bomb disarmament with IC3 as reparation for their heinous crimes against the Starways. Most died in training, and no one lasted longer than two years.

Except me. Anger boiled through her chest at the thought of her unusual luck. *Even the devil doesn't want me.*

141 inhaled sharply as the alien lifted her repaired hand, the skin intact and healthy, better looking than the rest of her battered forty-year-old body.

"Back then, we were not able to destroy the sh'nar, so we hid the weapon on Cerreca, a planet hazardous to our species, not thinking that anyone else would seek it out." Raza turned to the other aliens still interacting with their holograms. "My people are monitoring the traffic in our star system. There are many new starships near Cerreca. We are worried they will find the sh'nar. We don't want to bring war to the galaxy...or worse."

Raza lifted 141's restraints. Sitting up, 141 regarded her healed hand, marveling at a beauty she never associated with her own flesh.

"I can manipulate your biology, enable you tolerate the environment. Will you help us?"

Flexing the hand into a fist, 141 felt the crinkle of the new skin, the softness of a palm free of callouses.

"Why me?" 141 whispered, expecting to hear something about her almost impossible record of bomb disarms and high-risk salvaging.

"Because of who you are."

141 looked away. "I wouldn't know what you mean. Everything I am has been taken away from me."

The alien touched her arm again, sending a rush of warmth traveling to her chest. "Not everything."

Discomfited by her touch, 141 wrenched her arm away. As she

made to jump off the table, she stopped herself, thinking of the Warden's threat: *"Do this job, dud, or you'll rot in isolation —forever."*

Flashes of light caught her eye as one of the other aliens highlighted an orange and green planet surrounded by starcraft. *Must be Cerreca.*

Up until now, if she had failed any of her missions, only she and any other dud out in the same field would be compromised. This posed something new, something she hadn't—

Have I?—

—experienced before.

"Please…" Raza said, yellow eyes pleading. "Our people—the entire galaxy—needs you. I fear what the sh'nar would do in the wrong hands."

"Meaning?"

Raza's voice tightened. "Genocide."

The sweat beading across her brow surprised her, as did the pounding of her heart. Impressions from her recent nightmare resurfaced in discordant images, as did the cold voice that haunted her dreams.

"141…"

"One condition," she said, squaring back to the alien. The blue being regarded her with unwavering curiosity as 141 let the silence stretch out between them. "Wipe my memory totally clean afterward."

"You remember your past?"

"No," she said, dropping her voice to a whisper. "Just bad dreams."

Raza tilted her head, but didn't question why 141 didn't barter for freedom, or even her name. "As you wish."

* * *

Where am I?

141 found herself in another plane, surrounded by soft white clouds. A night sky, filled with a thousand stars, provided light, enough for her to see the figure floating toward her.

Raza? *She didn't believe her eyes, or the delighted smile upon the alien's face as she reached out to her with lucent blue hands.* I must be dreaming.

No, impossible; not the way the alien's skin felt against hers. Soft and warm, she hadn't felt such tenderness in—

Sirens wailed. White clouds and the night sky disappeared in the wake of a thunder-clap explosion. A mushroom cloud billowed out from behind the alien, harsh, red light shooting out from the base.

"141," a disembodied voice shouted, filling her gut with ice. Distorted faces appeared all around them, eyes burned from their sockets, mouths trapped open in a scream.

"Don't," the alien said as 141 pulled away, "you have to remember!"

141 shot forward, heart thudding against her chest.

"You're okay; you're just waking from cryosleep."

Blue hands settled her back upon a soft bed as her eyes adjusted to the lights.

"Where…?" she rasped through parched lips. She lie in a transparent half-cylinder, much more advanced-looking than the clunky coffins IC3 used to for cryosleep transport. Instead of the ugly prisoner uniform, she wore a sleek black suit that reminded her of the cutting-edge space tech she'd seen in the Homeworlds.

"You're safe aboard my ship." Raza appeared above her, a smile gracing her already beautiful face. "And you have the most interesting dreams."

Was that really her? As 141's cheeks bloomed red, she rationalized away what she didn't want to believe. *No; she must have been reading my cryo-readouts.*

"While you were in cryosleep, I made some adjustments to your body habitus," Raza said, interacting with a hologram projecting from the sleeve of her robe. The outline of 141's body appeared in yellow light, with glyphs drawn over her vital organs.

"Cerreca's atmosphere is mostly ammonia and sulfur. I've lowered your body's oxygen requirements and enabled you to withstand hotter temperatures."

Sitting up, 141 studied the hologram more closely. "What else?"

"Bolstered your immunity, and augmented neural activity in preparation for a lower oxygen supply."

141 caught a glimpse of her reflection in the half-cylinder, seeing the same tired eyes and haggard face she remembered. "Am I still human?"

Raza turned off the projection. "I would never change that."

With a shrug, 141 climbed out of the half-cylinder and looked for the rest of her accessories to cover her bare feet and hands. The alien vessel, designed with minimalistic interfaces and pearlescent, curved surfaces, looked nothing like the rusty old tankers she was used to traveling in. Even the other cryocylinders, five of them in a row against a digital readout, looked far more advanced than—

(Home.)

The thought startled her, as did the flash of brown hair and hazel eyes that skittered across her awareness. In that moment, she remembered the feel of silk sheets rustling against her bare skin, and the weight of someone's arm draped across her chest.

"Stay with me..." a familiar voice whispered.

No—

Bracing her temples, she stumbled the wall and slid down to a crouching position.

I can't—

A barrage of emotions flooded her mind, bringing tears to her eyes.

—don't want to feel—

Raza rushed to her side and ran her hands along 141's neckline. "It will pass."

"What's happening to me?" she said, holding her breath until the confusing sensations dissipated.

Supporting her by the waist, Raza helped 141 over to a bench near a console.

"Altering your neurons may have triggered some residual memories."

"No," she said between breaths. "IC3 took everything."

Raza laid her hand on 141's chest. "Not all memories are stored in the same place."

"That's bull." 141 grabbed the alien's wrist. "Make it stop."

"I can't; not until you complete the mission."

"Fine," she said, shoving off the bench. "Get me the weapon specs."

"You won't need them; your experience will guide you."

"Whatever," 141 said, resuming her search for the rest of her biosuit accessories.

"What do you fear?" Raza's yellow eyes searched 141's face. When 141 wouldn't answer, she pointed to a locker storage unit next to one of the cryocylinders.

141 punched the glowing blue button above the locker, and a door popped open. Inside the locker she found a helmet, gloves, boots, and a techpack to sling over her shoulders. "Just let me do my job."

Raza sighed, the sorrow in her eyes hinting of all the thoughts left unspoken. "As you wish."

Raza's radioed voice barely registered over the screaming winds. "...lifeforms close..."

Dammit, 141 thought, tapping her helmet. Raza had given her only three hours to find, disarm, and then return to the drop site for extraction—all while competing with the other factions hunting down the sh'nar.

If I even have an hour, 141 thought, shielding her eyes as she looked up to the tortured sky. Blue lightning branched out across the knotted black clouds, explosive thunderclaps following close behind. From the readouts on her sleeve and the toasty feel inside her suit, the temperature had already shot up to104 degrees Celsius, and things would only get hotter as the early morning progressed to the scorching midday.

Well, it's not raining glass. Yet.

141 removed the crystalline map from her techpack and held it up in front of her, trying to get a sense of direction over the hard-scrabble landscape. Jagged spires, shaped over the centuries by the winds and rain, reached out like charred fingers rising from the grave.

This can't be right. The green blip on the map wanted her to head south, but Raza had told her the sh'nar would be west, near acid pools. Given that Raza's people had purposely tried to lose the weapon on the inhospitable planet, she didn't expect it to be easy. *But not like this,* she thought as the map sputtered, then shut off.

"Raza," she shouted into her helmet mic.

"141..."

The voice came out of nowhere, cutting through the winds.

No, she thought, looking out into the desolate horizon. *It's not the voice from my dreams; Raza did something to me.* Still, a chill ran up her spine.

Not knowing what else to do, 141 picked her way through the towering silicate formations until she came upon a trail of blood splatter and shredded biosuits. By the scorch marks and carnage, she guessed a battle had broken out between the different factions.

I must be close.

Thunder boomed, rattling her bones. 141 paused, not from the overhead clash, but from the voice that whispered in her ear. *"141..."*

I'm losing it. Sweat slid down her neck and pooled around the seal for her suit and helmet. A terrible knowing, one that she could not rationalize, stole her breath and quickened her heart. *My nightmare...*

It's here.

"... okay?"

Raza's static-filled voice broke her trance. Inhaling sharply, 141 calmed herself. *Complete the mission. Then I'll be free.*

Erased, forgotten. That's all she wanted. No more nightmares, visions of pain and suffering, or disembodied voices crying out her name; no more ghosts of a past that no one, least of all her, wanted to remember.

"I'm fine," she said into the mic. *I won't have to be me much longer.*

Fighting the winds, she pressed forward, climbing up and over a striated shelf. When she crested, she gasped. Desiccated bodies littered the periphery of the gouged-out crater while dozens of aliens from various factions stood in a staggered ring around a gigantic monolith the size of a four-story building. Hypnotized by an unseen power, some of them grasped at the air while others shivered and shook.

The voice called to her from the black stone etched with glowing red glyphs in the middle of the crater. *"141..."*

No, she thought, unable to resist the urge to walk forward. With each step down into the bowl, she came closer to the pillar jutting out from its impact point in the blackened ground.

This is wrong—

Sirens shrieked, warning of an imminent attack.

Not real, she told herself, pressing her gloves against her helmet to quell the deafening sound.

The sirens faded away, replaced by a low hum coming from the monolith. Clenching her jaw, she tried to change directions, but her legs wouldn't respond to her command.

STOP.

As the invisible force drew her forward, 141 caught glimpses of the terror-stricken faces of the various aliens swaying in front of the monolith. *Oh, Gods—*

Beneath the transparent visors she saw their wounded eyes, bloodied and sunken, and caved-in mouths.

Terror seized her heart as she gazed upon the towering structure. *I can't disarm this—*

"141..."

The voice plunged into her, infiltrating her bones and blood, sucking the air from her lungs. Left breathless, she halted in place, a few meters from the monolith, aware of the many sets of eyes sinking behind her own.

Who are you? she thought as something cold and slimy slid down her spine.

"141..."

Body stiffening, she lost feeling in her limbs, and her vision dimmed. Any sense of fear and violation drifted away as her own sights turned inward, and the true depths of her nightmare came to light.

* * *

"Commander, we're in position," one of the helmsman shouted over the battle-noise coming from the holographic war globe projected in the center of the bridge. "Your order, Sir?"

Standing over the command station interface, she looked at the statistics scrolling down the secondary display. Her warship had taken minor damage after a failed attempt to communicate with the Grogons resulted in a firefight.

We'll try again, *she thought, wanting to reinitiate the translation program and find a way to communicate with the new alien species.*

"Communication from Central Command," the helmsman said, relaying the coded message to her console. The text appeared in bright blue next to her ship's readouts.

141.

Her heart froze. Order 141; the release of the military's secret planet-killing bomb.

This doesn't make sense. *The Grogons posed no real threat, and their species—and countless others inhabiting the Earth-sized world—had yet to colonize other planets.*

"Commander," the helmsman said, pointing to red dots on the

war globe. "The Grogons are coming about for another attack run."

The order flashed on her ship's readouts.

This is wrong. *But she had no other choice, lest she risk losing her post. And after twenty years of service and relationships lost, she couldn't imagine doing—being—anything else.*

"Order 141," she said, typing in her authorization codes.

"Launching," the helmsman said as the internal sirens wailed. "In three...two...one..."

* * *

141 gasped, heart thudding against her chest, resurfacing from the tidal wave of memories.

I remember.

Standing in front of the humming monolith, she bridged two realities.

I dropped the bomb. Shaking, she gulped for air as her nightmares congealed, forming a haunting vision she finally understood. *I destroyed the Grogon homeworld—*

Lightning tore apart the skies, but 141 drew further inward. *The military took away my name...*

And after disavowing her in the wake of the scandalous genocide, stripped her of rank, stole her identity and designated her as 141. No chance for goodbyes, not that she had seen her estranged wife in over four years.

They lied, she thought, remembering the scathing reports about her character, the public shaming and awful renouncement.

"For your heinous actions against the Grogons, we revoke your citizenship and reject you as our sister," the Starways President announced over the intergalactic broadcast.

No longer human. Heat stacked upon heat in her chest. *They took everything from me.*

The monolith's hum rose in pitch, overpowering the wind and thunder with its shrill cry. Red glyphs grew brighter, the ground beneath her vibrated. In her peripheries, she caught sight of the other aliens disintegrating as a savage hunger blanketed her mind.

"141..."

Rage, unlike anything she had ever felt before, lit up every cell in her body, setting her insides afire.

Give me justice, she thought, reaching out to the monolith. As soon as the tip of her glove touched the smooth surface, her senses extended beyond her body, channeling through the sh'nar and across the galaxy.

She found the Warden first, sitting in his office, filing a false report about her disobedience. Transcending physical bounds, she wove her fingers around his neurons and yanked back. The Warden screamed, bucking out of his office chair and clawing at his temples.

She moved on, already bored by his fading cries. Desiring a greater satisfaction, she turned her sights to military outpost constructed next to the devastated Grogon homeworld.

You made me kill them for an outpost? she thought, gathering the legion's soul-lights in her hands. She squeezed her fingers down, crushing all 700. *Criminals.*

On the fringe of her awareness, she heard the sh'nar's raucous tones escalate. Disinterested, she reached out farther into the cosmos, finding countless planets and populaces to ensnare. *You all abandoned me.*

Anger boiled through her, magnifying in bands of red light that projected from her fingers. *I will end you all.*

"Screw it," she heard herself say, vision splintering.

With the galaxy in her clutches, she felt the tickle of the chibi mouse's whiskers against her skin as it plucked the food from her injured hand.

No, she thought, resisting the sentiment of the memory. *I didn't save it.*

Other memories blossomed forth, competing with the dark force captivating her heart. She remembered Raza's touch, the way her lucent fingers mended her wounds, the alien's essence delving deeper than her lacerated flesh.

Nobody's touched me since—

Her mind made the long-forgotten connection.

Sienna.

Anger surged anew in her heart as she recalled the terrible moment when she lost her wife.

Don't take her away from me!

But pleading with the surgeons lowering the mind-wiping halo onto her head did nothing, not when they believed her to be the genocidal commander.

Falling to her knees, she extended her reach as far as the sh'nar would take her, past the known galaxy, into the deepest reaches of space, grasping at all the soul material she could see, ready to wipe away all the light of the universe.

"Hold me." Sienna, faced away from her and dressed in civilian clothes, dabbed at her eyes with a tissue. "Well?"

The commander walked over and wrapped her arms around her wife's slender waistline, settling her head into her perfumed neck.

"Don't forget me while you're up in the stars, all right?"

Never. *Not even after seeing the divorce notice waiting on her desk as soon as she hit orbit.*

The pulse in her veins quickened, the stentorian cry of the sh'nar reaching its peak as the memory faded away, and she found herself stretched out across the heavens.

I am a killer.

Then stillness, silence, as the collective universe held its breath, awaiting her reckoning.

Three.

I am—

She smelled her wife's perfume, saw Raza's smile as her blue hands glided across her skin.

Two.

I am...

(—forgive me.)

Gray whiskers tickled her fingers. Hope, possibility, in the face of death, reminded her of choice.

One.

Tears falling from her eyes, she embraced all that she was, and called out her name.

* * *

"I could have ended the universe."

Raza looked at the commander with the same knowing smile as she ran her lucent fingers up her body, repairing her damaged tissue with ease. For a brief moment, the transparent half-cylinder beneath her vibrated as the alien starship broke from Cerreca's orbit, and jumped to light speed. "The sh'nar was created to respond to the strongest desires, and empower that person to right the world. Given your history, we knew it would react to you."

"But I'm a murderer."

"Yes, and you have suffered for this," Raza acknowledged, helping her sit up.

Thinking of the Grogon homeworld, reduced to ashes and rubble, she whispered: "I have."

"In remembering all your past—not just the loss and tribulation, but also the reasons for life, for hope and choice—you found cause not to repeat your mistakes."

"Yes." Silently, she added: *I am not 141.*

"This is the conviction that shut down the sh'nar's power."

"But I killed the Warden…that entire legion…"

Raza held on to her arm. "Your humanity saved the universe."

"I guess," she said, regarding her revitalized body in the breaks of her white patient gown. Forty, going on twenty—at least that's how her joints felt and skin looked. "So, what now?"

Raza brushed back the loose strands of hair from the commander's face. "We will take you wherever your heart desires."

Home.

She hadn't thought of such a thing in years.

Where would it be?

"Take me to your world," she answered.

"Not Earth?"

Shaking her head, she took Raza's hand in hers, and held it close. "To new memories—and better dreams."

Raza smiled. "Alright then, Commander."

"Call me Ceri."

BIO

L.J. Hachmeister is an author and registered nurse from Denver, Colorado. When not touring comic cons, she practices a lot of Brazilian jiujitsu and Doce Pares Eskrima, and chases after her two rambunctious dogs.

L.J. is represented by Paul Stevens of the Donald Maass Literary Agency.

10

VALENTINE BLUES

JAMES A. HUNTER

The kids in Valentine, Nebraska just aren't right. Not anymore.

They're Dangerous. Unpredictable. *Hungry*. As violence breaks out and people start dying, butchered in their homes, only Yancy Lazarus—bluesman, gambler, mage, and former wet-works man—can put things right. Well, he can try…

* * *

Something was wrong in Valentine.

I could feel it in the air, beating down on my senses like an invisible sledgehammer.

My El Camino rumbled beneath me as I cruised along US 20, nearing the edge of the sleepy town, a few worn buildings poking up along the horizon. I leaned over and cranked down the window, letting the wind whip into the cab, filling the interior with the scent of fresh-turned earth—musky and rich—and the sweet aroma of wildflowers offset by the pungent smell of cow shit. I breathed deeply, inhaling a great big whiff of country air, then exhaled it slowly through my nose.

Great swathes of dusty dry yellow stretched off to either side of me, a flat land deep in the heart of a drought, but ahead lay a patch of green, like an oasis in a desert. I turned an eye skyward, searching the clouds above for any telltale sign of the strange energy bearing down on me, but the sky was clear as far as I could see. I turned my gaze back to the two-lane cut of asphalt lazily meandering off to the left. A "Reduced Speed Ahead" sign popped up on the right, so I dropped down from sixty-five, coming damned near to a crawl as I passed by the first few buildings on the edge of Valentine.

Off to the left lurked a recently renovated motel, the Trading Post, laid out in a "U," the grass out front lush and inviting, a series of squat bushes lining the roadway. The motel vanished in a blink, replaced in short order by a run-down gas station, followed by a few rows of single-wide trailers, many old and worn. None of 'em looked occupied. The run-down trailer park disappeared behind a clump of leafy trees as the road straightened, swelling into a four-lane boulevard, lined on either side by gas stations, hardware stores, a couple of fast-food chains, and a spattering of rough motels with names like the Waterfall Inn or the Motor Carriage Lodge.

Cheap tacky places that appealed to approximately no one, anywhere, ever.

I travel a lot, living out of the back of my car, moving from state to state, town to town, bar to bar, eating cheap bar food and playing the blues for beer money, so I know a thing or two about sleepy towns. This place? This place was a Podunk shit-speck—maybe eight or nine hundred people—the kinda town folks drive through, but only because they were on the way to someplace better, more interesting. The shops lining the streets damn near shouted that fact at the top of their lungs: all catered to the weary travelers looking for a bite to eat or a place to catch a wink.

Podunk to the core.

Not that I have anything against Podunk shit-speck towns, mind you. Not the kinda place I'd ever want to settle down in, obviously, but small towns are the best places to shoot the shit with crusty old-timers over at the VFW hall. Tradin' war stories, having a few laughs, killin' time.

I stared at the shops as I cruised, my eyes picking over the long shadows cast by the fading sun, searching for signs of life, but everything seemed dead. Cold. The air washing into the cab felt heavy with arcane power, some powerful construct laying over the entire town like a smothering pillow.

Eric Clapton blared from my speakers, but with a grunt of irritation I flicked the power button, killing the gritty tunes so I could get a better read on the town. The music died, replaced by silence. An unnatural quiet radiating from the buildings and the streets. A hush that demanded compliance. Valentine felt like a friggin' library, presided over by some haughty, overbearing lady with boxy glasses and a motherly cardigan, eager to bring down the gavel the moment some snot-nosed kid broke the peace.

I rolled up to a three-way intersection guarded by an unnecessary stoplight looking down on an otherwise empty street. There were cars around, true—lots of older American made trucks, a few newer SUVs in various makes and models, a couple muscle cars with peeling paint—but they were all parked along the streets, empty. On the surface, everything looked fine. No sign of trouble. No evidence of rioting. No burnt buildings or broken store windows. The stores, though mundane, looked neat and clean, carefully and lovingly maintained. But no people.

Not a one.

I stopped at the light even though I had a green, loitering for a moment as I drummed my fingers on the steering wheel, the sound unnaturally loud in the stillness. Straight ahead, flanking the US 20, lay more motels and fast-food joints. Then the road broke away, clearing the shit-speck town, cruising on for another three hundred miles until it turned into Interstate 25 in Wyoming. To the right, though, lay North Main Street, a quaint two-lane, slicing deeper into the town, leading back into the residential area, eventually turning into the US 83, which headed into South Dakota.

I was bound for Rapid City, which meant that bastard road was on my route.

For a long beat, I considered just gassing it, laying my foot down flat against the pedal and driving right on through this shithole. Skip Rapid City entirely and head west into Wyoming instead. After all, one town was as good as another, since I didn't actually have a place to be.

I idled at the intersection a spell longer.

Yep, the smart thing to do was to keep right on truckin', put this place firmly in the rear-view, and leave the residents of Valentine to deal with their own bullshit. Whatever bullshit that happened to be.

I frowned, sighed, then reluctantly gave the Camino some gas and wheeled right, puttering onto North Main Street and deeper into the heart of the town. Dammit. Idiot.

Stupid, bleeding-heart moron, is what I was.

I passed a few more shops and city buildings, all made of old red brick—a post office here and some kinda historical center there—before finally passing into a winding neighborhood loaded down with cute, double-story cookie-cutter houses that could've filled the suburbs of any city in America. Lifeless trucks and motorhomes dotted streets and driveways. Too-green lawns stared at me as I rolled past, mocking me with their vitality while the rest of the town remained dead and quiet. Still no friggin' people. Zippo.

I started taking turns at random: a left on West Second followed by a quick right onto North Edna, my gaze constantly sweeping back and forth. Constantly searching for any indication of what in the holy hell had happened here.

Each turn brought me further into town, offering me more views of the same quaint, rural neighborhoods. Creepy as hell. Like driving through a modern-day ghost town. I slowed the Camino to a crawl as I hooked a right onto Third Street and caught sight of red and blue police lights strobing ahead, tattooing the paneled siding of a ranch-style up on the left. The den window, looking into the home's interior, had been shattered. Pieces of glass littered the lawn while the curtains fluttered in a soft breeze. The front door stood ajar, yawning like a mouth, and a suspicious patch of red decorated the front walk.

The cruiser—a deep blue sedan with *Valentine Police* sprawled across the side in blocky letters—had mounted the curb, coming to a rest on the well-manicured front lawn. The driver-side door sat open, but there was no sign of the cop. No movement. No sound. Just the strobing light, *whoosh-whoosh-whoosh-whoosh,* washing over the house again and again and again.

I kept right on rolling, not wanting to get out until I had a damn compelling reason to do so.

Three blocks later, near the intersection of West Third and North Wood, I saw the kids.

A bunch of 'em, ranging from scabby kneed preschoolers to surly eyed high schoolers. They loitered around a sprawling brick building—a looming sign labeled it as the Valentine K–12 School —the younger ones hanging from monkey bars or swinging on the playground, while the older ones milled around in small pods on the blacktop and the connecting field. A couple played basketball, a few listlessly kicked a soccer ball back and forth, most shuffled absently from foot to foot. Uniformly, though, they did everything in complete silence.

No one talked or laughed, which was as downright unnatural as things got. Me? I'm not a big fan of kids—they're loud and obnoxious, plus they reek of responsibility, which isn't really my bag. But even I know kids well enough to say they don't ever do anything in complete silence. Ever.

Game was definitely afoot. Some kinda creepy-ass Children of the Corn game, which was *no bueno* and instantly set my teeth on edge.

But, I'd already sorta committed to figuring out what in the hell was going on here, so against my better judgment I eased the car to a stop. A host of empty placid faces swiveled toward me, fixing on the Camino like a pack of uber-intelligent, rabid wolves. Dammit. With another sigh, I shifted the car into park, popped the door, and slid from the driver's seat, stretching my weary legs with a groan. I peered over the roof at the kids and casually reached for the monster hand cannon tucked away in a shoulder rig beneath my leather jacket.

I fingered the pistol grip for a moment, feeling the worn wood inscribed with runic symbols of power, then shook my head, deciding against it. Scary asshole kids were blastin' out creepy vibes by the truckload—practically screaming *I'm gonna murder you and turn your skin into a fleshy bathing suit* through a megaphone. But, they were just *kids*. Kids clearly in need of intense psychological counseling and possibly an exorcism, but I couldn't just start shooting indiscriminately. Not yet. Poor scabbed-knee bastards could *actually* be possessed, so it wouldn't be smart to start fixing a potentially short-term problem with a cylinder full of long-term, irrevocable solutions.

A pair of high school kids, a boy and a girl, promptly turned, regarding me through hazy, hooded eyes. The boy was your typical corn-fed, football-playing farmhand: big ol' son of a bitch with sandy hair, thick shoulders, and a pristine letter jacket in blacks and reds. The girl, trailing just behind him, was a prom queen in the making—thin build, crisp cheerleader uniform, and shockingly blonde hair tied back in dual ponytails.

"Nice town you got here," I said with a lopsided grin, desperately working to beat down the slobbering-fear-badger clawing at my insides. "Don't suppose one of you would mind pointing me in the direction of an adult. Any grown up really—cop, politician, your local grocery store bag boy. As long as they can vote I'm interested and if they can buy beer all the better."

Naturally, they said nothing, their blank faces hardening as they shuffled toward me, lethargic at first, but only for a moment. Before I knew it, the pair broke into a lurching run, eating up the distance between us. A flash of movement in my peripheries caught my attention—I wheeled in time to see more kids emerging from the houses across the street. They too were lurching my way, closing in with the hungry, coordinated movements of a hunting shark pack surrounding hapless prey.

* * *

The kids were friggin' rabid, but I wasn't quite ready to put them down for keeps. Thankfully, I still had plenty of options aside from the ol' hand cannon. I breathed out, clearing my mind, dispelling fear and worry, and opened myself to the *Vis*—the cosmic power underlying matter, existence, Creation—just waiting to be exploited by someone with the right talent. Like me. A mage. True, I'm basically a homeless, wandering degenerate, but I'm also a former wet-works man for the Guild of the Staff, which meant I had a thing or two up my sleeve.

Time came to a herky-jerky crawl as energy flooded into me like a crashing tsunami. Heat and life filled me up, sharpening every sense, infusing my limbs with power and strength.

Everything came to a grinding halt, slowing to half-speed, then to quarter-speed:

The high schoolers barreling toward me seemed to hit a wall of invisible molasses; their movements slow, exaggerated. A glance back revealed a cadre of middle schoolers, most sporting jeans and collared T-shirts, headed for me. On instinct, on the level of subconscious thought, I thrust both hands out, conjuring a swirling cloud of silver fog, a force construct, which stretched and curled out in every direction.

Time snapped back into full speed all at once, the tendrils of creeping power engulfing the kids closest to me, bands of raw energy smashing into 'em like some giant hand, swatting 'em away in a wave. Bodies flew into the air, scattering from the force of the blow. A few kids skipped over the grass—twisting, rolling, bouncing, skidding—while others flipped through the air, ass over teakettle. A flash of guilt poked at me, but I shoved it away. Kids were tough, I reminded myself. Maybe they'd have a few bruises come morning time—assuming they were human, which was no certain thing—but mostly they'd be fine. Probably. Possibly.

Then, before they could gain their feet and force me to make a real fight of it, I shoved the Vis away, closing myself from the alluring power, and slipped back into the cab of the Camino. Definitely time to beat feet. I pulled the door shut with a *thud*, dropped 'er into gear, and slammed my foot down on the pedal. The Camino's fat tires squealed, leaving rubber on the asphalt as the car rocketed forward.

I stole a hasty look in the rearview mirror, relieved to see none of 'em were pursuing me.

Nope, not following, but most were back on their feet, and all were staring at me with blank faces and empty eyes. Something flickered *beneath* the skin of the corn-fed jock in the letter jacket: a ripple of motion—waves washing over the surface of a pond. His hazy, distant eyes seemed to shift for a moment, blue irises giving way to golden eyes slit horizontally with a ribbon of black like a goat's eye. That kid wasn't a kid. I couldn't be sure what the hell he actually was without knocking the holy crap out of him and dispelling his flesh-suit, but he sure as shit wasn't human.

Great. Perfect. Asstastic.

I kept on straight, blasting through a couple of stop signs, eager to leave the satanic school behind, then swerved left onto North Main Street, rear end sliding into the turn—

I mashed down on the brake a split second later, jerking the steering wheel left to avoid the line of cars running across the street in a makeshift roadblock of steel and glass. Dammit. On my left was an Ace Hardware store, on my right yet another beat-to-shit motel, but beyond that, on the other side of the car blockade, was the police station: a boxy two-story building of more red brick, with a marble face and wide doors. More cars lined both sides of the street, and it looked like someone, or several someones, had fortified the station—turned the place into a friggin' doomsday bunker. The door and windows were boarded over, and curled strands of razor wire cordoned off the walkway, leaving only a narrow gap that led to the door.

Could be, I'd finally found the adults.

Carefully, I threw the Camino into reverse, parking off to the side so some reckless yahoo, like me, for example, wouldn't rear-end my baby. I slipped from the car, scanning the building for signs of life. Things looked quiet, but I'm an old hand and a former Marine—spent time in Okinawa with the 3rd Battalion 3rd Marines, then later did a stint over in Nam—so it didn't take me long to catch the glint of a scope on the roof. The shooter was obviously in the prone, doing a damned good job of keeping hidden, but that scope told me everything I needed to know.

Cautiously, I edged between the cars blocking the street and approached the building, hands raised, palms open—the universal symbol of surrender. I did, however, open myself to the Vis, drawing in a trickle of power, preparing the weaves for a quick and dirty friction shield just in case the guard on the roof got an itchy trigger finger.

"Go ahead and stop right there, mister," came a hard-edged voice as I neared the C-wire barrier. "I don't fancy shootin' you, but you better believe I'll pull this trigger if you gimme cause. I fought in Phantom Fury—part of sniper a unit with Three-One. I could drop you at a thousand yards before you blink."

"Well, Semper Fi," I said with a nod, "but there's no reason to go and do something like that. I'm thinkin' you and yours have some weird-ass shit hittin' the fan around here, am I right?"

He didn't answer, but through my heightened senses, I heard him shift uncomfortably under my accusation.

"Listen, bub," I said, shooting for calm, friendly, "I think I can help you, but not if you turn my head into pink mist, you trackin'?"

Another tense pause, followed by the squawk of a handheld radio. "Go ahead and lay on down," he finally replied. "Get your face flat against the ground, hands up and visible. The sheriff'll be out in a minute."

I complied, squatting, lowering myself onto my belly, scanning the door.

A long squeak broke the tension as a woman, maybe mid-forties and trim, with a tangled swatch of golden hair, stole toward me, sidearm drawn and at the ready. She didn't speak as she moved, instead she slipped over and cuffed me with a quick, practiced ease, before pulling me to my feet and leading me into the building's interior.

Silently, she guided me down a corridor lit by harsh sodium lights overhead, my black boots clacking on the linoleum flooring. We passed a receiving station, manned by a pair of overweight, forty-something men with flat tops and camo jackets. Beyond them were people—more adults packing the station. The douches at the desk regarded me with open hostility and made to get up, but the sheriff waved 'em off and pulled me into a tiny cubbyhole of a room with a single exit, an innocuous circular table, and a couple of padded office chairs.

The sheriff lowered me into a seat, cranking up on my arms, situating them behind the chair, all without unlocking the fancy steel bracelets. With the kinda power I had at my disposal, a pair of cuffs wouldn't deter me from breaking loose if I really wanted to, but I wasn't here to pick a fight, so I kept my cool.

The sheriff lowered herself into a seat adjacent to mine, letting out a long sigh as she scrutinized me, parceling me up, filing away every detail. She was older than I'd first pegged her, maybe fifty, with dimpled cheeks made for smiling and fine crow's feet at the corners of her eyes. She looked tired, though, deep purple bags under gray eyes, frown lines creased into the skin by her mouth.

"I'm Sheriff Copeman, Heather Copeman," she offered. "My man up top says you might know something about what's going on in our little slice of paradise. That so?" She leaned forward, elbows resting on her thighs, gaze intense and burrowing. "Or maybe," she said, "you're working with that shitheel, Piper. Come to try and push us into paying. Threaten us maybe?"

"Look," I replied with a shrug, "whatever's ailing your town,

I'm not a part of it, Sheriff. I swear. And I sure as shit don't know who this Piper clown is. Never told your man I did. I said I think I might be able to help."

"Uh-huh." She nodded, unconvinced, leaning back in her seat, folding her arms across her chest. "Since you're not involved in any of this," she said with a frown, "I'm wondering just how exactly you think you can help us. I don't even know how I can help us, Mr. …" She paused, lips pursed in thought. "You know, I never did get a name from you. Care to fill that in for me?"

I cleared my throat, shifting awkwardly in my seat. I had sort of a questionable relationship with the law due to some of my various assignments for the Guild. As a result, I was on a number of different watch lists, though generally I had no problem keeping my head down and my profile lower than dirt.

I could've lied, but at this point I wasn't sure it mattered. "Yancy Lazarus," I said eventually, fidgeting in my seat, readjusting my ass in the squishy chair.

"If I run your name, am I gonna find anything?" she asked, glowering at me.

"Could be," I said with a noncommittal nod, "but I'm thinkin' you got bigger things to worry about—like that roving mob of bloodthirsty teens over by the school. The ones that have you hunkered down on DEFCON five."

"And what do you know about them?" she asked, focused as a laser.

"I know they look like townies, but aren't. They aren't even human. Considering the level of paranoia on display here, I'm guessing they've probably done some spectacularly horrendous shit."

She stood, turned away from me, and started pacing back and forth, arms squeezing tight against her ribs. "Well, those are some awfully wild claims, Mr. Lazarus. Everything okay up here?" She reached up and tapped at her temple with one finger. "'Cause you sound a few cans short of a six-pack."

I snorted, then shook my head with a roll of my eyes. "Don't give me that. You know it's true—otherwise you'd never have a jarhead up on your roof, ready to blast a civilian in the face. That sorta reeks of desperation and fear."

"Fair enough," she said, her feet still restlessly carrying her back and forth across the narrow room. "But you seem to know an awful lot for someone uninvolved. We're pretty jumpy around here, so maybe you can shine some light on what you *think* you know and how you happen to know what you do." She stopped abruptly, spinning, then slamming her hands down on the table. "Sound fair?"

"I don't think you'd believe me if I told you," I replied with another shrug.

"Mr. Lazarus," she said, righting herself, "for the past week, this town has been cut off from the outside world. No radio traffic, no phone calls, no internet. Over the past week Valentine has seen twenty-three homicides—kids murdering their parents. Tearin' them apart with their bare hands, then eating the remains. I saw a six-year-old bite through the carotid artery of her grandmother. Lapped up the blood like a goddamn cat. I'm past the point of disbelieving anything. *Anything*. So give me your best shot."

I smiled and with a whisper of will conjured a floating orb of flickering flame the size of a softball, which burned like my own personal sun. "Convinced?" I asked.

She stared at the orb for a solid half minute, the light shining in her tired eyes, mouth slightly agape. "Holy Mary Mother of God. Okay, good enough for me," she replied, reaching over and keying the radio at her shoulder. "Harlan, this is Copeman. I need you down in interrogation ASAP, over."

* * *

Sheriff Copeman loitered in the corner, legs crossed, one hand resting on the butt of her Glock, a permanent scowl etched into the lines of her face. She was cagey and understandably so, considering the circumstances.

The guy across from me, Harlan—first name, not last—was exactly the opposite: easygoing, lots of friendly smiles, unflappable nature. I'd been expecting a meathead, lots of muscles and tattoos, but Harlan was a short, unassuming man with a slight build, a balding head, and a clean-shaven face. A mousy fella wearing desert camo, his long barrel rifle resting against his leg while he sipped at a cup of coffee from a Styrofoam cup.

"Piper," he said tentatively, unsure how to begin, where to go. "Well, he came to us about two months back. A drifter. Real odd duck, though. Sorta thought he wasn't right in the head." He tapped at his noggin. "Gave me a bad feelin' from the get-go."

"Can you give me any kind of description to work with?" I asked. "Small, tall, fat, skinny, giant pointy horns, or maybe a snake tail? Anything would be great."

Harlan canted his head, then gave a little shake. "Sorry. Fella had a real forgettable face. Pretty average—white, 5'5", brown hair, little pudgy around the gut. But I can't remember him, not really. No one can."

I grunted. A glamour, probably. Only thing that'd explain it. "What'd this guy want? Did he threaten you in some way?"

"No, no." He waved one hand complacently through the air, brushing away my question. "He offered to help us. This fella, he came over to the mayor's office, walked right in like he owned the place. I do security for the mayor—well, *did* before …" He trailed off. "Before his son ripped out his throat." He looked down, avoiding my scrutiny. "Guess that don't matter much now. Anyway, we had us a real bad drought this year.

"The worst one I can ever remember. Farms were drying up. Crops dying. Then in comes this hobo, no offense meant"—he nodded at me—"says he could get rid of the drought. Had this little flute. He'd twirl it around and around. Said he could play a tune and end the drought." Harlan snapped thin fingers. "Said he could end it just like that. But he wanted fifty thousand for his effort.

"Well, the mayor, he agreed 'cause he reckoned it was a bunch of hogwash and he really just wanted the guy gone." He paused, sipped his coffee, then drummed his fingers on the table. "Piper, well, he nodded, smiled, and slipped away. And you wouldn't believe it, but the next day that drought broke. A week later Piper, well he come back, says he wants his due. The mayor had me kick his ass right outta town—no good to have some loon like that hanging around. But that's when he made his threat. Said we'd broken faith. Told us he'd get his fee in flesh and blood. Now here we are." He sighed and shrugged.

"So," Sheriff Copeman said, "what can you tell us?"

I leaned back into my chair, looking up at the pock-marked ceiling tiles. "Not much without meeting this guy. But from the gist of it, I'd say you made yourself a deal with a fae lord or maybe some dusty old fertility godling. Things like that don't really give a shit about money, so it was probably running a con the whole time—he expected you to break the deal, opening the door for whatever shiesty business he's got in mind. Like I said, though, I don't know how to fix it until I figure out what he's done to the kids."

"So what do we do?" the sheriff asked, eyes narrowing, forehead creasing.

"You?" I shook my head. "You folks just hang tight. I'm gonna head out and see if I can't pick a fight with this Piper asswipe. Figure out what we're up against."

"How you reckon you'll do that?" Harlan asked, perking up at the idea of a little ass-kickery.

"Don't worry about it. I got a feelin' he'll come out of the woodwork once I start blasting holes in his shithead army of nightmare kids."

It took only a little haggling before Sheriff Copeman agreed, turning me free, then escorting me from the premises.

"Good luck," Harlan called down to me from the roof as I weaved through the C-wire barricade. I shot him a quick wave, then beelined for Third Street, not bothering to get in the Camino. Didn't want to risk this Piper guy denting up the bodywork—taking a shot at me is one thing, but no one touches the Camino. It took me maybe five minutes to get back to the K–12 school on foot, but I'd attracted attention long before I ever reached my destination.

Blank eyes watched me from house windows while ghostly shapes slipped from shadow to shadow, alley to alley, street to street, tracking me, though never closing. Cautious, now that I'd tipped my hand.

A ring of kids waited for me at the four-way intersection of Third and North Wood, fanning out in a tight horseshoe by the school. Twenty of 'em, easy. A daunting number for sure, but even more so because I'd seen double that when I'd first stopped at the school. So the question was, where were the rest of the little turds? With my luck, probably closing in around me like a noose, hemming me in tight so I wouldn't be able to run. That was okay, though. I wasn't planning to run. Not this time.

Letter-Jacket and his bouncy cheerleader girlfriend broke apart from the rest of the pack, apparently the impromptu leaders of this merry little gang of horrors.

"Glad to see you're both doing okay after our little tussle," I said, drawing my pistol from its holster, canting the gun so I could check the revolver's cylinder for rounds. "But here's the thing, if you screw around with me again, I promise you're not gonna walk away. So, let me just make this real simple—I want to talk to your boss, Piper. If he's not here in"—I bobbed my head from side to side—"let's say two minutes, I'm gonna start shooting. Find out what's under those flesh-suits."

Letter-Jacket hissed as he dropped into a crouch, limbs elongating, joints cracking, fingers stretching into spidery appendages. More kids started dropping, shifting. A few at first, but more every second. Morphing, their rudimentary flesh-suits melted away, revealing pasty long-limbed critters of ropey sinew, bleached skin, and pouching potbellies that skittered around on all fours. Each had a chinless frog-like head, attached directly to their rib-lined torsos; they stared at me with yellow goat-eyes, their fleshy lips pulled back from blunt, yellowed horse teeth.

Yep, definitely not human. No doubts in my mind now. Oh,

also, grade A nightmare fuel. I'd really been hoping to bluff my way through this encounter, but apparently the freaks surrounding me didn't mind taking things to the next level. Great. Just my friggin' luck.

A battle cry went up a moment later, a chorus of awful voices shrieking and warbling, the sound hoarse, raspy, and sharp—a dog whistle made for human ears. Almost as one, they came at me in a wave, scampering on hands and feet, shuffling forward with a lopsided gait that nevertheless ate up the space between us quick as hell. I bolted toward a nearby truck, leveling my gun, going to town as I ran.

I aimed at what remained of Letter-Jacket and squeezed the trigger a pair of times—the gun barked in my hand, spewing a flash of fire from its muzzle. Most Rube handguns won't do much against the movers and shakers of the supernatural community, but my piece wasn't any regular handgun. Nope, not even close. It was a specialty item crafted by the *Dökkálfar*: .44 Magnum, dark hammer-forged steel, six-inch barrel, etched with runes and mystic symbols, swirling and twisting with artful flourishes.

Only bad, bad things lay at the end of the muzzle. Which Letter-Jacket found out.

The first round went wide, lodging itself in the wall of a nearby building, but the second shot caught him in the jaw—the side of his ugly-ass mug exploded in a shower of skin and black blood. He let out a gurgled shriek of pain and surprise, then spiraled to the ground, groping at his ruined face as he died.

I kept moving, dropping another of the encroaching Pasty-faces before scrambling into the back of a beat-to-shit pickup. Fighting from the high ground was always smart, even if the high ground ended up being in the back of a truck. *Pop-pop-pop*, I squeezed off my remaining three rounds, blasting one of the spidery-limbed dickbaskets in the stomach, punching a softball-sized hole of shit-kickery clean through its center. Another of the Pasty-faces—a short little freak that'd probably been masquerading as a toddler—I dropped outright. Its headless torso flopped to the roadway.

The cylinder ran dry, and though I had a speedloader in my pocket, I stowed the gun instead. A great tool, my hand cannon, but against a small army, thirty strong, I'd need more than bullets.

With a snarl, I pulled in sweet, life-giving Vis—my senses sharpening, strength flooding my body, time taking a shuddering breath—and thrust out my right hand, conjuring a spear of fire, thick as my wrist. Flame washed over the wave of creatures closest to the pickup, tongues of orange and yellow lapping at exposed skin, setting pilfered clothes ablaze. The front row fell back yowling, arms waving and flapping in the air. A few dropped to the ground, rolling in manic circles to put out the flames, but most simply ran around in terror, streaks of oily smoke trailing behind them.

That move got their attention awfully quick.

More pressed in, though, only to drop as the sharp report of distant gunfire split the air with a thunderous crack—rounds shearing down bodies. Not my handiwork either.

I took a hasty glance back toward Main Street and thought, for just a second, I saw the glint of a rifle scope, though it was probably my imagination. Still, it had to be Harlan. God bless that hillbilly hick. The firing continued in earnest: the shots slow, steady, methodical, and *precise* as a surgeon's scalpel. Every round found a target—sinking home with a deadly thud and a spray of black gore, dropping opponent after opponent.

The mad rush slowed, faltered, and died as the strange pack of critters surveyed their fallen dead, too-large eyes shifting suspiciously between the corpses and me in turns, confusion evident on their gruesome faces. Obviously, these clowns had expected some easy game, but were now reconsidering their options. I still wasn't sure what exactly I was dealing with here, but that hesitation told me a couple of things: one, they weren't keen on dying horrible deaths and two, they weren't nearly as tough as some of the nastier things in Outworld.

Both damn-good points to know.

"Yeah, that's right, assholes," I called, shifting from foot to foot, hand still outthrust—a loaded weapon ready to maim or kill. "This isn't gonna be a walk in the park. Now, like I said, get me your boss, Piper, or things are gonna start getting ugly—"

The melodic sound of a flute cut me off mid-sentence, its graceful trill parting the tension in the air and stilling the assembled mass of ugly-ass critters in an instant. The sound of that music swirled and danced around me, thrumming with ancient, potent power. Some kind of Vis-wrought glamour, meant to control and manipulate emotion and thought. The friggin' working pounded at my brain like a sledgehammer, demanding I cease my murderous tomfoolery. Demanding I relax, submit.

"That'll be quite enough," a man said as the music died.

The speaker in question stepped out from between two houses near the end of the block and ambled my way, his steps light and carefree. At a glance, he looked human—average height, unremarkable build, dusty brown hair, and a plain, if pinched, face sporting a five o'clock shadow. He wore faded jeans, a deep brown poncho, squared-toed cowboy boots, and a garish white Stetson. Guy looked like some sort of Old West gunslinger, except instead of a pistol he carried an ancient wooden flute, painstakingly carved with intricate vines and thick leaves.

"Yancy Lazarus," he said, drawing ever closer as the long-limbed freaks scuttled out of his way, subjects scraping before their king.

"Got it in one, bub," I said with a nod. "I take it you're Piper?"

He bowed with a fanciful flourish of his poncho, like some kind of matador acknowledging his adoring public. "So I am. And let me say what a pleasure it is to meet you—it's not every day I run across such an esteemed former member of the Fist of the Staff. You've got quite the reputation in certain circles, Mr. Lazarus."

I shrugged one shoulder and hawked a fat loogie to the ground to show him what I thought of his pleasantries. "Listen, guy," I said, "I'm not interested in any ass kissing. Let's just cut to the part of the conversation where you tell me who you are, what in the hell you're doing here, and what it's gonna take to get you to go away and give back the kids you took."

"A man of business," he said with a smug nod, then twirled his stupid flute around and around in one hand. "People, they call me the Pied Piper—"

"Like from that Brothers Grimm story with the rats."

"One and the same," he said with another bow and flourish. Friggin' weirdo. "I also happen to be a lesser lord of the Spring-lands. Now, in answer to your questions, I am here conducting business and there is naught you or anyone can do to get the missing children back. The governing officials of these fair lands entered into a binding agreement with one of the *Daoine Sìth,* then reneged on their word." He pouted, tut-tutting as that damned flute spun round and round. "Very bad form, I'm afraid. Now, I am simply exercising my right to recompense."

"By taking their kids," I said, folding my arms, offering him a cold, flat glare.

"That is my chosen form of compensation, yes. Now, I know a thing or two about you—information gleaned from some of my kith and kin—so I know my decision might rankle you. The fact remains, however, that I am acting lawfully and within my rights. They entered into an agreement and failed to follow through, and this?" He spread his hands, gesturing toward the crowd of heinous monsters.

"Well, this is the consequence. Now, I am prepared to let your assault on my children go, since you acted in ignorance, but if you interfere with me or mine again I shall take it quite personally. Are you prepared to commit yourself to such unpleasantries for people you don't even know?"

"You threatening me, asshole?" I asked, voice a growl, as I conjured a sphere of crystalline ice in my palm.

The Piper dipped his head and held up a hand in a placating gesture. "Haste and anger make fools of us all, Lazarus. So please, just consider my offer, won't you? Otherwise, we may find ourselves at an unfortunate impasse. And I think you'll find I can be a formidable adversary, despite your"—he paused, eyes narrowing, head tilted to the side—"*unique* skill set." Then, before I could reply, he twirled on his heel, poncho spinning in a whirlwind of cloth, and started playing his flute. A jaunty tune that urged you to move and dance. To follow. To obey.

And his pasty-faced brood did just that. The beasts turned and trailed after him.

* * *

"So what did you find out?" the sheriff asked.

I absently ran my palms over my dusty jeans. The damn interrogation room felt claustrophobic, despite the fact that I knew I wasn't being charged or held—guess there's just something about police stations that give me the jitters.

"Not much I didn't already know." *Except that you might be royally boned*, I thought. As much as I hated what was going on in Valentine, if these idiot Rubes really had entered into a legally binding contract with the Piper, there wasn't much I could do for 'em. They shouldn't have screwed around with something they didn't understand. There were a lot of nasty things out there in the big wide world; most were predatory, looking for any excuse to attack. The law of the friggin' jungle, right there.

Harlan pushed his way through the door a moment later, carefully balancing a large plastic trash can full of sloshing water.

"Just set it here," I said, waving him over. The man complied, confusion running across his face as I removed my socks and dipped my toesy-wosies into the water with a soft sigh.

"I'm sorry," Sheriff Copeman said, eyeing the trash can, then rubbing at one temple, "but what exactly is this going to accomplish?"

I sniffed, then wiggled my toes. "It's magic stuff," I replied, even though it's not really magic—more like advanced physics than weird rituals or any of that occult bullshit. "Don't worry about it. I just need to hammer a few things out." I closed my eyes, letting go of my fear and anxiety over this whole clusterfuck, feeding all of those unhelpful thoughts and emotions into the fires of the Vis as I conjured a weave of water and will, boring deeper inside myself. Seeking to connect with my inner man.

And by "inner man," I mean Cassius Aquinas, the shit-talking water elemental who lived inside my head, permanently bound to my subconscious mind.

When I opened my eyes a heartbeat later, I was no longer gazing at Sheriff Copeman in the boxy interrogation room. Instead, I stood on a narrow street lined on either side by two-story buildings and lit with the yellow glow of evenly spaced street lamps and neon signs in a riot of hues: sapphire blue, fallout green, look-at-me red. Most of the buildings had balconies jutting out over the wide sidewalks, which were filled with umbrella covered tables, all absent of guests. Bourbon Street, smack dab in the New Orleans French Quarter.

Except it was quiet, still, and lifeless—a thing which could never be said of the real Bourbon Street.

My brainscape, a metaphysical representation of my psyche, which naturally resembled the Big Easy, with its hot, muggy nights, over-the-top eats, and outta-this-world music scene. Here I was at home. Here I was safe and the aches and pains of real life were like distant memories, hazy and faded at the edges. The air filled with the scent of slow roasted pork—tangy, smoky, sweet—while licks of gritty blues swirled around me, thick as cigar smoke. I inhaled deeply, letting tense muscles relax and unknot.

"Yancy," came a voice from behind me. My voice to be precise. I glanced left, watching a dark figure, bathed in weak light from one of the hanging lanterns near a brick-fronted eatery, saunter toward me. He held a stout glass of scotch in either hand; a fat cigar hung from the corner of his mouth. He extended one turquoise-tinged hand, offering me the second glass as he drew up next to me.

I took it with a thankful grunt and a nod, then pulled a long slug as I regarded the man. Cassius Aquinas. An Undine—a creature of water and spirit, permanently grafted into a piece of my soul. The very embodiment of my subconscious mind. Minus the seawater-colored skin, he could've passed for my twin: an average guy of maybe forty with short-cropped, dark hair and an unremarkable height and build.

"You been paying attention to this horseshit in Valentine?" I asked without preamble.

He titled his head and took a deep drag of his cigar, then nodded in confirmation.

"So you got anything for me? Seems like this Piper douche is the kinda guy you mighta heard of in your past life."

"Yeah," he said. "Yeah, I know him. It'll be easier to show you, though." He placed one hand on my shoulder, fingers sinking down, then wheeled, dragging me with him. With a step, we *shifted*, leaving behind the comfort of the French Quarter, manifesting in a sprawling room with plush carpet, dark wood wall paneling, and mahogany furniture—all old, finely made, and smelling of lemon oil and leather. Cassius's office, I guess you could call it. I took a seat in a padded leather club chair and gazed up at a ginormous wall-mounted flat screen.

A picture of the Piper appeared on the TV, except now he was dressed in some stupid, frilly Shakespearian getup with a wide collar, puffy sleeves, and a ridiculous floppy hat. Complete tool.

"That's what he looked like the last time I ran across him," Cassius said, sweeping his free hand toward the screen. "But he goes back further than that—he used to go by the name Silenus." The picture on the screen blinked, resolving into an image of a potbellied, goat-legged yahoo with a pipe. "That was when he was still living the high life with Dionysus, back in the days when Greece was still a major player. Silenus is a minor satyr deity, I think. Asshole's fallen a long way since then, though." He paused again, drawing a long pull on his cigar. "He's been running con games since the fifth or sixth century."

"What kinda cons?"

Cassius shrugged, a look of disgust creeping over his features.

"A tasteless, unimaginative one. Nothing like what I did to those pricks in *Glimmer-Tir*—and he only works his hoodoo on Rubes, which is about as lowbrow as you can go. Ol' Silenus there runs the same friggin' play every twenty or thirty years. Rolls into some little flyspeck town or village, uses his fertility-god powers to whip up some kinda problem.

"Plague-rat infestations were his tragedy *du jour* in the middle ages, but he's got control over the weather, crops, all kinds of shit. Anyway, after he stirs the pot, he swoops in, fixes the problem *he* created, and demands payment. Not a bad grift, I guess, but lazy as hell. Then, obviously, when the townsfolk don't pay, he takes kids. Guy's a grade A shithead. No one likes him. No one."

"Why kids, though?" I asked with a frown, rubbing at my chin. "What's he do with 'em? Is it some kinda virgin sacrifice thing?"

The picture on the TV flickered again, and Silenus's goat-legged image was replaced by a photo of the nasty Pasty-faces. "You know what satyrs and seahorses have in common?" he asked.

"What? No. How the hell would I know that? More importantly, *why* in the friggin' hell would I know that?" I replied, staring at the drink in my hand. "They both start with *s*, I guess."

"Yes, they both start with *s*, clearly that's the connection." Cassius offered me a colossal eye roll. "Seahorse *daddies* give birth. Same thing for satyrs. Piper takes the kids in order to hatch a fresh brood of changelings. He gives birth to a horde of the shifty shits. His revolting offspring, in turn, kidnap a bunch of kids, steal their identities and memories, infiltrating the home, then eat the parents. Once the changelings are mature and the mental link becomes useless, Piper eats the kids, thus closing the whole disgusting cycle."

"Holy shit," I said. "That's brutal. Like pushing someone into a wood chipper, brutal."

"Right?" Cassius said with a shake of his head. He hunched forward, swirling his drink, staring at the swishing vortex of Bourbon, then offering me a sidelong glance. "You gonna go after him?"

I looked away, unwilling to meet his eye, and pinched the bridge of my nose with a grimace. *Was I gonna go after him?* Maybe coming to Valentine in the first place had been a mistake. Piper didn't want me here, and he sure as shit wasn't gonna stand in my way if I decided to hop back in the Camino and split. The folks of Valentine were the ones that entered into the contract. They were the ones that'd screwed the pooch, not me. The universe was giving me a chance to walk away—I could wash my hands of Valentine and leave guilt free.

Well, mostly guilt free.

My mind turned toward those kids. A bunch of kids that'd die unless I put my own neck onto the chopping block. I scowled. Sighed. Tossed back the remainder of my drink in a single gulp, the booze hitting my belly like a splash of napalm.

"You're such a bleeding-heart moron," Cassius said. "Complete moron. If you kill us, Yancy, I'm nominating you for the Darwin Awards."

I waved his insults off. "Yeah, I know. I keep thinking the same thing." I grimaced. "But those kids, Cassius."

"Fine, idiot. Whatever." He crossed his arms and scowled at me. "Piper's got this thing for abandoned cave systems, alright? And the closer to a body of water the better." He grumbled for a moment "If you can find his lair, you'll find the kids, and you'll find Piper. But watch out for that stupid-ass flute of his. All his power is music based—he uses that thing as a focus to channel the Vis. Shut down that flute, you'll shut him down, too."

I opened my eyes, Cassius gone—vanished back into my subconscious—the interrogation room unchanged. I pulled my feet from the water, weaved a small flow of air and heat to wick the moisture away, then shimmied back into my socks and boots. The sheriff stared at me from the corner, her lips turned down in irritation, hands planted on her hips. "So," she finally snapped as I adjusted the cuff of my pants, "what did you find out with your 'magic'?" She used air quotes around the word, as though she couldn't really believe what she was saying.

"We need an area map," I replied, "preferably a topical one." I paused, jaw clenching. "I'm also gonna need a local guide—one familiar with the cave systems in the area. And a mechanic. One who knows his way around a badass sound system."

The sheriff squinted at me in suspicion. At last, though, she dipped her head. "Harlan," she snapped, digging out a pair of keys from her front pocket, "go find me Vick Larsen, then head up to my office." She plopped the keys into his hand. "There should be several area maps in the top right drawer of my desk. I've got a cave survey in there, too. Grab 'em all and get back here ASAP."

"Sure thing, Sheriff," Harlan said, with a dip of his chin.

"Okay, Yancy," the sheriff said, fixing me with a hard-eyed death stare. "I feel like I've been pretty damn cooperative, considering the circumstances, but now I want you to tell me what you know."

So I told her, giving her the details Cassius had passed on to me. Harlan came back a few minutes later with an armful of maps and a burly bearded man in coveralls, who I assumed was Vick. "Alright," I said as Harlan unfolded the maps on the round table, "this is how we're gonna beat that assclown …"

* * *

I squatted down, fingers trailing over the dusty ground as I surveyed the narrow opening of a cave mouth on the outskirts of town, near a spit of water the locals called Mill Pond. The cave entrance wasn't much more than a tight fissure in the rocky face of a barely there hill peppered with trees. "You're sure this is the place?" I asked Harlan, who stood to my right, a compact M4 with a broomstick slung across his body on a tactical sling.

"It's bigger than it looks," he replied evenly, eyes picking over the map in his hands. "The entry's tight, but it oughta open up into a pretty good size cavern not too far in. Place don't go real deep, but there's nothing else in the area. If you're right and Piper's holed up in a cave, then it's here or nowhere."

"Is it big enough to hold forty or fifty kids?" I asked.

He shrugged. "You ever been in there?" Harlan asked, turning toward the sheriff, who lingered just behind him.

"Once," she replied, grip tightening on the heavy-duty bolt cutters in her hands. "Long time ago, though, back when I was still in high school—local kids come out here sometimes to drink beer and fool around. At least that's why I came out here in high school."

"Well," Harlan said with a drawl, "I guess we just need to take a looksee, then we'll know for sure."

"Yeah, alright." I stood, brushing my hands against my jeans before turning back toward the coverall-clad Vick, our car audio-system expert. "You hooked up and ready to rock?" I asked, nervously eyeing the substantial set of speakers and subwoofers positioned around a Valentine patrol car. The Camino's sound system—a truly heartbreaking sight. I ran a hand through my hair and took a great big ol' breath, tearing my eyes away from the damage. If my hunch about Piper was wrong, I could be setting myself up for colossal, certain-death failure. And not just me. If I called this wrong, Harlan and Sheriff Copeman might end up equally dead.

The greatest casualty of all, though, would still be my poor car.

Vick nodded at me, then turned his face and spit into the dirt—a big ol' brown blob of chew-laced saliva. "Everything's good as you're gonna get 'em," he said solemnly, then rubbed a thick, scar-laden hand over one of the black boxes. A pet lover admiring someone else's dog.

"Well, I guess there's no way to put this off any longer," I said. "Let's just get this shit over and done with." I clapped Harlan on the shoulder, then set off. I slid my pistol—freshly reloaded—free from its holster and conjured a wavering orb of soft blue light, which floated an inch above my outstretched left palm. Harlan eyed the little working askew, still clearly uncomfortable with all the wonky supernatural bullshit. "Sheriff"—I glanced at the salty law-woman—"no matter how things go down in there, you work on getting those kids out, trackin'?"

She nodded, face hardening in resolve.

"Groovy. Sheriff, you're behind me, Harlan, you've got our six." Without waiting for a reply, I set off, wiggling through the slash in the rocky outcropping and pushing inward. The tunnel, if you could call it that, was a tight, claustrophobic thing, big enough to accommodate me, but just barely. After about ten feet of pressing rock, though, I squeezed into a rough passageway, maybe five feet wide and seven high, that cut deeper into the hillside before curving away. I trudged on, movements slow, careful, quiet, ears straining to hear anything while my blue orb battled against the gloom of the cave's interior.

"Trying for stealth at this point is futile, Mr. Lazarus," came Piper's voice from somewhere up ahead, the words oddly distorted as they reverberated off the stone walls. "This particular cave carries sound exceptionally well, so your arrival hasn't gone unnoticed."

I crept forward another few feet, goosebumps breaking out along my arms.

The passage led to an irregular room—three or four thousand square feet—just as Harlan had predicted. Greasy firelight, burning from a handful of rusty miner lamps propped up on old crates, illuminated the rough-walled cavern, casting flickering shadows over everything. Along the right-hand side of the cave was a series of cages: beastly things of thick rebar, locked with even thicker chains, containing kids.

Lots of kids.

A good chunk of Valentine's young folk had been sorted more or less by age, then rudely crammed together, with no room to fully sit and certainly not enough to sleep. Each cage had a plastic bucket in the corner, which must've served as a shitter. The children themselves were dirty and hollow eyed, their cheeks gaunt, hair disheveled, skin sickly and pale. And they were quiet; not a one of 'em made so much as a peep. No one cried out for help or shouted in protest. No one banged a fist against the prison bars.

They had the look of coma patients, which meant they were in a trance of some sort—probably part of the binding ritual, attaching their minds to the changelings that'd stolen their identities.

And speaking of the changelings, they were present and accounted for, too. Yay for me. Piper sat on a rickety wooden rocking chair like it was a grand throne, and spreading out around him in a loose semicircle were his kids. None of 'em had bothered to don their flesh-suits or hide their disgusting, unnatural appearance.

"I was afraid you'd do something irrational," Piper said, giving me a lopsided grin as he tented his fingers. "That's what my kith and kin all say about you. That you have more misguided virtue than common sense. Still"—he paused, picking up his flute, running slender fingers over the carefully carved leaves and vines—"I wonder what you hope to accomplish here? Look around, Lazarus, and tell me how you think to seize victory. You're badly outnumbered and the terrain favors me and mine. So, last chance, turn around and take your lackeys with you. Leave my brood be, or perish."

"A lot of supernatural shitbirds bigger and tougher than you have made that same threat," I replied with an indifferent shrug, "but here I am, alive, kicking, and getting ready to turn your family into meat-paste. So, I'll make you the same generous offer. Stop now, leave those kids alone"—I jerked my head toward the cages—"tuck your tail between your legs and run, and I won't turn you into something I can sweep up in a dustpan, *comprende*?"

"Ah." Piper's grin faded, vanished. "And so we've arrived at that unfortunate impasse I spoke of earlier." He raised the flute to his chin, ready to play. "How do you propose we proceed, Laz—"

Pop-pop. I didn't let him finish the sentence, firing a pair of rounds his way while I broke left.

In a blink, Piper had that stupid flute to his lips; shrill licks of music swirled and twirled, echoing through the room, battering at my ears and senses. A shimmering wall of twisting green light—shifting in hue from emerald to jade—exploded before him, the hasty construct intercepting my slugs with brilliant flashes before they could sink home and end Piper. Simultaneously, the changelings sprang to life, surging forward in howling rage in response to Piper's music.

Gunfire erupted from my right as Harlan opened up on the charging doom beasts, placing precise groupings into the mass of pale bodies.

I hooked left, squeezing off a few more rounds, capping the Pasty-faces nearest to me. "Get the locks off," I yelled at Sheriff Copeman.

What I really needed to do was call up a whirlwind of flame and roast all these sons of bitches wholesale, but I couldn't risk it, not until we got those kids away. Changelings fell, shrieking, to the floor, limbs missing, bodies leaking out fetid blood, only to be trampled underfoot by their kin.

My pistol ran dry with a click, and I stowed it with practiced ease before drawing a Vis-imbued K-Bar at my hip—perfect for hooking and jabbing in a tight space like this. I dropped back a step, pressing my back against the jagged wall, then called up a spear of silver force, which blasted into the encroaching horde of creatures, smashing them into the ranks pressing in behind them. I glanced right: Harlan was standing near the entrance, laying down suppressive fire while the sheriff fought at the locks with her bolt cutters.

This was taking too long. Harlan was doing a damn fine job of holding back the changelings, but eventually they'd overwhelm the sheriff and that'd be endgame.

With a snarl, I drew Vis into my body, then shoved that terrible power into the ground, reaching into the deep places of the earth. The room trembled, quivered, and the dusty earth cracked as spear-shafts of granite sprouted from the floor. Sharpened javelins of rock skewered the changelings en masse, impaling emaciated torsos, ripping through arms, feet, and legs. The Pasty-faces mewled in pain as they struggled to fight free from the sudden forest of razor-sharp death.

All the while, the Piper played on, his face darkening, but his fingers never ceasing their frantic dancing—

One of the changelings broke free, a huge yawning wound in its belly, and threw itself at me. Before I could do jack-shit, jagged teeth sunk into my calf. A burst of pain lanced up from the wound, tap dancing its way through my body. Holy horsecrap, did that smart. With a howl, I lashed out with the K-Bar, stabbing down into the creature's skull, sinking the blade to the hilt. I jerked the knife free and booted the suddenly limp corpse away from me.

I took a quick peek out of the corner of my eye: Sheriff Copeman had gotten the locks and chains off the cages, but despite the cage doors hanging wide open, the kids didn't move. Didn't try to run. *Piper*—his damned music was filling up their heads, bewitching them into obedience. "Call Vick!" I shouted, limping right, positioning myself in front of flute-playing asshole in the Stetson. The sheriff tilted her head and spoke into the radio at her shoulder.

Piper, still protected by his conjured force shield, regarded me with cool hate.

A second later sound blared around us—an up-tempo track, *à la* Eric Clapton. Hard bopping piano runs and silky-smooth guitar riffs rattled the walls with thunderous volume. Piper continued to puff away at his stupid flute, but the noise was drowned out by Clapton belting out the lyrics to "Sweet Home Chicago." A nasty smile, mean and feral, broke across my face as the caged kids came to themselves, Piper's musical spell broken by the sheer awesomeness of the blues.

It took only a handful of seconds for Sheriff Copeman and Harlan to evacuate the captives, ushering 'em out in a panicked rush. By then, the changelings were finally starting to pull themselves free from the spears of rock and regroup, but it was a damnbit too late for that to matter. I slipped over to the tunnel entry, keeping my back pressed against the wall. Finally, Piper stopped playing, horror dawning on his pinched face as he realized how fundamentally screwed he was. I stowed the K-Bar, flipped him the bird as Clapton played on, then threw out both hands, unleashing a wall of flame that burned like the inside of a friggin' volcano.

Piper caught fire, his arms waving madly as he stood and rushed me. I conjured another hasty wall of bedrock spikes across the exit—the only exit—barring his path, consigning him to a long and, hopefully, unpleasant death. Asshole. I gave him a small wave, *bye-bye*, and turned away as he and his body-snatching brood burned, cloying smoke wafting up behind me, awful heat beating at my back.

Good riddance.

* * *

I puttered down Main Street, more Clapton washing over me, pouring from the open windows as I rolled along, puffing on a well-deserved cigarette. Vick had done a masterful job getting the speakers back in. I glanced up to my rearview mirror, caught a glimpse of Harlan and the sheriff waving at me. I stuck a hand out the window, returned the gesture, then put my foot to the pedal.

BIO

Hey all, my name is James Hunter and I'm a writer, among other things. So just a little about me: I'm a former Marine Corps Sergeant, combat veteran, and pirate hunter (seriously). I'm also a member of The Royal Order of the Shellback—'cause that's a real thing. I've also been a missionary and international aid worker in Bangkok, Thailand. And, a space-ship captain, can't forget that.

. . .

Okay … the last one is only in my imagination.

Currently, I'm a stay at home Dad—taking care of my two kids—while also writing full time, making up absurd stories that I hope people will continue to buy. When I'm not working, writing, or spending time with family, I occasionally eat and sleep.

11

THE TRAGEDY OF JOHN METCALF

YUDHANJAYA WIJERATNE

It was a little after dawn, and John Metcalf was above Bali, scrunched up in an aircraft. Not as the pilot, no, that would have been far too glamorous; he was just one more passenger in a crew of hundreds, scrunched into his slight-too-small seat, legs cramping slightly.

The asshole in front of him had just reclined his seat, and that made John's little foldout tray jump out and smack the book from his hands. John wished he could lean out of his seat and call the man an idiot, but instead he sighed and twisted awkwardly in his seat, groping for the book. His eye came level with the porthole.

And that was when he saw the ghost aircraft. The cross shape. The wings. The plumage painted on the tail. It sailed towards John over the sun-struck clouds, growing larger by the second. And then was right *there*, its metal fuselage right in his face, and he was staring at giant letters emblazoned on the craft. He recoiled and hit his head on the tray table.

"Sir?" said a concerned voice. He blinked. The aircraft was no longer there. In its place was a very pretty and very young-looking flight attendant in robes of blue and silver. And the passenger next to him, an old Indian gentleman who looked quite startled at his antics.

"N-nothing," John said lamely. His groping hand stumbled upon paper, and he fished out the book he had been reading. *The Doomsayer Journeys,* by some bloke named Wetherell. "Sorry, just dropped my book."

The flight attendant nodded primly and moved on, robes sliding back to reveal an extraordinary amount of creamy leg. Both John and the Indian gentleman stared appreciatively, and then pretended they hadn't. John stared out the window awhile, then dismissed it - probably lack of sleep. He went back to his book. By the time they landed in Constantinople he was deep into Steve Wetherell's prose and the only thing on his mind was the impending destruction of a planet he'd been rooting for several hundred pages. And of course there was an unlikely hero, and a mad emperor, and a warrior princess, and a planet-sized ordinateur. Just what the doctor recommended.

It was with a great sigh that he finally handed the book over to Ottoman Customs. There was some stuff in there about God, and however fictional, the Ottoman Empire took this kind of stuff seriously. The emin at the gate took the book, leafed through it, and tossed it into a bin labelled CONTRABAND.

"Any other items you want to declare, sir?" he asked, staring down his razor-sharp mustache at the contents of John's briefcase. "What are these utensils, powders, vials?"

"I'm a doctor," lied John fluidly, producing his papers. "The powders and vials are medicine. Agues, fevers and dementia. Here's my letter of invitation. I think you'll find everything in order."

The emin made a show of reading the letter from the Süleymaniye Complex.

"Western medicine," he said distastefully, but they both knew the score. Nobody would dare stop a doctor, especially one with the seal of the esteemed Complex. He stamped John's passport and waved him in. "Be safe, heal well, Doctor. Welcome to *Kostantiniyye.*"

John exited the airport with a spring in his step. A taxi trundled up to him almost immediately. A thickset, scarred face poked its head out.

"Good to see you, John. Hop in."

"Good to see you too, Victor."

Inside the luxurious darkness of the taxi, John Metcalf opened his briefcase.

It was true, what he had said - the powders and vials were medicines. But not all of them. He brought to his eye a very special vial, filled with a completely colorless liquid, obtained at great cost from one of the most secretive *ayurvedic* medicine-men of Bali.

In a sense, he was a doctor. Had they put him through a lie-detector, no untruth would ever have registered. He certainly thought of himself as a curer of certain disease. It was all about framing. John Metcalf cured vanity, hubris, and power.

John Metcalf was an assassin.

Twenty minutes later, the taxi dropped him off at very particular church known to be attended by some very particular functionaries in very particular governments. He took perhaps twenty minutes. Anyone passing by who happened to be Sensitive would have smelled the stench of magic being done, but it was the church - there was always magic being done. In twenty minutes, Victor, this time driving a sleek, black car stamped with the coat of arms of the Süleymaniye Complex. John, the smell of magic following him like hot iron filings, walked out slowly and carefully, wearing the robes of a priest, and got in.

That evening, three hundred people took Holy Communion at the newly rebuilt church of Hagia Sophia. Among them were visiting ambassadors from thirteen countries that the Ottoman Empire desperately wanted to court. Within days, all of them were all dead. Despite absolutely no trace of poison or magic in their bodies, accusations of murder filled diplomatic cables. The Ottoman government went into a state of high panic. Within weeks, both the German and the Austro-Hungarian Empires had threatened war, and a Dr. John Metcalf had shown up at the British embassy, asking for asylum from the growing political instability. He was just one among hundreds. They were processed instantly.

"Well done, John," said Victor, back when they were both safely on the ground in London. The scarred man drew out a book. *The Doomsayer Journeys.* "By the way, Management wanted me to give this to you. Said you might just have time to finish it on the next assignment."

Not for the first time, John wondered how Management knew these things. And, on the heels of that, he remembered the ghost aircraft. It had gone completely out of his mind.

"Bit creepy, if you ask me." said Victor.

John shrugged, picking up the book. "You'll get used to it," he said. They all did. Or they all died. That was how it worked with Management. He reached for the bottle of whisky he kept in the bottom-right drawer for times like these. Black Lake, Irish, '86, a good drink for anyone with Sensitivity. He poured for both of them.

They knocked back their whiskies in silence. It hit their throats and spread warmth like a cancer, sending tendrils of softness into their bodies. John's Oculum Sphere, left to idle on the table, briefly glowed a dull gold.

"Good whisky."

"Good whisky, yes."

Silence for a while, broken only by the pouring of another.

"So I know they say not to ask -"

"Then don't."

But Victor ignored him. "How long you been doing this, John?"

He thought about it. It seemed like an eternity. "Nine, maybe ten years," he said at last. "Doesn't matter."

"That's a long time. When do I get out, John? When am I going to be done?"

John looked at the scarred man with sympathy. Victor, despite being three times John's size, and a fantastic getaway driver, was still young in these matters. He debated giving his apprentice the speech again. A magician's choices came down to very few in these times; either you worked for the Church, or you worked for the Caliphate, or you worked for the Management, or you were dead, carved up in a gutter somewhere or screaming as they nailed you to a cross and set a fire in your flesh. It was simple reality.

"We're out when Management says we're out," he said. "You know the score. It's a hard world for people like us. You know the Church keeps tabs."

Victor made a face. "What about you, John? You have dreams, maybe? Things to do? You tell me you're okay with spending ten years living like this?"

"I had dreams," John said, not without a touch of bitterness. "But I learned they're a luxury for people like us, Victor. All this crap other people talk about. Aspirations. Morals. God's commandments. All of it's a story. There's only life. We do what we have to do to stay alive."

Victor was still making that face, so he poured him another glass. "It helps if you don't count the years," he said. "Think of it as just one day, always starting over, and it's given to us when we wake and taken from us when we sleep. All that matters is what you do with that day that's given to you."

"I can't live like that, John," said Victor. The drink seemed to give him courage. "Look, you don't have to live like this either. You're powerful, John, you're on a different level, you're telling me you can't decide to do your own thing one day and give them a good run for their money?"

"And do what? Spend a few years with the Church and Management hunting me?"

Victor's eyes were gleaming: perhaps with alcohol, perhaps

with fire. "You'd be free, John, *free.* Doesn't that count for something?"

Ah. The topic had emerged, somehow. John dreaded this talk of freedom. His wife had talked about this, often and loud.

What did freedom even mean, anyway? Freedom to live like dogs, forever looking over your shoulder, knowing you would die screaming? Or freedom to travel the world, with a dignified death at the end of it? There was a price to be paid either way. But not many people understood these things. They believed in ideals. Some believed in God's commandments. Others in freedom. Or love. Or glory. Or any number of useless fictions. And then they got angry when the world failed to give them space to act these scripts they had written for themselves.

John wanted to tell Victor this - to drag the fool up by his collar and show him the photograms of himself, years ago, to point to that starry-eyed idealist, and say *this man is dead,* and point to that other set of photograms, the ones he kept in the darkest drawer, and say *this is why.*

"I'd rather be able to drink a good whisky than be free," he said instead, pouring again. "At least I get to choose what my cage is made of."

They drank in silence. Eventually, Victor shook his head, presumably to clear himself of his disgust. "So are you going to tell me what comes next?"

"Moscow," said John. "Management wants a bit more fuel on the fire."

They drank again and began debating the assignment. Then, because it was protocol not to spend too much time with each other, John let Victor out the back door and watched him drive off.

"Good man," he said to himself, thinking about the poison he'd added to Victor's whiskey. Management's orders. The man was fraying. Either he did it or they did it. And John had chosen to give him a painless death - better than dying screaming in a Management cell somewhere.

He made his way back to the house and went up the creaky

stairs to his study and the bottle of whiskey. On the table, a photo of a woman stared at him in judgement. Underneath it, in slim gold letters: *Lisa Metcalf, 1980-2018. Requisat Au Pace.*

Only with Lisa had he ever been able to be himself. To everyone else he was the Inquisitor, the boss, the apprentice, the merchant of death, the faithful hand of Management.

"I'm sorry," he said to the photo. "I didn't -"

In his head, he could still hear her voice, gentle yet firm. *Didn't what, John? Mean to kill people? Didn't mean to turn out like this? You had a choice, John. We all did.*

John Metcalf, magician assassin, put his head down on the table and began to cry. Not for the hundreds dying in Turkey; not for Victor, who by now would be weaving very slightly; not for Management, with its dark master plans. He cried for himself, and for Lisa, and for the dark world that had made him who he was. The lights darkened in sympathy.

* * *

Meanwhile, in a world not too far removed, Dr. John Metcalf, physicist and engineer, sat in his study. He seethed.

It wasn't fair. It wasn't right. Ten years of research, almost on the verge of breakthrough, and the bastards had cut his funding.

He had tried, of course. He'd raged. He'd yelled. He'd made every single phone call he could - to the University, to the funders, to CERN, to the Department of Defense, and even, giving up every last shred of dignity, to Lisa, because ever since the divorce she'd been hanging out with some venture capital types who had serious money. But the Dean was apologetic, the funders disinterested, the Europeans thought he was mad, the DoD wanted only to know the military potential, and Lisa - well, Lisa had shrieked in laughter and kissed him goodbye, but not before sending him a photo of herself in the arms of some oil tycoon.

He was so far gone it barely hurt anymore.

So he had done the right thing. He'd dismissed the staff, even

Victor Klein, his faithful research assistant. Klein had a good brain on him and didn't deserve his career tanking because of the project. And here he was, drinking cheap whiskey.

"Face it, John," the Dean had said, trying on that fake-consoling voice of his. "Theory is all very fine, but it's been ten years and we haven't got a single good paper out of this. We need more than just potential. We need results."

There was just one last place he could take his work to: Moscow. The university would disavow him, of course, and the DoD would call him a traitor, and god alone knew what yarn Lisa would spin from it. But this was his magnum opus, and there was no way in hell that he would let it die like this.

* * *

Which is how, in two different worlds, two different aircraft bearing two different John Metcalfs bore down on Moscow. One was an old Snapdragon, its whale skin bags full of hydrogen, its steel and wooden carriage creaking ever so slightly. The huge Church-sanctioned Mobius engine spat out fire. The other was an Airbus A330, all steel and electronics. John Metcalf the magician saw the ghost aircraft again, just before his own landed. Both Metcalfs disembarked, disturbed by their own thoughts.

And both, in an act of remarkable coincidence, found their way to the same rambling street on the outskirts of the Moscow State University. There, under the iron-grey skies, occupying almost an entire block in a lazy, gone-to-seed fashion, was the hotel they had been directed to. It had probably been fit for princes a century ago. Now it loomed dark against the sky, a lone steeple inclined at an ominous angle, and the windows seemed to stare at them like empty eyes. Beggars sat outside the gated doors.

"The Grand Moscow Hotel," said John Metcalf, the physicist. His contact in Moscow had said they'd meet him here tomorrow. Damned odd place for a meeting, unless one had a flair for the gothic and a pressing need to be away from anything useful. Still, it was Moscow...

"The Grand Moscow Hotel," said John Metcalf, the magician, squinting. It was completely unlike Management's usual accommodations. They usually went for bright, expensive places, the kind of place you would least expect an assassin to work from.

Still, it was Moscow.

"Three days," they said to the reception desk, and in two different worlds were given the keys to room 222. Both settled down, and both went to work.

John Metcalf the physicist examined the room - large, but rather threadbare. Some rather despondent-looking bags of tea and a slightly melted-looking electric kettle occupied an otherwise usable desk. He changed his clothes, plugged the kettle in and spread out his papers, going through the draft one last time in hardcopy. There were still some things to fill in, proofs they hadn't got around to exploring, definitions that needed work, or at least a mention…

There was a knock on the door.

"Who is it?" said John the physicist. He flung open the door. A thin young man in a badly fitted grey suit almost toppled in.

"Yes?" said John imperiously.

The thin man scowled. He was clearly not used to people yanking the door open just as he was about to pick the lock. "The Director will see you day after tomorrow," he said in heavily accented English. "He says, bring your research. But you waste his time, you not receive his funding, not a cent, nyet."

"Thanks for the message," said John, excited and irritated at the same time. "Next time, call. Or text. I have a phone, you know."

The man gave him a look. "Day after tomorrow," he repeated heavily.

"Alright," said John. "Now are you going to stay in my room? Because if not, I'd like to get some sleep."

The thin man seemed to realize he was in John's room. With a curious look at the papers on the table, he brushed past John, and disappeared into the hallway. John stared after him, slightly disturbed, then closed his door and went back to his table immediately.

Christ. Seven in the morning. Seven. He had only so many hours....

He began to work feverishly.

* * *

Meanwhile, John Metcalf the magician spread out his copy of the Litany of Babel and rifled through the spellbook. The target was a politician, with armed bodyguards. He needed something long-rang, something almost untraceable...

Not Abraxas' Mirror. Not Bacon's Disembowelment. Not -

Aha. Theodric's Basilisk.

The Basilisk was a truly nasty spell. Cast right, it reconfigured every living cell within a certain radius to a stiff calcium approximation of itself. Not exactly turning a man to stone, but close enough for Management work.

That night, he put on his dark clothes and made his way to where Management had said the target would be most vulnerable: a mansion to the East, heavily guarded with cameras and sharpshooters. Daedric's Ghost let him slip inside the outer wall with relative ease, and he cast Frost's Revealing as he ran, outlining the location of every guard on the perimeter. It cost him a lot, but within moments he was at the inner doors, the guards no wiser for it. A magnificent marble hall and a gleaming wooden staircase greeted him. He wove a Lesser Spell of Unnoticeability around him and took the stairs, flying wraith-like past maids dressed in too-short uniforms and sneering, suited guards. The spell ran out just as he got to the study.

He knocked.

"Come in, Vasily," said a rough voice inside.

He slipped in. There was a man inside with his shirtsleeves

rolled up. He was sweating slightly. Another one of the maids in too-short dresses cowered and whimpered in a corner. The man turned, a look of surprise sketching itself on his face, and John cast the Basilisk. The man calcified before his very eyes, the look of surprise now permanent.

Perfect.

A whimper from the maid in the corner.

Oh no. Not perfect. The Basilisk had caught her, too, grabbing her by the legs and slowly creeping up her body as the spell took hold.

John crouched, aghast.

"I'm sorry," he whispered to her. "I'm so sorry."

She mumbled something. It sounded like she was begging. Then it crept up her chest, and he knew her heart had stopped. Only her eyes remained moving till the end, pleading, and then they, too, froze over.

John stood there for a long time, cursing himself. He had come prepared to kill any number of guards, but not the innocent.

Still, he was a professional. On the way back he knocked a guard out, tinkered with his memories to show the politician casting the spell on the maid and it backfiring in his face. He laid the guard by the door, and left by the window, creeping under the silent stares of the maid and the master.

And then he ran all the way to the hotel, feet pounding, heart hammering away in his chest, tears gleaming in his eyes. The Russian moon looked down at him without pity. His feet took him on a long and meandering route unthinkingly, just in case someone tried tailing him. He made it to the room and collapsed, trying to choke down the sobs.

The image of the maid, frozen, pleading. And, hot on the heels of that: Victor, sharing his last whisky. Faithful Victor, whose only crime had been to doubt.

There had to be a better way to make a living.

There was a knock on his door.

In an instant he had cast Revealing. One person behind the

door, no ill-intent, but plenty of fear. A snap of his hand and Blindness danced like a black blame in his left hand. He opened the door with his right.

It was a thin, young man, dressed in the ill-cut clothes of a valet. He was sweating and his eyes were huge in their sockets. "Simon 13-4," he rattled off. "Sir, they know you're here!"

"Who knows I'm here?" said John cautiously, putting the Blindness behind his back.

The young man almost staggered with disbelief. "They know!" he almost wailed. "Oh, God, please tell me I didn't get the wrong door. No, it's you, isn't it? Metcalf 6-8? Please, sir, hide, they're almost here. The operation's compromised. I don't know anything else -"

John stared at him, slightly disgusted.

"-but we can't leave, the place is surrounded," the man babbled. "Look, I'm going to make a run for it, sir, please tell Management I'm sorry, it's all gone south, Kovrova and Yeltsin are dead-"

He stopped as John's hand came down on his shoulder in a grip of iron.

"Shut up," said John calmly. "Or I'm going to stuff Blindness down your throat. Now take a deep breath. Good. Now tell me. How many are there, and what do they have?"

When the young man had finished, John let him go.

"Sit," he barked. "Make yourself some tea."

He paced the room, thinking. Thirty men in anti-magic armor, lead discs sewn into their coats. Shotguns. And a hegumen of the Russian Orthodox Church with five heiromonks backing him up. A full exorcism team.

Slow, but effective. They'd crawl through every damn level of the building. The exorcism team would pick him out from three floors away. And after that there was nothing he could do. Management would never retrieve a compromised operative.

There was only one thing to do.

He cast a memory modification on the babbler, something so

overpoweringly powerful that he almost accidentally turned the boy into a simpleton. He dialed it down just enough to make Simon, whatever-his-number-was, forget everything he ever knew about Management. Not much, as it turned out. He stripped out memories wholesale, turning the man into nothing more and nothing less than his alias as a low-paid valet at a shoddy Moscow hotel. He left a small set of instructions.

Moving jerkily, Simon - now Damir Yakovich - picked up the heavy Litany of Babel from John's desk, tucked it under his arm, and turned back to John with a glazed look in his eyes.

"I'll throw it in the incinerator, sir," he said in heavily accented English.

"Good man," said John. He watched the valet shuffle down the corridor, closed the door, and sat down, cross-legged.

There was a spell. In case of complete compromise. In case of inescapable situations. It was taught only to those whose compromise would do great damage to Management, and it was never meant to be used idly. They hadn't told him exactly what it did, but they had told him it would change his life.

He breathed in, found the balance, and began chanting.

Dark flame erupted his right hand, violet from his left. The chandelier overhead crackled and sparked, the bulbs exploding instantly as the current through them briefly became a hundred times more powerful. The furniture shook.

Ripples of space-time spread out from John Metcalf, twisting the past, twisting the future, twisting the present, making things *just so*. There was a brief sense of warping, of terrible *wrongness*, and the magician collapsed on the floor.

* * *

When he woke, he was slumped over his desk, and there was a terrible taste in his mouth, like copper and sulfur mixed together.

Everything looked different. And, when the taste cleared, everything smelled different. Then something kicked in his head, and he realized the room was still very much the same - an ugly, faded thing with the same layout. Nothing had really changed.

It still looked different, though.

He flexed himself off the chair, and winced as a completely unfamiliar set of aches and pains exploded in his hip and arms. He felt weaker than he'd ever remembered being. Experimentally, he flexed and snapped his fingers. The familiar Blindness spell erupted into black flame over his hand.

Well. Whatever it was, it hadn't taken his magic away.

There was a hunched old man in the bathroom mirror. With a start, he realized that it was him. His hair was grey, and his posture terrible, and the body he had always kept fighting fit was all but dissolved under a layer of unhealthily loose skin.

He debated a shower, but it was too cold. Instead he wrapped himself up in the robe, shivering. On the desk were papers. He wiped his drool off them and examined them. There were a lot of ordinateur printouts, all neat figures and lines, and stapled in between, page after page of notes, all in his own handwriting.

He read them. It looked like - wait, this was simple: it looked like someone was trying to derive Ogden's Cross, the basic examination of space-time, from first principles. It was basic, first-year stuff.

Not someone: *himself.* A version of him, in this universe. And judging by the way the papers had fallen, he'd been trying to finish the theorem in a great hurry.

The spell knocked on his mind. *Finish it,* it suggested. John Metcalf the magician picked up the pen, pondered its strangeness for a minute, and began to write.

When they knocked at his door at 7 AM, he was sixty pages into Ogden's proof of the reversible causality of time. By 7.30 the Director for Theoretical Sciences, a gruff, impatient man with an enormous belly, had swept into the hotel and begun to make noises. By 8 he had commandeered a key from the reception. Accompanied by his squad of flunkeys, the Director marched into 222 and flung the heavy door open.

"Bloody English!" he roared.

The English physicist raised an eyebrow at him and held up a hand for silence. "I'll be with you in a moment," he said. He scribbled on a page, stacked it neatly on top of a sheaf of notes, and pressed them into the Director's pudgy hand.

"There," he said. "Whatever that was all about, I'm sure you'll find it satisfactory. Now if you'll excuse me, I'm going to go have that shower."

The flunkeys gasped. So unaccustomed was the Director to being treated like this that he, too, fell silent. Then his icy eyes saw the first page, and the second, and before long he was sitting on the creaking bed reading page after page after page. An aide bought him a cigar and he lit it.

"By God, man!" he exclaimed when John emerged from the bathroom. "This is incredible!"

"I try," said John, towelling his hair.

"But this proof! Teleportation! You've modelled it! The mathematics!"

"Well, it only works on inanimate objects," said John, slightly confused by the enthusiasm but relieved that the spell was guiding his camoflauge. "Living things don't work, unfortunately, they end up rather dead. I suspect it's something to do with consciousness being quantum. And it won't work over large bodies of water. And really small things and complex machinery tend to glitch the hell out, no idea why. But other than that, if you want to move, say, a ton of sand, that'll work perfectly. All you need is enough energy on this end. But this is really basic stuff, of course. There's refinements you can do to improve the accuracy…"

The Director stared at him in incredulity. "By God!" he repeated. "By God! Such clarity! Such precision! And you say they did not accept this in America?"

"Well, you know how they are," said John vaguely. He had absolutely no idea how they were, but this seemed to work most of the time.

It worked now. The bed creaked alarmingly as the Director got up. "Dr. Metcalf," he said. "I apologize for startling you in coming in. Clearly you are a genius, and as they say, genius must be left to work in peace. We will approve your request for funding. Nay, we double it! It will be a pleasure to work with you to realize your vision. Indeed, for such a breakthrough in the fundamental sciences, it is, dare I say, only a matter of time before you win the Nobel Prize itself..."

He held out one pudgy hand.

The spell nudged John again. "I'm looking forward to it," he lied. "I hate to ask this of you, but can we continue the discussion tomorrow? I'm afraid I have a bit of a headache."

"Of course," said the Director, rather subdued now, and withdrew. As his retinue shuffled nervously after him, John heard him whispering, "By God! By God!"

* * *

He was still unconscious when they broke the door down. Men in black moved slowly into the room, clanking with every step, sweeping every nook and cranny. Then they parted. White robes walked in and knelt beside John. There was pin-drop silence.

"This is the heretic," said a voice in Russian.

"Are you sure?" said a younger voice.

The hegumen drummed his fingers, staring down at the body. He said a small prayer. There was a brief flash, and John stirred and blinked owlishly at the wizened priest staring down at him. There was a powerful sense that something was wrong.

"Oh, shit," he said. "Did I miss the appointment?"

"My son," said the hegumen sternly in English, fingers casting the Litany of Confession. "What magic have you performed? What is your role with the Management? Confess, and your death will be painless."

John stared up at him. "Magic?" he said, completely nonplussed. He got to his feet, swaying slightly. "Magic?" he repeated incredulously. "Really?"

Then he caught sight of the men with guns pointed in his direction and swallowed. "Look, I don't know what the hell you mean," he said hastily, his voice trembling a little. "My name is John Metcalf. I'm a theoretical physicist. I do math, not magic. I have an appointment here with the Director of Theoretical Sciences at the Moscow Institute of Fundamental Research. I'm an English citizen. Please put the guns away and leave."

The hegumen stood up in a rustle of vestments. "He thinks he tells the truth," he said softly. He unraveled the Litany of Confession.

"We found traces of magic on a valet, sir," said a heiromonk nervously. "A rather powerful memory spell. Boy can't remember anything. But it has his signature all over it."

The hegumen looked John up and down and made the sign of the cross. "Cursed are they who lie to the Lord our God," he said, with spite.

One of the men raised his gun and hit John on the head. There was immense pain, and then darkness.

When he woke again, the priests were gone, the men were gone, and his skull hurt like ten thousand hangovers. He tried to move, and discovered he was chained to a stone wall. The stench of urine hit his nostrils. Through blurred eyes he made out a white shape behind a red glow.

"Help," he said weakly.

The white shape resolved itself into a priest wearing ornate robes. The red glow sharpened into a cross, heated to red-hot, heading slowly towards his naked body.

"Confess," said the priest softly.

In the darkness, John Metcalf, the physicist, began to scream.

* * *

Five years later, in a different world, a man named John Metcalf sat with the President of the United States.

He was a legend in his own time. The whole world knew the story - the reclusive genius, working for decades on a new theory of space and time, something practical, being turned down by every place he applied to for funding, save one. How that first breakthrough - paired with a great deal of smart tech and investment - had led to revolution in every single sphere, in everything from large-scale transport to the space effort to - and this was really important - reshaping the contours of countries so they could better survive climate change.

And John Metcalf hadn't stopped there. From that great brain had poured forth a stream of new theories and inventions that would have made Isaac Newton green with envy. The Metcalf Theoretics had given the world new ways of harnessing energy; they turned seemingly impossible problems - like solving world hunger and ending armed conflict - into trivial matter conversion solutions that aid workers deployed by the thousands every day. Even things like PTSD and Alzheimers were a thing of the past, thanks to Metcalf's latest batch of NeuroCare products.

And if he had profited from it, what of it? Surely Metcalf, who changed the world deserved to be the richest man who walked the Earth. Millions worshipped him. Billions respected him. He was the Man of Science, the one who conquered the darkness, and showed humanity its true potential.

The President was thus rather nervous, though she did a fine job of not showing it.

"Congratulations on the Nobel Prize, John," she said. "Though I'd have preferred it if you gave us a leg up every now and then, you know, instead of giving everything away. So what next? You're practically overthrowing a new industry every year, so hit me."

John smiled vaguely, knowing it infuriated her and she could do nothing about it. "It is what it is, Madam President," he said. "As for my next research...who knows? Perhaps you might think about my automation proposal. I feel we could do a lot with the GOLEM model. I'm sure you've seen the demos. Life-size robots you can reprogram with just a sentence. Perfect for every type of labor. Who wouldn't want one?"

"Indeed," said the President. "But you're aware it's political dynamite right now? This is going to take a lot of jobs away, John, and that's not going to go well."

"And you wonder why the Russians are the first to get around to implementing my ideas."

"True." She fished around for another topic. "I'm sorry to hear about your wife."

Something happened to John Metcalf's face. It shut off like a steel trap. Suddenly the lights seemed to dim.

"She did try to come back, once or twice," he said. "But I'm used to thinking of her as dead."

"Good," said the President. "Then you won't mind what I have to say next. Metcalf 6-8, your return to the source world has been authorized. Management would like you to take on another mission. It is to be your last field operation. You'll wake up in your old body, which is currently shackled down in a Church cell in Russia, not too far from the target."

John Metcalf stared at her, incredulous. Then a slow grin crept on to the steel of his face.

"No," he said slowly. "I don't think so. I rather like it here, you see. It's nice not to take orders for a change. To be at the very forefront. I'm going great good here, Madame President. I'm sure you understand."

The President tried not to sweat. "These are orders from Management. I was sent here to deliver them to you-"

"You don't seem to understand," said John. "I'm done with Management." He waved a hand at the world outside. "This," he said. "This is my life now. I do good. I help people. And I haven't even finished with what I remember of the Litany of Babel."

"They said you might say that," said the President, whose real name was Sarah 10-3. Her fingers closed on the silenced pistol taped under the desk.

John Metcalf reacted instantly. Blindness sparked from his fingertips.

"I have dreams again," he said softly as she collapsed. "You won't take them away from me."

Then he cast a memory spell on the cameras.

By the time the Secret Service broke the door down, convinced that someone had set off an EMP in the Oval Office, the President was stirring. John Metcalf, the world's foremost genius and inventor, knelt by her body, cradling her.

"Somebody call an ambulance!" he shouted. "She had some kind of seizure!"

The President opened her eyes, and with the utter vacancy of a child, began to drool and gibber on the floor.

Of course they detained John, but only very briefly. After all, everybody knew the kind of man John Metcalf was, didn't they?

The moment he got out, he dialed his Tactical Unit. To them he described every single detail he knew about Management's tactics, their operations, the kind of equipment they might have on this side. And they, being extremely lethal mercenary bodyguards, nodded and asked him where he wanted the bodies if they found any of these people. That done, he spent the next few days tripling the watch around the people he had met in these five strange years, the people he really cared about.

The spell nudged him. He had to go to the funeral, of course, it was what the other John, the John-from-this-world, would have done. And so he did. He endured the rather ornate ceremony, made a fine speech, and drove past the graves to him home.

That was when he saw the casket.

It lay on the earth beside an unmarked grave, glimmering softly in the fading light. He could see the grass through it. And, if he squinted, a broken body inside. Something with only one arm and legs that were stumps.

John parked his car - a nondescript station wagon that his fans loved to praise as a symbol of his humility - and ambled over to the casket, peering into it. The more he concentrated, the more he could see - the burns, the stitches, the skin peeled away in vicious stripes.

So they had caught him and finally killed him. The body still had his face, of course. And inside, no doubt, John Metcalf from this world had died screaming and confused, tortured beyond madness and despair.

Just like that maid, from what felt like a lifetime ago. Just like Victor.

John thought about them, a little saddened. Life was poor, nasty, brutish and short. It always had been.

But perhaps, in this new world, he could make it a little better for everyone, if only as a way to atone.

He went around to the trunk of the car, retrieved an old and battered copy of *The Doomsayer Journeys* and a bottle of whiskey. It wasn't the old Black, but it was close enough. He raised a toast to the ghost casket and tried to find words to say.

There were none.

"To us," he said at last. "To a different world."

Then he sat down and began to read.

BIO

Yudhanjaya Wijeratne is a data researcher and former journalist as well as a Nebula Award-finalist. He spends his time filling notebooks with strange ideas and code. He's run news operations, designed games, and fallen off cliffs (most of these things by accident), but he's known in his native Sri Lanka for bringing data analysis to political commentary. He's currently working on the Commonwealth Empires trilogy for HarperCollins.

12

EFFIGIES IN BRONZE

COLTON HEHR

I stand before you, O King, priests and oracle, kith and kin, and the Creator grant me the tongue to speak all that I have seen and done. I pray to the Creator, Molder of Men and Clay, that the oracle divines truth from my words. Just as she hears the spirits and knows their will, let her see in me the truth of words and deeds. All that happened is as I tell you now.

It began when we came upon the village. Not the whole vanguard army, just my spearmen and I, I in my chariot, and with us a band of archers led by Lugal, whose bald pate I can see even now among the crowd of listeners. We had ranged ahead of the army, and the swift horsemen farther afield than we, on the trail of the Kascians. We thought to find them among the hills and cedar trees where they might have hid from our horsemen, but instead we found a village, rude and unwalled. A cairn, stone piled on raw stone, stood in the center of the cluster of huts. Children, young and naked and dirty, ran round the hovels' walls of mud-daubed reeds. The cairn marked it as a Kascians camp, but it looked little more than a handful of farmers—a dozen huts, crudely built.

A faint thread of tracks led to the village. We thought it a few of our foes, breaking away from the main force. Now, I knew it to be a goatherd's trail, or a path for some villager to draw water from the nearby stream. We had discovered the tracks there and assumed our foe had crossed running water to cast confusion on his trail.

I arrayed my spears, bronze points gleaming in the noonday sun. Our pursuit of the Kascians bands took us from the sea's edge, and we could no longer see wine-dark waters on our eastern horizon. Below, between the rising crests of two hills, the village sat, silent and ignorant of our presence.

I went to Lugal's archers and sought him out, looking for the silver clasp on his thick girdled belt, a twin to the one that I wore. He and his archers were preparing their bows. I found the sight strange and told him so.

"We have the enemy before us and ample arrows, cousin. We go to our work." Lugal strung his bow, a weapon of yew and horn. I saw him lance a man through a bronze corselet, leaving the man dead in the dust of his chariot from two hundred paces, with that bow. "Up, men! String bows."

I grasped hawk-eyed Lugal's forearm and held him fast. "Cousin, hold a moment. Men, loosen your bows. Put away those arrows that prick men out of their chariots and darken their eyes."

"Your poetry flatters, Esar. What troubles you?"

"This village is a slick of mud compared to Eridu. Look—see you any men? Gleaming bronze, shields and spears?" I held out my other hand to the squat of ramshackle huts. "Your enemy is somewhere beyond this place. This holds no glory for your arrows or my spear."

"A dozen huts might hold twice as many foes. Let our arrows fall among the Kascians. We might yet see bronze's flashing gleam." Lugal gestured with one of his arrows. "Let this dart of mine find its mark."

"Cousin, the Sage Iodonna taught our people their virtues. Did she ever say there was glory in fletching your arrow in an old man's back, or in seeing a child fall beneath your chariot's wheels?" I squeezed his forearm tightly. "Mercy. You will send more Kascians to their forefathers before we see Eridu again. We will return home more than captains and soldiers—heroes for an age."

Lugal smiled. "You have always held Iodonna's teachings foremost in your heart, Esar."

I let go of his arm and turned, motioning for my spearmen to stand down, to unshoulder their bronze burdens from chafed and aching shoulders.

"All the same—fire at all." The soft hiss of an arrow in flight sounded behind me. "We must be sure, cousin."

Lugal pulled another arrow from his quiver. He was setting it to string when I rounded and bulled into him, shoving him to the ground with my shield's broad face. The arrow snapped in his hand and he stood, casting its feathered end at me. I threw down my shield in anger.

"You sack of wine! Don't treat me like a cur." Lugal flung his bow to the ground and strode towards me.

"You make a cur of yourself, nipping at the old and the young with your arrows!" I caught him mid-stride and we struggled for a moment before I cast him to the ground. Lugal, you stand among the witnesses here, and I tell you: you have always been a favorite kindred of mine, but you should have known who of us held the advantage in wrestling, even in anger.

"You would strike a kinsman? That is beneath you." Lugash, sharp eyes glowering with anger, glared at me.

"And attacking a village is beneath you. I save you from yourself." I took a deep breath and settled myself. My men bristled behind me, and so too did Lugal's before me. I wanted no quarrel between us, as kin or as captains.

I held out my hand to Lugal. "I acted in haste. Forgive me, but I would not have you lessen yourself with the blood of these people."

Grimacing, his lower lip split, Lugal took my hand and I pulled him up from the ground.

"An accord," I suggested, "Let us show the villagers we are here, in strength and bearing sharp bronze aplenty. If they hide warriors, these men will rush to meet us. If not, the villagers will flee. We will fire the buildings with these swift arrows of yours, to be sure that no enemy ever hides in them."

Lugal picked up his bow and nodded, wiping blood out of his curled beard. "As you say, cousin. All the same, I will speak to your elder brother. You are stronger than me—there was no need to treat me so foul."

"I agree. Consider it an urge to do right by a man well loved by his kin. I will pay whatever recompense my brother sees fit, to you and to the Creator."

"Damn you, but you are a hard man to hate." Lugal laughed and slapped my bronze-scaled cuirass. "You heard him. Make fires. You, Esar—take those spearmen, and make the air ring with spear against shield. Let those below hear us."

I embraced Lugal, our quarrel forgotten for the time being. "It will be like waves beating on the shore. Shields!"

* * *

We left the village in ashes, its people fled, no warriors within. We returned to find the army encamped, ditches dug, cedar spikes laid and guards posted. Tents by the thousand dotted the ground, many smaller ones clustered around a larger like cubs clinging to their mother. My own tent, and those of my men, sat near the largest in the camp, where Eshua held court among the noble-born sons of Eridu.

Lugal had raced ahead in his own chariot, so that a quick-footed courier waited for me at the camp's entrance, its packed-dirt path flanked by upright poles of painted wood.

"Eshua, Under-the-King, requests your presence."

I gave the man a silver piece. "Make a libation of wine at the camp's shrine for me. Keep the rest of the libation for yourself."

The courier tucked the coin into his belt. "Gladly. To the Sage?"

"And to Ninurta. We need the spirits' favor."

"I will see it done, captain."

My brother sat on a broad, low stool of cedar and river rushes in his tent. His armor sat on the floor beside his chair, still earing the dust of the day, and grim clung to his bare arms and legs, darkening the linen of his tunic where the armor sat heaviest and hottest. Only his attendant remained with us, mixing date wine with water in a bowl. The table in front of Eshua was low and broad, and many clay tablets sat on it. Missives from the king, messages from the other armies, and one attempt at a rough map of the mountains that yet laid northward.

We disagreed on many things, but none respect your willingness to work and share alike with the others of our city, my brother. There he sat, receiving his captains, still in his marching tunic and sandals, unwashed and no doubt unfed.

Eshua served a small bowl of watered wine to me with his own hands and took one for himself before we spoke. The rest he sent to the nearest group of soldiers outside. Once his attendant left to portion out the remaining wine, my brother spoke. "Lugal brings me distressing news. He said that my youngest brother quarrelled with our cousin. Struck him, even. Is that so, Esar?"

"Let doubt depart from heart. Lugal spoke true."

"He claims it came from dealing with a Kascian village."

"It did."

Eshua slapped his thigh. "Does dust dry mouth, or wine drown tongue? Tell me why!"

"He wished to attack. Our foes would have been but lambs—women, a few men, children. Folk with wheat-reaping scythes and stout staffs against spear and bow."

"Your devotion to the Sage's Path is why your siblings love you best among our father's children, but we are not in Eridu giving bread to our fellows." Eshua tugged at his dark beard and leaned forward. "We ride to rid our city—and the others—of the Kascian hordes. That means bronze, brother."

"Against soldiers, not some shepherds."

"I share your faith in Iodonna's ways. They are how we exist in harmony with our world and our Creator. All born from the clay of Eridu do, but we may have to fail in those vows to win this war. If so, we can beg forgiveness from the Molder of Men and Clay, beseech the spirits' aid, and redouble our devotions—after we win."

I drank from my wine bowl to gather my thoughts and then spoke. "The Sage did not set a path for our people that we might walk it or stray as we will. We cannot go our own way when her virtues become as burdens on our backs. That is when we must stay true, Eshua."

Eshua held up a hand. "Enough. We will speak of this another time. I have word that our scouts have found tis Merabanna's band again. We continue our march at dawn. They go still to the mountains, and we will follow them."

I stood and bowed. "As you say, brother."

We grasped hands and I left. Kin or not, Eshua commanded the army. He is the king's scepter and sword. I left the tent and obeyed, though my heart sat heavy with fear and concern for my brethren.

* * *

We put feet to ground early the next day, just as my brother promised. We marched steady throughout the morning, watching as the sun burned away the mist and the cedar trees gave way to hard scrub and rocky, thin soil. I marched with my men, letting my attendant—a young cousin from some distant family lineage—drive my chariots and my two strong horses. Some captains kept to their chariots, but I kept to my spears, to the men who wielded them. This I learned from Eshua, who believed that the noble-born captains ought to live and die alongside the common soldiers, as we and they are brothers born of one city. Our fortunes and fates are bound.

When the army halted, I went ahead with some of the scouts who had made promising discoveries on the trail. We came again to a village, but a wall rung round this town, and hundreds of tents bordered that wooden bulwark. It spread out through a broad, gently-sloped valley, and even from a distant hilltop I could make out the telltale glint of bronze among the tents.

When I returned to the camp, Namhu waited for me with my men. The magus sat at our cooking fire, showing the men the length of shaped brass, capped with carven chalcedony that he used for his thaumaturgy. Some gave him wide berth, other eager ears.

Namhu and I embraced when I drew near. I have known Namhu nearly all of my life, his father the charioteer for mine. Though he didn't lack for his father's talents, he has gone on to master the subtle energies of the world, as many here today know well. His thaumaturgy has driven many a stone block into place and brought rain to more than one thirsty vineyard.

Nearly anyone could wield the wand he carried on his belt, charged with energy as it was, but few possessed the will or the training to manage that wild storm of power. A magus's focus was a tinder waiting for an errant spark, in the wrong hands it became a wildfire.

"What brings you to my tent, Namhu?" I led him inside and offered him a crust of bread and a small, clay pot of honey. He refused, but I indulged, eating while I yet had time.

"You missed your brother's assembly of the captains." Tan brushed his fingers through his beard. Like all magi, he wore it shorter than was usual in Eridu. Long beards make for ample fuel, he says.

"I was out with the afternoon scouting party. I wanted to see this village the morning scouts mentioned."

"Your brother means to attack it before dawn's light tomorrow. He wants to overrun it—first with flames, then with bronze."

"Sound thinking. He means to catch them while most slumber. He will fire the tents?"

"And the village." Namhu crossed his gold-girded arms over his chest, charms and talismans jingling. "I like it not—my flames were meant for more than turning some farmer's hut to ash."

"What would you suggest?" I asked.

Kohl-ringed eyes hooded and squinted with contemplation. "Fire the tents. The gate and section of the wall nearest us, too. Drive the villagers away, force the warriors to face us in the field."

"I'll broach the idea with Eshua. May my brother see wisdom, honestly offered."

My brother did not receive Namhu's wisdom as graciously as I hoped, nor did he believe his plan to have issue.

"We cannot go into the village and strike down all we see. You know what the scouts saw, just as I do." I stood before him again, and again we argued in private, without the other captains. The privilege of brotherhood.

"The Kascians do it. Think you that they built that village? They took it, no doubt after putting the people to the bronze."

"Are we Kascians, brother? If they lay waste to a city, leave its people to the carrion birds—do we do as they do?"

"It would be justice, fairly given!"

"It would not be our way on the Path! If we do as they do, what difference separates us? Virtues we no longer hold to?" I slammed my fists on the table hard enough to slosh watered wine and rattle bowls. "We cannot become as they are and still be who we are. Who we ought to be."

"You would let the Kascians burn us from the earth and cut the Eridui root and stem from the world before you strayed from the Sage's Path, Esar."

"No, but I would not take their path and forsake the one Iodanna laid before us. I would not walk that road simply because it was easier than our own."

Eshua glowered, sun-bronzed face darkening with blood beneath his beard. "You go too far. Cease arguing, close mouth and lend ear! I lead the army; the king gave me the point of his spear to drive away our foe—not you. We will do as I say. You will do as I say, be it as captain or as brother."

Tension flared between us, glowing hot as bronze does when poured molten into a casting mold. For a moment we both stood, staring at each other. If we were not kin, one of us would have surely struck the other.

My brother tugged at his beard in frustration before smoothing it out with his fingers. He sat back down and motioned to my chair. "Come. Sit. You mean well, I know. Angry words, spoken in fervent faith. I would not have my own blood think me without devotion."

He took an unfired clay tablet and watered it. Once smoothed beneath his hand, he began to write with a blunted river reed on its surface. "You must stand by your faith if you demand a measure of mine, Esar. Tomorrow, you go to their village under flag of truce. Tell them what you will, ask what ever you think they will agree to, but not let nothing of my strategy pass your lips."

"And if I forge no pact with this Madrubanna?"

"Then I will attack as planned." Eshua rose and placed his clean hand on my shoulder, the other grimed with water and clay. "If they will not accord with you, then they must reckon with me. The village makes no difference in the matter of our city's safety."

At dawn, I rode out into the valley. A standard bearer rode with me, his chariot beside mine as we made our way down the rough, hoof-beaten path. I drove the team myself and left my kindred charioteer in the camp. Not for you, this meeting—still too young to keep voice firmly in mouth, dear cousin.

Eshua sent a messenger before me and the Kascians waited for me in front of their camp. All their warriors in their hundreds stood before the tents, arrayed by clan kinship, sheathed in bronze and leather. Plumed helmets swayed in the morning breeze, horsehair and feathers added to the heights of the wearers. At the forefront of this panoply of men stood one alone, gray of eye and gray of hair. A band of beaten silver hung around his wrist and it shook when he raised his hand in greeting.

I stepped off of my chariot to meet him. His face looked cut from granite and crudely done, at that, eroded by hard living. He spoke our language well, though simply and sometimes with pause as he searched for the proper word or phrase to suit his desires. His careful words cloaked a studied cleverness that many here, general or priest, would tell you does not exist among marauders like the Kascians. I tell you now, what I convey to you now is just as we spoke.

"Welcome, honored foe. Take this: my vow of your safety, for all to see."

Madrubanna held out a dagger, its edges blunted and its point rounded. I tested it with a thumb; the blade would have struggled to cut an unbaked mud brick. I tucked it into my belt. "Gratitude. Fear of offense stays my voice. What do your people call you?"

"King. King Madrubanna, lord of twelve clans of the Kascia. Eight, now, after your campaign against us." A Kascian approached. Before us he drove a post into the ground with a weighty mallet. To this we tied our chariot teams. Afterward, the standard bearer took his place behind me. Madrubanna bid us to follow him.

"Your messenger said you wished to discuss peace." Gray-eyed Madrubanna led us to a table set up near the tents, within javelin distance of his assembled clansmen. "We have little to speak of. You are Esar, yes?"

"I am." I took the reed and whicker stool he indicated. A Kascian pair, man and woman, brought us fermented milk and bread, brick-hard and salted. I followed the king's example of dipping bread into milk.

I do not believe the fare will become popular here in Eridu, but I ate it out of politeness. "Why not? This war cannot go on forever."

"It need not. We fought to take your cities. Now we fight to tire you. Eventually you and your kinsmen will grow weary of war and return to your high-walled cities of brick and stone, and we shall take pasture land here on your frontier."

"We scatter you at every turn. You tore down the walls and temples of Yisuz. The Twelve Cities will not set bronze aside until the Kascians are gone, be it from our land, or to their ancestors." I caught myself and drew up short. "It need not go so far. Your people can leave. Sue for peace, go back to your homeland. We do not thirst for blood."

"We cannot. Home is lost to us. We die going forward into your bronze, we die going backward to the icy steppes where once we rode. Better to gamble against your cities." Madrubanna spoke plainly, eating and munching between words.

"Then go east, take ship to sea. There are other lands. The Kascians are warriors, kings would pay to set your bronze against foes. Pay in land and in silver."

"We would not be slaves to some king behind his wall. Then what? Servitude? Whoring ourselves until our people are wasted in the wars of others?"

Mudrabanna shook his hoary head. "No. We will fight here. If you beat us back, then we will run. To fight again, or to flee. No peace until this gamble is played to its end."

"Then fight, King, but send the people of this village away, lest our arrows fall on those without bronze. We Eridui have no desire to slay children, nor your valued elders."

Stormy-browed, Madrubanna stared at me. He took off his silver band and gave it to me. "My gift, for your mercy. A strange man you are, to save the son of a foe who might grow to hate the slayer of his father. That is the blood price—for the lives of children yet saved."

The king motioned to the hills. "Go. I will do as you say, but when we next meet, it will be as foes, honored or otherwise. I will add the silver buckle of your belt to my others, if the gods will it. If not, then you already have your loot from my corpse."

The stony face did not change, but I needed no second dismissal. I left the Kascian clan-king there, brooding in the wan light of morning.

* * *

Eshua's magi fired the tents as the sun rose. The village sat lifeless behind them, as a chest of silver emptied of its riches. The Kascian warriors streamed out as we came rolling down the hill. They met us with bronze, some without armor and none of them with their vaunted war horses, which remained corralled.

This is war, for those among you who have not gone through it:

It is loud. Bronze clashes on bronze just as the storm spirit splits the sky and roars its fury with earth shaking thunder. Men groan and scream, you feel the stamp of feet rattle in your breast as you march, line by line with your fellows, shields forming a sheet of bronze between you and hated foe. Noise weighs on you, clogging your ears and your heart.

The enemy comes on to you, they shout their war cries, and then it is that crash of shield on shield. A man aims his spear for your heart. Your shield turns it aside, your own bitter bronze buries into his belly. His eyes darken, his soul departs, he falls at your feet. A friend collapses in the line, feathered arrow sunk in neck. He dies, blood gushing from wound and mouth.

It goes on this way for ages, all choking dust and thrusting spears. Then it is done, all at once and without pomp. You see the backs of your foe. They break, crumbling. Arrows chase after them; some fall, but others reach their herd of horses, and they go like a storm's wind, fleet and sudden.

After, you are mired with blood and grime, caked with it—arms, feet, face. Armor, once polished and shimmering, is dull and tattered, shield's face scarred and pitted. There are faces among your soldiers that you see no longer and cannot find. Later, someone will find them among the dead and, with luck, save them from the crows' greedy beaks. As for the wounded foes moaning on the field? You go among the bodies, finishing them where they lay whenever you find them.

No, I cannot remember how many men I slew. Three, perhaps four. We were not in the thick of the fight, but on its flank, driving inward from the left. By the time we pushed our way into their center, many of the Kascians were turning and fleeing. No, I did not see King Madrubanna, though he surely fought.

Eshua gave us scant time to rest. Enough to wash our hands,

wet our tongues, and dress our wounds. From the time of of the sun's rising fully above the horizon til the time it sat at its zenith, and then we clasped armor, hefted shields, and began the march. My brother left a few men in the valley to count and bury our dead with proper funeral rites.

Hear me, oracle: that march weighed heavier on me than did the battle. We trudged onward in the heat of the day, battered and aching. The hills gave way to stony detritus and hardy, straggling grass as we began a steady ascent into the mountains.

In the welter of bloodshed, where do Iodonna's virtues arise? Where compassion? Where humility, where wisdom and harmony with the natural order? There is no order when men bear bronze against men except that which we try to impose on it with commands and serried ranks.

And yet, some men revel in it. They tire of feasting and drinking, of love and worship, but never of bloodshed, of glutting the tellurian spirits with gore. For all our disagreement, I at least know for a certainty that my brother cannot be counted among those men. And still, our argument tugged at me, dragged me into a gloom. I wondered if Eshua might be right and I wrong.

Virtues cannot be found among bloodied bronze and ruined bodies. It can be found before and after, but not in battle. How then, to apply what the Sage taught us? If not Iodonna's path, then what guides our steps? I can see no kinship between Iodonna's teachings and war. The virtues are in harmony with our nature, but what aspect of man makes a farmer set aside plow for sword? It does not exist! War is a thing men are driven to by need, as an ox is driven to the butcher block with goads and whips, because it is frightened by the smell of blood. It goes no more willingly to slaughter than we.

Whether or not one follows the Path, they cannot love war and yet be whole of heart. He may revel in the moment, find glory in defense of home and hearth, but none find joy in their own dead kin and still claim devotion to gods or spirits.

Night fell and my heart was as lead in my heart. We camped in the rocky heights, crags and jutting stone all around us, the ground reaching upwards in a sweep that disappeared beyond our camp fires. I prayed to the Creator, I made oblations of sweet wine and burned herbs to the spirits, but if they heard my pleading, they gave no answer.

Soon after I awoke, two soldiers, whom I did not recognize, joined me in my tent. They shouldered spears and shields and offered open hands to me in greeting.

"Does my brother have need of me?" I asked.

The look on their faces twisted, like a man with spirit-plagued bowels. "Honored servant of the king he is, Eshua wishes you to remain in your tent."

"Until when?"

The other man spoke, low and quiet. "We know not, Esar."

"What reason has he given?"

"He fears." The man licked his lips, eyes shifting from me to my sword, which laid in its sheath on the ground beside my reed mat. "He fears you will do ill out of desire to do right. We would not bar your way, but by his command."

Only when the man spoke did I realize that anger had crept up from heart into throat, tightening the muscles in my shoulders and making the muscles bunch and bulge with tension. I unclenched my teeth and waved away the man's unspoken apology. "We all must do as commanded. I cannot hold anger in heart at you for that. For Eshua, it is a different tale."

I sat down on my mat and held out a hand. "Go. One of you tell him I wish to speak to him. You have my sacred word that I will remain."

One of the men left. The other relaxed and let his shield hang from its strap, jabbing his spear's butt-point into the hard ground.

"Who captains you? And who leads my men?"

"Your spears serve Eshua directly. I am under Lugal. He favors the bow, but many of us bear spears and shields for him."

"A worthy captain and honored kinsman." I motioned to the wooden plank that served as my table and board, where a pitcher of water and a few bags of dried fruit rested. "Eat, if you wish. When I leave my tent, it will not be through you or that other man, but through my brother. We have no quarrel."

The spearman half-smiled. The left side of his face scarcely moved for the angry scar that gouged his cheek. "No, but my gratitude. We only know other captains by the word of their men. I'm glad that your men's boasts are true. My fellow and I—we thought you would surely rage at us."

Inside I fumed! Indeed, I raged, a storm blackening the sky as it comes down from the mountaintops. I held in my fury and did not let the soldier see my lightning or hear my thunder. It was as I told him: he was not at fault for the orders given. The sun rose high in the sky before my brother came to my tent, girded in bronze. I rose from my mat so quickly that it startled both he and the spearmen.

"You take your time in coming, brother. What cause do you have for all of this?"

"I have your own cause, Esar. In battle, you lead as well as any, but you are too quick to set aside bronze and make a brother of your enemy when they still hold war in their heart." He held out a hand to the flap of my tent. "You confuse the men, make them hesitate, and we cannot afford to stumble!"

"If I make the men wonder, then you ought to, too."

"I do!" Eshua rarely raised his voice. His shout filled the tent, and his hands became grasping claws in frustration. "Every choice I make might lead us to doom. I can only do what will keep our city safe and our men alive. If those choices don't accord with the Sage's wisdom, then I must bend or else we all break!"

My brother regained his calm and shook his head. "If I go astray, then it is up to you to lead me back—after we have settled the matter of the Kascians. No more talks, no more peace offerings. We scatter Madrubanna's forces or we grind them into the dust, and we do so before next dawn's coming."

"Stay here, Esar. I cannot let you trouble our campaign any longer." Eshua turned and left the tent. I began to follow him when the two guards closed ranks and barred my way. Even though I had given them my word, I still saw worry on their faces, and so I did not try to push through them. I was angry with my brother, but I knew his heart—being a leader of men, making decisions that lead to the life and death of others is a strain on any man. I argued with him not to make the burden heavier, but to lighten it.

Time passed slowly, only marked by the sound of moving men and the arc of the sun as its spirit drove the burning disc through the sky. When my tent flap next opened, Lugal strode into my tent. His spearmen offered terse salutes.

"Leave us. I wish to speak with my kinsman alone."

"Captain, Eshua speaks with the will of the king, and he ordered us to remain."

"I know who my cousin is and what he does. He serves the king. I serve Eshua. You serve me. Is that not so?" He slapped the flap of the tent. "Go. Wait outside. If any ask, tell them you do so at my will."

When the guards left, Lugal turned to me. "You've been absent from the assemblies more often than usual, cousin. Your brother says you won't be in the coming battle."

"By his decision, not mine."

Lugal paused a moment, hand resting on sword hilt. "Nor mine. Cousin, I have seen the Kascian camp. They are few, and few among them are warriors. Perhaps a few hundred, all told. We have bickered on the matter before, and I have not always agreed with you, but this time—this time you have the truth of it."

"What did you see?"

"The Kascians, camped in a shallow basin at the end of a ravine. The ravine opens up and bottoms out, shallow nearer the ravine and steeper as it does. They cannot hope to escape us before tomorrow by scaling the cliff face that they camp beside. Not in a single night."

Lugal used his hands to map out the basin. Hard granite, bowling outward before sweeping upwards mercilessly, nearly a natural wall, save for the random outcroppings and jagged cuts of the stone where it is cloven by time and age.

"Esar, the Kascians are camping in a grave of their own making. If we march to battle, I am afraid that we will bury all of them. A few arrows into a village is one matter, trampling the old and the young beneath our feet another. I cannot do it."

"Speak to Eshua. You and the other captains can sway him."

"We cannot. We are divided, and it would take all of the captains standing united to bar his path. He is still our leader, as we are the leaders of our men. Where he goes, we follow. It is your privilege as blood to speak out against him, but even that has its limits."

Lugal strode over to me and took my hand in his. "Cousin, if given opportunity—could you do something?"

I squeezed his forearm. "There might be something I can do, if given my freedom."

My cousin laughed and nodded, as much to himself as to me. "Your brother may whip me but perhaps the Creator will be look kindly on me for this."

He stepped past me and over my reed mat and drew out his knife. Placing a hand on the tent to tauten the linen, he stabbed his knife into the fabric and slashed a rent down it. He turned to me and motioned to the tear. "Go. I'll remain for a time."

I embraced Lugal. "Sage's blessings on your house and heart, cousin."

The tear came up to my chest, but I ducked and slid through as a fish darts through the river reeds.

I made my way through the camp to where the magi stayed. They camped among themselves, for the sake of the men—the loud noises and unnatural smells accompanying thaumaturgy can unsettle horse and man alike, if unused to them. Even I, growing up in the company of many magi, find some of the arcana to be strange and fearsome.

Everywhere, men readied themselves for war. It was no different among the magi tents, so few paid me any heed when I slipped into Namhu's tent. He sat among his esoteric tinctures and crystals, a bowl of barley porridge still steaming before him.

"Esar. Your brother said you were to remain in your tent."

"That is so. He doesn't know I'm here."

Namhu frowned. "That reeks of ill omen."

"Not as ill an omen as what my brother intends." I told him what Lugal told me and the frown on his face grew, his brows furrowing, his features growing stormier by the moment.

"Eshua is a good man. He will see sense when we approach, surely," Namhu said.

"I think him the best among men, but I see the burden he bears as our leader. I fear it drives him to act in haste. Namhu, lend me your wand." I held out my hand to him, and that made the magus hesitate.

I see him now in the crowd of listeners. I know that he told the oracle he gave me the wand after some discussion. I would tell you otherwise—that I struck him, threatened him, and took the wand from him, to save him from being brushed with the tar of my own deeds. He is too good a friend, though, and the oracle would see through my lies.

I cajoled him into giving me the wand. Though the act went against his better judgment, I believe it accorded well with his heart, for he works to follow the Sage's Path as we all do, and he knew what sins waited for us at the far end of that gorge.

He sighed and drew the wand, putting it in my hand. "What you do is folly. Don't let it be fatal, too."

I left his tent in haste and made my way to the corral. I found my chariot and its team. Swiftly, I hitched horses to chariot and leapt in. We plunged out into the camp, throwing men into disarray. Shouts followed in my wake, curses of anger or surprise left behind me. As I drew near Eshua's tent, his voice joined the outcries. He ran out towards me, arms waving desperately.

His orders to stop and his upthrown arms did little to slow my chariot as we ran out of the camp, startling the guards on post. I was sure that my brother intended to have men give chase, but my team was swift and I had the advantage in distance already. My chariot bounced and rattled hard on the stone as we rode, jostling me as I held tight to the reins.

A long, towering-walled gorge led into the basin where the Kascians camped. The gorge was the only way through that our scouts found: trying to go over the steeper slopes and sweeps would have taken days, and there was no guarantee of reaching the basin that way. Nor could we hope to bring horse or chariot over such terrain, it would have maimed steeds and snapped chariot axles with the effort.

That made my task easier, though I scarcely grasped my own intent.

I halted deep into the winding gorge and turned my team about. I cracked the whip and shouted until the horses raced back towards the camp, chariot jouncing and wobbling wildly behind them. What I planned would have scared a horse too much for the animal to be useful, and I saw no point in endangering them.

The walls of the gorge towered over me, as tall as any ziggurat in Eridu but made of solid stone, the ravine carved out as if by sword-stroke. The base of the ravine's walls were closer together, and it widened onto the open sky near the top, the nearly-sheer walls beginning to slant away from one another, as if slouched by their own immense weight.

The wand felt warm to the touch as I drew it out from my belt. An inner illumination glowed from within the pale chalcedony on its tip and a subtle tremor emanated from the length of polished bronze. I cannot pretend to know the esoterica of what magi do, but like many noble-born, I knew enough to dabble in the inner arts, to be unafraid of the magus and what they represented.

For lack of finesse, I chose to rely on power, which Namhu's wand held in ample supply.

I leveled the length of bronze at the top of one wall and bent my will to the task. I felt some of my self flow forth through the focus. For a moment, I became as the spirit of the sun: bright, iridescent, and reaching out beyond my flesh with a flush of force like blood rushed by quickened heart's beat.

My arm's fervent shaking drew me back to my flesh. The power of Namhu's wand pulled me like an unseen hand, drawing my arm across so that I made a sweeping flourish, coruscating light playing across the stone above. More out of fear than cleverness, I tried to bring my arm down, fighting against the tug of the wand.

I brought the walls of the gorge down with it.

Some of you gasp and murmur at my claim, but banish doubt from heart: it was as I say. No, the Kascians had no magus, no chanting shaman who covertly aided me. Ask any magi that campaigned with Eshua, they slew Madrubanna's shaman in one of our very first battles, blasting the man's very spirit from his body.

The wand nearly leapt from my hand. By the time I sundered my will from it, the gorge was giving its raging death cries. Divorcing myself from that wellspring of power lanced darts of agony into my flesh. It felt as though my arm was plunged into boiling pitch, as though flesh bubbled from bone. When I finally drew the chalcedony tip towards the ground, the wand burst apart in a flash of light. It washed over me and cast me to the ground as a child throws away an ill-favored toy. Agony followed, like nothing I have ever felt.

The wand and my right hand were gone. My arm terminated several inches above where the wrist ought to have been, skin charred and scorched black, curling like aged parchment.

I speak of it now, but there are no words for what I felt. Pain in ample measure, yes, and a mute sort of surprise. I think my heart dulled itself against the horror, lest it drive me into madness. Pain, hurt, agony, terror—these are words, but only pale ghosts of what they represent when I tell you of this maiming.

With ruined limb, I picked myself up off the ground in a lurch, moving like a man deep in his bowl of unwatered wine. I nearly lost my life then, when the shattered ravine walls fell into their death throes. Boulders the size of chariots tumbled down and crashed to ground with such force that the stone shook beneath me.

One missed me by a mere stride's length as I stood, bounding past as if cast from a sling or skipped across a river.

I ran. To the Kascian camp or to ours, I knew not. The quaking ground nearly took legs out from under me, and I could only wobble around the raining stones, each a death sentence written in granite. Behind me, I heard one of the ravine walls shift, cloven like the hoof of a goat. The sound of it coming apart shook breath from chest. A gust of wind and a cloud of billowing dust overtook me, flinging me to the ground. Dust filled mouth and nose, stinging eyes. With both breath and sense nearly knocked from me, heaving and coughing, I rose among the cacophony again.

I cannot say where the stone that struck me came from. Only that it must have bounced or rolled, since I find my mouth absent several teeth on one side. It struck clean, though, for the world went dark suddenly, night shading my eyes while I was mid-stride.

Of what occurred after, you must ask others. I have only dim, fever-warped recollections of being dragged on a litter, of sinking in and out of dreamless slumber, time and again, without grasping the passage of days. I am told that they found me beneath a pile of stones, battered, broken, but breathing. The Kascians, I hear, were gone by then, but that my brother found a cairn at the far end of the ravine where the basin begins. I have the topmost stone here with me. It bears my name in rough strokes.

None have see nor heard Madrubanna's remnants among their fellows. While recovering, I followed the war closely. Kascians remain, roaming the land beyond our many rivers, but the greatest bands have broken before our bronze. Clans cast themselves outward, like strands of linen being torn from one another as a garment shreds. Already, city begins to look at city with renewed suspicion or greed—I see it in your faces that you worry as much about our neighbors as about the last of our invaders.

Whatever wars come, I am not for them. The magi of Eridu worked wonders and wrought for me a hand of bronze and glass to replace the one I lost. It works nearly as well as the original. They could not do as well for my eye—see the right one, how milky and pale it is? I see but shadows and morning dew, too dark or too bright for fighting, for swinging sword or casting javelin. I may as well be blind, where matters of war are concerned.

I am not glad to suffer these wounds, but I do not begrudge them. Nor do I regret the choices that brought them upon me.

Once, worry gnawed on heart and I wondered if my brother's way was true. Suffering and time spent recovering have brought clarity and banished doubts.

It is for you, O king, and you, priests, to decide my fate. That I leave to you, but I take for myself certitude: I have followed the Sage's Path in word and deed and did only as Iodonna bid us all to do.

As goes my fate, so too goes yours as you accord with my way or with my accusers'. I tell you now as I told honored kinsman: the Path was meant to be walked. The ways of our foes must remain theirs and never become ours; to forgo virtue for equal measures is to aid them in disrupting the nature of Creation. We must all fail in our pursuit of the Sage's Path but that does not mean we can do so willingly. To stray of our own accord is to stand against the harmonious nature of the Molder of Men and Clay.

I see Eshua, Lugal, and Namhu still among those who gathered to hear my testimony before sovereign and oracle. I hope that, hearing my words and knowing the truth of my heart, they will forgive any wrongs I wrought against them. If I sinned or stood against my kin and my countrymen, it was to keep them from committing acts even worse than my own.

It is not for me to say if my intent outweighed my folly. I have told you my decisions. Now, you must make yours and I must go with them.

BIO

Colton Hehr is a speculative fiction author who received his first publishing credit as a winner of Writers of the Future in 2017. He is employed by the Oklahoma Department of Mental Health and Substance Abuse Services, and is currently nocturnal. He lives in Norman with his significant other, Ariana, and hopes one day to own many, many dogs.

13

DAILY BREAD

E.A. COPEN

Layovers could be hell, especially in the City of Angels.

I'd been there only a handful of times over the last two decades, always just passing through, but that time was different. I felt it when I stepped out of the cab and into the street. Stale urine, burned rubber, and curdled dairy smells filled the air, the perfume of all forgotten ghettoes of modern American cities. It was the scent of desperation, of poverty. Dreams gone bad.

At the corner, a bleach blonde in torn fishnets and a blue jean skirt held a cigarette between two fingers, one stiletto heel resting on the rotting carcass of the building where she conducted her business. For a couple of tenners, I could buy ten minutes behind the dumpster in the alley, and she could get her fix from the dealer on the opposite corner. She took one look at me and decided the cigarette was the better investment of her time. Her loss.

The building in question was run-down, painted grey by neglect and exhaust. A tin roof drooped in the evening heat, mirages rising from its sun kissed surface to dance in the twilight smog. Wire mesh painted diamonds in dirty glass behind chipped lettering and flickering neon promising beer on tap. Batwing doors harkened back to a time when the west was a different sort of wild, the hopeful sort, a time of Manifest Destiny and golden prospects. Now they were props placed over a tired door that'd been kicked in too many times. Two-by-fours graced the door at the cross sections and dusty plywood patched the broken footplate.

White wooden cut out lettering named the place: DAILY BREAD.

I shouldered my leather bag, plucked the cigarette from between my lips, and ground it into the pavement underfoot before checking my watch. I still had six hours and a parched throat to kill.

Inside, weary old men sat in pews shaped like stools topped with torn leather and duct tape. A pyramid of glass bottles bathed them in the neon light of their prophets named Coors, Corona, and Yuengling. Above the altar of glass, a reporter lead tonight's downtown sermon. Protestors had taken to the streets to march on the unbelievers again. They carried signs demanding miracles and speaking prophecies of destruction. Judgement was at hand and God was coming.

About time, if you asked me. I had a few choice words for the Almighty, most of them spelled with four letters or less.

"Josiah? Josiah Quinn, is that you?"

My heart kicked into a staccato marching rhythm. Cold sweat formed on the back of my neck just like it did every time I heard her voice for the first time. Christ, after so many years, you'd think I would've gotten used to it, or at least come to expect it. But she still managed to surprise me every time.

Maggie was a Nebraska ten with her straight auburn hair, light freckles, gray eyes, and full cheeks. Every farmhand's fantasy back in Omaha, probably. But then, there's not much in Nebraska but cornfields and simple living. No one had told her a Nebraska ten was a California six and she'd fancied herself an actress some years back. I stopped in once every few years, just to see how she was getting on.

I flashed her a big smile. "Maggie Dale! 'ow ya goin'?"

Maggie dropped off the beer she was carrying at the nearest

table and bounced over to me for a hug, all smiles. I forgot all about how thirsty I was. *Tell her*, whispered a voice in my mind. *Help her.*

But I couldn't, not and maintain my cover. She was better off never knowing who and what I really was.

I put my hands on her shoulders and leaned back for a look. "A jumper in the L.A. heat? Aren't you warm?"

She rolled her eyes and pushed my hands away. "Nice to see you too, stalker," she said and gave my shoulder a weak punch. "And here in the States, it's called a sweater, not a jumper. You want your usual?"

I slid onto a bar stool and nodded. "Surprised to find ya still here, Mags. What about that big break?"

Her cheeks dimpled with a wholesome smile. She slid behind the bar and grabbed a cloudy glass to fill it with beer from the tap. "Oh, it's coming. Brett says he's going to introduce me to a producer soon. A real household name, Josiah. Said he liked my audition reel, believe it or not."

Mags placed the beer in front of me. I stared into the piss-colored drink, wondering how she could still be so stupid. Of course, look at her parents. Maybe it was a genetic failing, still being young and dumb enough to believe in her dream. *Give it three years, girl. See if Tinseltown doesn't chew you up and spit you out, older, wiser, and more broken than before. It happened to me. It'll happen to you.*

It was a neon sunset. Shades of electric orange lay atop a blanket of cool blue. Airplanes raked streaks of pink across the sky like fingernails clawing at flesh while I sat on Skid Row, desperate for a fix.

I was a fifteen-year-old boy, and only two things mattered in life: music and sex. One of the two was bound to get me into trouble. Figures it'd be the music and not the sex.

It was the summer of '95 and the music scene had lured me across the Pacific from Sydney to Los Angeles. I fancied myself a drummer. But then, so did thousands of others who were better than me. Within two weeks, I was out of money and on the street with the rest of them. It didn't matter. Music was my drug, and so every day I sat on a corner where I thought someone might notice me and tapped with my drumsticks. Except I didn't do it with my hands. No, not me. I was too good for that. A prodigy. I'd crafted a spell that made the drumsticks move all on their own. The gimmick bought me a sandwich and maybe some stale coffee, but little else so far. I was still waiting on that big break, and so sure it was coming.

Black shoes and dark trousers stepped up to my station, too nice to be in that part of town so close to dark. He'd be dead before he got out of the hood, killed for pocket change and fresh socks. Not that I cared. Maybe he'd give some of that change to me and I could eat well for once.

Black Shoes stood and listened to me play a minute before he crossed his arms and said, "Nice parlor trick."

I reached out to grab the drumsticks, interrupting the spell to look up at him. He was dressed like an idiot in all black, probably baking in the heat, especially in that long leather trench coat. His hair was long and all black too, making his pale skin stand out even more. The guy looked like a damn vampire. If his money spent, what did I care? But he'd just insulted me. I wasn't getting any cash from him. Maybe I'd take that coat from his corpse later. It'd make a nice blanket. "Drop me some change or fuck off, old man."

Slowly, Black Shoes turned his head first one way and then the other as if looking for someone. "I don't see a line of patrons waiting to buy your next meal, Little Drummer Boy."

I gestured with one of the drumsticks. "Fuck. Off."

Black Shoes grinned, showing perfect white teeth, and extended his hands above my head. The drumsticks flew from my hands to his, except when he closed his fists around them, they were inanimate slabs of wood no longer. They'd transformed into beautiful striped sphinx moths that perched on his fingers.

My mouth fell open. It was one thing to use magic to make a few sticks dance to a rhythm, but it was another thing entirely to transform dead hunks of wood into living, breathing creatures. It broke every law of magic that I knew. "How?"

The wizard with the black shoes lifted the moths for me to see them better and smiled. "Come with me and I'll show you."

I let the drumsticks clatter to the ground, rose, and followed.

His name was Christian Lenore and brought me back to an expensive, modern flat on the top level of some downtown high rise where he let me shower and sleep in a featherbed. I sank into it and didn't move until the pounding of loud bass woke me well after dark.

Still dressed in my ratty street clothes, I wandered to the bedroom door and pulled it open on a party in full swing. Loud music, dark and sensual, pumped through the air like a heartbeat, alive and vibrant. Colored lights swam across the ceiling in dizzying patterns while bodies moved all over the apartment, red plastic cups in hand. I swam through the sea of people in a daze at first, until I spied Christian leaning against the counter chatting up a busty, dark-haired girl. She was closer in age to me than him, but that didn't seem to be slowing him down any.

"Josiah!" He waved me over and handed me a cup. "Glad you made it."

"A little hard to sleep through the party of the century." I drank expecting beer, but that wasn't what was in the cup. Whatever it was, it was stronger and burned going all the way down. I wanted to spit and cough, but the girl was watching so I just cleared my throat and pretended it didn't bother me.

Christian gave me a knowing smirk and gestured to the woman. "This is Evette. Evette, Josiah Quinn."

Evette's smile had dimples. I didn't stand a chance. "Are you British, Josiah? I couldn't help but notice the accent."

"Australian, actually. Well, I was. I consider myself a citizen of the world more like."

She shifted closer to me, brown eyes sparkling. "Really? Christian tells me you have the gift. Can you show me?"

* * *

"Josiah?" Mags ducked her head into my vision. "Is everything okay? You checked out on me for a minute."

"Been a long year is all. This Brett, he your agent?" The beer was awful. Americans and their shit excuses for beer.

Mags shrugged. The movement made her hair shift, revealing a dark spot behind her ear, an ugly yellow bruise that was already mostly healed. "He's more of a publicist, I guess. Enough about me though. What've you been up to?"

My latest trip had been to Berlin where I'd retrieved an artifact for the Vatican. A bishop had been holding a relic hostage, threatening to destroy it if his superiors went public about how he abused a coupla grade school boys. The church paid me a hefty sum to retrieve the object and convince the bishop to come forward on his own. He took some convincing, the kind that left my knuckles raw and bruised.

I shrugged and leaned forward on my arms. "Went to Berlin on holiday. You ever been?"

"No, but I'm sure you'll tell me all about it." She smiled as she filled a glass for someone else.

"Lovely place with friendly people. Some might say too friendly."

"There's no such thing." Mags reached to pass the beer to someone. Stretching her arms tugged the sleeve of her turtleneck back. Another bruise, this one darker. One bruise was an accident. Two was trouble.

I grabbed her arm and pulled the sleeve back further, revealing the shape of it. A full ring of dusky fading gray lined in red. If she'd given me a chance to flip her arm over to examine the underside, what were the chances I'd see five distinct impressions in the shape of fingers? Pretty damn good, I wagered.

But Mags jerked her arm away and tugged the sleeve down. Her jaw clamped, and she went back to work, trying to pretend I hadn't just seen what I saw.

"Mags…" I tilted my head to the side. "Is that who Brett is? Why'd you let him do that to you?"

"He doesn't do it all the time." Her voice was small, doubtful. "Just when he's been drinking and I get on his case. He's a good guy. He'd never hurt me."

"Maggie, be honest with me." I tugged on her sleeve.

She pulled away. "I have to work, Josiah."

I frowned and watched her scurry to the other end of the bar to smile and chat with other drunks. *I love him. He'd never hurt me.* Now where had I heard those words before?

* * *

I was hooked the second Christian introduced me to Evette, and he knew it. The two of us hit it off straight away. She liked the same music as me, wanted to travel the world like me, loved magic just like me. Even if she hadn't, she was a girl and she knew I existed. That automatically meant I was going to try to get her to sleep with me. I just didn't expect to succeed. After all, why should she be interested in a homeless fifteen-year-old boy whose magical skill began and ended with parlor tricks?

By midnight, the crowd had begun to thin out and the music had gotten darker, more screaming vocals and heavy guitar riffs. Small crowds of people gathered in the living room to jump and crash into each other, laughing like idiots whenever they fell and got up bloody. It was a music driven possession, this strange yet familiar worship of heavy metal. Familiarity. Comfort, even in that strange place, though I still felt on edge.

Evette's hand closed on my arm and she leaned in to say in my ear, "Are you okay?"

Reason told me she was only touching me, so close to me because the music was too loud to hear her otherwise. The rest of me was convinced if I asked her to go back to the bedroom with me right then, she'd do it.

"Just a little overwhelmed," I shouted back. "Is Christian's place always like this?"

"Not always." She shifted, looking through the crowd as if she'd spotted someone she'd been searching for. "He's a good man, you know? Christian. He'd never hurt anybody."

Her words seemed strange, out of place. I considered for a minute how unusual it was, and then dismissed it. She was only trying to put me at ease in a strange place, after all. I tried to follow her gaze, but there was so much movement under flashing lights that it was impossible. "What are you looking for?"

"I'll be right back," she said. Before I could object, she was gone, pushing her way through the crowd. Evette slid into a corner with her back to me, talking to a man in a netted shirt.

A few moments later, she burst out of the crowd, all smiles, and tripped into me. I caught her and helped her get her balance back. She smiled and we both laughed at her clumsiness like it was the funniest thing we'd ever seen.

Until it wasn't funny anymore because somehow her lips were pressed against mine. Her tongue glided against mine soft and wet, all except for the small lump of sweet tasting candy she slid from her mouth to mine. It was dry as chalk. I pulled away and plucked whatever it was from my tongue to examine it. A little white pill with a smiling face stamped on it.

"It's no big deal," Evette said. "It makes everything better. Unless you're not into it."

Who was I kidding? I was into whatever would get me into her pants. "No, it's cool." I put the pill back into my mouth and swallowed it, sticking my tongue out for her to check.

Evette threw her arms around me and stuck her tongue down my throat like she was trying to suck out my soul. With how things turned out, maybe she was.

* * *

I dropped a twenty on the bar and left before Mags came back. I couldn't look at the bruises anymore. Why had she come back to this God-forsaken city? Why had I? It called to us, this spawning ground.

Outside, beetles threw themselves in vain at the orange light of a street lamp proving easy prey for hungry bats. Roaches buzzed their wings in dumpsters to attract females, driven by thousands of years of evolution to mate and die in the same rotten sewage where they were conceived. Carapaces, legs, and antennae twitching, writhing in confusion, they were little more than puppets and evolution held the strings.

I rejected the smog and exhaust-rich air in favor of tar and nicotine. The familiar buzz flowed into my chest and out through the rest of me. My heart pumped it on, unable to tell the difference between deadly poison and life-saving oxygen. Relief dawned top down, calming the pacing man inside. I closed my eyes and exhaled, but instead of release, I imagined Maggie's pain.

It wasn't just the bruises on her head and arms that hurt. It was in her chest, that feeling of lost control, diminished worth. The death of the superego in favor of the id.

Another buzzing set of wings lost in the squalor of garbage.

* * *

I woke up in a strange bed. Something was inside my head, pounding behind my eyes. I felt sunken, drained. It was as if someone had sucked the life out of me from the lowest section of my belly.

Evette was next to me, snoring with her arms above her head on the white pillows. The blanket laid low on her stomach, leaving her chest exposed. Sun cut through the blinds, sharp and blinding to me, yet she was like a cat in a sunbeam. Content just to be.

I considered waking her up for another go when the door

opened and Christian stepped in. With a curse, I scrambled to cover myself and Evette. That's right. This was Christian's bed. How the hell had we wound up here? *Where else would you go, idiot?*

"Christian, I—" I broke off whatever it was I was going to say when I saw the box in his hands. It was covered in circles and runes. Even with my inexperience, I could feel the magic radiating off the box from a distance. It left me awestruck. "What is that?"

"This," he said as he placed the box in front of me, "is your first lesson. How do you feel?"

Evette shifted in the bed next to me, sitting up. She didn't even bother covering herself.

I frowned. "I don't know. Does it matter?"

"Of course it matters, Josiah. You have the gift, yes, but you need to learn to harness it. Make it yours. To do that, you'll need a better understanding of its source. Magic is in your blood. All around you. But harnessing it has a cost." He opened the box. Inside, something formless and bright pulsed in time with my heartbeat. "Go ahead," he urged. "Touch it."

I raised my arm and slowly reached for the glowing orb only to pull my hand back at the last second. "What's the cost?"

A curious light danced in Christian's eyes. "It costs what all power costs. Pain. Death. Suffering. We live at the expense of other, smaller beings. Predators survive because prey exists. The strong survive. That's the way of the world, Josiah. But you can't know how strong you are until you've been pushed to your limit. You must know pain. Conquer death. Embrace suffering. Endure the pain in this box and you will unlock a new understanding of the power within you." He pulled the box back a few inches. "Unless you are too afraid. In which case, you can collect your things and go."

"No!" I shouted, probably too eager.

Christian smiled. "Prove it. Put your hand in the box."

Fear beat in my neck. I swallowed it, but it didn't fill the pit in my stomach. Sweat trickled down my spine as I stared down the ball of thumping magic. My fingers hovered over the box, feeling the steady beat. A bass line. It was music in magic form. Beautiful.

I put my hand in the box.

* * *

I flinched awake choking on a scream and gripping my hand in front of my face. A terror rhythm throbbed in my veins, making my stomach reel in disgust. Red mottled skin hovered in my vision, broken in the center by thick scars cut and burned there through years of use. The back of my hand. The arcane arts were not for that faint of heart.

Police sirens screamed one or two streets over. Probably what woke me in the first place.

Dizzied by the nightmare, I rose and went to the toilet for a piss that I had to work too hard to coax out. Dehydration probably. I'd spent the day before drinking coffee, whiskey, and beer. For a minute, I worried it was something worse. I was getting older. With all the abuse I'd put my body through, it was only a matter of time before it gave up on me. It might be cancer. God, I hoped it wasn't cancer. I had seen great men, true forces of nature, die penniless and alone because of cancer. But then, those men had never put their hands in Christian's bloody box.

All the great poets of the world could gather and debate on how to describe the box and they would all come to the same conclusion. The box was sentient pain. Not normal pain, no. Normal pain, a man could adjust to. The body compensated, shutting things down, acclimating to whatever new level of hell the nervous system encountered. The pain in the box wasn't like that. It shifted, flexing, growing, devouring.

My hand went to my stomach. Sometimes, I had nightmares about it eating me from the inside out. The empty pit that was left in me after that first night with Evette grew into a black hole and sucked the rest of me in. At the center of the black hole was that box, like it was supposed to mean something. But it didn't.

Nothing meant anything, not when I could cheat. Not when I had magic. When you had magic, you made the rules. That was Christian's way, and he had passed it to me. The bastard had filled me with his hate and called it love, and the memory of it and that stupid box made me sick.

In the bedroom, the cracked red display of the alarm clock announced it was three in the morning. My flight to Okinawa had left without me hours ago. Okinawa could wait. I needed to meet Brett. Maybe I would make a box for him.

* * *

Christian's cult had nine members, four teenage boys close to me in age, and four girls, all of them between eighteen and twenty-two, plus Christian himself. Over the course of the first month, I met all of them. We got on well enough, but mostly, I was with Evette, spending every spare moment I could with her. Christian never let me have her alone again. Not until I proved myself, he said.

There were drugs, music, parties and power.

And we would do magic. Real magic, not just the low-level tricks he showed me at first. The more he gave, the more I demanded. I was an addict. The same way my body needed air, my mind needed the magic. It sustained me, became my reason for waking, for breathing, bathing, existing. Every moment became dedicated to learning the next incantation, the next symbol, mastering the next summoning.

Inside two years, I was Christian's second in command. He gave me unrestricted access to everything, including Evette. I felt like I had won.

What is it they say about reaching the top? Once you do, there's nowhere to go but down.

It was the Fourth of July and there were fireworks exploding in the sky. Christian was throwing a party on the roof, but Evette and I didn't go. Instead, we hid in the bathroom with a paper sack full of plastic test strips while she pissed on them and then waited three minutes for lines or crosses to appear.

I leaned against the locked door and crossed my arms. "Do you really think the fourth one is going to say anything different, Evette?"

She massaged her forehead and let out a quivering breath. Her voice was strained, panicked. "I can't be pregnant, Josiah. You don't understand. I can't."

Evette was right. I didn't understand the problem. If she didn't want the kid, she'd just do what Deirdre and Ellie had done. Both of them had been pregnant too. Christian sent them away somewhere until it was all over. Like a little vacation. They'd be back soon.

"It's no big deal," I said. "We just need to go to Christian with it. He'll take care of it, just like he did with the other two."

Her hand slid down to cover her mouth. She choked on a sob. "I can't. I won't." She got up from the toilet and gripped me by the shirt. "You have to help me get rid of it."

I raised my hands. "You need to tell him, Evette. He should be a part of this."

"No!" She threw herself into me, sobbing against me. "Please, you can't tell him!"

Invisible hands choked me. Still a boy myself and I had fathered a child with this woman. Someone who could never be mine. Not truly. I didn't love her. Not like I loved magic.

I could have her if we left, I thought. We could walk out the front door while everyone else was upstairs, drinking and doing their small magic. No one would stop us. But if I left, there would be no more lessons. No more power. No matter how good I got, I would always be second best to Christian. We would live on the run, always afraid that he was coming for us. What kind of life was that? A seventeen-year-old father, a twenty-two-year-old mother, on the run from a sorcerer with limitless power? We would be dead inside a week.

I pushed her away from me. "It's not my problem, Evette. Do what you've got to do."

She fell to her knees on the bathroom floor behind me as I opened the door. I left her there, sobbing and alone.

Everything that came after was entirely my fault.

* * *

The air in the motel room grew heavy. I struck a light and watched the flame dance in the wind coming through the open window. More sirens had joined the cry of the first, painting the alley below in flashing blue and red watercolor on black. Whatever was going on down there, it had nothing to do with me.

I lit my last cigarette and smoked it, trying to remember the beat to a song I'd once written. The rhythm eluded me, so I wrote a new one in my mind. This new song began slow, quiet, steady, a predator studying his prey. The predator moved in the shadows, gathering evidence using a new magic: Internet and background checks for the low-low price of nineteen ninety-nine. Credit cards. Bank accounts. School records, all easy enough to find if you knew where to look.

Public records told the tale of a violent man named Brett Trace with multiple arrests, dropped charges for assault and sexual battery. He was a small-time porn director, preying on would be starlets. Brett was a predator too, but a much smaller one. He was a house cat hunting an injured mouse and he'd drawn the attention of a lion.

The cigarette burned low and the sun rose. The siren song died hours ago, replaced by car horns and shouting. The rumbling of a predator's empty stomach. Los Angeles had awoken.

I looked into the face of a dead man on my screen. "Hello, Brett," I said before crushing out the cigarette and rising for the hunt.

* * *

Months passed. I spent them learning Enochian, which Christian called the language of angels. A language of power words wrapped in magic. Flawlessly, I folded them into my practice while everyone else struggled to grasp the most basic concepts. They hated me for it.

I stopped seeing Evette. Our child grew, and no one said anything about it. I thought more than once about bringing it up to Christian, but it didn't feel like my place. I wasn't growing an eight-pound sentient tumor in my belly, so I felt I had no say in what was done with it. Evette would do what she wanted, and if she didn't ask me to acknowledge it, I didn't care.

It was an April night with the cries woke me. My eyes fluttered open to the steady tapping of rain on glass. I'd fallen asleep on the floor, twisted in the arms of whatever initiate groupie was available. Her arm was still on my chest. I pushed it off and staggered to my feet, pulling up my pants as I stood.

Another muffled cry cut through the room. It was coming from the bedroom. Why was the door closed and the light on? It was three in the morning. And where the hell was everyone? I searched the mess of bodies on the floor. Everyone with any real power, our entire inner circle, was missing. Maybe Christian had called them together for a late-night ritual. If so, why hadn't he woken me?

Every step closer to the door felt heavier. Magic made the air tremble, synced to my heartbeat just like the light in the box. It vibrated over me as if I were standing in front of speakers right in the front row, punctuated by another pained cry. Fear pierced my spine. Evette.

Possessed by some new sense of devotion, I stormed to the door and threw it open, only to pause dumbfounded by what I saw.

The seven other members stood in a circle around the bed, which had been moved to the center of the room over an intricate summoning circle. An identical circle had been painted on the ceiling and on each wall.

Evette was tied to the bed naked, one limb to each corner. Someone had shoved a gag in her mouth, which explained why her screams had been muffled. She was cut open, thick sacs of bloody jelly lying around her. So much blood… it was everywhere. There couldn't possibly be any of it left inside her.

Christian stood at the head of the bed, his ritual knife in hand, except it wasn't Christian. It was some strange, angelic imitation, a version with bloody white wings. Gore dripped down from the feathers in chunks, staining him and the floor. He was a newborn child, covered in afterbirth. His box of pain stood open next to him, the light strobing too fast. In his arms, a bloody mass squirmed and gurgled, desperate to draw its first breath.

It took me three, maybe four seconds to deduce the purpose of the circles, the patterns and what they meant.

"Good of you to join us, Josiah." Christian raised his head.

I stared at the scene in shock. "What did you do?"

"She was going to kill it. I couldn't let her do that." He shifted the child so I could see. "Come hold your daughter, Josiah."

My legs were numb. I couldn't move, not even if I'd wanted to. Evette was dead, and Christian was covered in her blood, holding my child. And Christian had wings. This couldn't be real.

Christian crossed the room and grabbed my arms. He forced me to hold her. I didn't want to. I wanted to drop her and run screaming. Evette was dead, and it was my fault. The baby girl cried and turned her head, searching for Evette to feed her. But Evette was dead.

Steel flashed, and I found Christian holding his knife out to me.

"I don't understand." Tears fell when I blinked. "What's happening?"

"Complete the ritual," he commanded. "You must kill the child and claim the power of her soul so you can rise as I have done. Then we will be gods, you and me. No secret beyond our reach. We can enter Heaven itself, Josiah. Angelic blood flows in our veins! Why do you think you take to this so easily? You're more than this weak world. More than human." He pressed the knife into my limp hand. "Be strong! Do it! Join me!"

I looked down at the squirming baby in my arms. She was

smaller than a doll. Tiny, red, barely formed. She couldn't even open her eyes. Killing her would be so easy. I didn't even need the knife. All I had to do was drop her, put my foot on her head. One twitch of my arm and she would be gone. Just like Evette.

I closed my eyes. Magic brushed against me, as thick in the air as the blood smell. Power was shed at death. The more painful the death, the more raw power became available. It was one of the first things Christian had taught me. I touched the magic Evette had shed and nearly recoiled. So much… She must've been in such terrible pain. There was easily enough power to fuel a summoning. I couldn't save Evette, but I could use the pain of her death to avenge her.

I grabbed the magic, gathering the power to me, letting it rise like a pillar of flame around me, bending it to my will.

"What are you doing?" Christian snarled.

I didn't answer. There were no more words for him, for a madman so drunk on power and secrets that he would murder one of his own. I wouldn't be that. I couldn't become that. No, just being part of that made me unclean. I needed to be *clean*.

The magic surged when I spoke the words of my native tongue. Enochian bounced off the walls, the sharp edges of words shattering the glass window panes. I squeezed my eyes shut tight. All around me, desperate screams erupted along with the wet sound of exploding meat and crunch of breaking bone.

Christian screamed my name, but the whirlwind of flame I had called up destroyed him too. It burned him to ash along with the rest of them.

I pulled my daughter to my chest, shielding her from it while she cried. *Don't worry, child. I'll protect you. I will always protect you.*

* * *

For the next twenty minutes, I prepared the circle on the hotel room floor and fed it my blood. Ten more minutes of focused chanting, and a dark spirit surrounded by flame coalesced in the center, answering my call. "Josiah Quinn," spoke the demon. "We meet again."

"Valefor," I said in the form of a greeting. "I'd offer you a ciggie, but I'm fresh out."

The lord of the Hellhounds' red eyes lit up brighter. "This had better be good, conjurer."

I rubbed my chin, wishing I hadn't smoked everything all in one go. "D'ya fancy another hunt?"

The fire died. I kicked out the groupies and stole everything worth selling out of Christian's apartment. With the money, I bought a few supplies for the baby and a bus ticket to the cheapest place on the list. Turned out, that was Omaha, Nebraska.

Once I got there, I spent three days doing research, talking to the local clergy, and narrowing down my options. There was a couple just outside of town that everyone seemed to know. Good people. No connection to the occult, to magic, to any of it. God fearing, they said, but not too much. Just enough. Boring, normal people.

Their little farm also happened to be situated on the same plot of land as an old church. With a large enough cash donation, I was able to get a priest to consecrate the four corners of the property. After he left, I laid my own protection spells, as many as I could without drawing too much attention. All the effort created the equivalent of magical dead space. Even if she was my flesh and blood, she'd grow up with no access to magic. I made sure of that.

Then, with the help of a social worker and a judge, both of which were paid handsomely and sworn to secrecy under the threat of a death curse, Harold and Barbra Dale became parents.

I stood on their porch, ready to hand my daughter over to the Dales, but hesitated. There it was again, that awful empty feeling in my gut. *This is where she's safest*, I told myself. *I don't know anything about raising children. I didn't even graduate high school.*

Barbra held out her hands and pushed her thick cheeks up into a welcoming smile.

I placed my daughter in her arms. The hollow feeling in gut turned into a familiar black hole. "What'll you call her?"

As soon as Barbra took her, I knew I'd made the right choice. She looked down at the sleeping baby, her face full of love. I could never look at her like that, not after all the ugly things I'd seen.

Barbra smiled. "Maggie."

Harold nodded and repeated. "Maggie."

"It's a good name," I agreed. "Well, take care."

I walked to the property line, lit a cigarette, and gave Maggie the last gift I could. With a drop of my blood, I sealed the final spell over the property and everyone still in the house, erasing me from their memory.

* * *

At seven thirty, I got out of the cab in front of a squat, run-down hovel with a broken-down car out front. A rottweiler barked at me from the other side of a chain-length fence when I shouldered my bag. I looked at it, focusing my will and forcing it to meet my eyes.

The dog quit barking and sat, panting.

The front door swung open and my prey stepped out into the open. "Butch, I fucking told you—" He broke off when he saw me.

Brett was a typical asshole pimp. The fact that he rented a room to shoot his films didn't make him any less of a pimp. White singlet, gold chains around his neck, tattoos, ball cap, pack of cigarettes in his shirt pocket. Fuck me, he had a soul patch. What a fuckwit.

He squinted at me and came to the gate. "Can I help you?"

"Brett Trace?" I mispronounced it on purpose.

"No, it's Brett Trace. Like race. You don't pronounce the e."

What a fuckin' idiot. Never give a wizard your name.

I shifted my bag. "Thanks for giving me your name. Now, let me tell you who I am. I'm the fella about to give you a very bad day if you don't break off all contact with Maggie Dale immediately and permanently."

"'Scuse me?" He crossed his arms. Typical alpha male move. Trying to make himself look bigger. If ever we fought, I'd melt the flesh from his bones just as fast as I had Christian Lenore. "You want to run that by me again, pal?"

"How about a demonstration?" I extended a hand.

The gate he stood in front of swung open, hitting him in the groin. Brett doubled over, cursing, but I was just getting started. A quick chant, a small infusion of will, touch the charm in my pocket, tap into the connection I forged earlier with the rottweiler and...

The rottweiler's eyes flashed red as Valefor possessed it. He surged forward, barking and snarling, but stopping short of doing any actual mauling. Brett's terrified cries must've woken the whole block. His bladder and bowels let go as he sank into a quivering, shrieking mess. I didn't blame him. I screamed the first time I saw a real Hellhound too.

"Maggie Dale," I repeated, shouting over the hellhound's howls. "You're going to leave her alone, Brett. Forever. Or I'll be back, and next time I won't keep my demon on a leash."

"Okay, okay! Anything! Just make it stop!"

I recalled Valefor with a word and stepped forward to lift the cigarettes from Brett's shirt. "Thanks for the smokes," I said and walked back to my waiting cab.

The neighbors had just started to come out to investigate when we pulled away.

I hopped a plane to Omaha and a cab dropped me off at the Dale farm at dusk. It was abandoned now. Barb had passed on, and Dale had Alzheimer's. He was in a home over near Lincoln, fading fast. Mags visited whenever she could, but not as often as she liked. The judge I'd bribed died of a massive coronary, and the social worker was in a train accident that left her in a coma.

Only the house and I knew the truth now, just the way it ought to be.

I walked up to the rotting porch and sat on the sagging stairs to light a cigarette. All around, wild corn grew, tended by ghosts, serenaded by crickets singing for their mates. Poor buggers didn't know they'd be dead come winter. Yet the human race soldiered on, driven by instinct, sustained by a false hope that the next time, they'd do better. The lie that we would give our children a better world persisted, stretching back into the dark ages. Unless something changed, the lie would never be enough.

The sun set and I stood, shouldering my bag once more. Okinawa was calling. I flicked the smoked cigarette off into the tall weeds and started down the dusty, dirt road. "Until next time, Maggie Dale."

BIO

E.A. Copen lives in Southwest Kentucky. While working a boring retail job, she entertained herself with stories of the fantastic, some of which became books like Guilty by Association, Death Rites, and Broken Empire. She speaks three languages fluently: English, Latin, and sarcasm. E.A. is currently studying to become proficient in memes.

14

THE DEMONS OF ARAE

CHRISTOPHER RUOCCHIO

THE MOUTH OF HELL

Fire screamed all around us, and the violent shock of atmospheric entry that shook the ship beneath my feet was like the coming of an avalanche. Faceless men stood about me, gripping their restraints. The red glow of the emergency lighting reflected off their featureless ivory masks.

The thunder stopped. We were falling through clear air beneath yellow skies.

Arae.

"You're sure they're on Arae?" I remembered asking before we set sail from Nessus on this expedition.

Captain Otavia Corvo had only shrugged her broad shoulders. "It's your Empire's intelligence, Lord Marlowe. They said they tracked this lost legion of theirs to within a dozen light-years of the Arae system. If they're not on Arae, they're somewhere in the Dark between, and we'll never find them."

An entire legion had vanished. Four ships. Twenty-six thousand men.

Gone.

At first Legion Intelligence had suspected the Cielcin. The xenobites needed to eat, after all, and four troop transport ships with the legionnaires already on ice for the long voyage were indistinguishable from meat lockers where the aliens were concerned. But when we arrived in Arae system, we found something we hadn't expected.

"Pirates?" Corvo didn't believe it. I could see it in the way her brows arched above black eyes. "What sort of pirates could capture a Sollan legion?"

We all knew the answer. I could feel the eyes of my officers on me, as if each man and women were daring me to say it first. I glanced from one to the other: from the Amazonian Corvo to her bookish second-in-command, Durand; from green-skinned Ilex to solemn Tor Varro.

"Extrasolarians." After Vorgossos the word carried a poisonous aftertaste for me and for every member of my Red Company. The Extras had been an Imperial bogeyman for millennia, the sort of monsters mothers scared their children with. But I knew now. Those men who—fleeing Imperial control—fled to the blackness between the stars, to rogue planets and lost moons far from the light of Imperial order, had bought their freedom with a piece of their own humanity. As a boy, I'd believed the Chantry's proscription against intelligent machines and against the augmentation of the flesh was nothing but reactionary cowardice.

I know better now.

Monsters are real, and I had met them. Met not only with the Cielcin who threaten mankind from without, but met also with the monsters we'd made in our own image and in the image of our inner demons.

Repulsors fired, and our descent slowed, forcing my bile up as we came out of free fall. I shut my eyes, mindful of the quiet chatter of my men through my suit's comms, of the way the thermal layer clung to me beneath the armorweave and ceramic plates. I still felt half a clown wearing it.

I was no soldier, had never trained to be one. I'd wanted to be a linguist, in Earth's name!

But I was a knight now, one of His Radiance's own Royal Victorians. *Sir* Hadrian Marlowe. And after Vorgossos I knew there was no going back.

I undid my restraints and moved into the middle of the cabin, conscious of the faceless soldiers watching me through suit cameras. My own suit worked the same—though my black visor was fashioned in the image of an impassive human face and not a blank arc of zircon. Almost it seemed I wore no helmet at all. Images from outside were projected directly onto my retinas, and but for the indicators in my periphery that indicated my heart rate and the integrity of my Royse shields, I saw plain as day.

"They're putting us down close to the door as they can!" I said, voice amplified by the speakers in my breastplate. "Petros's team should have those gun emplacements on the south ridge down by the time we make landfall. Pallino's got the north. The Sphinxes have air support! All we have to do is back the Horse!" They knew all of this already, had gone over the assault plan with their centurion before we'd left the ship, but it bore repeating.

"You ready, Had?" that same centurion asked me, clapping me on the shoulder as I took my place front and center by the exit ramp.

Beneath my helmet mask I smiled and returned the gesture. "Just like the coliseum back on Emesh!" I seized hold of one of the ceiling straps to steady myself as the dropship banked into an arc.

"Let's hope!" Siran replied. The woman had been by my side a long time. Long before Vorgossos, when I had been little more than a slave in the fighting pits of Count Balian Mataro.

Turning back to face the fifty men that stood in the cramped hold of the *Ibis*-class lander, I got a clear look at myself in the mirrored glass at the rear of the compartment. Like all Sollan Imperial combat armor, my suit's design recalled the style of ancient Rome, the shape of it speaking to cellular memories of ancient power. The muscled breastplate was black as anything I had seen, embossed with the trident-and-pentacle I had taken for my sigil when His Radiance the Emperor restored me to the nobility. Beneath that I wore a wide-sleeved crimson tunic darker than the ones worn by legionnaires. Strapped pteruges decorated my shoulders and waist, marking me for an officer. Black boots and gauntlets contrasted the Imperial ivory and scarlet, and I alone wore a cape: a lacerna black above and crimson beneath.

How had I ended up here? I'd left home to go to school, to join the scholiasts. Not to fight a war. Still, I raised my voice. "Some of you won't have fought the Extras before! Soldiers of the Empire, whatever comes at you you *will* hold your ground!"

My tutor always said I had too-developed a taste for melodrama. Maybe he was right. Or maybe whatever gods there are share my love of theater. Whichever is the case, no sooner had a said these words did the landing alarm blare and each of us felt the *Ibis* buoy on its final approach.

The landing ramp slammed downwards, admitting the orange Araenian sunlight.

I turned and drew my sword, kindling the weapon's exotic matter blade with a button press. Liquid metal the color of moonlight gleamed in my gauntleted fist, and I was first onto the shattered tarmac and the approach to the pirates' fortress.

The mountain rose before us, the last lonely peak in a chain that broke upon the salt flats of the *Soto Planitia.* Arae had never been settled—its air was carbon monoxide and ammonia, and there was little water. But for the remains of a few mining expeditions the pirate fortress was the only settlement on the planet. I could see the fingering shapes of antennae and other comms equipment bristling on the ridge line above, and the smoking ruins of gun emplacements where Petros had taken our Fifth Chiliad and wiped out the artillery.

Battle raged about us, plasma fire splitting the cancered daylight like lightning, black smoke rising from bodies and from the wrecks of ground-effect vehicles and three-legged machines that I think had governed themselves.

And ahead—between the two reaching arms of that final mountain—stood the *Horse.*

Our colossus.

The titan stood nearly forty meters high, its legs more like the arms of a crawling man than those of a horse in truth. The earth trembled with each mighty step it took, and the men who stood against it could not so much as scratch its armor with their arms. Beyond it, the hardened outer wall of the fortress rose two hundred feet above the landing field, black as the space we'd come from. A stray shot pinged off my shield, and not ten yards off the tarmac exploded as a plasma cannon struck ground, sending dust and bits of shattered concrete fountaining skyward. Above, three of Sphinx Flight streaked overhead, single long wings tacking like sails against the wind, filling the air with the thunder of their drives.

"Why haven't they cracked the wall?" I asked, toggling to the officer's channel.

"It's shielded, lord," came a thin, polished voice. "Crim took a few shots at it with the Horse's artillery, but we'd have done as well to scratch at it with our fingernails."

I cursed. "How are they powering a shield of this size, Lorian?" I asked, "I thought your people didn't pick up a fusion reactor on your scans."

From his position on the ship in orbit, Commander Lorian Aristedes wasted no time in answering. "Could be geothermal. Arae's core runs hotter than most thanks to all those moons. I've ordered sappers. If they can attach a plasma bore directly to the door, the shield won't matter."

"We'll clear the tarmac then," I said in answer.

I did not hurry, but allowed the bulk of our soldiery to fan past me, soldiers moving in groups of three behind their decurions. One of the colossi's massive feet descended, cracking the pavement. The earth shook, air filled with a noise like drums.

For a moment, all was silent and still. Far above, a cloud passed before the swollen circle of the sun.

An awful cry resounded off the surrounding rocks, high and shrill.

"The hell is that?" Siran's words came in clear over my armor's internal comm.

A terrible sense of foreboding blossomed within me. Some kind of alarm? I half-expected to see the light of sirens flashing in the gray stones above us, but there was nothing.

"On our left!"

"I see them!"

"The right, too!"

I turned my head, trying to see just what it was the others were seeing through the smoke and the ranks of men to either side.

Then I saw them, and swore.

They must have come from bolt-holes hidden in the arms of the mountain. Hundreds of them. They had no arms, nor shields—but they needed neither. The SOMs feared neither death nor pain, and came forward with the focused scramble of a swarm of ants trying to bridge a puddle with their own bodies.

They were men once. Before the Extras carved out their brains and filled their heads with kit, before they meddled in the subtle language of their genes to harden them against the poisonous air. They had no will any longer. They never would again. They were only tools, puppet soldiers controlled by some intelligence—human or artificial I dared not guess—in the fortress ahead of us.

"Hoplites!" Siran exclaimed, singling out our heavy, shielded infantry. "Shield walls!"

All about us, the army shifted, hoplites shifting from the point position in their little triases towards the outside of our line.

"Fire!"

The hoplites opened fire, phase disruptor bolts crackling in the warm air. Siran seized my arm, "We need to get you to the Horse, Had."

She wanted to escort me to safety, to get me out of danger and the enemy charge.

She wanted me to abandon my men.

"No!" I shook her off, then toggled my comm once more. "Commander!"

Lorian Aristedes replied at once, "Yes, my lord?"

"Order Sphinx Flight back around! Strafe the enemy line!"

The ship's tactical officer acknowledged and relayed my orders.

The SOMs were still coming, loping across the flat ground to either side. How many armies had died thus? Smashed between the horns of the enemy? Shots rained down from above, and turning I saw men standing on the platforms above the Horse's thighs and the fell light of the colossi's rear cannons gleaming. It wouldn't be enough, and it was only then I realized the source of that awful keening sound.

The SOMs were screaming, howling like a band of blue-faced Picts out of the deepest history.

Then I realized Siran's mistake. Ordering the hoplites forward was standard procedure: they had the expensive shielding and the disruptor rifles, the heavy firepower. They were meant to shield the more numerous peltasts, who—without shields and with lighter armor—were cheaper to outfit and less costly to replace. But the peltasts carried bladed energy lances.

They had spears.

We had no time.

"Peltasts!" I called, transmitting my words to everyone in the line. "Forward! Forward!" There was a fraction of a second's hesitation. I suppose I cannot blame them, the order was unorthodox in our age. But they got the message when I added the crucial word: "Bayonets!"

A double line of light infantry stepped forward, allowing the hoplites to turn and fall back towards the center of the column. They moved with gearwork precision, the result of weeks of careful drilling and a course of RNA learning drugs. From above, it must have been beautiful, and for a moment I envied Lorian Aristedes and Captain Corvo their bird's eye view. The peltasts lowered their spears, beam weapons firing into the galloping horde. I saw SOMs fall smoking from laser burns, only to be trampled over by the ranks behind. The puppets did not care for the loss of their brethren, did not care that they were charging without so much as a knife at two triple lines of armed Sollan legionnaires.

My men all did their best, but stopping the onslaught was like trying to block the tide. The enemy crashed against us from either side, throwing themselves against our spears like fanatics, only from their brothers to vault *over* them and hurl themselves at us. From the rear, the hoplites fired over the heads of the lines before them until the air was thick with the static aftershock of disruptor fire.

Where was the air support?

One of the puppet-men leaped fully over our line and landed in the narrow gap left between. For a moment it just stood there, processing, as if not quite sure what to do. It turned its head to look at me, and I think it understood who I was. The man it had been was shorter than I, bald as an egg and pale, skin burned and peeling in the chemical air. How it breathed at all I couldn't say, though the gleaming black implants in its chest and throat perhaps had something to do with it.

It lurched towards me, and before Siran or any of the hoplites could intervene, I pushed past them and lunged, sword out-thrust. The highmatter blade passed through the SOM's flesh as easily as through water, and it fell with no legs to support it. For a single, awful moment, the upper half of the once-human form dragged itself forwards, clawing towards me until one of my guards shot it with a disruptor.

A metallic screaming filled the air, and glancing up a moment I saw the blade-like profile of five lighters burning across the sky. Sphinx Flight. Plasma fire picked its way in twin rows along the enemy line, parallel to our own. One of the SOMs fell smoking at my feet, and I slashed it in half for good measure. The earth groaned once more as the Horse advanced, closer and still closer to the wall and gate of the enemy fortress just as Sphinx Flight wheeled round for another pass.

I seized Siran by the arm. "Order everyone towards the Horse! We need to deepen the lines!"

She nodded and went about her orders. Turning, I proceeded up the no-man's land between our lines, cutting down those enemies who'd made it through. "Commander!" I almost yelled into the line. "Find Petros and tell him to get his men down here. It's time they were the ones surrounded!"

If young Aristedes replied I did not hear it. One of the SOMs threw itself at me and I had to duck to escape it, keeping my sword up so the creature cut itself in two for its trouble. Blood and something the color of milk spilled out and beaded on my cape. Disgusted, I shook the garment out and continued my advance. Behind me, the line was falling back, collapsing into a kind of mushroom shape as it thickened and grew shorter, making it far harder for the SOMs to clamber over.

The Sphinxes wheeled about once more. Plasma fire split the air and tore through the enemy. I'd nearly made it to the rear legs of the Horse. Ahead men were climbing the legs of the colossus to reach the platforms where their brothers rained fire down from above. The sound of the lighter craft overhead screamed across the sky, and I saw their wing-sails flatten to yaw them round for another pass.

Our lines were holding, thickened as we were into a tight box about the rear legs of the Horse. Where was Siran? I could hear her voice on the comm, ordering the ranks of our line to rotate, fresher troops in the rear replacing the spent men in front. Looking past those leading men, I saw a sea of scabrous faces, hollow eyes and grasping fingers spreading back as far as the southern ridge of the mountains. And behind them?

I thrust my sword into the air and let out a cry.

Petros and the Fifth Chiliad had come. Another thousand of our troops crashed into the hollow men from behind, splitting the attention of the fell intelligence that governed them.

"Concentrate air fire on the northern side!" I ordered, turning Sphinx flight away from the narrowing slice of the enemy between us and Petros's relief force.

Fire reigned.

* * *

Smoke followed.

Not even the airless vacuum of space is so quiet as the battlefield when the fighting is done. Pillars of oily smoke held up the sky, and though my men busied themselves unloading the plasma bore from the Horse's underbelly and the winds scoured in off the salt falts of the *Soto planitia,* I heard nothing. I stood watching from the shadow of the massive gate, my guards around me and my friends: Siran and Pallino, who had come with me out of Emesh.

Thus we waited.

The plasma bore had the look of some swollen jet engine mounted on four legs. It took a man to pilot it—no daimon intelligences here—and the tech moved forward step by lurching step, extending the cigar-shaped body of the bore forward like a battering ram against the gates of ancient Jerusalem.

As the ground crew busied themselves with their preparations, I cast my eye skywards, past the circling shapes of Sphinx Flight and the sulfurous clouds. Somewhere above our ship waited, locked in geostationary orbit above us. The SOMs had been a nasty welcoming party, but everything had gone according to plan in the end. One of the once-human creatures lay not far off, dead eyes staring at the umber sky.

"Do you ever wonder who they were?" I asked aloud, indicating the corpse. There were burn lines on his flesh where the disruptor fire had fried the implants that enslaved him. I hoped that —for a fleeting moment, in the instant before he died—the fellow had remembered who he was, and that he was a man. I wondered what his name had been, and if he'd remembered it before the end.

"Some poor sod, most like," Pallino answered in his gruff way. "Merchanter or some such as got skyjacked by this lot."

Cape snapping about myself, I advanced and turned the fellow fully on his back with my toe. The man was bald as the first one I had cut down and pale almost as the Cielcin who drink the blood of worlds. My heart fell, and I swallowed, kneeling to get a better look at the tattoo inked on the side of the man's neck. It showed a fist clenched around two crossed lightning bolts above the Mandari numerals 378.

A legionary tattoo.

"I think I know what happened to our lost legion."

Silence greeted this pronouncement, deeper and darker than the quiet that had come before. I stood, turning my black-masked face toward the towering expanse of grim metal looming from the mountainside before us, and at the vast war engine and our army arrayed beneath it.

The silence broke with a great rushing of wind as the plasma bore roared to life, sucking at the air around us. The mouth of the plasma bore was pressed right against the bulwark, passing clean through the high-velocity curtain of the energy shield that guarded the gate.

The metal began to glow and run like water.

It was time.

THE CAPTAIN

All was dark within but for the flashing of sirens warning the defenders that their fortress was breached. I followed the first wave of my men over the threshold, the heat of still-cooling metal beating on my suit despite the coolant sprays the plasma bore released when its work was done. There I stood a moment, surveying the hangar before me, the parked shuttles and stacked crates of provisions and equipment.

"Search the shuttles and drain the fuel tanks!" Pallino called out, signaling a group of his men to advance. They did, moving off in groups of three, rifles and lances raised.

"Mapping drones have gone ahead, my lord," said Petros. He saluted as I drew nearer, his fist pressed to his chest. He extended his arm as I acknowledged the salute. "It's a fucking maze."

A wire-frame map of the fortress was even then sketching itself in the bottom left of my vision. The levels that rose stacked above the hangar bay seemed straightforward enough, but the warren of tunnels and caverns carved deep into the living rock at the base of the mountain were anything but.

"I don't want anyone wandering off," I said to Petros and Pallino. "Groups of two and three decades should stick together. We should assume there are more SOMs where those others came from." If the entirety of the 378th had been taken and converted by the Extras, it was very possible that thousands more lay in wait for us, but I couldn't help thinking that if such were the case, these pirates would surely have deployed them *before* we breached their fortress. Perhaps some of our soldiers we still alive. Perhaps most of them were.

My officers turned to go about their duties, and I was left with Siran and a vague sense of deja vu. The caverns—vaguely damp and lichen-spotted—reminded me of the city on Vorgossos. I shut my eyes, as if by doing so I might retreat to some other place: to the cloud forests on Nagramma where Jinan and I had hiked to the old Cid Arthurian temple; or the foggy coast at Calagah. Instead, I saw swollen hands rising from black water and the countless blue eyes of the Undying King of Vorgossos, and despite the warm wind from the Araenian desert outside, I shivered.

"Get a seal on that door!" I said, gesturing at the smooth hole the plasma bore had put in the main gate. "Static field will do! I don't want anything impeding our exit should it come to that."

I could still feel those bloated fingers on me, and shook them off with the memory of their touch. This was not Vorgossos. This was Arae. On Vorgossos I had been alone, but for Valka. Here I had an army at my back, my Red Company.

"Lord Marlowe," came the voice of some centurion I did not recognize, one of Petros's men, "we've captured their captain. We're bringing him to you."

Unable to suppress a crooked smile, I said, "No need, centurion. We'll come to you."

* * *

Sunlight fell through windows narrow as coin slots high on the high chamber's walls. The turret was in the very highest part of the mountain fortress, and through the holograph plates that imitated larger windows I could see the Horse; the arms of the mountain spread out below; and the infinite, sterile whiteness of the *Soto Planitia* beyond.

The man who sat in the chair between four of my soldiers wore an old gray and white uniform. His face was as gray, and his hair with it. He did not *look* like an Extrasolarian. He looked...*ordinary,* the very model of the old soldier. Indeed, he reminded me of no one so much as Pallino: aged and leathered, with a sailor's pallor and sharp eyes—though unlike Pallino this man still had both his eyes. The fellow had the stamp of the legions about him. A former officer, most like. Such men often turned mercenary, if they did not turn gladiator. I knew his type.

"What's your name, soldier?" I asked in my best aristocratic tones. There was enough of the Imperial iron left in the man to straighten his spine at the sound of it.

"Samuel Faber, sir. Captain of the Dardanines." From his accent I suspected the man was at least of the patrician class—though certainly he was not palatine.

"The Dardanines?" I echoed, stopping five paces before the chair. Turning to survey the room, I caught sight of the dozen or so other officers who had surrendered with Captain Faber.

Faber cleared his throat. "Free company."

"Mercenaries?" I said, and arched my eyebrows behind my mask. "Foederati?" But it did not matter, not then. I pushed on to more pressing matters. "Where is the Three Seventy-Eighth?" I saw a muscle in Captain Faber's jaw clench, but his gray eyes stayed fixed on my face. He did answer. "Legion Intelligence tracked a convoy carrying the 378th Centaurine Legion to within a dozen light-years of this system, captain. I need to know what you did with them." I did not say *What you did* to *them.*

Faber was silent for a moment, and when he did speak it was with the air of one resigned. "I know who you are." Seeing as he had started talking, I did not interrupt, only tried not to glance towards Pallino where he stood near at hand. "Is it...true you can't be killed?"

I did look towards Pallino then. The old veteran alone of those in the room knew something of the answer to that question. Voice flattened by the suit speakers, I answered, "Not today, captain. Not by you." The man seemed to chew on that a moment—or maybe it was only his tongue. He looked down at his scuffed boots and the gunmetal floor, arms crossed. "Tell me: How does a man go from a posting with the Legions to kidnapping one for the Extras? Was the money that good?"

I expected the man to rage, expected that there must be enough of the Legion officer he had been left in him—and enough honor—to insult him. I wanted him to stand, to take a swing me, to give me an excuse to put him right back in his seat. The man had sold human beings—his fellow Sollans, his fellow soldiers—to the barbarians who dwell between the stars.

I did not expect him to shake his head and press his lips together, as if he were afraid to speak. Taking a step forward, I asked again, "Where is the legion, Captain Faber?"

Nothing.

Gesturing to Siran, I stepped aside, saying, "I had hoped it would not come to this." I had seen video of the mercenary captain relayed to my suit before we'd boarded the lift to come upstairs, and I'd guessed at his legionary past. Four men entered the command chamber a moment later, carrying a fifth between them. They stopped just before Faber's seat and dropped the body there, face down.

The SOM did not move.

For a moment, I said nothing, only hooked my thumbs through my belt and waited for the shoe to drop. Faber must have felt it coming. Kneeling, I turned the dead man's head with one hand, presenting the fist and crossed lightning bolts of the 378th Centaurine. Then nothing needed saying, and Faber found he could no longer look at the dead man or myself. He looked rather at the dozen of his own lieutenants who knelt on the ground to one side, manacled with guns aimed at their backs.

"We're both soldiers, you and I," Faber said into the vacuum growing between us, and for once I did not argue the label. He was nodding steadily, hands clasped in his lap. "I've done things I'm not proud of, Sir Hadrian, for the Empire and after. But that's *the job.*"

"These were your brothers, captain," I said, more regretful than angry. The anger stayed far below the surface, churning like a river of eels.

"It was the job," he said again. "That's what they paid us for. Tag a convoy while the men were still in fugue, bring them here. It's not even hard if you know where the ships are going to be—but they did. They must have a mole in Legion command."

I took a step that put me between Faber and the corpse on the floor. "Who is they? Who are you working for?" Faber only shook his head, still not making eye contact. I could see the whites there, and the way his hands shook. Was he afraid? Not of me, surely?

Letting out a sigh, I reached up behind my right ear and clicked the hard switch there before keying a command into my wrist-terminal. The sigh turned to hissing as the pressure seals in my helmet relaxed. The black titanium and ceramic casque broke into pieces that folded flower-like away from my face before coiling into the collar of my hardsuit, and for the first time I looked down on Faber with my own eyes.

With a rough hand, I pushed back the elastic coif that covered my head and shook out curtains of ink-dark hair. Coming to within two paces of Faber's chair, I crouched to put us at a level. "You were a soldier, you say. Then you know we can take the answer from you. I would prefer not to have to." Reaching out, I seized Faber's clenched hands with my own, looking like some parody of the vassal kneeling before his lord, of the devoted son before his father. I squeezed. "Who hired you to betray your brothers?" I glanced back at the dead man behind me. I could see Faber was looking.

Then his vision shifted and we regarded one another eye-to-eye. "You don't understand. These people. The things they can do..."

But I had been to Vorgossos, to the lowest dungeons of the Undying. I knew full well what horrors, what abominations mankind was capable of in the name of *science,* of *progress*. I had seen the body farms, the surgical theaters. I had seen armies of puppet SOMs larger than this, and had seen machines to violate every natural law. I knew exactly what the Extrasolarians were capable of—knew it was every bit as vile and unthinkable as the rape and pillage the inhuman Cielcin carried out as they conquered our worlds. And worse. Worse because the Extrasolarians were human, even if they tried not to be.

"Give me a name, Faber. Please."

The man swallowed. "You have to take my people out of here."

"You are in *no* position to be making demands," I said, standing, my finger in his face. I turned my back on him, pondering what to say next.

"You misunderstand, Marlowe. That's not a demand. It's the terms of my surrender." I stopped mid-step and turned around, hands back at my sides. I waited him out. The man had been in the Legions, surely he knew that the Empire would put every one of his men in a prison camp for the rest of their lives. Surely he knew his own life was forfeit. For an officer of the Imperium to take up arms against the Empire was a grievous crime, one the Emperor would never forgive. "Passage out of here for every one of my men, even if it's to Belusha," he said, naming just such a prison planet as I'd imagined.

"What are you so afraid of, Captain Faber?" I asked. "Your employers, plainly, but why? The fortress is ours."

The older officer glanced at the dozen or so of his men again, then once more at the SOM dead at his feet. "MINOS, they're called MINOS."

I blinked, "Like the Minoan king?" Minos was a character out of ancient myth, the ruler of vanished Crete. It was he who had built the labyrinth into which Theseus had ventured to fight the Minotaur. Thinking of Theseus brought a grim smile to my lips, and I saw once more a stony shore. A black lake. Slippered feet standing on the surface of the water. And against a wall of bare stone a tall red fountain rose dreadfully distinct.

"The what?" Faber said stupidly. "No, I—I don't know." He wrung his hands, eyes fallen. I let him take the time he needed; could sense the stripped, exhausted gears in his mind still turning. "Have you ever heard of the Exalted?" he asked, voice very small.

"Yes." The Exalted were amongst the most dangerous of the Extrasolarian tribes—if tribes was the right word. They had abandoned their humanity—they would say *transcended* it—replaced their bodies with machines, altered their neural chemistry to suit their whims, discarded their humanity like so much rotting meat. They crewed massive interstellar vessels and never set in to port, fleeing from the Empire and the Holy Terran Chantry as shadows flee from the sun. Many had lived for eons preserved like medical specimens in jars of their own making. It is the Exalted every little boy and girl in the Sollan Empire grows up afraid of. It is they we imagine when he hear stories of the Extrasolarians and the things they do to innocent sailors.

"MINOS *makes* them. Designs them. And they make..." he nodded weakly towards the SOM still lying at his feet, "...those things."

"And they hired you to acquire materials," I said. "They're building an army. For whom?"

The Dardanine captain screwed his eyes shut. "I don't know. I don't know. On my honor."

"Your *honor.*" It was all I could do not to sneer. "Your *honor,* M. Faber? Just what honor do you think you have?"

"Enough to plead for my men," Faber replied without hesitation. "Do with me what you will, but get them out of here. And get out of here yourselves. If you know what the Exalted are, you know what trouble you'll be in when they arrive."

"They're coming here?"

"Most of the MINOS staff fled the moment your ship came out of warp, but not before they summoned the others."

Petros barked a laugh, "At warp? That'll take *years!*"

"No," Faber said flatly.

Petros hadn't been with us at Vorgossos. He didn't understand.

We might only have hours. Maybe less.

All at once, Captain Faber's surrender took on a more dire cast. It was as if the sunlight had changed, or the sun itself had gone behind a cloud. "This has gone on long enough, captain," I said, falling back on the aristocratic sharpness with which I'd begun our little meeting. "If what you say is true then we haven't much time. If you want your men to live, you will surrender any of these MINOS people still on base and for the love of Earth and all that's holy you will tell me where my legion is."

THE LIVING FAILURES

It was so cold in the depths of the fortress warrens that I'd had to put my helmet back on. Frost misted the air and massed on the coolant lines bracketed to the walls, reminding me of veins in the limb of some giant. Far above, bay doors of steel and reinforced concrete stood closed to the yellow sky. Through that aperture—hundreds of meters long—the Dardanines had lowered dozens of troop transport units: ugly, rectangular pods each holding two centuries of Imperial legionnaires.

"How many are left?" I asked.

"Thirty-seven, lord," Petros replied.

"That's what? Seventy...four hundred soldiers?" I drummed my fingers against my side as I ran the numbers. It wasn't even a third of the full legion. I tried not to imagine where those other men had gone. Turning to where two of Petros's centurions stood near at hand, I said, "One of you: head up top and signal the *Tamerlane.* Tell Aristedes to deploy the cargo lifters, double time. Are we any nearer finding the controls for the bay doors?"

I directed that last bit to everyone in the vicinity, voice amplified by my suit's speakers.

A decurion answered in a thin voice, "My lord, we're locked out of the control room."

"Where?"

"Here, lord!"

The door looked to be solid steel, the first in an airlock that separated the landing bay from the inner fortress when the roof was open to the sky. Just as my man had said, the control panel beside the door was blacked out, dead as old stone.

No matter.

"Stand back!" I said, holding out one hand to fend my soldiers away. I drew my sword, kindled the blade. The highmatter cast spectral highlights—white and blue—against the brushed metal walls. Its cutting edge was fine as hydrogen, and I plunged the point through the reinforced steel as easily as through wax paper. Moving steadily, I carved a hole in the door just large enough for a man to step through. The door fell inward with a slamming sound like the unsealing of a tomb, and—sword held out before me—I stepped inside.

Into darkness.

I activated my suit lights, revealing abandoned banks of control consoles and inert projector plates. My men followed me over the threshold, and behind them I heard someone—Siran, possibly—

calling for a scout drone. The device whizzed over my shoulder, emitting a faint, ultrasonic whine as the scanning lasers fanned across the room before vanishing through an open door at the far end.

Pausing, I tapped one of the consoles. It flared to life, holograph readout filling the space above the desktop. "Get the techs," I ordered one of the others, "tell them to get those bay doors open. We need to lift the survivors out, double quick. The rest of you: with me."

Captain Faber had said the MINOS staff had fled the base when we attacked. That had been a lie. We would have noticed any ship attempting to leave Arae when our assault began. There had been none.

They had to be down here somewhere.

I have seen more than my fair share of dark, demon-haunted tunnels in my life. I have said before that light brings order to creation, and that in darkness order grows ever less. The magi teach us that before the First Cause and the cataclysm that birthed the universe there was only Dark, and that it was from that darkness—the infinite chaos and potential that exists in the absence of light—that *anything* might happen. And so *everything* had happened, and the universe had emerged, birthed not—as the ancient pagans would have it—by the declaration of a deity, but born of the limitless chaos that comes in the absence of light.

That is why we fear the Dark. Not for what it contains, but for the threat that it might contain *anything*. Aware of this fact, I pressed down the hall after the drone, following the path laid out in the display at the corner of my vision. Doors opened to either side, revealing store rooms and offices and what reminded me of nothing so much as medical examination rooms. Cold sweat beaded on the back of my neck. A powerful sense of dread settled on me, crouching like a gargoyle. It was almost like being back on Vorgossos, in the dungeons of the Undying.

"My lord!" a voice rang out from behind me, and as I turned the soldier added, "Over here!"

I joined the man in the arch of a broad doorway opening on a round chamber. The roof above was supported by a single central pillar, and the floor was a tangle of cables, as if someone had pulled apart and rewired several machines in a great hurry.

And then I saw them, sitting in seats around the outer wall, each slumped as if in slumber, hands unfeeling in their laps. There must have been three dozen of them, men and women alike.

None moved.

"Dead?" Siran asked. "Earth and Emperor protect us. What is this?"

Lowering my sword but keeping it lit, I approached the nearest corpse. She didn't look like an Exalted. None of them did. Each of the dead men seemed human enough. On a whim, I flicked my suit's vision from visual light to infrared, saw the cooling nimbus of life's heat fading in her core. "Still warm," I said, and fingered the braided metal cable the dead woman still grasped in both hands, tracing its course from the floor all the way up to the base of her skull. "They're not dead," I said, and with a vindictive turn of my wrist I slashed the cable with my sword. "They're gone."

Two the soldiers nearby made a warding gesture with their first and last fingers extended. One asked, "What do you mean, gone?"

"Synaptic kinesis. I've seen it before," I pointed to the column in the center of the room with my sword. "That's a telegraph relay. This lot wired their brains in and broadcast their minds offworld. Probably to a ship. They'll have new bodies waiting for them." They'd discarded their old ones like sleeves, abandoned them here to rot. The eels churned within me once again, and I turned my head. It was easy to imagine the Exalted growing these bodies for just such a reason: to wear for a time and discard. I was prepared to bet my good right hand that the true owner of the flesh before me was some brain trapped in a bottle up in the black of space like some foul djinni. "Once we get the soldiers out, bring atomics down. None of this can be left. And don't *touch* anything. Who knows what they've left behind."

No sooner had the words left my mouth then a shot rang out,

and turning I saw one of the bodies tumble from its chair with a smoking hole in its chest. "Hold your fire!" I called, raising a hand.

"I thought it moved, sir," the soldier said, voice higher than I'd expected. "Like the ones up top."

"No, soldier. We've nothing to fear from these."

Have I said the universe shares my love of theater?

Something shot out of the darkness and sliced clean through the armorweave at the base of the man's neck. There was no noise save the sigh of impact and the dull smack of blood against the wall behind him, no crack of gunshot or crash of bullet against the wall. He took a moment to fall, and in that space whatever it was hit another of my men.

"Shields up!" Siran bellowed into the sudden stillness.

I saw a flicker of movement out the corner of my eye—the trailing hem of a robe. I started after it, Siran close behind. Had some of Faber's men not surrendered with the rest? Or had one of the MINOS personnel remained behind when the others fled by their unholy road?

The tunnels ahead were a labyrinth still incompletely mapped. We were near the bottom of the fortress now, almost to where I guessed the geothermal sinks and the power station must be. All the world was low ceilings and blind turnings in the dark, the walls lit only by the rare sconce, fixtures yellow with neglect. I could just make out the sound of soft footfalls on the ground ahead, and skidded round a corner in pursuit. Once or twice I saw a human shape round a bend ahead.

There!

A stunner bolt flew over my shoulder from Siran's hand. Was that a gasp of pain?

"Missed," Siran spat, making the word a curse.

She was right. It must have been a glancing blow, for when we caught up to the next bend there was no one there, but I knew what I had heard. There was a door up ahead on the left, and it stood open. Inside, the shadowed hulks of nameless machines stood in rows.

"Reinforcements are right behind, Had," Siran said. "We should hold."

"And let them escape?" I said, brushing past. I knew what Siran was thinking, that this was some kind of trap. But if what Faber said was true, this whole thing was a trap and the Exalted would be on us in hours.

I stepped inside.

Immediately my shield flashed as the strange bullet impacted against it.

It flashed again. Again. Held. The icon in the side of my vision indicated the shield was still blue.

"You should have hired better mercenaries!" I called out, not seeing my quarry among the slumbering machines. "Your Captain Faber's surrendered!"

"He bought the time we needed!" a cold, high voice returned. "You see my fellows have already escaped." I scanned the darkness ahead of me, but save the tongues of chilly fog twisting in the air, nothing moved. I swept the beam of my suit lamp ahead and above me, searching the narrow catwalks and raw plumbing.

Nothing.

"You work for MINOS?" I asked, signaling for Siran to cover my back.

"I'm certainly not one of Faber's little boys," came the reply. "And I know all about *you,* Lord Marlowe. The Emperor's new pet. Killed one of the Cielcin clan chiefs did you? Is it true you twisted the Undying's arm to do it? The Lord of Vorgossos does not bend easily. I didn't think he could bend at all."

Behind my mask, I smiled.

After a moment's silence, I said, "Who did you sell the legion to?"

No answer.

No surprise.

I tried a different tactic, anything to keep her talking. The longer she kept talking, the better the odds were my reinforcements would catch up. "MINOS produces the Exalted?"

"Abstraction. Body modification. Yes," the voice floated down from above. "We provide design and fabrication work for the captains and the clans. Life extension. Maintenance of the cerebral tissue—some of our clients are thousands of years old, don't you know? Whatever they dream—and can afford—we make real."

Still searching for her, I passed a bit of machinery like a vast, squat drum. Frost rimed its surface, but something there—a glimmer of movement, perhaps?—caught my attention. If there was something inside I could not see it, but I sensed something there the way the swimmer senses the passage of a fish in dark waters.

"What are these?"

"Prototypes," she said. "Failures."

"Failures?" I drew back.

On our private band, Siran said, "I see her, Had. Up and left. She's limping." I looked, and seeing understood why I hadn't seen her sooner. She was far too cold to be human, and my suit's infrared pickups nearly lost her against the awful chill in that room.

"Progress is never without loss."

"On the contrary," I said, and it was my tutor who spoke through me, a response out of childhood, "any progress which is accompanied by loss is no progress at all."

"Spoken just like an Imperial dog."

"Or like someone who reads."

Siran fired, stunner flash splitting the gloom. She struck true, and I heard a clatter as a body hit the catwalk above.

"Good shot!" the woman's voice rang out. "You got me!"

Siran froze before she could start her search of the room's perimeter. Over the comm, I heard her whisper, "What the hell?"

"Some sort of nervous bypass," I answered over the private channel. "Kept her conscious. Is she moving?"

"No."

"Get up there and lock her down before she recovers." That at least had explained how the woman had kept running after we shot her in the hall. "We'll put her in fugue and bring her back with the rest."

Not so fast! The woman's voice crackled over the speakers inside my helmet—over the private frequency. Damn these Extrasolarian demoniacs and their machines! *It's you who won't be going anywhere, Lord Marlowe!*

I switched off my communicator with a glance, sealing my suit off from Siran and the datasphere. The last thing I needed was this Extra woman crawling around in my armor's infrastructure, shutting off my cameras or my air. I had visions of being trapped there, locked and blind in my suit, waiting to be found by the Extras Faber warned us were coming. An unceremonious end to Hadrian Marlowe, Knight Victorian.

But the MINOS woman had something else in mind.

A light cold and blue as forgotten stars blazed in the drum—the tank—before me, and a moment later something huge and heavy thumped the glass *from the inside.* Hairline cracks spiderwebbed from the point of impact, and I lurched backwards, scrambling to put as much space between myself and the *thing,* the *failure,* that lurked in the woman's tank.

It struck again and the glass *splintered.* Super-cooled fluid flooded out, changing the air to a thick, white fog that dragged the *thing* within outward like an unborn calf from the corpse of a stranded whale. The thing within lurched on unsteady limbs, hands and feet of steel clanging, scraping the ground as it struggled to rise, to right itself.

Words fled me, and my mind with them, and for a single, terrible moment it seemed I stood once more upon the shore of the sea beneath Vorgossos, with that great daimon of the ancient world rising to meet me.

"Hadrian!" a voice cried out. Siran's voice—and I remembered.

Remembered who I was and what I was there to do.

Remembered the sword in my hand.

The failure pushed itself to its feet, and hunched and lurching as it was still it towered over me: ten feet or twelve of white metal and jointed bone. It had no face that I could see, for like the helms of our legionnaires its visage was blank and pitiless as ice. It lunged towards me, clawed hands outstretched, but it lost its footing and crashed to its knees. One of the arms biforcated, the upper half folding up and out from its shoulder like the pinion of some dreadful wing. Seeing my chance, I lunged, hewing at the creature's arm. The highmatter blade bounced off, ringing my hand like a bell. Wincing, I recoiled, boots unsteady in the rapidly warming coolant. I might have known. I had fought the Exalted before, on Vorgossos and after, and I should have guessed this creature's body would be proof against highmatter, forged of adamant or some composite whose molecules would not be cut.

I bared my teeth.

Things had just gotten a great deal more difficult.

Siran opened fire, violet plasma scorching the side of its head. She might have been throwing rocks at the Horse for all the good it did. The beast turned to look at her, and I fancied I could see the wheels of its still-organic mind turning. I could see common metal shining in the elbow and shoulder joints, beneath the armored carapace. It had weaknesses. I took a measuring step closer, hoping to try to my luck. I didn't make it far. The third arm that sprouted from the top of its shoulder whipped round like a peasant's scythe so fast it *vanished.* My reflexive flinch was far too late, and I was saved the impact only by the energy curtain of my shield flashing about me.

Letting out a piercing cry, the living failure rose once more to its feet, one leg sliding out from under it. This time it steadied itself, one massive hand striking the wall of the tank beside it. I wondered what was wrong with it. Something in the way the Exalted's mind interfaced with its new machine body? Something that made it slip and stagger so?

"Stand aside, beast," I said, aiming my sword at it like an accusing finger. I had fought worse and more dangerous creatures than this. The beast howled again and cracked its third arm like a whip as it advanced, loping forward on legs bent like a dog's. As a young man in the coliseum on Emesh, I had battled azhdarchs and ophids, manticores and gene-tailored lions large as elephants. And once, after our victory on Pharos, I had faced a charging bull with no shield and only a rapier for defense.

The principle here was the same.

By rights, the abomination ought to have been faster than me, fast almost as that evil appendage that sprouted claw-like from its shoulder. By rights, I should already have been no more than a dark smear on the floor of that hall.

Siran shot it in the head, for all the good it did. The creature shook it off like a slap. There was something in the way it shook its head that was familiar to me, pulling its ear towards its shoulder in sharp, repeated movements. I had no time to think about it, only about the way its fist slammed down like the hand of God. I threw myself sideways, aiming a desperate cut at the side of one knee. The blade pinged off the metal, and just like the bull on Pharos I swung round my enemy like a gate about its hinge, undoing the magnetic clasp of my cape as I went and tossing the garment aside.

"Go find the doctor, Siran!" I ordered, "Don't let her get away!"

"And leave you?"

"Go!" I ducked a mighty swipe of the creature's arm and stepped forward. I'd seen a slight gap where the ribs ought to be, between the armored breastplate and the interleaved segments that passed for a stomach. How thin it was! Too long and too narrow to be human anymore. If I could get the point of my blade in that gap...there might be something underneath, some delicate system or piece of the mostly discarded flesh.

I did not find out.

The *knee* lanced out to meet me. Not fast—certainly not fast enough to engage my body shield—but it did not need to be fast. The knee was titanium wrapped in adamant and zircon. There were softer statues.

My armor alone saved my ribs and the heart and lungs beneath them, but the wind was driven from me. I flew backwards as if thrown and struck the wall behind me so hard I imagined the dull metal cracking like glass—or maybe that was only my skull.

Where were the others?

My vision slipped and blurred, righted itself only when I forced myself to slow my breathing and the mutinous hammering of my heart. It was coming, and there I was resting with my back against the wall like some derelict watchman. It leaped towards me, and it was all I could do to roll away as the machine collided bodily with the wall just where my head had been. I regained my feet, glad of the positive pressure in the suit forcing air into my lungs.

There!

Before the beast could turn, I lunged, the point of my sword burying itself in the back of the Exalted's knee. Common metal parted like paper, and a violently white fluid bled out, running down the ivory calf to the floor. The scythe-arm lashed against my shield then, and slowly began to wind itself about me. I stumbled backwards, but the thing wound itself about my chest. I could feel the thermal layer hardening to protect against the pressure. The creature turned, reached down towards my face with a six-fingered hand.

Six-fingered.

"Iukatta!" In my winded state, the word was little more than a whisper, but my suit amplified it to a shout. *Stop!*

The beast dropped me, surprise evident in the way it just *stood* there.

"Nietolo ba-emanyn ne?" the creature asked. The alien within the machine. *You speak our language?*

I made the sharp sound that passed for *yes* in their tongue. The Cielcin tongue. "What have they done to you?" It wasn't possible. The Cielcin and the Extrasolarians…working together? But no, the Cielcin clans had been dealing with the Extras since before they invaded the Empire—since before we had even known they existed. That they would work together against the Empire should not have surprised me, and yet...seeing the xenobite standing there encased in so much Extrasolarian kit...I felt a thrill of holy terror.

The creature's blank faceplate opened like a jewel box and folded away, revealing the milk-white flesh; the eyes like twin spots of ink on new paper, large as my fists; and the teeth like shattered glass. "They have made us strong," it said, gnashing its teeth. "Strong enough to defeat you *yukajjimn." Vermin,* it said. Its word for human.

"Strong?" I echoed, drawing back, putting distance once again between me and this Cielcin-machine hybrid, demon and daimon. "You can hardly stand." And no wonder. MINOS and the Exalted had had thousands of years to perfect the systems that bonded man to machine. The Cielcin were not men.

"We were only the first."

In the quiet of my heart, I imagined armies of such creatures falling from the sky to sack world after imperial world. Dust to dust by the million, humans carried back to the stars and the dark ships the Cielcin called home. I remembered the slaves I had seen, mutilated by their alien masters, and I knew at once what had happened to the rest of our lost legion. MINOS had offered them to their Cielcin friends in payment or in tribute. They were dead, and worse than dead: still living. This was something new. In all my years of fighting, this was something I had never expected: the black marriage of Cielcin and machine.

"Who is your master?" I demanded, "Which clan? Which prince?"

"You cannot stop him. Or his White Hand."

"Iedyr Yemani?" I repeated the words *white hand,* not sure I had heard them correctly. Not sure I understood. "Who is *he?"* Its prince, certainly. Its master.

"He will tear your worlds from the sky, human!" the Cielcin roared, and beat its chest with its hands. "He has conquered an army for himself, and he is coming!" Then the creature pounced, thinking me distracted. But I was ready, and lunging aimed my sword at the creature's unprotected face. It was my only chance.

My only hope was that whatever was *wrong* with the hybrid would slow it down. As it hurtled towards me, claws outstretched, I saw the visor begin to close like an eyelid snapping shut. The adamantine faceplate slammed with the point of my sword caught between its flanges, and almost the weapon was wrenched from my hand. I grinned savagely.

It had worked *exactly* as I'd planned.

The beast landed badly, and its ruined knee went out from under it. It fell with a crash, and I leaned all my weight against the hilt of my sword. I bared my teeth, eyes stretched wide as I pushed the sword downwards. The point moved only slowly, metal grinding against liquid metal as the highmatter sank home, piercing flesh and bone. And brain.

Like a muscle relaxing, the visor fell open once again, revealing the neat hole between the massive eyes, and the black blood running like tears.

I found Siran and the MINOS doctor moments later. My fears were justified. The doctor—a small, gray woman dressed in white —had indeed possessed some implant or artifice that had saved her from the stun. While I'd been distracted with her *experiment,* she had crawled along the catwalk to a room overlooking her lab.

Siran handed me the gun as I entered, cape firmly back in place. It was a strange thing, silver and strangely organic. I looked down at the body at my feet and the name embroidered above the breast pocket of her lab coat.

"Severine," I read aloud, eyes wandering to the perfectly round hole she'd punched through the bottom of her jaw and out the top of her head. She had carefully missed the delicate hardware at the base of her skull. "She escaped then?"

"Like the others?" Siran asked, "Guess so. By Earth, Had. This shit's beyond me." Her blank-visored face turned up to look at me, looking for all the world not so different from the helmet of the creature I had slain. "Are you all right?"

I caught myself rubbing my hands—as if trying to remove

some spot on the black gloves. "They were mingling the Cielcin with machines. That's what that thing was."

"Are you serious?" I could imagine the look of shock on her face, eyes white and wide in the dimness.

"The body is just down there," I gestured to the room below. "We'll need to bring it back with us, and everything we can get from these machines." Breaking off, I looked round at the banks of computers rising all about us, the machines through which the ghost of Dr. Severine and her fellows had escaped. "The Cielcin said its master had raised an army. That it was coming for us."

The centurion—my friend—moved to stand beside me, her arms crossed. "The Cielcin have been invading for hundreds of years. That's nothing new."

"No," I said, shaking my head. "This time it's different." I let my hands fall, looked back through the open door to where the failed hybrid lay on the floor. "A Cielcin prince willing to work with the Extras… The world is changing."

"Lord Marlowe!" a voice rang out from below, "Lord Marlowe!" The questing beams of suit lights blazed up from below. My men had found us. Too little. Too late.

I did not step out to speak to them at once, but turned to Siran. "Something's coming. Mark my words. This war of ours is about to get a good deal worse."

BIO

Christopher Ruocchio is the author of The Sun Eater, a space opera fantasy series from DAW Books, as well as the Assistant Editor at Baen Books, where he co-edited the military SF anthology Star Destroyers, as well as Space Pioneers, a collection of Golden Age reprints showcasing tales of human exploration.

. . .

He is a graduate of North Carolina State University, where a penchant for self-destructive decision making caused him to pursue a bachelor's in English Rhetoric with a minor in Classics. An avid student of history, philosophy, and religion, Christopher has been writing since he was eight-years-old and sold his first book—Empire of Silence—at twenty-two. The Sun Eater series in available from Gollancz in the UK, and has been translated into French and German.

Christopher lives in Raleigh, North Carolina, where he spends most of his time hunched over a keyboard writing. When not writing, he splits his time between his family, procrastinating with video games, and his friend's boxing gym.

15

A TALE OF RED RIDING: SEDUCTION OF THE WEREPIRE

NEO EDMUND

Glimmering light of the blood-red moon filtered down through the branches of the ancient oaks. The stench of blood and decaying flesh tainted the sweltering night air. Deafly silence stifled the land. Every living creature, big and small, cowered in the shadows, pinning hope against hope not to be discovered. An insidious beast had been ravaging the western territories of Wayward Woods for weeks on end, with no end in sight.

"A *wererpire*," the Alpha Huntress Red Riding muttered with a sarcastic sneer. "Do you have any idea how dumb that sounds?"

"No dumber than your endless yap-trapping when we're supposed to be doing the stealthy hunters' thing," said Wolfgang Helheim, Red's handsome yet rugged hunting companion. As usual, he was wearing ripped jeans and a dingy gray tank top. Red would often complain about his grungy appearance, though in truth his rugged bad-boy persona made her blood boil with *want*.

Side-by-side, the teen warriors slogged along a murky path. Their eyes keenly surveyed every nook and shadow, well aware that they could fall prey to an attack at any instant. On most nights they would have already taken their werewolf forms, but instead opted to hold off until absolutely necessary, much due to the western region's insufferably hot weather. This was also why Red chose to leave her red cloak at home and instead wore only faded jeans, a black tank top, and knee-high boots.

"There's no point in being stealthy when the thing we're hunting probably already knows were here," Red said. She raised her head the way a canine would to take a few sniffs of the air. Her Alpha werewolf powers gave her the tracking skills that a bloodhound would envy. Somewhere in the near distance, she caught the scent of a creature with a lycan like aroma, but it lacked the sweltering warmth she would expect. The creature smelled almost icy cold, though Red couldn't say for certain.

Wolfgang snapped a look back over his shoulder upon hearing the sounds of feet scampering in the nearby brush. "Maybe the werepire wouldn't know we're here if you weren't so busy with your yap-trapping."

"Maybe so. Maybe not," Red said and raised a half-cocked fist. "What I do know is that if you say I'm yap-trapping one more time, my fist and your face are going to have an up-close and personal discussion about it."

"Wouldn't be the first time. Won't be the last," Wolfgang said with a smug-shrug. "That is, unless your yap-trapping causes us to get bitten by the werepire and we end up turning into depraved killing machines."

"At least then you wouldn't have to listen to my endless yap-trapping about how dumb you sound when you say stuff like that," Red said.

Wolfgang snarled. "The only thing dumb going on here is that after two-years of living in Wayward, and all the menacing monsters you've put in the ground, you still doubt the existence of things like werepires."

Red gritted down, fighting back her instinctive need to snark back. If she had learned anything during her two-year sultry relationship with Wolfgang, these sparring matches could go on for hours, and usually ended with them stomping off in opposing directions.

A bellowing howl from a mighty beast thundered in the near-distance. The tone sounded both depraved and desperate. Red and Wolfgang stopped cold in their tracks, waiting and listening for a tense moment.

Wolfgang faked a throat-clearing cough. "This would be the part where you've come to accept that werepires are a real thing and ask me to clue you in on what to expect when we encounter one."

Again, Red fought back a snarky remark. As much as it irritated her to admit it, she was starting to suspect Wolfgang was right. "Fine. Tell me every little thing there is to know about werepires."

Wolfgang reached over his shoulder and pulled out a katana style sword with a glossy black blade. He began to hack and slash through a patch of thorny foliage that was obstructing the path. "Didn't your granny ever teach you to use the magic word?"

Red's angst was boiling hotter by the second. She knew exactly what Wolfgang was getting at but wasn't about to entertain his antics. "My granny has taught me a lot of magic words, one being a spellcraft that can make an adversary burst into flames."

Wolfgang slipped his sword into the leather holster over his back and apprehensively turned to face Red. "Are you serious or seriously messing with me? Because the way you said that, I seriously can't tell."

"Only one way to know for sure." With a deadpan glare, Red took a step closer to Wolfgang so they were standing nose to nose. "Look into my eyes and tell me where your future lies."

Wolfgang gazed into Red's eyes and caught a glimpse of tiny flames dancing in the center of her pupils. "If I were a guy of lesser quality, a thing like that might get me all hot and bothered."

"Me thinks you're giving yourself just a bit too much credit, Wolf Boy," said Red.

"Don't say I didn't warn you, Alpha girl." Wolfgang took a few steps back and yanked off his tank-top, then used it to wipe the sweat from his brow.

Red looked away, doing her best not to gawk over his muscular chest and rippling abs, but the sight alone was enough to twist up her thoughts with want. "Now you're just being ridiculous."

"You like when I'm ridiculous," Wolfgang said with a seductive rumble and took a step closer to Red.

"Not in life and death monster hunting situations, I don't." Red bit down on her lip. Her heart fluttered. Sweat trickled down her brow. He was getting to her in all the worst ways. She hated that he held such power over her. "Now put your shirt back on so we can get back to tracking down this werepire."

"I thought you didn't believe in werepires." Without breaking eye contact, Wolfgang took another step closer to Red so they were again standing only inches apart.

Red began to tremble. The sharp points of her werewolf claws were poking through the tips of her fingers. "I didn't believe in the big bad wolf until I met you."

Wolfgang gently put his hand on Red's chin. "And as it turns out, the big bad wolf isn't nearly as scary as you thought."

"Not scary at all, actually." Red's expression twisted into an impish grin. "More like a lost little puppy, sad and hopelessly in need of attention."

Wolfgang snarled a bit, but managed to maintain his seductive stare. "And then you came along and for the first time in his sad, lonely life, he knew what it felt like to be loved."

"*Bwahahahahahaha!*" Red burst out laughing. "Almost had me there, Wolf Boy." She shook off the moment and nudged past him, continuing off down the path. "Now put your clothes on and get to stepping."

Wolfgang bitterly bit down on his lip and quickly put his shirt back on. Brimming with disappointment, he scurried off after Red.

For the next half hour, Red and Wolfgang continued along the murky path without a word spoken between them. All along the way the air got hotter and the stench infesting the night air grew fouler. This made it all the more difficult for Red to track the scent of her prey, though she remained steadfast in her intent to win the night.

Their trek came to an abrupt end upon reaching the base of an expansive stone wall. Black vines grew all along the surface of the granite barrier that spanned for a hundred yards in both directions and towered fifty yards in height.

"Whoever built this thing really doesn't want visitors," Red said, her eyes surveying the wall's surface, plotting a course to scale to the top.

"According to legend, the dividing wall was built thousands of years ago by the Empire of the Kupa King. The Kupas lived in total isolation from the world and would kill anyone who tried to get inside," Wolfgang explained. "And before you get any ideas, the top is covered in razor vines, along with the bones of everyone who has ever tried to get across."

"Thanks for the info, captain melodrama," Red said. "Any suggestions how we get over the thing?"

"Unless you plan on sprouting wings and flying, it's fully impossible for anyone or anything to get over the thing," Wolfgang said.

Red took a quick sniff of the air. "You say that and yet somehow the thing we're hunting is on the other side. In fact, I can smell its trail going all the way up the wall."

Wolfgang stepped near the wall and sniffed around. "I don't smell anything but a whole lot of razor-rat dung."

"Only one way to know for sure." Red gritted down and let her werewolf claws rip through the tips of her fingers. Ignoring Wolfgang's warnings, she jammed her claws into the stone wall and began to nimbly climb her way up. After a struggle that lasted for several minutes, she finally reached the top, where she cautiously peered over. Razor vines swarmed along the upper surface, which was nearly ten yards in width.

Carefully rolling up onto a small open space, she took a

moment to catch her breath. Upon closer inspection, she was startled to see the vines were formed from iron and every inch was covered with twisted spikes.

"You know how much I hate to be an *I told you so,* but *I told you* so," Wolfgang shouted from below.

"Yeah. Yeah. It's not all *that bad,*" Red replied.

"As-if!" Wolfgang said.

"Guess you'll never know because you're too much of a fraidy-cat to climb up here and see for yourself." As Red looked around the area trying to find a way through, she noticed the skeletal remains of numerous armored warriors intertwined in the vines, just as Wolfgang had warned.

"Maybe you're too much of a fraidy-cat to admit that I was right about there being no way to get through," Wolfgang shouted.

"No way for normal people, but I'm not normal people." Red gritted down. Extending her hands forward, she focused her thoughts and let the power of the Alpha flow through her body, from her toes to the tips of her fingers. "Flame on!"

Whoosh! A mystical wave of blue flames with a blast radius of several yards erupted from Red's hands. The metallic vines quickly heated to a glow under the searing inferno. Molten drops began to dribble down from the vines. Red continued the assault until the vines were reduced to smoldering puddles of liquified iron.

For a lingering moment, Red stood gasping in awe over the power she had unleashed.

"Hey, Red, you are coming or what?" Wolfgang called out, his voice now sounding from the direction of the inner side of the wall.

Quite confused, Red nimbly made her way around the steaming puddles and glanced over the edge. Wolfgang was indeed standing down below, looking up at her with a gleaming grin. "How the freak did you get over the wall before me?" she asked.

"Oh, I didn't get over. I used the tunnel about twenty yards to the north," Wolfgang said. "At least now we know how the werepire got into this place."

Red growled through clenched teeth. Without another thought, she stepped right off the edge and jammed a clawed hand into the wall. All the way down her claws ripped through the stone surface, slowing her descent enough so she could make it down without hitting the ground at breakneck speed. The instant her feet touched down, she stormed directly to Wolfgang and grabbed him by the shirt. "Why didn't you tell me there was a freaking tunnel before I climbed up that freaking wall of doom?"

"I didn't freaking know until I searched the area and found the freaking thing," Wolfgang smugly replied. "Took me less like two minutes. Maybe next time you'll think things through before you go racing up the wall of doom."

Red bitterly snarled and shoved him away. "Let's just find this stupid werepire and get this night over with."

For the next several minutes, Red and Wolfgang cautiously made their way through the crumbled stone ruins of the ancient city. They trekked along cobblestone streets where countless dome-shaped structures stood in ruins; the dwellings of those who lived there long ago. All along the way there were statues of armored centaurs, pointing their swords skyward.

Red took a quick sniff of the air, catching the distinct scent of the creature they'd been tracking for hours on end. "We're close. Maybe this would be a good time to tell me exactly what the freak a werepire is, and so help me if you say it's a vampire that has the power to transform into a werewolf, I'm going to—"

"Going to what? Rip me a new one?" Wolfgang interrupted. "Because that's exactly what we're dealing with. A werepire is a werewolf that got bit by a vampire and now it has to suck the warm blood of the living to stay alive."

Red stopped cold and pressed her hands over her eyes, trying to calm her thoughts. For a girl who grew up in a big city orphanage, such creatures only existed in myths and fairy tales. "So, it has to be warm blood, not just like any blood?"

Wolfgang reached over his shoulder and pulled out his sword. "A werewolf is a living creature, so it needs to stay warm, but a vampire is an undead, so it's naturally cold. For a werepire to stay alive it has to constantly drink warm blood."

"But why does it have to be blood? Can't it just drink a lot of hot stuff like coffee and coco?" Red asked.

"Because the vampire half needs the blood to survive. It's the perfect food to satisfy both halves," Wolfgang explained.

"I guess that makes about as much sense as anything else in Wayward," Red said and wiped a hand across her sweaty brow. It probably also explains why a werepire would want to live in the hottest place in the land."

"That's what I would do if it was me," Wolfgang said.

Red reached behind her back and pulled out the Alpha Sword from a leather holster. This mystical relic was more powerful than any weapon in all of Wayward. "That also makes our werewolf blood the tastiest item on the menu. Even more so if we transform," she said.

Wolfgang nodded in agreement. "Now you're catching on. Just the smell of our werewolf blood would drive him berserk with hunger."

"True, but it would also help to draw him out, or at least get him to stop running," Red resolved.

"Oh no!" Wolfgang held up his hands defensively and took a big step back "I am not going to play the part of live bait to trick that thing into a trap."

"Fine, then I'll do it myself," Red looked up at the moon and raised her fists skyward. The blood in her veins heated to a boil. Every muscle in her body twitched and trembled. She sprang to her feet, raised her arms, and roared like a raging beast. Razor-sharp claws ripped through her fingertips. Short brownish-red fur covered her from head to toe. Canine ears poked from the sides of her head. A moonstone embedded into an amulet hanging on a gold chain around her neck illuminated with lunar energy. Her red cloak materialized, along with a sleek, form-fitting suit of armor, covering her chest and back and extending to her knees like a metal skirt.

In the near distance, a beast roared with ravenous hunger.

Wolfgang grimaced. "Welp, so much for being stealthy."

Red dashed away, venturing further into the city ruins. Many of the buildings reminded her of the stone pillar structures of ancient Rome, and though the original inhabitants were long deceased, none of the structures were uninhabited. Murderous beasts driven with predatorial hunger had made themselves at home, and they were all aware that Red and Wolfgang were lurking about.

"Red, the werepire isn't the only dangerous thing in this city that wants to kill us," Wolfgang called out as he dashed to catch up with Red.

Just then, a hissing pack of flesh-eating razor-rats leapt in Red's path. Without slowing a bit, she raised the Alpha sword and unleashed a rapid series of lightening quick swipes and slashes. It took her mere seconds to send the reviled creatures to their unwitting demise.

"You were saying?" Red called out to Wolfgang and raced around a street corner.

"These are just low-level combatants," Wolfgang shouted and continued racing after her.

Red took another sniff of the air and caught the scent of her prey a few hundred yards ahead. She rounded another corner and soon came upon an expansive amphitheater that had been constructed in the depths of what resembled an impact crater, hundreds of feet deep. There were enough stone benches to seat many thousands of onlookers.

Red came to an abrupt stop upon reaching the amphitheater's upper rim. As she stood gasping to catch her breath, she gazed down into the crater, where she saw a stone stage, carved from a single slab of glossy black stone. While this in of itself was an impressive site, what caught her attention was the young man sprawled out on a metallic black throne on the center of the stage. His shoulder length locks of hair that flowed ever so slightly in the breeze. He wore a puffy white silk shirt, only buttoned halfway up so his muscular chest was well exposed and his form fitting black pants left little to the imagination.

"Oh my," Red gasped.

"Oh my?" Wolfgang grunted as he stepped up behind Red. He glanced down into the amphitheater and saw the young man that had inspired her *wanting* reaction. "Red, you cannot tell me you're hot on that creepy-creeper."

"Can't I?" Red said, her eyes already glazed over as if in a hypnotic trance. "He's just so pretty."

"Pretty!" Wolfgang grunted even louder than before. "Red, are you out of your mind? That jerk is the thing we've been running our tails off all night trying to find."

"Stop lying," Red said, shaking her head in outright disagreement. "That hot dish of man chowder couldn't possibly be a werepire."

Wolfgang glared down at the pretty young man and clenched his fist. "Snap out of it, Red. That murderous beast wouldn't hesitate to make you into a steaming caldron of vampire porridge."

"I could live with that." Red began stammering down the stone steps, ascending deeper into the amphitheater and closer to the pretty young man.

"Snap out of it, Riding." Wolfgang said, following close behind her. "You're falling under his spell like a fly fluttering right into the spiderweb."

"How overly dramatic of you, Wolf Boy," Red muttered. With a firm shove, she pushed Wolfgang, causing him to stumble off his feet and flop down onto a stone bench. "Now sit, boy."

"Sit?" Wolfgang wailed.

"And stay. I've got this one." Red didn't have to look back to know Wolfgang was gnarling in outrage, but in that moment, she just didn't care. All rational thought had departed her. "This one is all mine."

The pretty young man finished sucking a mouthful of blood out of a razor-rat and then flung its lifeless carcass aside. He then raised a hand and made a rather dramatic proclamation. "It is said that the Kupas dominated the land for a thousand generations, both with malevolent military might and benevolent intellect. None who lived under their reign ever went without a roof over their head or food in their belly. The Kupas gathered in this very theatre night after night to worship their king who they believed to be a god."

"That's a really neat story," Red said, deeply infatuated by his seductive persona

"It is, though I suspect you did not travel all this way for a history lesson," said the pretty young man. "You came here seeking me and for that I am so very grateful. I receive so few visitors.

"I bet you get so very lonely," Red said, continuing down the steps, her eyes helplessly locked on the pretty young man. "Sounds to me like you need a friend to keep you company."

"Major gag factor," Wolfgang said.

"Stifle it, Wolf Boy," Red replied, just as she reached the base of the stage. "I'm talking to the pretty man right now.

"You flatter me." The pretty young man took a long stretch and flicked his locks of hair from side to side. "It is not every day I receive praise from one of such revered prominence."

Red gave him a curious stare. "Are you saying you know who I am?"

"Everyone in Wayward knows who you are, Red Riding." The pretty young man fluttered his long eyelashes and gave Red a flirtatious smile. "Or should I say, her grand highness, the Alpha Huntress."

Red giggled like a giddy schoolgirl. "Oh please, Red will do just fine."

"As you wish, Red," the pretty young man said with another flutter of his eyelashes.

"And what can I call you?" Red asked, well aware she was blushing bright.

"My dear Red, you may call me any name of your choosing and I will come upon your command," the pretty young man said.

"*Ugghhhhhhhh!*" Wolfgang groaned. "Red, just stake the

bloodsucking meat-sack so we can get back to your granny's place in time for breakfast."

"Wolf boy, so help me if you don't shut that yapping trap," Red warned with a raised fist.

"It would seem your friend does not much care for me," said the pretty young man.

"Don't mind him. His boy brain gets all jealous when I talk to strangers," Red said, slowly walking up the three steps leading up to the stage.

"Are you afraid of strangers, little Red?" the pretty young man asked.

"Depends on the stranger," Red said meekly. "If you told me your name, we wouldn't be strangers anymore."

"Very well. You may call me Valerie," said the pretty young man.

"Valerie!" Wolfgang burst out laughing. "Were your parents expecting to have a girl?"

Red threw Wolfgang a callous glare. "Wolf Boy, one more insensitive comment like that, I'll drag you to the nearest veterinarian and have you snipped."

"Whoa!" Wolfgang scoffed. "One more insensitive threat like that, you'll be looking for a new boyfriend."

"Forgive me, Red." Valerie said and sat up straight in his seat. "I was unaware that you two were involved."

"Don't worry about him. We're not *that* involved," Red said coyly.

"Oh, that is it," Wolfgang wailed. "I am so out of here."

"As if!" Red replied. She knew without looking that Wolfgang was pacing around in a steaming fit of irritation, but he wasn't going anywhere.

Valerie sneered with a hint of amusement. "So, what happens now, Huntress? Are you here to lay me to rest?"

"I'm not entirely sure." Red took a few steps closer to Valerie. "Do you deserve to be *laid* to rest?"

"I do not believe so, though it is not difficult to conclude that you came here to do precisely that. Am I wrong, Huntress?" Valerie asked.

"Not even a little," Red admitted and took a few more steps closer, so they were now a stone's throw apart. "But that was before I met you. Before I saw just how pretty you are."

Valerie snickered. "I have been called many things in my centuries of existence, but never once have I been called *pretty*."

Wolfgang again groaned. "If you two keep this up, I might just stake myself."

"I thought you were leaving, Wolf Boy," Red replied to Wolfgang and then took yet another step closer to Valorie. She reached up and used the back of her hand to wipe the sweat from her brow. Her blood was boiling hotter by the second.

"No need to soil your hands like that, Huntress." Valerie stood up from the throne and slowly pulled off his shirt, revealing his rippling abs. "May I?"

Red was uncertain what he was getting at, but she was too busy gawking at the sight of his bare chest to care. "You can do whatever you want."

"*Arghhhhhhh*!" Wolfgang grumbled.

Valerie strutted over to face Red. He then used his silk shirt to gently wipe the beads of sweat from her brow. "That's better."

"So much better," Red muttered. "What happens now?"

"What do you want to happen?" Valerie asked with a scent of seduction. He slowly leaned in close to Red so they were looking deep into one another's eyes. "Speak your desire and it will be yours, Alpha Huntress?"

Red gazed deep into his hypnotic eyes, "I—I—"

"Do not burden yourself with words. I already know what it is that you desire," Valerie said, this time with a hiss in his tone.

In a flash, Valerie transformed into a werewolf with black fur, pointy ears, and razor-sharp vampire fangs. He leaned in close to Red's neck, his fangs hovering just above her shoulder. Red stood trembling, petrified, unable to think, her thoughts coupled with fear and wanting desire. She knew that Valerie was a beast of unnatural seduction that wanted only to drain her life's blood, though in that moment she couldn't think of a reason not to let him have his way; at least not until she felt the tips of his fangs touch her flesh.

In a heartbeat, Red's blood heated to a raging boil, her hand balled into a fist, and with a mighty upward thrust, she pummeled him in the jaw. Valerie didn't know what hit him. He simply fell backwards and crashed onto the floor with a thud.

"*BAMMMMM*!" Wolfgang cheered. He raced down the stone steps and then leapt up onto the stage. "I knew you were faking that giddy-girl routine."

"Who said anything about faking?" Red whipped her head from side to side, trying to shake off the trance. "He might be a life-sucking menace, but he's still a hot cup of man chowder."

Valerie arose to his feet, as if lifted by unworldly forces. "You disappoint me, Alpha Huntress. I would have made you immortal. We could have had love eternal."

"Not gonna lie. You kinda had my attention at immortal, but fully lost me at love eternal," Red said.

"It really does sound super boring!" Wolfgang agreed as she stepped up next to Red.

"Does it really?" Red asked, giving him a sideways glare. "So how long before you get super bored of me?"

"That's just argument bait and I'm not biting," Wolfgang said, shaking his head in outright refusal. "At least not until after we put a stake in mister man chowder."

Valerie giggled diabolically. "You cannot believe a crude shard of wood could be enough to lay end to my immortal existence?"

"Guess I never really thought of it that way," Wolfgang said with a shrug, then reach over his shoulder and pulled out his sword. "Maybe an old fashion beheading will get the job done."

Wolfgang made a lightening quick slash of the sword, directly at Valerie's throat. An instant before the blade connected, Valerie leaned back, just enough to evade the deadly strike.

Valerie laughed diabolically. "That might have actually worked, had you not announced your intentions. Next time you'd be wise to simply attack without—"

SLASH! Red unleashed a mighty swing of the Alpha sword. Valerie's body flopped to the ground and his head went sailing across the stage, where it crashed down right on the throne. "Thanks for the advice!"

"Showoff," Wolfgang said.

"You wore him down for me," Red replied with an impish grin.

"Alpha Huntress." Valerie's voice spoke from the direction of the throne. "You never asked me what became of the Kupa Empire?"

Red and Wolfgang snapped a look over to the throne. Valorie's head was laying on its side. The eyes were open and glaring right at them with a blank expression.

Red took a nervous gulp. "Did that thing just talk?"

Valerie's head began to speak. "The Kupa Kingdom was invaded by a gang of greedy giants who saw the Kupa's immense wealth as a thing to be owned by the few and not shared by the many. Though the Kupa army was great, they were ultimately conquered, and their corpses consumed."

"How the freak is he still alive?" Wolfgang asked.

"What part of immortal are you failing to understand?" Valerie's asked.

Valerie's headless body snapped upright and slowly ambled to its feet. Before Red and Wolfgang could think to react, the headless body reached out and locked a hand around Wolfgang's throat. Sharp talons ripped through its fingertips, piercing deep into Wolfgang's flesh. The headless body then pummeled a fist into Wolfgang's face, knocking him half out of his senses.

"Hey, hands off my man," Red shouted.

Valerie's free hand swung wide, bashing Red in the face, hard enough to knock her backwards. Valerie's body then flung Wolfgang headfirst at Red like a rag doll. The impact sent them both crashing down onto the stone stage.

The Alpha sword fell from Red's grip and hit the floor with a clang.

Valerie's body began stammering towards the throne.

Wolfgang clutched a hand to his wounded throat. "Bet you don't think he's such a hot cup of man chowder now."

"More like half a cup, but he's still pretty steamy," Red admitted. She nudged Wolfgang aside and hopped to her feet, just in time to see Valerie's body stepping up to the throne and picking up its head. "You gotta be kidding me," she muttered.

"It's not too late for us, Alpha," Valerie said as he reattached his head. "Immortal love can still be ours."

"Pass." Red scrambled over and scooped up the Alpha sword.

Valerie cracked his head from one side to the other and began walking towards Red. "Alpha, you must understand by now that your mortal weapon can do me no lasting harm."

With the Alpha sword held at her side, she timidly trembled as Valerie slowly approached. It took every bit of her will to save herself from again falling under his hypnotic prowess, but that will was fading fast.

"Stop resisting me. Submit to my will. Accept my gift of immortality," Valerie said, gazing into Red's eyes. "We both know you want that."

Red reluctantly shrugged. "Not gonna lie. There *is* a part of me that wants that." She then glanced back at Wolfgang, who was on his knees and still clutching a hand to his wound. "But for whatever reason, there's a part of me that cares more about that mangy mutt than spending an eternity looking at your pretty face."

"Then you leave me no other choice. I shall rip the life from you and drink every last drop of your blood," Valerie said and slashed his talons at Red's throat, but she stepped back and swung the Alpha sword, hacking his hand off at the wrist.

"That might have actually worked, had you not announced your intentions," Red said. She then unleashed a rapid series of hacks and slashes, first chopping off his arms at the shoulders, and next his legs at the knees. The body parts flopped to the ground one at a time, followed by his limbless torso.

"Holy chop suey," Wolfgang cheered as he stammered up next to Red. The disembodied limbs were flopping around trying to make their way back to the body. "On a scale of one to ten, this has a creeper factor of about eleven."

"More like ninety-nine," Red said. "The big question now is, what are we going to do with him?"

Valerie burst into a manic fit of laughter. "Foolish Alpha, what part of immortal are you still not getting? I am invincible. I am—"

"Knocked out cold." Wolfgang said and kicked Valerie in the head, hard enough to knock him senseless, but far from deceased.

"Thank you, but he's not going to stay out forever," Red said, clutching a hand to her head, trying to make sense of the situation. "I guess we could try burning him, but that just seems so gruesome."

"Nothing could get more gruesome than this," Wolfgang said and glanced up toward the upper rim of the amphitheater. "Or could it?"

Red snapped a look up and saw what Wolfgang was looking at. A flock of flesh-eating razor-rats, thousands in numbers were stalking down the stone steps. "Wolf Boy, I think we better get out of here."

"Agreed," Wolfgang said and slowly backed away. "I think pretty boy Valerie is about to become a whole new flavor of hot man chowder."

BIO

Neo Edmund (WGA-W / SFWA) began his Hollywood career appearing on numerous television shows, most notably as on 100+

episodes of Mighty Morphin Power Rangers! Optioning to pursue his passion for writing, he transitioned into the creative side of the film & TV industry, and currently writes teen and YA books, most notable his Red Riding Alpha Huntress Trilogy and numerous Power Rangers books!

16

THRESHOLD

TODD FAHNESTOCK

The human lay dying in the grass because it was the law, and Mother stood at a distance, waiting. Stars shone brightly between the trees, but there was no moon. A warm breeze blew, carrying the scent of fallen leaves.

Six other *syvihrk* clustered around Mother, blending with the long shadows. As *Syvihrk vik Kalik*, the leader of her people, Mother had been notified the instant the human had been found lying within the borders of Sylikkayrn. Now it was Mother's duty to watch him die or ensure he passed through Sylikkayrn without knowing who lived here.

Stavark hid in the trees, far enough away that even Mother could not hear him. He wondered if he would cross his threshold tonight, from *syvihrk-lan* to *syvihrk*. Stavark didn't know when the threshold would come or what it might look like. He only knew that once he crossed it, he would no longer be a child.

Surely this must be it. No human had passed the borders of Sylikkayrn in Stavark's lifetime. He waited a moment to see if he felt different.

Would he know when he became an adult? Would there be a

transformation? They said the threshold was a decision that must be made by the *syvihrk-lan* alone. Adults made their own decisions. Children did not. Had he already become an adult by making the decision to sneak out of his home tree and follow Mother to this place?

But he didn't feel different, just...scared that he might get caught and vaguely ill at watching an impending death...

He clenched his fist and told himself to focus.

Mother could not see the human, of course. For as long as Stavark could remember, she had been blind, her eyes dark like tarnished silver. But she had other ways of seeing the world. She could smell the blood scent that lay over the wet and earthy aroma of autumn. She could hear the human's shallow breathing; she could even feel his life dwindling. She had taught Stavark how to do that, how to sense the living without seeing them. The life of a creature created an aura around them. The more vital the creature, the greater the aura. If a *syvihrk* was sensitive enough and well-trained, he could feel that aura like heat radiating from a sun-baked rock.

Most importantly, Mother had taught Stavark how to listen to his heart, how to sense rightness and feel when nature was out of balance. Stavark was her *syvihrk-lan*; she'd taught him everything important.

She had also taught him that humans were destroyers. Contact with them was forbidden. Humans stole the *maehka* from the lands long ago and caused the great dying. They were *vanvakihrk*, creatures of violence and self-serving hunger, and they could never be allowed to know about Sylikkayrn. That was the law.

But as Stavark strained to hear the wisdom in his heart, he couldn't feel the rightness in the law. He did not see how letting the human die helped the balance of nature. His stomach turned, and he wanted to vomit.

Is this my threshold, then? To know and understand the wisdom of the law?

The aura of the human's life grew colder with each rattling breath. It would be soon.

Hope and duty twisted inside him. He reminded himself that the *syvihrk* weren't killing the man… Some other creature, perhaps even a *volverka,* had caused that bleeding wound in his leg. The *syvihrk* were merely following the law, letting nature take its course. Balance would be restored naturally…

But if the law was right, shouldn't Stavark feel that rightness in his heart? He didn't understand the pulsing conflict inside him.

"Pick him up," Mother said suddenly. "Take him to the Life Tree."

One of the *syvihrk* gasped. Stavark's leg twitched. His foot shifted and made a scuffing noise that almost gave him away.

But Mother's shocking statement felt right. His heart became lighter. The rightness was near, almost within reach.

"*Syvihrk vik Kalik,*" one of her entourage, a *syvihrk* named Gessek, said. "Do you mean, after he is dead?"

"Take him now. We will heal him. Take him to the bole of the Life Tree," Mother said as though it was an everyday command.

Nobody moved.

Mother pressed her lips into a line, stepped from concealment, and crossed the distance with gliding, certain footsteps. She felt nature with her entire body, not just her eyes. She didn't need to see to find her way. She knelt next to the human, then turned her face toward her reluctant attendants. After a tense second, Teyva and Mallock also left the trees. They approached cautiously, as if the human might leap up and sting them like a giant tree scorpion. After another breathless moment, two more *syvihrk* followed.

Gessek and Sayla remained behind, standing in open-mouthed shock.

The four who had obeyed Mother lifted the human, and he groaned. They carried him up the main path into Sylikkayrn.

Stavark desperately wanted to follow, but he held back, waiting until Gessek and Sayla raced in another direction. There was no turning back for Mother now. The deed was done, the law broken.

Gessek and Sayla would hit the city like a stone hits a quiet pond, sending ripples to every *syvihrk* in Sylikkayrn.

Stavark felt fear, excitement and a fierce pride. The ill feeling in his belly eased because Mother had followed her heart, followed the rightness. He was proud to be her *syvihrk-lan*. And he was also proud of himself. He, too, had sensed the rightness. His heart had spoken, and he had heard it, even if the other *syvihrk* had not.

Was that his threshold? To know the difference between fear and wisdom? Was he a true *syvihrk* now? He wasn't sure.

When everyone was far up the path, backs to him and barely able to be seen, Stavark stood up from his hiding place and used his new ability. He stepped into the silverland.

The main path, the tall trees, the green grasses, even the night sky and the stars above...all suddenly became glistening silver, gleaming and completely still. He jogged lightly to the east first, far away from the frozen forms of Mother, the other *syvihrk*, and the human they carried. When a *syvihrk* moved through the silverland, it caused a silver flash that others could see. But so long as Stavark stayed far enough away, they would never suspect he had been here at all.

Last week, Stavark became the first of his people to enter the silverland. No other *syvihrk* had done it in centuries, not since the humans stole the *maehka* from the lands. When Stavark opened the silverland for the first time, he thought he'd crossed his threshold and become a true *syvihrk*, but Mother said he hadn't. She also said he needed to keep his ability a secret until they understood why only Stavark could do it.

Stavark raced home, left the silverland, climbed up the outside of his home tree and threw himself into his hammock, breathing hard. There were no scents at all in the silverland and the air was thin. He waited, eyes open, staring at the interwoven branches of his ceiling until his breathing calmed. He heard Father moving about in the family room below, waiting up for Mother. Stavark heard when Mother returned, heard Father's quiet voice greeting her. They talked for a time, then Mother left again.

Stavark held perfectly still. This wasn't the end of it. She was going to talk with the council of elders about the human. He twitched, looking toward his window.

I should stay here. I've done quite enough for tonight...

But what if this was his threshold? Tonight. Now. What if he passed up his chance while sleeping?

No. He couldn't simply wait here. That was ridiculous.

When he was certain Father had gone back to bed, Stavark crept out of the home tree once more and padded through the streets to the center of Sylikkayrn.

The Life Tree loomed over a circular clearing. Thirty *syvihrk* holding hands couldn't reach all the way around the trunk. The Life Tree speared high into the night sky, higher than any other tree in the forest. Its soft, silver leaves glinted like small crescent moons in the starlight. Two guards stood sentry at each of the four archways in the trunk; no one could enter or leave without being challenged, and there were no windows to slip through.

Not on the first floor, at least.

Stavark glanced at the oval windows on the second floor. The lowest was more than twenty feet off the ground, and there were no branches between here and there. But then, Stavark didn't need branches to climb a tree anymore...

He stepped into the silverland and ran toward the trunk. Everything slowed in the silverland, even the pull of the ground. Stavark could not fly, but he could run up a vertical surface much further than he could when he wasn't in the silverland. The bark felt like flat ground to him, but slick like he was running across a frozen lake.

He sped up the tree to the nearest window, made of silver-bound, colored pieces of glass that had been cleverly crafted into a raven with spread wings. He opened the window slowly and carefully. Too fast, and it would shatter. The silverland made Stavark's strength enormous on still objects. He darted through, landed lightly inside the room and eased the window closed.

He stepped out of the silverland and placed his hands on his knees, breathing hard. There were endless advantages to the silver-land, but traveling through it was unbelievably strenuous, harder than running a dozen miles. He tried to keep his breathing quiet. If he was lucky, none of the guards had seen him. At most, they might have caught a glimpse of silver light, but as Mother had kept his ability secret, they probably wouldn't know what such a flash meant.

As Stavark recovered his breath, looked up and—

And found the human watching him, sitting up on a large hammock in the center of the room. They were alone together, and the human was just as brutish as Stavark had been told.

Of course, Stavark had seen the human in the glade, but that was from a distance. And the man had been unconscious, helpless. Now he was awake, and Stavark could see the violence in every part of the human. His big arms, wide shoulders and thick fingers resembled that of some muscled beast. His blunt cheekbones, doughy cheeks and round chin were covered with dirty-looking whiskers. His hair was mud-brown, and it curled down over his face, covering one of his mud-brown eyes. There was no curly hair in Sylikkayrn. All *syvihrk* had ivory skin, straight hair and silver eyes, like captured droplets of moonlight. This human looked like he'd crawled out of a badger's den. He blinked, like he thought he was hallucinating.

Stavark's heart lodged into his throat. He'd only come to take a closer look. He'd assumed the human would be downstairs, in one of the large rooms, unconscious. Stavark thought about leaping out the window and running home.

"You have flashpowers," the human rasped. He cleared his throat. "The gift of the quicksilvers. You have it," he said, and the hoarseness had vanished, transformed into a deep and rumbling voice, deeper than any *syvihrk's* voice. It should have frightened Stavark, but somehow it was soothing. "I'm sorry. You don't call yourselves quicksilvers. It's *syvihrk*, correct?" the human amended. He shook his head. "My apologies. That was rude."

Stavark looked closer at the human, at his manner and his

clothes, and suddenly he didn't seem so brutish. His linen shirt was dirty, yes, but it had fine lace at the throat and cuffs. His black leather vest, though scarred and worn, bore decorative embossing. This wasn't a violent animal; he was simply…different than a *syvihrk*. The human shifted on the wide sleeping hammock, which was secured to the ceiling by four thin poles, then propped himself up on one elbow with a wince of pain. "You probably don't call them flashpowers either, do you?"

Was this Stavark's threshold? Surely having a conversation with the human was enough! Even adults did not do that. Stavark swallowed. He had a choice. Either he could run, or he could stand his ground and speak with the man.

"How do you know of us?" Stavark asked. After a moment's hesitation, he found the courage to approach the hammock. "Humans do not know the ways of the *syvihrk*."

"Most don't." The human swallowed and winced. "But I do. I find lost information. Things forgotten. Books mostly. I read."

"Everyone reads," Stavark said.

The cocked his head, as though he found Stavark's comment interesting. "Not in the human lands. Not anymore."

"What do they call you?" Stavark asked.

The human gave a soft chuckle, and it was also strangely soothing. Stavark expected the human to be feral, with burning eyes of greed and malice. But he wasn't like that at all. "They call me Reader Orem, actually," the human said. "At least the ones who speak to me at all."

"Your people do not speak to you?" Stavark asked.

"They don't like what I do."

"That you read?"

"Among other things," Orem replied.

"Did they wound you?"

"No."

"Humans love violence," Stavark said. "They hurt for no reason. They murder."

"All humans?"

"Yes."

"Have you met them all?"

Stavark pressed his lips together. "I do not need to meet them all. I do not even need to meet one of them."

"More than one, you mean," Orem said. His lips quirked in a smile.

Stavark's face burned, and his anger rose. But Orem was right... Stavark *had* needed to meet this human. He'd been driven to come to the Life Tree for that very reason.

"Amarion is a dangerous place right now," Orem continued. "People are afraid. Most humans feel books are the reason for their hardship. They think knowledge is a threat, but actually it's the other way around. Ignorance is what will kill them."

Stavark's heart beat faster. To his shock, he agreed with the human. "It is better to know than not to know," he murmured.

The human cocked his head again, and his eyes narrowed. "How old are you, *syvihrk*?"

"I am…not *syvihrk*. I am *syvihrk-lan*. I have twelve turnings of the seasons."

"*Syvihrk-lan*…" the human said, and he narrowed his eyes as if thinking. "Is that a diminutive? For children?"

This human wasn't the feral beast Mother had described. His eyes twinkled with intelligence. He liked learning, liked knowing. Stavark could feel the heat of the human's aura, pushing toward him.

"Do all *syvihrk* have your… What do you call your flashpowers?" Orem asked.

"We do not name it that way. I step into the silverland. I move through it. I step out."

"When did that happen exactly? Or have you always had it?"

The human's insight bordered on supernatural. Stavark's fear prickled across the skin of his arms like creeping frost. "Last week," he said. "And for none save me."

Orem raised his eyebrows. "Only you?"

Stavark said nothing. He'd already said too much. What was he thinking, giving such information to a human?

"Gods..." Orem murmured, more to himself than to Stavark. "Any threadweavers here?"

Stavark hissed. It was the human threadweavers who had stolen the *maehka* in the first place, twisted it to their own selfish desires. "No *syvihrk* is a threadweaver! Only humans are so arrogant."

Orem paused, then said, "Many wondrous things were created with threadweaving. Once upon a time."

"There is nothing wondrous about twisting nature."

Orem pursed his lips, and he paused a moment before saying, "You know what your people have told you, *syvihrk-lan*, but you to not know the whole the truth."

"And I should accept your lies instead? You are human. You cannot see truth."

Stavark thought Orem would lash back, but he didn't. Instead, he watched Stavark—not like one enemy watches another—but like a *syvihrk* watches a *syvihrk-lan*, trying to help, trying to teach. "You're correct, of course," Orem said in that comforting, rumbling voice. "I'm blind to many truths. There's so much I don't know. But I am looking. At least I am doing that."

"You think the *syvihrk* are not?" Stavark asked.

"Are they?"

Stavark opened his mouth to retort, then realized his anger had run away with him. He did not know the answer to Orem's question, not a true answer. He only knew what Mother would have him say: Humans are *vanvakihrk*.

He suddenly realized he did not feel that truth in his heart. The stories of humans told one thing. Stavark's own experience—here and now—told something quite different. He could not say for certain that this human was *vanvakihrk*, a selfish creature bent only on his own satisfaction. He'd seen nothing with his own eyes to confirm that, not yet.

"Tell me, do you know about what is happening to the lands right now?" Orem asked.

To a human, everything of consequence happened only to them. Mother said they had no care for the lands, for nature, only for their own grimy cities of stone, but that wasn't what Stavark heard in Orem's voice. Orem wasn't talking about the incessant skirmishes of human kingdoms. He was talking about the lands as Stavark knew them—all the lands—the trees and roots, the sky and water, the grass and ground, the humans and the *syvihrk*, too…

What is happening to the lands right now…?

Stavark thought of the *volverka* that had ravaged Sylikkayrn last month, a horror from the time of Dervon the Diseased. Like Stavark's new ability, such monsters hadn't been seen for centuries. It slew two *syvihrk* gatherers and one *syvihrk* tree guard before it was caught and killed. The *volverka* looked like it might once have been human or even *syvihrk*, but twisted, elongated. It had midnight black skin, shiny as if oiled, and spindly arms that could throw a *syvihrk* twenty feet.

After a long pause, Stavark finally answered the human's question in a soft voice. "The lands are sick. Sicker than they already were."

The human raised his eyebrows in surprise, then nodded a quiet approval.

"But you humans caused the sickness," Stavark said. "You caused the great dying, stole the *maehka*. You brought the *volverka*."

"*Volverka…*" Orem puzzled through the word like he had *syvihrk-lan*. "A *volverka* is a monster? Does it have thin limbs? Long teeth? A small head?"

"You've seen them." Stavark felt ill thinking that there were more *volverka* in the lands, running free, killing…

"We call them darklings."

"They are here because of *you*," Stavark said.

"Not this time. Yes, human threadweavers caused the great dying. And yes, if this word *maehka* is what I think it is, we stole that, too. But we didn't summon the darklings. I *do* know where they're coming from, though. I just…I can't fix it by myself."

Orem turned an intense, unmistakable gaze on Stavark. "I need help."

Stavark took a step away from the hammock. After all the humans had done, after all they'd twisted and destroyed, Orem dared to ask for help? *Stavark's* help? The arrogance of the man!

"Your ability to use the silverland makes you one of the most powerful beings in Amarion," Orem pressed. "You could fight a darkling…a *volverka*…and win."

Stavark's heart beat faster. As fast as a *volverka* was, it wasn't faster than one who could walk through the silverland. The human's words rang true. Stavark felt confused, lost, like he had swum into the waters of a lake and suddenly the shore had disappeared.

"You are human," Stavark spat. "You lie. You are selfish and self-serving!"

"Am I lying about the sickness? About the *volverka*? Is it selfish to want to return the lands to what they once were? To bring back the *maehka*?"

No and no and no and… Stavark's head spun. He couldn't find the lie in the man's words, couldn't find the rightness in his own heart, couldn't see past the veils of his own fear and anger.

He backed away another step. This was why *syvihrk* were forbidden to interact with humans. Mother was right. She was always right.

"I should never have come here," he whispered.

"And I say you were meant to. You, the only *syvihrk* who can step into the silverland. Me, the only human who sees what's happening and wants to help. We were meant to find one another."

Stavark fled. He stepped into the silverland and raced to the window. Too quickly, he shoved it open, and cracks spiderwebbed on the frozen, silver panes. The instant he left the silverland, the window would explode, blowing shards of glass to the ground below. He didn't care. He jumped out, slowly fell to the silver ground, and sprinted into the silver woods. He didn't stop until his lungs were nearly bursting, until he reached his hammock in his own home tree.

He lay there, lungs burning, straining as he sucked breath after breath. He'd made a horrible mistake. This was why *syvihrk* and humans could not interact. Humans were a mass of confusion and deceit, and Stavark had somehow been tainted by it.

Yet this human had wisdom. He spoke truth. The lands *were* sick. And yes, Stavark wanted to bring the *maehka* back…

But that was impossible. The idea of a *syvihrk-lan* going on a human quest was ridiculous. Mother and the elders would see it as an abduction, and that was worth a war with the humans, especially if the *syvihrk-lan* abducted was the only one who could open the silverland.

He twisted his fingers together like the branches of the ceiling overhead.

"Stavark?" Mother's soft voice came through the door. Stavark jumped like someone had poked him with a sword. He almost fell off his hammock. Mother parted the leafy vines and stepped inside his room. "You're still awake," she said, so calm compared to the frantic beating of his heart.

She walked smoothly to the center of the floor, made of thick and thin branches so expertly grown together that they made a perfectly flat surface. Her arms were folded, hands hidden inside her sleeves, and she waited for him to speak first.

He held his tongue.

Finally, a smile turned up the edges of her mouth. "He who speaks first reveals most. Well done, *syvihrk-lan*. But set your mind to rest. You need not hide what you've done, for I already know. For one who is listening, the air rings like a bell when one steps into the silverland. The old texts talk of music in the trees of Sylikkayrn when all *syvihrk* could use the silverland. I heard you tonight; I knew you followed us. I know you were there when I made the decision to heal the human."

Stavark didn't breathe for a moment, waiting for her to condemn him for talking with Orem. She held her head slightly cocked to the side, as though she could hear the cold sweat seeping into his palms.

He suddenly realized she didn't know he'd gone to the Life Tree, didn't know about his conversation with Orem. It was the only reason for her calm. Stealing out to look at the human was one thing. Talking with the human was…what? Horrible. Possibly treason. He kept his mouth clamped shut.

"I am sorry, my son, that I let you follow. I see now that I was wrong. I could have stopped you, but I thought allowing you to see the human would be educational. I often forget just how young you are. I'm sorry you had to see that. And…my failure."

"Failure?" His whirling thoughts stopped at the word.

"Perhaps I thought to show you a *syvihrk's* compassion. Perhaps I thought…" She trailed off, then shook her head. "It doesn't matter now. It was a mistake. And a hard lesson will follow for me, I'm afraid." She drew a deep breath and let it out. "But I will bear the consequences."

"What consequences?"

"Some of the *syvihrk* no longer trust that I should be the *Syvihrk vik Kalik*. They may choose a new leader."

Stavark's whole body ached. Suddenly, the rules of his people felt like walls around him, close and confining. Mother had listened to her heart; she'd chosen the right. How could they punish her?

"What will they do…with the human?" he asked.

She sighed. "That is another hard choice, but one I won't fail to make this time." She reached for his hands, and he made sure to take hers quickly with the tips of his fingers so that she would not feel the sleeves of his tunic, so she would not know he was still fully dressed. "I think it likely that you, Stavark, will one day serve as *Syvihrk vik Kalik*. Like me, you must learn to make hard decisions. I hope you will let my mistakes guide you. I hope you will be a better leader than I have been this day."

"What will they do with him?" he asked again.

"He woke tonight. Woke and saw the bole of the Life Tree,

broke the window in his room and saw all of Sylikkayrn. Perhaps he was trying to escape; he wouldn't say. I thought…" she hesitated, then sighed. "It doesn't matter what I thought. I will pay the price for my mistake, and now so will he."

The realization struck Stavark, a stone to his chest. "They're going to kill him," he whispered through numb lips.

"Please understand, Stavark. They must."

"No."

"We cannot afford to set the human free to tell others about Sylikkayrn."

"But Mother, *syvihrk* do not kill. You taught me that. On a hunt, yes. To defend the right, yes. But not this. Not murder. The human is helpless."

"Not murder, my son. A restoration of the balance."

"Balance? We are choosing to end a life!"

"We are choosing to save the *syvihrk*. The human is a plague that will spread. If we spare him, more will come with their violence and their greed; it will cost the lives of many *syvihrk*. No. He will be stopped here, now. It was the law, and a rightness, to leave him where he had fallen. I turned from that rightness. Now, his death falls upon my shoulders."

Stavark's hands gripped hers harder. "You must stop it."

"I must wield the blade."

"Mother—"

She pulled her fingers from his and stood up. "You do not see it yet, *syvihrk-lan*, but you will. I apologize that I have filled your head with such concerns. Someday, they may be yours to bear, but not tonight. Please, go to sleep. Rest knowing that we do what we must for your safety and the safety of all others in Sylikkayrn." She turned and walked to the curtain of leafy vines. "I love you, Stavark. Tomorrow the sun will rise, and once again we may seek the right."

His breath came fast, and he held back the ideas that sprang to mind. She would not listen to his words anyway—he was only a *syvihrk-lan*—so he must speak with actions. And also, if he told her what he planned to do, she would try to stop him.

But he needed to say something; his silence was conspicuous. He searched for words of truth, and he found them.

"I love you, Mother," he said softly. "No matter what you decide. No matter what....burdens I may someday bear. Know that I love you, and I always will."

She smiled. It was the smile of a mother to a *syvihrk-lan*, to a son who had not yet crossed his threshold.

His heart hammered. He knew what his threshold was now. He saw it before him, and it was more horrible than he could have imagined. The consequences could burn him for life.

Mother left the room.

Stavark laid back, staring at the ceiling of twisted branches, paralyzed.

This will be the last time I look at my ceiling...

Fear crept over him with cold, prickling feet, but the warmth of the rightness radiated out from his heart, spreading into his head and belly, his arms and legs. It pushed the fear away, and he sat up.

Once more, Stavark crawled out his window, but this time he waited at the base of the tree, watching. Moments later, Mother left with the family sword in hand, a curved blade of silver and steel. He followed her silently, and this time he did not use the silverland.

Mother met four tree guards at the east entrance to the Life Tree, and they had Orem. His legs were bound at the ankles. His wrists had been tied behind his back. No other *syvihrk* were present, of course. A murder in Sylikkayrn would have to be committed in secret. The elders would say the human had died of his wounds. Deception... It was a lie from *syvihrk* to *syvihrk*, and it hurt Stavark like someone was squeezing his chest. The world was upside down when *syvihrk* lied and humans spoke truth.

Mother led the way, and the guards carried Orem to the place where they had found him. There, they pushed him to his knees.

When Orem saw the sword in Mother's hands, he began to struggle, but the four guards held him fast.

Doubt flapped about Stavark's head like raven wings. Fear prickled his scalp. But he would not flee the horrible sight. His body felt like wood, hard and ready, his heart warm with rightness.

Mother had turned from her heart's wisdom. *That* was her mistake, not healing the human. She had been swayed by fears and doubts and had fallen into turmoil. Now she was about to commit an atrocity.

I will save you from yourself, Mother, from those who mistake fear for wisdom. And if the human's words are true, perhaps I can save the lands as well.

Mother raised the sword.

Stavark stepped into the silverland.

The grim tableau froze. He strode to the still silver figures and took the sword from Mother, gently peeling her fingers away from the hilt one at a time. He went to the guards and tapped the sword's pommel against the back of each of their heads. Then he cut Orem's bonds.

Breathing hard, he stepped out of the silverland. The four guards fell like sticks. Orem jerked as his arms and legs sprung free. Mother gasped, staggering, her hands suddenly empty.

"Go," Stavark whispered in Orem's ear. "Run east. Do not stop."

Orem staggered to his feet, still unsteady from his injuries. Stavark waited while the human shuffled east in a limping jog.

Even over his own labored breathing, Stavark could hear his mother's heavy breaths as she realized what was happening, but he kept his gaze on Orem until the human vanished into the trees.

"Stavark…" Mother said, but his name stuck in her throat. In all his life, he'd never seen her at a loss for words. Finally, she recovered herself. "Go," she breathed. "Catch him. Bring him back. We will… We will fix this."

But he was her *syvihrk-lan* no longer. A *syvihrk-lan* only wondered if he had crossed his threshold. A *syvihrk* knew.

Stavark had made his choice—an adult's choice—and he would live with the consequences forever. There was no wondering. He was a *syvihrk* now. He'd crossed his threshold.

There were words he could say to explain to her, to tell her why he'd made his decision, to tell her why he could not heed her demand, but she had been his teacher. It was not his place to give a lesson to her. It would be an offense to try, so he didn't. They were both *syvihrk* now. What he *could* say to her, he already had said to her.

But it was Mother, after all, so he repeated it. He owed her that much.

"I love you," he said softly. "No matter what you decide. No matter what burdens I choose to bear. Know that I love you, and I always will."

Then he ran after the human, ran to join his quest to save the lands.

"Stavark," Mother called after him. "Stavark, come back!"

Blinking through silver tears, Stavark kept running, and he left his mother behind.

BIO

TODD FAHNESTOCK is a writer of fantasy. His epic fantasy works include the *Threadweavers* series (*Wildmane, The GodSpill, Threads of Amarion* and *God of Dragons*), *The Heartstone Trilogy* and *The Whisper Prince Trilogy.*

He is also the author of the bestselling *The Wishing World* series for middle grade readers, which began as bedtime stories for his children. Stories are his passion, but his greatest accomplishment is his quirky, fun-loving family. When he's not writing, he goes on morning runs with his daughter, bounces on the trampoline with his son, and instructs Tae Kwon Do at Family Tae Kwon Do of Littleton. With the rest of his free time, he drives the love of his life crazy with the emotional rollercoaster that is being a full time author.

17

THE LAST DEATH OF OSCAR HERNANDEZ

RUSSELL NOHELTY

The last time I died wasn't much different than the first time, or the twelfth time, or the thousandth time, or...

...well, you get the picture. I've died quite a few times before, and every single one of them sucked equally.

There was immense, searing pain, followed by a loud snap as my soul disconnected from my body. After that, I floated in the cold, dark, nothingness of space until my soul was yanked into another body. Sometimes, it was a baby. Sometimes, it was a dying adult. Sometimes I was on another planet, acting like I understood R'lyehian or why aliens had three heads.

Those times were few and far between. Most of the time, it snapped into a middle-aged man, on Earth, who lost their will to live, and I took over after their soul faded from their body.

I was an anomaly when it came to death, but not in a good way.

For most people, their past lives were wiped from their minds at the moment of death, before they dealt with the void or the agony of rebirth, but lucky me, I got to experience it all, every single time, as if it were my own personal Hell.

I suppose it's possible that this was my Hell, and I was

condemned to cycle through it until I learned some sort of cosmic lesson.

But the joke's on whoever created this screwed up universe, because I'm a horrible student. I haven't done one worthwhile thing in 3251ish chances at life—I may have missed a couple here or there and I'm horrible at math.

3251 chances at life, and I'm pretty sure I'm not going to get many more chances. Or at least that's what I've been told.

Or, more accurately that's what I learned through my travels. In my many lifetimes I've traveled to the tops of the Himalayas and explored the bottom of the Marianas Trench trying to find answers trying to unlock the secrets to my plight, and why every time I come back I feel less tethered to my body.

All I've been able to figure out is that the human soul has a shelf life, like cheese. The longer it sits out, gathering mold, the more it rots.

Rot.

I've thought a lot about rot the past ten thousand years, or so. The rot, was more apparent with each generation of humanity.

Sometimes, I would reincarnate on another planet, and would hope humanity would figure it out by the time I got back, but they never did.

Sure, sometimes they made a breakthrough. Sometimes they banded together to save the planet, but more often than not, humanity rotted with each subsequent generation.

I saw it when we couldn't come together to fight global warming and the planet destroyed itself. I saw it when a third and fourth World War decimated what little remained of our species. I saw it when we promised to be better, over and over, but then couldn't even keep that promise for even a decade.

I was no better. I felt like I was supposed to become something better than what I was, but every time I came back I drifted further and further from that person, until I was nothing but a shell of my former self, unable to remember what it even meant to be good.

I felt my soul rotting with the rest of humanity, but I didn't want that to happen. I didn't want my soul to rot away.

Not until I could become a hero, whatever that meant. When I was a child, I thought that being a hero meant spandex and capes. After I died a few times, I thought it meant living as long as possible in this horrible world. A few times I thought it meant accruing enough power and money that you could pass it on to the next generation.

Now, I've forgotten what any of that meant. Was it doing the most good, or the least bad? What about doing bad for the sake of good? Does that count? All the moral philosophers I've read in my many lives and I'm still not sure.

I don't have any time left, either. It felt as though my soul lost elasticity to this body, like chewing gum that has lost its flavor. It was harder to stick with every reincarnation, and this body was the hardest yet.

Oscar Hernandez. That was my name once, when I was born the first time, or at least the first time that I remembered. I stopped paying attention to each individual reincarnation and now just focused on my original body. What did I want? What was I here for?

I've still not figured it out, and if I don't do it right this time, there might not be another go around to figure it out.

"Hey, mister?" I heard from across the park from where I sat on a metal park bench. There was not much grass in Los Angeles any more, not that there was much to start with, even during my first life. This grass was plastic of course, as were the trees, but the humans playing in the park were real. At least, they seemed real.

I looked up to see a little girl in pig tails waving at me. She wore a polka dot dress with grass stains on it that scraped all the way down to her knobby knees. She looked happy, which was something that wasn't normal in this day and age.

We had long since killed the sky and were forced to live inside bubbles of our own design, which filtered the smog outside and made it breathable. Of course, that little girl didn't know any different. She just knew what she knew, which was that this was the way of the world.

"Yes?" I shouted back to her.

"Can you help me?" she replied. "I lost my kite up in this tree and if I don't get it back my mom's going to kill me. She traded a week's rations for it."

I sighed. I wanted to say no and brood more, but that's not what a hero would do. At least, that's not what I thought a hero would do.

"Sure," I said, pushing myself up from my seat.

My weary bones weren't what they used to be. I came into this body as a young man, full of vim and vigor, but over the decades my body deteriorated until it was almost unusable.

Yet, even though I felt like an old man, I was only thirty-five. Not uncommon for the times we lived in these days. The pills they gave us for calcium and vitamin C weren't the same as the real thing, as much as they said they were. I remember lifetimes in my distant memory where I lived until a hundred and fifty years old, and now, here I was, in the distant future, barely able to live to be what they would have called an adult a few thousand years ago.

"It's up in that tree," the little girl said, as she pointed up to a pink kite stuck in a fake plastic oak the city council planted in the middle of the park. It would have cost too much, and been too expensive, to plant a real tree, even if it did give off real oxygen instead of the fake stuff I breathed all day.

I stared down at the little girl for a moment as she radiated joy back at me. I didn't spend much time with children anymore. It was too sad to think about their shortened life. The shortened life their ancestors, me included, doomed them to, when we forced them to live in a hermetically sealed bubble and eating rationed powders for food. I wished, just once, they could have the joy of a freshly cooked steak. Maybe I should have thought of that before the last war, when we had a chance to save ourselves.

"What do you want me to do about that?" I asked, scratching my head as I looked up kite in the highest branch of the tree.

"Well, I can't climb it. The limbs are too tall for me to grab. Can you climb it and get it down for me, please?"

The truth was I didn't know if I had the energy to do anything more than exist, but if I wanted to be a hero, it meant occasionally acting as if I wanted to help people. Heroes helped people, if I remembered correctly.

"Sure, little girl."

"Becca," the girl said. "My name is Becca."

Becca was the type of name you heard a thousand years ago, but now names were more likely to be B'c'c' than anything normal that I remembered. I hadn't heard a name I would consider normal for hundreds of years.

"That's a pretty name," I said, walking toward the tall oak tree.

"I hate it," she replied. "Everybody makes fun of me for it."

I smiled at her. "Well, I like it."

She turned away from me. Adults weren't known to smile much, and that was inclusive of me. I hardly ever smiled or emoted in any way. Still, I couldn't help but seeing something of my past in her eyes, and it almost brought me to tears. It didn't, but it almost did, and that was more emotion than I had felt in quite a while.

"I'll get your kite down for you," I replied, latching onto the rubbery tree. "Don't you worry about it."

"Thank you, mister," she replied.

Helping people wasn't normal. Not anymore. There was a time when people liked being helpful, and polite, but those days were long gone. Now, people understood their part in the machine and worked to keep it going one moment more. There wasn't joy in a job well done. There was only the satisfaction of having lived another day, whatever satisfaction could be drawn from that, of course.

I pulled my aching body up to the next tree limb. My bones creaked inside me, and they popped as I struggled to climb higher into the sky. There were peacekeepers whose duty it was to help little girls with their problems, and make sure the city was running smoothly, but it was best not to engage them unless necessary. If you engaged them, you were seen as causing a problem for the city, and even a minor problem was met with a demerit. Enough demerits and you were labeled a threat to civilization and banished into the wastelands.

This isn't some great science fiction novel, where the wastelands were truly livable area, and the city had been lying to its denizen the whole time until a great man stood up and showed them the truth.

I thought that might be the case, two lifetimes ago, but when I tested the peacekeepers and was sent into the wastelands, I fried in the heat of the outside in less than ten minutes. Perhaps others lived. That was possible. I don't know. However, I knew that I didn't. I knew that the threat of banishment was real. All too real.

"How goes it up there, mister?" Becca yelled up to me from the ground.

"I'll be honest," I said, catching my breath as I rose another limb into the tree. "It could be going better."

I was already winded halfway up the tree, but I kept climbing. It reminded me of my younger days, and my earlier lives, when the trees crackled in your hands and sent splintered deep into your palms. They weren't nearly as spongy back then as they were now, when they were manufactured instead of grown. Finally, with a great heave of my body, I reached the highest branch where Becca's pink kite rested.

"Now," I said, huffing and puffing. "I'll ask you not to fly your kite anymore, please, when I get this down. It could get you in a lot of trouble if it got lost again."

"But what's the fun in that?" Becca said, looking up at me as I peered down at her.

"The fun is in living," I replied.

"Oh," Becca said, confused. "But what is the fun in living if you can't do anything fun?"

I shook the branch until the kite floated free, down to the ground, and into Becca's loving arms. "The fun is in not dying."

"That doesn't sound like much fun."

I couldn't argue with her, at least not about that. There was no fun in dying, but there was even less fun in living, especially if it meant living in a world with so little joy. However, that was my job, as an adult, to toe society's line, and make sure she grew up to be an adult, like me, even if all we gave back was our lives.

I placed my hand on the hollow rubber tree and made my way back down to the ground. When I finally had two feet on solid ground, I turned to Becca.

"Now, you be a good girl, okay?" I said to her.

"What does that even mean?" she asked, clutching her kite tightly in her hands.

"Honestly," I said, with not a hint of irony on my breath. "I don't know. It's just something we say to kids."

"Oh," Becca replied. "I guess I understand that."

I shook my head. "No, you don't, and honestly. I don't either."

A strong gust of wind blew through my hair. I looked up to see a Peacekeeper looking down at me from his shiny hover bike. As it drew closer to the ground, the wind kicked up faster and harder, until I fell over onto Becca, and we both crashed to the ground on top of each other.

A Peacekeeper, dressed all in black, covered in a helmet that hid any semblance of his humanity, swung his leg off the bike and unsaddled himself. In his hand he gripped a long, electric baton, the preferred weapon of their class. However, his other hand gripped tightly around a laser pistol which could evaporate a person in a matter of seconds, and they weren't above using it with extreme prejudice.

"Citizen!" The peacekeeper shouted. "You have been found in violation of code 124.329. Halt!"

I shuffled to my feet. "And what is code 124.329?"

"Flying a kite without a license and getting it stuck in a tree," the Peacekeeper said, stomping forward. "Please move aside, so we may process this dissident."

"Mister!" Becca yelled. "Help me. I've already got three demerits this year."

"That's insane!" I shouted, stepping forward to block the Peacekeeper from Becca. "This girl didn't do anything wrong. She was trying to have a little fun in this stupid world."

"Yes she did. She is in violation of code 124.329," the Peacekeeper said. "Please move, or I will be forced to use more aggressive means to force your compliance."

In all my previous lives, I would have stepped aside. I valued my own life above anything, especially if its continuation meant I didn't have to deal with the horrors of death again.

But today felt different. My gut burned with the fire and rage. I had to make sure the Peacekeeper couldn't ruin this little girl's life. Perhaps it also burned with the desire to make least one of my lives to matter, even if this was the last one.

"There's nothing you can do to me that will make me abandon this little girl."

The Peacekeeper didn't hesitate before he dug the electric baton into my side, and I fell to the ground in immense pain, as electricity flowed through me. Becca ran toward me as I toppled over.

"No!" I shouted. "Run!"

The Peacekeeper slammed his baton into me again as I screamed in pain. "Stop, citizen!"

As the peacekeeper shouted at Becca to stop, I placed my hands around the baton and yanked it away from him. I slammed it into his leg again, and again, and again.

"You will not hurt that little girl! You will not hurt--"

And just like the last time I died, I felt my soul yank out of my body. The Peacekeeper fired a laser beam into my gut, the same gut that burned with rage just a moment ago. Now it burned with laser fire.

There was no remorse toward my death in his eyes as he reached his gun up to fire on Becca.

In my last moment of life, I lunged forward and pulled the

Peacekeeper's gun down to the ground as it fired into the plastic soil. Becca ran down an alley and out of sight, just as I faded from existence.

I waited, in the darkness of limbo, for something to pull me back into a new body, but it never did. Instead, a blue light fell from the sky, shepherding me onward. Perhaps, finally, I found out what being a hero was all about. Or maybe, I was even more screwed.

I guess I'll find out soon enough, I thought, as I swam toward the light, and onto the next journey.

BIO

Russell Nohelty is a writer, publisher, and speaker. He runs Wannabe Press (www.wannabepress.com), a small press that publishes weird books for weird people. And the popular The Complete Creative (www.thecompletecreative.com) blog, where he talks about mindsets, strategies, and tactics to make it as a creative.

Russell is the author of *Gumshoes: The Case of Madison's Father, My Father Didn't Kill Himself*, and many other novels, along with the creator of *the Ichabod Jones: Monster Hunter, Gherkin Boy, Pixie Dust* and *Katrina Hates the Dead* graphic novels. He makes books that are as entertaining and weird as they are thought provoking and interesting

18

THE MAGPIE AND THE MOSQUITO

JOSH VOGT

Crouched beneath the torso of a reptilian gargoyle, Magpie tracked her pursuer by the light of the triplet moons. The archpath below spanned one of Falveron's many ravines. At this late hour, little foot or hoof traffic trickled through the area. In fact, the archpath would've looked empty to anyone else, but to Magpie's perspective the figure below stood out like charcoal against chalk.

Rather than crossing atop the span, the person clung to the side, traversing the bottomless drop by using ancient engravings as hand and footholds.

Magpie sniffed. Unlike the amateur below, her form-fitting suit—spun from smoke quartz—blended her in with the weathered architecture, just one more patch of darkness.

Despite the person's lack of subtlety, they'd managed to keep up with Magpie for the past hour. She'd picked up the tail on leaving the Felglass district just after sundown. Briefly, she considered making a game of it, seeing how long the other could keep up, until she realized her elderly bones might surrender first. With the sensitivity of her job this night, she couldn't afford any major distraction or delay.

She breathed in.

The weight of herself flowed down and into the city's living stones, leaving her feather-light and momentarily free of the fierce aches that plagued her knees and hips these days. Held in the breathspace, she launched from the parapet and floated down until she landed on the narrow ledge her stalker had edged past moments before. She exhaled and her body sagged as it returned to its normal weight. Her joints protested, but she held firm, a shoulder propped as if to chat outside a cafe.

"Trying to follow me is hardly wise," she said.

Her pursuer's head whipped around. The hood flopped back, revealing a young woman at least a third of Magpie's age. Black hair bristled across her scalp and scars crisscrossed pale cheeks. Had Magpie once looked so young, decades ago, before exchanging golden hair for silver, before age chiseled its lines across her flesh?

The girl shifted to face Magpie while keeping pressed against the stone. "I wasn't *tryin'*. I was doing a crackin' good job. Jealous, Maggy?"

"It's Magpie, you little skunk."

"Not skunk. Skeeter."

"I don't care what your name is, and that's a ridiculous one anyways."

Skeeter flashed an infuriating grin. "Better than any flea-bit bird."

Magpie leaned in. "You think you're the first to challenge me? Next time I catch you slinking in my shadow, I'll leave you as scraw-bait in the nearest sliver pit."

Skeeter drew herself up. "Not here to challenge. I wanna be your apprentice."

Magpie scowled. "No."

"I'll pay. Got coin. Stole it m'self."

"No."

"I'll wash your linens. Cook for you."

"No."

Skeeter's eyes went as hard as glass panes. "Then I'm gonna keep followin' and learn whether you want or not. Can't stop me."

That finally quirked Magpie's lips into a smile. "Oh, yes, I can."

Grasping one of the braided stonecords looped around her waist, Magpie whisked it off and snapped an end around Skeeter's wrist before the would-be-thief could jerk away. She pressed the other end to the archpath side. Living stone called to living stone, and so the earthspun cord melded seamlessly into the wall.

Skeeter shouted and yanked against the stonecord. As she pulled, Magpie aimed a kick into the girl's side and launched her off the ledge. Her cry turned to one of pain as the cord went taut. Grimacing against the pain crackling up her leg, Magpie waved farewell to Skeeter, who stared up as she dangled.

"You can't!"

Magpie shrugged. "If you had any potential as a thief, I shouldn't have been able to catch you so thoroughly off guard. Let this be your first and only lesson. Don't worry. Make enough noise and they'll send a Stoneskin to haul you up."

She breathed in. Her flesh lightened and a stamp of a foot launched her into the night.

* * *

For another candleburn, she bounded across the Ojama district. With each inhale, she leaped from balcony ledges to rooftops to temple spires to archways. With each exhale, her weight surged back, forcing her to strain against the sudden crush of muscles that wanted to drag her into a unmoving heap. When this night ended, she knew she'd feel like little more than a sack of brittle leather and bones. Her talent wearied her more with every passing year, exhaustion burning deeper, recovery taking longer—yet she only needed to endure a little longer. If all went according to plan, that is.

When she spotted the Registrant Spire, she scrutinized the

southern-facing windows on the fiftieth level. The triplet moons glinted off the glass of hundreds of stonesealed windows, all gleaming in the misty night...except for one empty slot where the living glass had been retracted.

Relief rippled through Magpie. Buildings formed of Falveron's living stone were anathema to thieves like her, who always needed a crack to slip through. It had cost her five years of planning and half a fortune to have that one window left unsealed for this single hour.

Three more breaths, three more leaps, and she landed within the Spire. She paused until enough strength seeped back into her marrow for her to stand on wobbling legs. She'd memorized the layout—another year, another dozen jobs to acquire the map—and so hobbled on without hesitation. Hesitation killed. Ignorance killed. Worse than death, though, would be capture. The Blooded would surely imprison her soul in a bondstone, turning her into one of their Stoneskin slaves. The thought alone made her clamp down on a flare of panic.

She eyed the walls for the telltale swirl of a Stoneskin summoning, but they remained quiescent. The Blooded were so sure of the sanctity of the place their soul-shackled guards patrolled the bottom ten levels, leaving mere wardstones to protect the upper sections.

Magpie could handle wardstones, thanks to the iron-etched charm hanging on a wire around her neck. The potent enchantment was one of the few vestiges she kept from the days when the old group schemed and stole together, living as friends and partners and lovers.

She brushed away tempting memories of better times, unable to afford more delays. Once the null-seal wore off on the window, she'd be as trapped inside as much as she would've been kept out.

Reaching the proper room, she eyed the gem-studded wardstone slabs on either side of the doorway. They glowed softly, but crossing between elicited nothing more than a prickle on her sternum; so long as she didn't touch them, they'd ignore her.

She went to one of the slotted cabinets against the walls and drew out granite trays on oiled wheels. Hundreds of cryshards glittered before her, each cut into infinitesimal facets.

Counting down the socketed rows, she picked out the violet orb she sought. Plucking this up, she dug out a paste imitation and clicked it into place. Then she held the true cryshard up for inspection.

Lines flared along the back of her eye, a flash of branching halls nestled in the heart of a flower-like structure. Yes. This one held the vault designs. Exactly what she needed to—

A low hum tickled her ear. She spun and eyed the wardstones, which dimmed as if a shadow passed over them. The hum rose to a buzz. A blow struck Magpie across her back. Gasping, she went to one knee, vision going dark. The cryshard flew from her hand.

When she regained her sight, Skeeter stood before her with the cryshard. "This?" She rolled the gem across her knuckles. "You crack a nut this big for such a teeny seed?"

Magpie reached out, but her old bones swayed and she stumbled, catching herself with one arm planted. "Give...it back."

"Naw." Skeeter tucked the cryshard into her tunic. "Gotta guess you wouldn't have tempted fate and fury if it weren't worth nothin'. I'll see it gets a good home."

She whirled and dashed off into the Spire halls. Clutching her side, Magpie lurched up and hobbled after. She breathed in, casting off gravity to speed after the girl—but her ribs spasmed and she gagged. Her weight crashed back as she fell from the breathspace; she staggered and rammed a shoulder into a wardstone. The gems blazed and a piercing whistle drowned out her pained cry.

The walls squirmed. Faces and hands thrust out of the rock, humanoid figures stepping free, formed of the very living stone from which they'd emerged. Eldritch glyphs and arcane swirls splotched their torsos while emeralds formed eyes on otherwise featureless faces.

Stoneskins.

In moments, eight of the guardians stood just a few strides

away. In their gemstone eyes, Magpie saw the trapped souls of former city residents. Some had given their lives willingly, believing such duty a thing of honor and glory. Others were formed from the souls of captured criminals, those who once undermined the Blooded's authority now serving them as enforcers, actions controlled by their bondstones.

For a horrified heartbeat, she searched those eyes for a glint of recognition or a familiar hue. Then she tore her gaze away and forced herself into a run. The Stoneskins followed and the floor trembled under their impossibly silent tread. She caught up with Skeeter just as the younger thief reached the still-open window. Skeeter held a white pebble between forefinger and thumb as she perched on the edge, poised to jump.

"No, don't!"

Skeeter sneered. "Slink off, scrawshit." She spat on the pebble and gripped it in a fist. When she opened her fingers, white powder coated her palm. The same buzzing from before filled the air. Arms spread, the girl dove off the ledge and plunged into the dark abyss.

Magpie stumbled over in time to see Skeeter sprinting down the Spire as if running along a wide-open road. She vanished into the gloom below.

Magpie gripped the sill so hard a fingernail cracked. "No..."

She started to turn back. There might be other vault schematics stored as backups.

The floor shuddered. Magpie cringed as the Stoneskins hove into view around the curving hall. In the same instant, translucent crystal crept in like fingers of frost, starting to seal the open window.

Magpie gulped a sob and breathed in. The weight of the world dropped away, but her heart hung like a dead stone in her chest, choking as she fled through the shrinking aperture.

* * *

Half a day later, Magpie struggled for balance as she flitted across the cityscape. Sleep—the one cure for spending too much time in the breathspace—had proven impossible with her mind a whirl of despair and desperate plans. So she'd risen, creaking and groaning, practically drizzling dust from her pores, and headed out to see the job done no matter the cost.

After calling in several beyond-ancient favors, she aimed for the Scourment, where a goodly portion of the city's castoffs and careaways lived like grist in a millstone trough. She despised using the breathspace during the day and despised Skeeter all the more for forcing her to do so. While most people never bothered to look up as they milled about the city, it'd only take one errant glance to have Stoneskins across the city put on alert. Her smoke-suit still helped her blend in, but not nearly as well as when the shadows gathered alongside her, old allies, the only real friends she had left.

With time a rapidly dwindling resource, she had no choice. By early afternoon, she'd found the proper tenement. Unlike the city-center structures, where the walls and windows flowed together like skin, here buildings were constructed of common granite and other dead stones, even dried and rotting wood, prone to all sorts of flaws through which she could flutter.

She crouched in the drafty rafters of the enchanter's hovel, watching him putter over a smelting pot and chisel table. After ensuring he had no wardstones or other lethal defenses in place, she breathed in and dropped from the heights.

She worked. Briefly. Then she leaped back up into the rafters and waited. Long.

Skeeter barged into the place as evening clouds drew curtains across the sun. The young woman wore a simple cloak, not going to any great lengths to conceal her diminutive frame or pallid features. Magpie breathed in again and dropped to the floor right behind the girl. She exhaled and staggered a moment before catching herself and speaking to the other thief's back.

"I want what you stole from me."

Skeeter whirled, one hand snapping out. Magpie's spine

crackled as she twisted to dodge a pebble. The stone struck the wall, shattering in a burst of flame and smoke.

Magpie turned back to the girl and waggled a finger. "Lesson number two. A thief should be composed at all times. Haphazard actions will cost you a job and possibly your life."

One blink to the next, Skeeter went from wide-eyed and tensed to acting as if nothing at all had happened. "How'dja find me?"

"Not many gutter skunks going around calling themselves Mosquito. Not many chanters who bother with pebble charms, either. Too unstable. But since they drain within a day or two, I knew you'd have to visit your supplier frequently to get them refreshed or replaced."

Skeeter glanced around the room. "Lopos still breathin'?"

Magpie went over and lifted up the low cot, revealing the enchanter lying gagged, bound, and unconscious.

Skeeter whistled low. "Snails and scales. I gotta admit, you are one tough old—"

"Say *bird*, and I'll put you with him, you little—"

Skeeter reached into her cloak. "Say *skunk* again and I'll call your bluff."

They matched stares until Magpie dropped the cot back into place. Time spent trying to shore up her ego was time wasted. She closed the distance between them, hand outstretched.

"The cryshard you took last night. I need it back."

"Fact is, you stole the shiny first, so me stealin' it from you don't count." Skeeter rolled a shoulder. "I sold it. Should've found me faster."

"You're lying."

"Why you so sure?"

"A lifetime of experience. You aren't connected enough to have hocked anything that valuable this quickly and you wouldn't pawn it so soon after the actual heist. You're foolish, but not stupid."

"Ain't those the same thing?"

Magpie contained her sigh, if barely. "The cryshard."

"Maybe I do still got it. What's it worth?"

"Many more lives than yours."

"I only got one and I plan to keep it."

"So suggest something else to barter with. Blooded Beast, girl, haven't you ever haggled?"

Skeeter sucked through her teeth. "I want you to teach me how you do that jumpin' trick. I ain't ever seen no charm or smokesuit let any folk act like they got wings."

"That could be...tricky." Truthfully, Magpie had no clue if she could teach it even if she wanted. She'd never met anyone else who exhibited the same ability, and didn't know if it was innate or an odd twist of the city's own magic. Still, the girl didn't need to know that. "Took me almost a decade to learn, but if that's your price, we can try. We'll discuss it once I finish the job."

"Finish? Y'mean gettin' the cryshard was just part of it?"

Magpie wiped across her face to hide a scowl. She must be more exhausted than she realized to let that slip.

Skeeter scooted closer. "Why you need this cryshard so bad? What's it for?"

Magpie grimaced. How much did this presumptuous spitshot deserve to know? What could she reveal to get the girl's cooperation without giving the whole plan away? She clenched her jaw, memories straying down too many well-worn paths. The words dammed up and then broke forth in a rush.

"I had a partner once. Silvia."

"Never heard of her."

"You wouldn't have. She worked under a different name. She..." Magpie shut her eyes briefly. "She gave me mine. We had bright dreams, all the ways we'd become rich and powerful. We had a plan to steal from the Blooded themselves, but she died before we could ever try."

"How'd she die?"

"Doesn't matter. Dead is dead. What does matter is that the cryshard contains the map for a major Blooded vault."

The girl's eyebrows bobbed. "Treasure?"

"What else is kept in vaults, hm? The layout details the wardstones, the rooms, and access points. I spent a decade earning enough favors and coin to find it and get into the Spire, and you use a few cheap spells to hop in after me and foul it all up."

"Hold a grudge much?"

"Before Silvia died, I swore to her I'd see our dream through no matter what." Magpie held her head up, unashamed of the tears tracking down her weathered, deep-channeled cheeks. "I have to fulfill my promise. It's the only thing I have left to live for."

Skeeter's winced. "What's with the weepsies? Wasn't you just talkin' about being composed?"

"Thanks to your bumbling, they'll know someone broke into their records last night. They'll have an idea of what cryshards were targeted and will eventually find the fake I planted. I figure I have a few days at most before they either move the treasure or shift the whole vault to another location. The map will be obsolete and..." She waved at her knobby body. "I hardly have the time or strength to start over."

Skeeter gnawed on a nail. "Then I ain't waitin' until you get back. I go in with you and start learnin' right away."

"It's not a two-person job. Not the way I've adapted it."

"Was once. Is now. I go in with you."

"You don't know what you're asking."

"Scrawshit. They say you were gutter-born too before getting a pocketful of shine."

"That was a long time ago."

"Don't matter. No one forgets the streets. We've both got grime cloggin' our veins to the last drop. But I'm moving up, whatever it costs me. That's why I picked you to follow outta the whole pile. You made a path out and I'm going right in your footsteps to the end." Skeeter struck a defiant pose. "So I'm your second skin startin' now until you can't teach me no more. No delays or no deal. No haggle. Besides, with two of us, we can carry out more coin."

Magpie sighed, too wrung out to argue further. Let the girl

damn herself. "Very well. But if you fall behind, you're left behind. I'll not coddle you."

Skeeter beamed. Enthusiasm and energy—the domains of foolish youth. "One last thing."

"What?"

Skeeter pointed to the bound enchanter. "What say we untie Lopos? I'm gonna need him to cook me up a good handful for the fun."

* * *

It took another day for Magpie to confirm their way in. She'd had her hunches, but the actual layout finalized the details.

The vault sat within the depths of the Tenfold Temple, north of the city center. A monument of living stone, it looked like an enormous six-petaled flower, each petal containing scores of chambers and halls that shifted according to the priests' whims. The core spire rose like a stamen, filled with Blooded ceremonial chambers.

Cloaked as supplicants, they entered through the main gates, just another pair of commoners among the throngs. Stoneskins stood at every door and hallway entrance, watching the crowds with eyes of every cut and hue. High above, massive chandeliers of gem-studded bones hung from the vaulted ceilings, filling the space between arches and alcoves where Blooded occasionally appeared to bestow blessing or judgment.

"Ready?" Magpie asked Skeeter once they'd mingled and shifted into position.

"Always been."

"Up we go."

Skeeter crushed a pebble in one hand while lobbing another over the crowd, as far as possible. Flames and smoke erupted, harmless in its flash, but plenty to send people screaming and running in all directions. Stoneskins headed that way, eerily fluid in their movements.

Magpie entered the breathspace and jumped. She flew above the distracted crowd until she reached and grabbed one of the chandeliers. It swayed beneath her restored weight, but held. She glanced over to Skeeter, who'd dashed up a column and now clung to the capstone with a skitterspell, the same she'd used to escape the Registrant Spire. Magpie nodded at a near alcove. A breath let her leap the distance, while Skeeter dashed upside-down across the curved ceiling and then sideways along the wall. They met within the opening. Skeeter peered down the hall beyond while Magpie braced a hand against the floor until her arms and legs stopped shaking.

They turned their cloaks inside out, revealing a grey-green pattern made to match priesthood apprentice robes. So disguised, they wound their way into the temple depths.

Even with the map Magpie had memorized, it took them another candleburn to reach the vault. They passed dozens of priests and other apprentices going about temple business, plus the occasional Blooded in yellow and crimson robes, their skin grey and smooth. Magpie had to quell a shudder at the nearness of the city masters, those who fed the living stone their own fluids in exchange for inhuman power.

They found the hall leading to the vault. Pairs of blade-wielding priests stood on either side of the twelve-foot high door—which stood open. Several Blooded clustered before the arch, with more muttering grating prayers off to the side. Golden falelights glowed in the vault's recesses, creating a false day that blanched the stone.

"What're they doin'?" Skeeter whispered.

"Looks like they're preparing to shift the vault," Magpie said. "Like I suspected. If we'd come a day later, it might not have been here at all."

She sprang up into the arched heights, taking quick, gulping breaths so she didn't regain much true weight as she flitted across the friezes. She shed her cloak and tucked it out of sight atop another chandelier. Skeeter climbed a pillar and followed suit. The both of them then slipped along the upper portion of the hall until they crouch above the priests' heads.

Magpie hung from a metal sconce for a few moments, gathering focus. Sucking as deep a breath as she could, she locked her lungs in place and dropped head-first. She grabbed the top lip of the doorway and flipped under it, planting feet on the opposite side and kicking off toward the rightmost passage.

She flew twenty feet before she touched down. By then, her pulse throbbed and her vision flickered with silvery spots. Her diaphragm cramped, trying to force a gasp out of her. She came into a crouch and peeled her lips apart slowly, letting the air out in controlled whoosh. Her limbs quivered, throat clenching, but she contained herself through sheer willpower as her body evened out.

Skeeter crawled down the wall and watched back the way they'd come, but none of the guards or Blooded appeared. Magpie rose and led the way on shaky legs.

The vault looked like expansive catacombs, a fitting comparison in Magpie's mind, considering what it held. Intersecting halls shot off into the distant dark, walls broken up by tall, thin arches. The cylindrical chambers beyond each arch held deep cubbies carved into the earth, and each space held twenty crimson gems in chiseled slots, all the size of Magpie's thumbnail.

After they passed the tent such set of chambers, Skeeter paused. "Why's it all the same? Don't they got nothin' but rubies?"

"They're not rubies," said Magpie. "They're bondstones."

"Bondstones? Blooded soul-magic muckery?" At Magpie's nod, she scowled. "You...you said there was treasure here."

"Priceless treasure."

"Whatcha squawkin'? Can't sell bondstones for spit. Stoneskins would find anyone who held 'em. What's the steal here?"

Magpie sighed and let her head hang. "Silvia didn't die, like I said. She was captured. Her soul was trapped in a bondstone and used to animate a Stoneskin, just like all other criminals the Blooded get their hands on. I'm here to find her bondstone, destroy it, and free her."

Skeeter grabbed her arm. "Y'tricked me!"

"Lesson three. The best lies are ones that have elements of truth to them." She shook the girl's grip loose and headed deeper in. "Feel free to sit and sulk, or take your chances and go back the way we came."

Muttering, Skeeter trudged after her. Magpie brushed any grains of guilt out of her heart. She'd warned the girl, after all, and she would've told a thousand lies more to ensure she reached this place.

She quickly lost count of how many bondstones they passed. Hundreds of thousands. Perhaps millions. The city had been settled for at least a millennia, after all, and there'd never been a shortage of those the Blooded punished.

The only mercy came in their being stored chronologically. Magpie eyed the glyphs above each arch, denoting various years and months. She discerned the descending pattern and headed that direction. The oldest bondstones were stored closest to the entrance, which made sense as the priests could dig out new chambers and expand the vault as needed.

It took them almost half a candleburn to reach the right storage slot.

"She should be in here." Magpie pointed to an alcove. "Keep watch."

Skeeter glowered but pressed her back to the wall where she could eye both directions. Magpie shuffled into the chamber and studied the bondstones. The gleaming crystals bathed the tiny chamber in a crimson glow.

She fixed an image of Silvia in her mind—not just her cinnamon-brown hair and willowy body, but also the sensation of her touch, her smoky scent, the way her leaf-green eyes lidded in thought as they worked up a new scheme.

She ran fingers over each bondstone in turn, projecting the gestalt of Silvia into each one, seeking an echo.

Silvia? she asked. The first hundred remained inactive. The second hundred denied her as well. She gave each a second or two before moving on. Three hundred. Four. Magpie fought off despair, fearing she'd read the cataloguing wrong. The vault would be sealed within another candleburn and they'd be entombed as surely as the rest of the souls. Should she tell Skeeter to get out while she could? Would the girl even listen to reason?

Mariah?

Magpie froze, her finger on the four-hundred and fifty-third bondstone. She blinked against blurring tears.

You shouldn't have come, Silvia said.

I'm here to free you.

But I'm still their slave. The instant you contacted me, I was forced to alert my masters that you've breached the vault. They're coming for you.

Magpie drew a tiny iron hammer from an inner pocket. *So long as they no longer have you, my fate doesn't matter.*

Sensations flickered through Magpie's mind, the faintest echo of memory. A press of flesh. A giddy laugh. A sob.

Mariah?

Yes?

I always knew you'd come for me.

Magpie kissed the bondstone and then set it on the edge of the cubby and swung hard. The gem shattered and the light at its core winked out.

No masters anymore, she thought. *Be free, beloved.*

She wiped her eyes clear as she emerged.

Skeeter curled her upper lip. "Y'get your precious treasure all sorted?"

"Job's done. Time for you to go."

The girl frowned. "Me? What about you?"

"The Blooded are coming. Stoneskins too." Magpie studied the walls, expecting an emergence any second. "My destroying the bondstone warned them."

"Did you know it'd do that?"

"I guessed it might. They know I'm here, but not you. That

gives you a slim chance to get out about before the whole place is sealed off."

Skeeter's eyes narrowed further. "So you was never gonna come back from this job to teach me. You planned to die here. That's another lie told and another y'owe me."

"I owe you nothing."

"What about thieves honor, huh?"

Magpie scoffed. "Keep swallowing that sort of dribble and you'll choke on it. Don't you get it? I'm done. This was my last job. I'm finally going to be free of this prison."

"What prison?"

"All of this! The whole damn city." Magpie swept her arms out and then struck her chest with a fist. "Everything here is just a chain that drags you down sooner or later. My bones might as well be the bars of an iron cell. Silvia should've been released from this cage years ago, but she wasn't even given that mercy. And you? The gutter's going to cling tight the rest of your life no matter how much you try to escape. I'm done with it all."

Skeeter thrust a finger so close the nail almost gouged Magpie's cheek. "So you're a liar and coward? Think you can wriggle out of our deal? Nothing doin'. We're out of here, both of us."

A chilly line settled on Magpie's forearm. She jerked back. Skeeter had wrapped the stonecord from the archpath around each of their wrists, sealing the tips back onto itself to bind the women together.

"Crooked Scales, you are a stupid fool after all. You'll die with me for sure."

"Quit moanin'. You think I didn't notice you only plotted the way in and not out? Fortunately, I got brights enough for two."

The young thief hauled her into motion with surprising strength. Magpie stumbled after, feeling like a child trailing its mother. Skeeter took turns without hesitation. They ducked into chambers a couple times as priests raced by, blades drawn. They double-backed from a few halls where Stoneskins stood as sentries.

Magpie considered making a noise to draw their attention and end the futile escape attempt.

Ten years spent planning for this one night. She'd never thought beyond it, expecting to die in the effort even if she succeeded. With it done, all focus and purpose fled. Only her ailing body kept her soul from drifting up and out of existence, and the guards would make short work of that.

Yet she held back, uncertain, without a plan to follow or trick to pull. Skeeter's determination snagged something deep inside and hooked her along. To have such a zeal to live...to defy the odds...had she so thoroughly forgotten what it was like?

Magpie tried to track their position and had a vague sense of being near the southern corner by the time Skeeter stopped and tapped on the wall.

"Vault's thinner here. Not much. Just a foot or two, but should be enough."

"So you've a spell to walk through stone?"

Skeeter smirked. "Sorta." She produced a pebble and cracked it against the wall. Fiery veins shot out and the stone began to melt, weeping black and grey toward their feet as the pebble sizzled deeper into the wall, glowing white-hot. Skeeter tilted her head.

"Huh. Bit brighter than usual."

Magpie spotted a crack threading across the pebble. "Is it supposed to—"

A larger fissure formed just before the wall exploded. Shards pelted Magpie, but she'd flung up an arm in time and most bounced off.

A big fragment struck Skeeter in the side of the head. The girl slumped and became dead weight on the floor. Magpie bent over to keep her wrist from being snapped. She peered through the smoke. The explosion had blown a hole in the wall large enough for her to squeeze through, but the edges already grew inward. It'd close in less than a minute.

Hardly knowing why she did, Magpie dragged Skeeter closer, shoulders and hips feeling ready to pop from their sockets. Just as she reached the opening, the wall swirled and a Stoneskin stepped out, blocking the way.

Magpie cringed back. "Please, kill me but let the girl go. She's done nothing wrong."

The Stoneskin studied her with emerald eyes for several heartbeats. Then the construct reached down and scooped Skeeter up. It ducked through the hole and the stonecord forced Magpie to follow right behind. Once in the hall beyond, the Stoneskin deposited the girl in Magpie's arms. The young thief barely weighed anything, all rangy muscle corded over thin bones.

Magpie eyed the Stoneskin in disbelief. Why would it help them?

The Stoneskin laid a hand on her cheek and held it there a moment. Despite the inhuman hands, the touch was impossibly intimate. And were those emerald eyes an oddly leafy hue?

One breath to the next, the Stoneskin crumbled into a pile of rubble. Magpie got the clear sense that the soul animating it had departed rather than been subsumed by the city—which was only possible if the associated bondstone had been destroyed, allowing the previously enslaved individual to act of their own free will.

Magpie wavered at this thought, but kept herself from stumbling and dropping Skeeter. Distant shouts spurred her to take one step. Then another.

She didn't recognize this portion of the temple but kept to the shadows and poorer-lit paths, steering away whenever voices or steps sounded ahead. In this manner, she wove through the structure until she discovered a series of empty side rooms. One held an open balcony overlooking an inner court. All the opening she needed.

As she balanced on the ledge, Skeeter moaned in her arms. Magpie glared down at her.

"Damn you for making me live. I'll never forgive you for this."

She breathed in. As she soared toward freedom, a whisper tickled her ear.

"Yeah, y'will..."

BIO

Author, editor, and freelancer Josh Vogt has been published in dozens of genre markets with work ranging from flash fiction to short stories to novels that cover fantasy, science fiction, horror, humor, pulp, and more. He also writes for a wide variety of RPG developers such Paizo, Modiphius, and Privateer Press.

His debut fantasy novel, Forge of Ashes, adds to the RPG Pathfinder Tales tie-in line. His urban fantasy series, The Cleaners, is published by Story Strong Press and includes Enter the Janitor, The Maids of Wrath, The Dustpan Cometh, and Fellowship of the Squeegee. Other works include Solar Singularity from WordFire Press and the Fate's Fangs tie-in novel. A Compton Crook Award and Scribes Award finalist, he's a member of SFWA as well as the International Association of Media Tie-In Writers.

19

MONSTERS

JIM BUTCHER

My secretary opened the door, leaned in, and said something.

I kicked my feet off my desk, wiped the drool off my chin, rubbed at my sleepy eyes and said, "What?"

"I said we've got a customer," Viti said. She was of average height, blandly attractive, and her body was vibrating with tension. "He's dangerous."

"You think everyone's dangerous."

"I think everyone's treacherous," she corrected me. "This man could kill you."

I tilted my head to one side and narrowed my eyes. "Oh?"

She nodded. "I don't know who he is. But he's a bad one, Grey."

I rubbed at my chin and straightened my clothes a bit. "Well. Show him in."

"You're sure?"

"Try not to kill him unless I specifically ask you to."

Viti gave me an offended glance, which I felt unwarranted, pressed her lips together, and went back out. I watched her go appreciatively. Viti and I are strictly business, but the woman is in shape.

Plus, I'm never sure when she'll try to kill me again.

It's complicated.

I went and got myself a fresh cup of coffee from the Keurig. It wasn't good for the environment, but neither was raising food. Or breathing. If humanity wanted to raise the difficulty on the survival game they were playing, that was their business. I'd be fine either way.

My name is Goodman Grey, and I am a professional monster.

The man who entered my office radiated danger. Medium height, medium build, excellent suit, absolutely amazing haircut. His posture said ex-military. The very faint scent of gun oil said he was armed. We'd never spoken, but I knew who he was.

If you were a bad person in Chicago, you knew who Gentleman John Marcone was.

"No thugs?" I asked, without turning away from my coffee prep. "No revenant bodyguards? No Valkyrie girl Friday?"

Marcone swept his eyes around the office and said, "I'm told your secretary is heavily armed and fidgety." He'd expected to be recognized. Well, maybe that wasn't unreasonable for the Baron of Chicago, the lord of its underworld.

"Exaggerations," I said broadly. "She's a kitten."

Marcone showed me his teeth. "Oh."

I waved him at the chair in front of my desk. He nodded and sat.

"Coffee?"

"Thank you, no."

I plopped back down in my seat, blew on the cup and regarded him through rising steam. "What brings you to Monster LLC?"

"Business," he said. "What do you know of a certain criminal organization originating in Los Angeles?"

"Eighteen?" I asked, "Or thirteen?"

"Does it matter?"

I shrugged.

"They're large, organized, well-funded and extremely dangerous," Marcone said.

"Business partners?" I asked.

I saw his teeth again. "It is occasionally necessary for us to interact."

"And there's a problem?"

"They broke my rule."

I sipped my coffee and regarded him for a moment. "No kids?"

"No kids," he replied, nodding.

"So how come they don't wind up rotting in a shipping container on a slow train back to LA or wherever."

That made him tilt his head and regard me closely. "Standard business practices aren't appropriate."

"How come?"

"Because children are involved," he said. "They've brought half a dozen of them into the country illegally. Their intention is to establish a brothel."

"Huh," I said, and sipped more coffee. "And?"

"If I act directly, I'd find myself at odds with their greater organization."

"Scared, huh?"

"Not particularly. But I do not wish to be distracted. And sending the Einherjaren after them would be… inappropriate."

"Like swatting flies with an elephant gun," I said.

"Just so. But, if they failed to heed my warnings about the unknown and unknowable dangers in that part of town…" He gave a very Gallic shrug.

"Uh uh," I said. "So, you want a discrete contractor? Or a discreet one."

"Both."

"Why me?" I asked.

He spread his hands. "There's another person I could go to. But even if he believed me and agreed to the job, he would complicate it unbearably. We'd be at war with Canada within the week. Somehow."

"Heh," I said. "Yeah."

"I need a professional. You come highly recommended."

"I don't like politics," I said.

"I'm not here to establish a relationship. There's a mess. I need someone to clean it up."

"Why me?"

He leaned back in his chair, steepled his fingers, and looked at me over them. "Because I'd rather not have dead children on the evening news. Bad for business."

I exhaled and eyed my coffee. "Kids, huh."

"I am told such things are within your idiom."

"You know my price?"

"I assumed it was a joke."

I looked at him with a flat gaze.

Marcone tilted his head and said, "My mistake." He reached into his pocket and withdrew a single silver dollar. He put it flat on my desk.

"Why one dollar?" he asked me.

"Got to pay the Rent, like everyone else," I said.

"To whom, may I ask?"

"You may ask," I said. "Where?"

He took a business card out of his breast pocket. There was only a phone number on one side. There was an address written in a terse, neat hand on the other. "Call this number when you're done." He rose and turned to go, then paused. "Perhaps you and your secretary should lower your voices somewhat when discussing potential murder. It might be off-putting to some clientele."

"Honesty is the best policy," I said.

"I concur," he said. "If this deal goes south, I will make your life an affliction."

"Fair," I said, "If you're lying to me, I'll come for you. Right through your Einherjaren. Right past your Valkyrie."

This time when he showed me his teeth, he was smiling. "Excellent. Good day, Mister Grey."

* * *

Viti drove me to the address on the card in her Volvo at 4 AM the next morning. It was, she assured me, the car with the highest safety ratings ever recorded. It was spotlessly clean. Viti was religious about maintaining equipment.

"You'd have thought it would be in a rougher neighborhood," she said.

We were stopped in a neighborhood in Wrigleyville, at a house that looked like other houses. Hell. There were angels standing guard around another house not unlike this one not three blocks away.

I wondered if the angels could see what was happening to the kids from there.

That's the thing about angels. They don't take contract work. Sometimes monsters do.

"It's tougher to get that elite business clientele to venture into bad neighborhoods," I said. "And people get sort of upset about operations like this if they're discovered. Even other criminals. So, it's only the rich clients who can put up enough money to make it worth the risk."

"Ah. I had assumed a different business model," Viti said. "With a larger but poorer client base."

"Poor people have to make their own fun," I said, studying the house. There were elegant security bars over the windows. Not unheard of, in this part of town. But not everyone had all the shades pulled all the way closed, either.

"Security door in front," she said. "Assume the back one will be reinforced as well. There are a number of fisheye cameras around the exterior of the house." She took up an electronic tablet and a stylus that wouldn't leave fingerprints on the screen, and tapped the device to life. "It's a wireless system."

"Place like that will have cameras in the rooms, too," I said. "Get me whatever you can. Be nice if I knew how many bad guys are in there and which walls are safe to go through."

"I killed every member of my graduating class," Viti said

absently, tapping away. "I once watched you torture a man to death."

"You did it to survive," I said. "I did that because the bastard had earned it. What's your point?"

"Are we not bad guys?"

"We are not bad guys," I said.

"In what way does that not make us 'bad guys,'" Viti asked. "Explain it again."

"If it helps," I said, "think of us as worse guys."

She lifted her head from the tablet, drummed her stylus against the edge and frowned at me. "In what way?"

"Meeting those guys in a dark alley would be bad," I said. "Running into someone like you or me would be worse."

"This is a moral framework that I have not encountered before," she said. "Dark Alley Theory. The implicit extension of such a theory is that anyone in the alley who is not some measure of bad is of necessity a victim."

"Nothing theoretical about that," I said. "Tell me how many victims are inside. Assume the children aren't hostile and will not need to be targeted."

Viti frowned. "Unwise."

I sighed. "Just do it, please."

"You are too trusting, Grey," she said. She went to work with half a dozen different software tools on her tablet. I'm not really into computers, if they aren't video game systems. Those I can manage fine. But Viti probably knew enough about computer security countermeasures to get her tossed into a number of cold, dark holes around the world, purely on principle.

"My God, they're using storebought," she said. "Who buys their security at Best Buy?"

"Show me."

Viti turned over the tablet to me and reached into a compartment in the driver-side door, her lips twisting with distaste. I took the tablet in hand and studied a black and white video feed. It was in surprisingly high resolution. Naturally, they'd want to invest in getting good pictures of their clients. It would make them easy to control.

I flicked through the array of feeds from the different cameras, which were scattered throughout the house as well. There wasn't much happening there that wasn't going to be recorded, and there was no reason to think that the bozos in the house were the only ones receiving the data.

"Little bit tricky," I said. "Can't just walk in there and take the kids unless I want to fight a one-man war with the whole organization."

Viti stared at me for an extra-long beat before asking, "Do you?"

"Ugh," I said. "It would take forever, and someone else would just step into their shoes a minute later. I'm a contractor, not a crusader. The job is these particular kids."

I could see them, on the screen. Four of the kids were in bed. Two of them were sitting at a table in the house's kitchen, looking exhausted, eating a sleepy breakfast. Some of the clients must come in before work hours. They were all maybe eleven or twelve.

Yeah. I didn't see any reason to complicate this particular contract with survivors.

They had one guy watching the monitors, one guy at the front, another at the back, and another watching the kids. There were automatic weapons in evidence inside. They seemed to like Uzis. They were wearing business clothes, to a man, but all the tattoos and the style of their haircuts put any doubts I might have had about their identity to rest.

I passed the tablet back to Viti. She had already withdrawn a wipe from the packet in the door, and she scrubbed the tablet's surface religiously before taking up her stylus again. She tapped away for a moment and said, "There's a transformer I can subtract a hundred feet away. That should take down the power."

"They'll have a generator," I said.

"Even one that kicks in immediately will force their computers to reboot," she said. "You'll have a window."

"If they're connected to the rest of the organization, someone will know when the power goes out," I said. "They'll send people here."

Viti's face brightened slightly. "Do you think they're that skilled?"

"If Baron Marcone wants to be indirect, I'd say there's good hope of it."

Viti lowered the tablet and peered around the street. "Nice firing lines."

"I don't want any collateral damage," I said. "People live here."

"Oh. Yes. People." Viti frowned at the houses around us, as if they were the problem. "I keep forgetting them."

"Can you get me a good clear image of one of them?" I asked.

She went to work on the tablet, and after a moment got me a good three quarters view of the gangster at the back door. She mucked with the image for a moment to bring out the bone structure of the guy's face a little better, and then held the image up.

I studied it hard for a second, fixing it in mind. Memorizing details and retaining them long enough to use them was an old habit.

"Okay," I said. "Take me to the end of the block. I'll walk in. You hit the transformer. Then stay out here, stay low, and watch my back." I opened the glove box, took out a slender plastic case, hit the power button on an earbud and slid it in, even as I passed the case to Viti. She got her own earbud and put it in. They smelled sterile. Viti cleaned them before and after each use. We ran a quick check and were ready to go.

She drove the Volvo to the end of the block and dropped me off, and I started down the darkened sidewalks under the shadows of the trees. I'd worn slacks and a business shirt, because they blended into the city landscape as well as anything, and as I walked, I thought about the face of the clown at the back door.

Then, with the effort of a task long practiced, I pushed the bones of my face into position and altered the shape of my mouth, nose, and eyes, until I looked enough like him to pass at first glance. I couldn't have gotten any more exact without a lot more imagery, or some of his blood, but it would be close enough to make his mother look a second time before she noticed.

Oh, didn't I mention? I'm a shapeshifter. It's kind of my thing. When I told Marcone I could get to him through his security, I wasn't kidding around.

When I was ten feet from the edge of the house's property line, there was a coughing sound and a loud clack—followed instantly by a rather spectacular crackling and snarling and a flare of blue-white light that threw the rooftops of the Wrigleyville houses into stark relief.

Then the lights went out.

And I walked right up to the front door and knocked.

I heard the guard at the front door start up out of his chair. The place had been soundproofed, but I'm not human. I heard him rack a round into the chamber of an Uzi and stand.

"Who the fuck is that?" he said, in Spanish, if it matters.

"It's me, man, let me in," I answered in the same tongue, with as little inflection as possible.

The door opened partially, inward, and a flashlight glared in my face. I held up empty hands and said, "What the hell?"

The guard hesitated. "How the hell did you get around he—"

I didn't wait for him to finish asking. The minute I was sure his mind was on something other than aiming the gun and maybe squeezing the trigger, I slammed the door with one knee.

I'm not human. My muscle doesn't work like human muscle. I've made sure of that. I'm not Hercules or anything, but if you aren't a professional strongman of some kind, you don't want to arm wrestle me. You'll lose a hand.

The steel security door was particularly heavy on its hinges. It hit him like a small truck and he fell back.

I was in position before his back hit the floor, driving the edge of my hand down onto his larynx. I crushed his throat flat to his spine, batted the Uzi out of his stunned hands and kept moving without stopping or looking back, while his body forgot how to breathe.

I dilated my eyes to considerably past normal human maximums, and the dim ambient light from the city outside changed the utter darkness to deep shadow and vague outlines. I moved silently and saw the light on the rear guard's gun coming from the back of the house, reflecting off the walls from rooms away.

I slipped into what proved to be a hall bathroom and waited. I could hear the rough breathing from the guard whose face I hard borrowed, the thud of his shoes on the floor, the scent of his cheap body spray. I could also hear the dead man as his body went through the process. He was making harsh gurgling sounds, and his heels drummed feebly on the floor.

The second guard came close enough to the bathroom door that I was able to reach out and snatch the Uzi out of his hands. I flung it away from him and through a section of drywall.

He was fast and good. He had a knife out before I came through the doorway and hit him, overbearing him. He drove it repeatedly into my ribs, half a dozen times in three seconds. While he did that, I jammed my left hand over his mouth, swatted his flailing left arm away with my right, and slammed a hammer-fisted blow into his temple.

Human skulls are fragile right there.

His broke.

I left the body behind me and rose, moving forward, toward the kitchen. My entire left side was on fire. I withdrew the knife and held it loosely in my left hand. An effort that required me to grit my teeth caused my spilled blood to seep back into the wounds and for the flesh around them to seethe and tighten and begin to go to work closing them. In five minutes, you wouldn't know I'd ever been stabbed.

Until then, though, I was going to be in agony, and there wasn't time to slow down.

"Grey," came Viti's voice over the earbud. She sounded calm.

"Flashlights just came on in the basement. At least two. I'm coming in behind you."

I didn't answer. Viti had been the survivor of a training program whose members had, as the culmination of their training, been assigned to murder one another. She had a gift. She would be fine.

My concern was the kids.

The kitchen door opened, and the guard there appeared, a small flashlight in one hand and a pistol in the other.

"What the fuck?" he blurted. "What happened?"

"He pissed himself when the lights went out," I said in a contemptuous tone.

The third guard lowered his gun a little and began to answer, but doing so had cast the light down over my bloodstained shirt. His eyes widened as he realized something was wrong.

I threw the knife at his head. It didn't hit him point first or anything like in the movies. But it was still a pound of steel, and I threw it hard. He went down, stunned, and I drove myself forward swiftly enough to be on him before he hit the floor. I got a hand on his pistol and twisted it aside. He fired a couple of rounds and I was able to aim them at the fridge. I slammed the gun against the floor until his fingers broke and then I clubbed him to death with it. It made a mess.

Like I said. Professional monster.

His flashlight rolled across the room and left the light shining upon the two kids. They were wearing big t-shirts and nothing else. They had slid out of their chairs and were doing their best to hide under the table.

"Hi guys," I said. "English?"

They both stared at me.

"Do you speak Spanish?" I asked, also in Spanish.

They nodded at me. They didn't look terrified. They looked like feral cats might: wary and searching for a means of escape. Too much had already happened to them for them to react the way kids were supposed to react.

I wished there'd been time to kill those bastards a little more slowly.

"You guys want to get out of here?" I asked.

They looked at each other. One was a boy, one was a girl. The girl looked back at me and nodded.

"Your accent is funny," she said.

"I learned a long time ago," I answered.

Boots pounded on stairs. A door in the hall flew open and three men came up out of the basement, half-dressed, fresh from sleep, guns in hand.

At the far end of the house, something went "clackclackclack-clackclackclack."

All three men dropped bonelessly to the floor. Their bodies died swiftly, each with a pair of small, neat holes in their skulls. A little .22 round has enough velocity to penetrate the human skull at close range if you know where to shoot, but not enough energy to leave it again. They just bounce around on the inside for a while.

Viti appeared from the shadows behind them, ejecting a partially-full magazine from a Colt Woodsman that had been fitted with a silencer. The girl isn't right—but she can shoot like no human I've ever known. She slipped a fresh magazine in and said, "We don't have much time."

There was a whirring sound from out behind the house, like a lawnmower, and the lights came back up.

"Good work," I said. "Get these two to the car. I'm going upstairs for the others."

Viti turned the gun on the kids, who flinched.

"Viti!" I said. "They're kids!"

"That only makes them smaller targets," she said. Her voice assumed an authoritative tone and she spoke in rough, clear Spanish. "You two. Come quietly or I'll shoot you."

Both kids looked back at me with wide eyes.

"We're good guys," I explained to them.

"We are not good guys," Viti protested in English. "We just talked about this. Why must you make it so confusing?"

I didn't have time to argue. I eyed her, wincing at the pain in my side and said, annoyed, "Just go with her, kids. Do what she says, and you'll be fine. Viti, we're going to talk about this later. And they go in the back seat, not the trunk."

Viti made an exasperated sound and seized the fallen flashlight. "Fine." She waggled the gun. "Move it."

The kids moved it. My secretary marched them out of their slavery at gunpoint.

"Monster LLC. We aren't pretty, but we get results," I muttered.

"We should put that on the business cards," Viti said primly into my earbud.

"Little too much truth in advertising," I replied, and headed for the stairs up to where the monitor room and the… dormitory, I supposed, waited for me.

I went up the stairs with my weight on my toes, and my toes at the very edges of the stairs, near the walls to hopefully minimize any creaks. I went fast. Stairways are great places to get shot, and I didn't feel like doing that. I fully expected the fourth guard to pop up and start riddling me with bullets—but I got up clean.

The upstairs consisted of a couple of client rooms, the security room, a bathroom and a locked and barred door to the dormitory.

The dormitory door had been unbarred, but was still closed.

The door to the monitor room was open. I checked. The room was empty.

I checked the monitors. The room's computers were just completing their reboot. They'd be recording again in a few more seconds, but since Viti had gotten clear and I was wearing a dead gangster's face, I didn't care much.

An electronic voice abruptly came over one of the PC's speakers in English. "Hey, asshole."

I frowned and checked my back before checking the source of the sound.

The monitor screen had come up again, and I stared at camera inside the kid's dormitory, where the fourth guard had evidently just gone. He now stood in the center of the room, facing the camera.

He was pouring gasoline from a plastic jerry can over the beds of the sleeping children. Even as I watched, he threw the empty container aside, scooped a Zippo out of his pocket, struck it alight and held it up. "Hey, asshole! Can you hear me yet? There's an intercom icon in the bottom corner of camera feed. Click it."

I did that and said, "I see you."

"Just watched your partner take those kids out," he said. "You're going to go join her. Get in that piece of crap car and drive away. I'm going to watch you from the window."

"Oh yeah?" I asked.

"Do not fuck with me!" screamed the guard, spraying it more than saying it. "You think I'm afraid to die?! I will burn these little assholes alive if you fuck with me!"

I thought he was panicky, desperate, violent, and would think no more of burning those children alive than stepping on an ant. Also, he was smart enough to know when he was in trouble. That didn't add up to a very good situation for those kids.

But he had used three sentences when one would have done. He was a talker. I could work with that. "You're a tough guy, huh?" I asked.

That set him off. He started screaming at the camera again. The soundproofing in that room was pretty good. I couldn't hear a thing that wasn't coming through the monitor.

I let him shriek and eyed his position in the room. Then I turned and walked briskly down the hall into one of the client rooms that had an adjoining wall. I eyed the room, touched a spot on the wall, then moved to where I'd have the most lead-up room, keeping my hand lined up with the invisible point I'd designated, while he continued cursing at me through the monitor down the hall.

Then I triggered an adrenaline rush. One of the fun things about being a shapeshifter is that I've got conscious control over all kinds of things that are usually autonomic.

And as I did, I triggered another change.

Time seemed to slow. The room, even lit only from the hallway and the monitor room, grew almost unbearably bright. My heart rate jumped, causing my vision to almost throb with each beat. My body temperature went up to over a hundred and ten Fahrenheit almost instantly.

And I changed.

I drew mass from the immaterial world, my body twisting and bending and swelling. Though it might have taken, at most, a second of real time, subjectively I had a really bad afternoon. Pain seared through my body as my mind told it what to do. Clothing ripped and tore. Muscles swole and shifted and knotted into vicious cramps. Tendons stretched and screamed. Ligaments twisted, warped, and stretched into new shapes. Skin stretched and tore and healed again, then erupted into a furious, agonizing rash of itching sensation as it erupted in hair.

It's the hands and feet and face that always hurt the most to change around. I don't know, maybe because they're just so specialized, so unlike those of other creatures—so human. The way my jaw had to dislocate was never any fun, but there had to be room for all the teeth. My skull shifted, my back cramped in a series of rippling pops. My hands stretched, the knuckles screaming and swelling and popping as my nails twisted and rolled and solidified into raking claws.

It's not just my face I can change around. Didn't I mention? Animals. Monsters. Just about anything I can imagine. Monster LLC. Hire one monster, get every monster. You won't find bargains like this at Wal-Mart.

God I love animal bodies. There's a sensation of pure joy in movement that you just can't get as a human being. You guys really are kind of pitiful, in the physical department. The kind of power that animal bodies offer, the speed, the coordination—there's just no comparison.

Hey, you know how a nine-hundred-pound Bengal tiger gets into a locked room?

Any damned way it wants to.

I went through the drywall and insulation between the two rooms with about as much effort as a dancer popping out of a cake.

I roared as I came, a coughing explosion of pure sound that hit the guard like a club. He staggered, his knees loosened by the roar, his expression dazed.

A single swipe of one sledgehammer paw struck the Zippo out of his hand and out through one of the room's barred windows.

Most of his hand went with it. The guard went down screaming.

Threatening to burn kids.

I came down on top of him, held him down, and started raking with my rear claws. It wasn't a death of a thousand cuts. He was gone before I'd given him a hundred, hundred and twenty, tops.

I spent most of my time in a humanoid form; usually, it's the most convenient for my lifestyle. Going back into it, at this point, felt something like a stretched rubber band snapping back into its usual loosened state. Steam and ectoplasm bubbled off of me, all the extra mass sloughing off into a clear gelatin that would evaporate more rapidly than any water, and I stood up out of it, snatching a gasoline-soaked blanket off one of the beds and wrapping it around me as I did. No sense traumatizing the kids any more.

It took me a little talking, but I got them to follow me out of the house. I got them packed into Viti's car. I'd ride in the trunk.

Then I paused and looked back at the house.

"Head for the office," I said. "I'll meet you there."

Viti frowned and said, "Don't take much time. They'll have backup here in another minute."

"I won't," I promised. "There's something else we need to do to finish this."

Viti tilted her head.

"I'm going to have some homework for you."

Viti smiled.

* * *

The next day, Marcone, with his big dumb Einherjaren bodyguard, was eating breakfast at an expensive sidewalk bistro in the Gold Coast when I called the number he'd given me.

He picked up a cell phone from the table and answered. "Marcone."

"Grey," I said. "Job's done."

"I saw, on the news," he said. "You were rather thorough."

"You approve?"

"I do."

"Then you're going to love this," I said, and sent him several pictures.

From another bistro across the street, wearing a very different face and body, I watched Marcone look at the images.

There were six pictures: Three high powered attorneys, one corporate executive, a city councilman and a notorious religious-political activist. Each picture was identical: a look-down at a dead body with small, neat bullet holes in the temples. On the chest of each body was a computer printed photograph of the deceased, engaged in acts of brutality with one of the children.

Marcone studied the pictures for a long moment. His expression never changed. Then he picked up the phone again.

"Where did you get the pictures?"

"Surveillance feed at the brothel," I said.

"Those people were assets."

"Those people were a market base waiting for a supplier," I said. "As long as they were around, you'd have this problem again and again."

Marcone's face was stony. After a few beats he said, "This could be considered an attack upon my interests, Mr. Grey."

I peered at him for a second, and then I chuckled. "Hah. You didn't know they were pedophiles, did you? Or they wouldn't have been working for you in the first place."

"Yet they were mine. Their loss represents considerable effort that must now be re-invested."

"I suggest you look at this as a glass half-full," I replied. "You didn't lose anything but liabilities. Your rivals had already compromised them with the photographs. Probably what they had in mind all along. I just saved you years of headaches and information leaks."

"You are playing with fire, Mr. Grey."

"Nobody should do that," I said. "That omelet looks tasty. But grapefruit juice?"

Marcone's face went blank. His eyes swept up and down the street.

"See you around, Baron," I drawled.

I finished my coffee, left the burner phone on the table, rose, and walked away.

I was just one more random face among millions. Marcone's eyes didn't track me.

How could they?

* * *

I got into the office, where we'd kept the kids overnight, on inflatable mattresses. There wasn't much floor left in the entry, where Viti's desk was. She was sitting behind it, looking exhausted.

I could hear the kids in my office, speaking Spanish excitedly. My office has a big TV, for when I feel like watching the news, which is seldom, and an X-Box for when I'm thinking hard about important professional things, which is constantly. My work ethic in that arena is second to none. The kids were in there, following in my footsteps.

"Grey," Viti said, as I entered. "This is hell. I will resign. I'm not kidding."

"I wasn't planning on keeping them," I said.

She reached for the phone. "I can call the authorities."

"Yeah, after what they've been through, we'll hand them to the government." I shook my head. "We can do better for them than that, I think." Then I grinned. I had an old paper-style Rolodex. I got into it, opened it to the right card and said, to Viti, "There. Call."

Viti frowned at the number. "Are you sure that's wise?"

"You kidding," I said. "It'll be fun."

She exhaled, eyeing me. Then she said, "Why do you help them, Grey?"

"To pay the Rent," I said.

She frowned. "No. You're already ahead for the year."

I frowned back. Then I said, "Do you remember being young? Feeling helpless?"

Someone who didn't know her well, meaning anyone but me, would not have noticed the darkness that slid into the backs of her eyes. "Yes."

"Me too," I said. "Seems like the kind of thing it would be fun to stop."

Her brows beetled. "Vengeance?"

"When I was young," I said, "they took a lot of things away from me. Maybe when I help those kids, I take something back."

Viti shook her head. "I don't understand."

"Stick with me," I said. "With any luck, someday you will." I put my hand on the table next to hers, close enough to feel the heat of her skin without actually touching her and said, "You're doing fine."

She nodded uncertainly and offered me a small smile. I nodded at her. Then I went into the office to play video games with the kids until the cavalry arrived.

I heard Viti make the call.

"Monster LLC calling for Harry Dresden," she said. "Please tell him that there are children who need his help."

BIO

Jim Butcher is the author of the Dresden Files, the Codex Alera, and a new steampunk series, the Cinder Spires. His resume includes a laundry list of skills which were useful a couple of centuries ago, and he plays guitar quite badly. An avid gamer, he plays tabletop games in varying systems, a variety of video games on PC and console, and LARPs whenever he can make time for it. Jim currently resides mostly inside his own head, but his head can generally be found in his home town of Independence, Missouri.

Jim goes by the moniker Longshot in a number of online locales. He came by this name in the early 1990's when he decided he would become a published author. Usually only 3 in 1000 who make such an attempt actually manage to become published; of those, only 1 in 10 make enough money to call it a living. The sale of a second series was the breakthrough that let him beat the long odds against attaining a career as a novelist.

All the same, he refuses to change his nickname.

CALL TO ACTION!

Thank you for reading Parallel Worlds. If you enjoyed these stories and would like to see more from any of these authors, please leave a comment/review. These help the editors and authors know their works are loved and valued, which means a higher likelihood of more anthologies featuring these writers and their stories.

Made in the USA
Las Vegas, NV
17 October 2022